"Why  *pered.*

He cou_____ds came
around ___ ___ _____ _____, turning toward him with passion-brightened eyes that raised the heat in his body like a tide.

"I've brought you a present." Her words seemed random, whimsically sincere, and they made him smile. Her cape fell in a black halo around her as she knelt by her cloth bag. He watched curiously as she drew out a dark object. It was a bird's nest.

"This one is special. It blew inside my open window while I was sleeping. At the time, I thought it had great significance, that it meant a wonderful thing was going to happen to me."

He started to go to her, but she shook her head. She looked frightened. "Alan, you have to understand. It can't be. For us, it's like the birds. We nest with our own kind. I know—I think I know—that you want something less. But what you want is impossible."

He wanted to be able to let her go, but his need was more potent than anything he had ever known. And it must have been that hers was also, because the strength seemed to leave her suddenly and she covered her face briefly with her hands.

"Touch me," she whispered. "Do it. Quickly."

Sunshine and Shadow

Sharon and Tom Curtis

BANTAM BOOKS
TORONTO · NEW YORK · LONDON · SYDNEY · AUCKLAND

SUNSHINE AND SHADOW
A Bantam Book / October 1986

ISBN 0–553–25047–7

Published simultaneously in the United States and Canada

*Bantam Books are published by Bantam Books, Inc. Its trade-
mark, consisting of the words "Bantam Books" and the por-
trayal of a rooster, is Registered in U.S. Patent and Trademark
Office and in other countries. Marca Registrada. Bantam
Books, Inc., 666 Fifth Avenue, New York, New York 10103.*

PRINTED IN THE UNITED STATES OF AMERICA

O   0 9 8 7 6 5 4 3 2 1

Dear Reader,

Sunshine and Shadow is the story of a desperate forbidden love between an Amish girl and an outsider, who can be together only if one of them will sacrifice everything.

We approached the idea of an Amish setting with delight. Not long ago, most of us were as the Amish are now. America was a nation of farmers. The fascination many of us feel for things Amish may come not from how foreign and apart from us they seem, but from how familiar. They are living our heritage, prospering in a history that is rapidly vanishing beyond their horse-tilled acreage.

Though Sharon's ancestry is not Amish, it is markedly similar. Her grandparents were Swiss Lutheran farmers, much like the Amish in their European background and German dialect. Like the Amish they were frugal, independent, great storytellers and great teasers, and patient with everything but conceit, affectation, and cows who sent them flying with a well-aimed hoof at milking time if their hands were cold. It was Sharon's grandmother who first hefted her up into the secret universe of a haymow, who showed her where to find lady's slippers in the woods. Among her grandmother's favorite stories are the ones about her country school days.

My own grandfather, James Eddie Curtis, was a farmer, poet, bluegrass musician, and storyteller from the hills of southeastern Kentucky. I have saved and cherished his letters to me. In 1974 he wrote:

> I brought down one of the old comfort quilts your great grandmother made in 1924. It needed four blocks replaced. I put in new ones, hand stitched, then cross-stitched the rail fence pattern on each seam with heavy silk thread...

SHARON AND TOM CURTIS

The letter and the quilt still exist, imparting a lingering warmth, both painstakingly created by hand, both intended to give love long after the giver has gone.

Our title, *Sunshine and Shadow*, was inspired by a famous quilt pattern, one much used by Amish women. With its exquisite blend of light and dark colors, the "sunshine and shadow" pattern is meant to capture symbolically the rich joys and deep tragedies of life, to remind us that the dark moments will pass and the peace and sunshine will return, and that each cycle has within it the power to enhance the meaning of its opposite. For us, this simple yet subtle concept held the essence of the love story in our book about two people who are at once torn from each other and pulled closer through their differences.

The more we learned about the Amish, the more our admiration for them increased, but I can date to a single moment the instant I fell in love with their culture. On a visit to a one-room Amish schoolhouse, I found a tiny *kapp*, what we might call a bonnet, lying on a desk where it had been left by a small girl at day's end. It was weightless, fragile, and so finely made that I could see my hand through it—revealing the care of the maker for the wearer.

That evening we took a ride in a buggy pulled by a pair of fine Morgan horses. We had already chosen the title for our book at that time, and so you can imagine our pleasant surprise when, at the end of the journey, the driver pulled back on the reins and spoke to his horses in a quiet voice; "Whoa, Sunshine . . . Whoa, Shadow . . ."

Love,
Tom and Sharon Curtis

Chapter 1

*H*e liked the monster. Some monsters had it. Some didn't. This one did. Take the Creature from the Black Lagoon, for instance, or the Rancor monster in *Return of the Jedi*. They had real charisma. If a monster had that "certain something," movie audiences were perfectly cheerful about watching him consume half the cast.

Alan Wilde looked at his monster, realized that it was going to become the central ingredient of an instant horror-film classic, and leaned back against the woven wire fence, sparing a warm thought for his Creature Design supervisor.

It was one of the few warm thoughts that had crossed Alan Wilde's mind in days.

The weather here didn't lend itself to warm thoughts. Here. Wisconsin. What addled chain of logic had led him to the conclusion that he wanted to make this movie in Wisconsin? It was hard to remember that the location was close to perfect for his purposes. His staff had hyped him on Greyling. They'd given him material from the Wisconsin Film Advisory Board glorifying this restored historical village, a kind of midwestern Williamsburg. They were renting the full five hundred acres, including the original coach house, reborn into a modern hotel, for the two months before it was open to tourists. His investors were happy; the rent was cheap.

Probably it hadn't been logic at all, only a flare of

self-deceptive arrogance. If Francis Ford Coppola could make a movie in Oklahoma, then Alan Wilde could make a movie in Wisconsin. Bad thinking. Very dangerous.

Wilde glanced around the high meadow, marred as it was by the more than fifty members of his crew, shapeless in unfamiliar woolens: the sound man, the mixer, props people, special effects, electricians, grips, the assistants to the assistants—the men and women who became extensions of the visions of his mind, the will of his muscles. The trailers and the tons of heavy equipment were becoming slimy with condensation in the cold, clammy air. The actors had had to work with mouthfuls of ice chips to keep their breaths from misting. The theatrical blood had frozen so often, they'd begun to use vodka instead of water as its base. Appropriately ghoulish.

This was the last day in April. The date on today's call sheet proclaimed it openly, but the mercury in the outdoor thermometers registered so low that it might as well have been the day after Christmas. It was supposed to warm up over the weekend.

Wilde had never been fond of spring. It was messy and unreliable, overrated—like success. Back in L.A., bodies were baking in the sun. Flowers were blooming on the hillsides. God help him, he was even beginning to miss the smog. It had to be more wholesome than this interminable chill.

Time crept, as it had so often for him lately, inching frame by frame as though he were running in slow motion to a Vangelis score. He had damned few destinations left to run to. He had the palacelike home in Beverly Hills with Japanese parchment screens and koa wood, and the pool he never had time to swim in. He had the obscenely expensive imported car that spent most of its time in the repair shop waiting for a vital piece of its imported guts to make its way through the intricacies of international mail. He had the Oscar that haunted him, the ghost of hungrier days. And he had the women who came and went like honeybees in his life, their presence leaving little impression on the curious silence in his spirit.

He ran a desultory finger along the fence wire, registering the abrasive filings of rust through his leather glove, and it occurred to him that he would never use his own character in a movie—the rich, cynical movie director. Yes, bored and cynical. Why did that sound like a law firm? Too obvious; too corny. Trite. What happened to people who turned into living clichés?

His script supervisor, Joan, was walking by, her runny nose bent toward her clipboard, her magnificent red hair turning to strings in the wind. He stopped her with a touch.

"How're you doing?" she asked.

"Coming to the conclusion that I'm bored and cynical," he said.

She slipped her hand under the lamb suede collar of his jacket, dragged down his head to tease her tongue slowly along the edge of his ear, and whispered a cure for his boredom. His body kept its chill, even though she was cute and trying so hard to please him. He took her chin lightly between his fingers and smiled, a smile that he knew hadn't reached his eyes when she pulled back, gazing at him, manufacturing a shiver that had nothing to do with the weather. She left him after a playful shake of her head.

It was unprofessional as hell to flirt with an employee on the set. People were staring at him, his reputation a cage around him. Each bar of that cage was forged from a half-truth, yet still the whole was as strong as iron. His genius, his promiscuity, his frigid emotions had become industry legends. And inside there was only a human being who was wondering how to stop discarding himself.

Max, his director of photography, came puffing up, his balding head stuffed into an Irish tweed cap. He was nursing a cold, and his handkerchief blew out from the side of his face like a white banner of surrender into the chafing wind.

"I don't like the light." Max glared up at the absent sun as if he wanted to replace it with a tungsten bulb. "What d'you think?"

They'd been fighting all day about the light. Wilde said, "I think that I'm bored and cynical."

"Yeah? Well, I think that I'm Ferrante and Teicher." Still looking upward he added, "Damn clouds."

Wilde took his D.P.'s shoulders in a friendly grip.

"You want me to help you with the clouds, Max?" He redirected his gaze from Max's crimson nose to the stratosphere. "Clouds!" he commanded. "Clear the sun!"

By odd coincidence one actually did, and a ray of sunlight shot down to the meadow at a long angle. Laughter ruffled through the crew. If they thought they were supposed to, they would have laughed at his reading of the back of a cereal box, and he knew it. But the laughter improved his mood anyway.

"Don't let it go to your head." Max grinned as he blew his nose. "You happy with the way that reflector's placed now?" He indicated it with the flexing of one shoulder.

Wilde grinned back, remembering the days when the perfect placing of a reflector would have been enough to make him happy. When had the cyclone of creative decisions ceased to excite him? He glanced north, following the line of wire fence as it rushed along the meadow's lip. Two crows perched there. *If the crow on the right flies first, I'll like the placement of the reflector. If the crow on the left flies first, I'll have it moved.* The breeze sprayed a fan of yellow grass against the fence, and the crow on the right launched itself into the wind.

"The reflector is fine." Wilde pushed off from the fence. *Scratch the self-doubt,* he told himself. *No one would believe it was in character.*

He walked across the meadow, dispensing directions, settling back into his role of Godfather and Khan in the same way that an actor settles into a monster costume.

The actor in this particular monster costume was one of his closest friends. Dash Davis—not his real name, of course—was a veteran of TV westerns, and "oh, yeah, *that* guy" face to millions who couldn't have matched it with a name. A cluster of wardrobe and makeup people had just finished twenty minutes' worth of work attaching the monster mask to Dash's head. One of them must have told Dash that the director was making his way through the busy crew, because as Wilde approached, the monster began to lumber toward him, hideous claws uplifted menacingly.

"Wanna kiss?" asked the monster, voice muffled by thick foam rubber.

Wilde dropped a courtier's kiss on one gory paw. "Fangs become you."

"Hell, this is the best I've looked in years. Will I play in Peoria?"

"You'll scare the hell out of Peoria."

Rick Lessa's self-satisfied smile lengthened as he stood back admiring his creation, one hand hooked in a belt loop, the other running lazily through his punk haircut. He'd created the monster—and was something of a monster himself. "And Alan will do big box office scaring the kiddies until they hide under their seats."

The remark irritated Wilde on several levels, but the directorial persona never betrayed irritation on a set. The actors were temperamental, the highly creative members of the technical crew were temperamental, the writers were temperamental. The more frantic the atmosphere became, the more calm Alan Wilde grew; the more patience he exuded. His pictures came in on time and on budget, even sometimes under budget.

"I'm looking for a PG-13, so the kiddies will have to sit this one out." He said to Dash, "What's it like in there? Can you see? Can you breathe?"

"Poorly. Very poorly. But I'm warm."

"Warm? The rest of us have forgotten what that feels like. Let's shoot this thing and go home before someone tries to wrestle you for that costume. If you're finished, Rick?"

In a series of complex and beautifully dovetailed movements, the crew prepared to roll film. It would be a minor piece of footage, an extreme long shot of one well-mangled victim and the monster, rattling around, barely visible inside a wall of foliage. Meaningless without the sorcery of editing and score. Simple, except that in making a film, the simplest act was elaborate.

Wilde relaxed into the security of his professional anxieties. Was the special-effects foreman overdoing the artificial haze? Were the reflectors anchored well enough or was one of them about to take off like a sail into the wind? Was Dash getting enough oxygen in there?

He watched a young technician with a battery pack and blow drier feed cool air full force into the monster's mouth. The cameraman focused on the horseshoe meadow of golden grasses where the victim lay. The monster went to lurk in the dense growth of trees.

Joan joined him and whispered, "I like the set. It looks very natural."

"It better, after the money we've sunk into it. . . . Two weeks of planting to make a pasture look natural . . ." Sound was up to speed. Film rolling. Quiet on the set. Clap board. Technicians busy making notations. "Okay. Action."

Moments passed. The corpse lay. The monster, unseen, began to touch branches eerily. The camera panned and the assistant racked focus.

Okay. Enough of this. Very nice, and all in one take. Let's get Dash out of that armor and call it a day. He was about to call out, "Cut. Print that."

All at once the monster burst from the trees, his grotesque form vaulting forward like a bounding elephant. He was followed immediately by a sprite of a girl in a long dress who was doing her level best to crack him over the head with a gnarled branch.

"What in the . . ." Alan heard his own shock. A babble rose from the crew, echoing his confusion.

"Hey, is this some kind of a gag?"

"What's going on? Where's Security?"

"Where in the hell did she come from? Is this in the script?"

"No." Alan took a swift step. "This is a total—" Total blank. Although distance obscured her features, it was clear that this was no gag. Every motion of the girl's body radiated terror. She thought she was fighting off a monster. Crazy. Yet riveting. Vintage "Saturday Night Live." Her full mauve skirts danced and caught in the high grass as she tore after Dash. The black triangle of a shawl was slipping from her slight shoulders. A wisp of a bonnet wanted to tumble from her dusky hair.

"Do you know what she is? Amish!" Joan, speaking quickly, had grabbed his arm. "You know, Amish. This area is full of them. . . ."

"Oh, my God, she's knocked out his eye!" Rick Lessa, his lips turning white, his breath appearing in short, angry-looking clumps of vapor, was standing straight as a rod. "Five days, I worked on that eye. I'll *kill* her."

Watching Rick take off at a run, Alan decided he really might be about to have a murder on his set. He was running after Rick when it occurred to him suddenly, surprisingly, that he was laughing, sweet, irresistible, genuine laughter.

Spring roared like a lion. The forest path bellowed the joy of the ripening season. The bracing air nipped at Susan Peachey. Her body seemed to be bursting with strange excitement. Exhilaration. Following the wooded trail, the children seemed to float behind her like dancing leaves. Their footsteps were nearly silent on the loamy earth, their cries filled with delight as they discovered each herald of the reawakening world. Robins had returned. Hepatica, bellwort, and wild geraniums were tucked like smiles in forest corners. Pussy willows grew like soft silver kittens on arching boughs.

Susan bent, calling the youngest children to her, putting her hand under the curling leaf of a jack-in-the-pulpit to uncover the tiny green figure below.

Without warning, the forest in front of her exploded in a violent shower of nodding branches. From the epicenter, something rose—a beast . . . a creature . . . a thing of nightmares.

She froze in horror.

The monster's eyes burned, twin flames in the pit of a carbon-black face. Under each lifting arm was a membrane that opened like a bat's wing. Its vast, hooked talons were spreading slowly. It was immense, macabre, silent.

Then, like a lightning bolt, it lunged at her and the children. Terror ripped a scream from her throat.

Susan had no time to think, no time to decide why the nightmare creature stalked a forest where she often walked. No time to plan strategies. She only knew that it was terrible, and savage, and she threw herself between it and the seventeen children who were in her care. It never would have entered her head to act in any other way.

She had chased it twenty feet into the clearing and hit it twice when it spoke.

"It's a costume, lady! A costume!" it said quite clearly.

She'd scarcely taken in that it had a voice when she realized that the peaceful meadow she had known all of her twenty-five years was filling with the strangest human beings she had ever seen. And they were running at her, yelling. A reed-thin person with spiky orange hair and a golden earring was having to be physically restrained.

"Let me at her, dammit. Five days of work . . ." he said with rasping fury.

Susan staggered backward. The grass seemed to shudder under her feet. The stick dropped from her numbing fingers, and she frantically ushered up a prayer.

The crowd swept apart to admit a man who passed through in a way that showed her the projection of power before it showed her the source. The man stopped not ten feet from her, and she had scattered impressions of height and graceful limbs. The breeze riffled through his thick, dark hair, stroking it.

His features were full of expression, more than she could absorb, revealing the complexity of the man within. Emotion played with captivating lightness on the clean contours of his face. His mouth was an elegant stretch, the span wide, the corners uplifted in a tender crook. But his eyes held secrets that took hold of her. They were a soft, very clear hue that so intermixed green and blue, it became impossible to discern the shade. The color was brilliant, the effect lavish, startling in its lightness against the sun-gilded richness of his skin. His gaze probed gently, briefly touching her body, stealing her breath. There was nothing left of innocence in those eyes, she thought.

"Not a child, after all," he said, his eyes continuing their slow warming.

She had never heard a voice like his—soft, the tonal quality harmonic, the vowels silky and spread, perhaps the residue of an accent from the American south. Only perhaps. She had little acquaintance with non-Amish tongues.

From her posture of frozen shock she watched him half-turn to the man with the earring and say in that soft, seductive tone, "Let's let her escape without violence this time. 'Vengeance is mine, saith the Lord.'"

"A tooth for a tooth, an *eye* for an eye," said the man with the golden earring, shaking off his captors.

"Possibly. But if anyone's going to yell at her, it's going to be me," he said.

He began to walk toward her, not quickly, not with a threat to his stride, but her sense of disorientation was so profound that she swung her body defensively backward. Something solid connected with her ankle. She lost her balance and fell, landing on her hip. Stunned, she inhaled the marshy perfume from the bruised grass around her as a chilly dew began to seep through her skirts. She caught sight of the thing that had caused her fall. Her hand, her hem, and one of her feet were resting on the ravaged and bloody remains of a human being.

She couldn't cry out—or escape.

Through the paralyzing agony of pity and terror, she saw wildly that the man with light eyes was covering his face with one beautifully gloved hand, shaking his head, making a gesture of mock weeping, commanding softly, "Curt, stand up before you give her a coronary."

Under her hand and foot she felt the damaged flesh stir, then tense. Her hands were clenched under the arc of her rib cage, pressing into her frantic stomach. The ruined body stood with a young man's grace and gave her a smile.

"It's not what you think." The compelling voice came closer, then the light-eyed man knelt, facing her. "This man is an actor. And though you won't be able to tell it now, or when he rolls out of bed in the morning, he's not dead." He directed a brief glance over his shoulder. "Joe, will you hand me some blood?" He turned back with a cup in his hand. "Fake blood. You see? You can taste the alcohol base."

His light eyes beating into her, he touched the cup to his wayward, smiling mouth and took a healthy swallow of the red fluid inside.

"Of course, it's much better with orange juice," he said, offering her the cup. "Try some—you'll see. Fake."

For a moment she was convinced she was going to be ill, and she bent the force of her will to keep that from happening. He must have seen—perhaps she turned green—because he removed the cup and offered his hand instead.

"I'm Alan Wilde, overlord of all this madness."

Susan watched his fingers surround hers, the supple glove leather imparting the deep warmth of his body. His grip was surprisingly strong, the tips of his fingers lightly stroking her tender inner wrist. Tattered heartbeats filled her throat.

"I'm sorry you had to stumble on us like this. To ward off the sane we hire security people, but they seem to have made themselves invisible. Are you all right?"

He released her hand, his fingertips trailing a slow caress over the contour of her palm, between her fingers. Her heartbeats grew quicker. Every rational process of thought had been engulfed by five minutes that went beyond the total of her life experience. Every sensation was heightened and stinging. Through the wreckage of her reason, she saw his brilliant, curious gaze fasten on her, searching, searching. It was as though they were alone together, and she realized with a jolt that he was finding her as foreign and puzzling as she found him. They were close only physically, an illusion of space. Their diverse cultures parted them, two strangers facing each other across a vast chasm. Inside his easy study of her she read prejudgment, studious interest, and something that might, on the deepest plane, have been ridicule. In spite of that, multiplying her shock, she felt the unfamiliar response of her body as it welcomed his touch.

Retreating from that knowledge, and from the gathering bitter embarrassment over what she could now see was her idiocy in front of these strangers, Susan demanded motion and support from her uncertain limbs, and rose unsteadily to her feet. The monster took an instant protective posture behind Alan Wilde, the huge form exaggerating a cringe.

Susan Peachey felt the rush of painful color to her face.

She faced the monster, trying to look with something like composure into one of its remaining bloodshot eyes. "I can see..." The words faded as her throat muscles constricted from tension. She took a breath and tried again. "I can see that I've made a terrible mistake. If there are any amends I can make—" The heat from the blush became suffocating.

Desperation or some more complicated emotion, one that she couldn't name, made her look sideways, her gaze arrested by Wilde's amused expression. Again she experienced that deep tug on her senses.

In that moment her mind cleared. Actors. Fake things. *Actors.* A glance at the hillside showed her the black box of a camera, the lens glaring down at her like the eye of some malevolent idol. She knew cameras. They intruded without care or compassion into the intimate passage of Amish life. They had come to John's funeral, feeding on the long, somber line of buggies. The sharp spots of heat in her cheeks turned to ice.

Her dignity returned in a flood. She didn't flinch. She didn't cover her face. As though it were happening to someone else, she heard her own voice give her name, and the direction of her home in case there were damages they wished to assess against her. Once more she issued an apology, this time resisting those light, translucent eyes, though she sensed the caress of their interest. That man's gaze must have followed her as she turned, because tiny eerie sparks played along her nerves. She began to run toward the children, where they stood saucer-eyed in the bushes, the youngest seeking refuge in the arms of the older ones. She swept up little Deborah, who was tearful, and led the others swiftly with her into the forest.

He continued to stare after her, fascinated, though the branches disturbed by her flying skirts had folded back into place, closing behind her like a turnstile to another world. Susan Peachey. Her name was so apt.

The director of photography joined Wilde. The D.P.'s cap was pulled down further, his collar was turned up, and the wadded handkerchief he was pressing crossly to his nose had reached a critical stage of saturation.

"Amish," he said, briskly sniffing. "And they say we have all the nuts in California. Alan, if you want another take we'll have to do it again tomorrow. Lessa says he'll be awake all night getting the monster prettied up again."

Wilde ended his dreamlike study of the misted trees. "It doesn't matter. We'll use the footage we've got. Tell them to go ahead and print it."

"I already have. Do you know we had film rolling until about a minute ago? I told them to cut it and print everything up to Dash's great leap from the bushes. Is that okay?"

Wilde recaptured the image of an earnest figure in long skirts, her face upturned in solemn apology to a monster, and remembered his own unfettered laughter. "No. Print everything."

"What's the point?" Max asked, face buried in innocent misery in the depths of his handkerchief. "Why spend the money to have a piece of film processed that has no earthly purpose—"

"I hire you to carry out my decisions, not debate them," Wilde said sharply. "Print every foot of film whether you think it has an earthly purpose or not."

Max's brow furrowed in amazement. Wilde was surprised himself at his own uncharacteristic flare of temper. Life was an intangible disappointment, and he often felt a nagging inner impatience with things, but he usually restrained it behind a shield of cool, practiced humor. But here was the impatience, rising to the surface like steam.

Max fed the handkerchief into his coat pocket and gave his director a doleful look that asked: why, if you have to be difficult, do you do it on a day when I have a bad cold? He said aloud, "You want a print from it, you'll get a print from it. We'll print you the damned leader if you want. Satisfaction guaranteed."

Wilde smiled a brief retraction of the anger, and when Max's expression thawed he began to walk up the hill, draping an arm around the older man's shoulders. The dispassionate narrator of his life pulled back again and observed with regret that there was little kindness in the affectionate gesture, that it sprang from a desire to charm and control.

Can you cure cynicism or is it a terminal condition? he wondered, and began, with inner desperation, to coolly tease Max, telling him all the ways that his cold was going to get pampered back at the hotel—chicken soup, bed, hot toddies . . .

Satisfaction guaranteed. Satisfaction had become like happiness to him—elusive.

Chapter 2

*T*hey screened film in the hotel library, a room that Alan had decided could be appreciated only by people whose tastes ran to heavy doses of Hemingway masculinity. The stuffed wildlife mounted on the walls was a maid's nightmare. Ben Rose, the producer, had said he hadn't seen so much oak paneling since Perry Mason's courtroom went off the air. They were already in Dutch with the management because someone on the crew had painted shark fins into the duck-pond landscape, and an elk's head had been filched from the wall and lashed to the nose of a caterer's van.

Wilde sat in a leather armchair watching the rushes from the day's filming. A ribbon of smoke rose from the cigarillo forgotten in his lax fingers and funneled into the wall-to-wall haze. He'd had bad news this afternoon. Ulcer-making news. Carrie Tippett, his female star—if you could put a label like "star" on a twenty-two-year-old who wore a retainer, and spent half the day under a Sony Walkman—had put herself into the hospital after a careless experiment with heroin. He'd worked with Carrie twice. She was not stupid, but her eye-opening Bo Derek facial features had little elasticity. The "face" couldn't act and the girl knew it. For Wilde's movies it didn't matter. Shakespeare this wasn't. He needed two things from a woman: great looks and great screams. Carrie knew she would never have more to offer a director, and it produced anxiety within her that ticked like a time-charge. On the phone this afternoon with Carrie's agent, Alan had gotten the bad news at about the same time that she should have been arriving from California for a two-day settling in before they began shooting her scenes on Monday. He'd responded with a moment of some little-practiced emotion that resembled heart-struck pity, but it had passed swiftly to anger as soon as he'd learned Carrie was going to recover.

"Next time she wants to try to kill herself," he had said gently into the phone, "tell her to put a gun to her head and pull the trigger. It may not be as chic, but it's a hell of a lot less agony than heroin, and cheaper."

The anger had continued in several variations through most of dinner. A waiter in a white jacket had been attempting to serve him coffee, when he had risen abruptly, going to the temporary location office to phone Los Angeles and order Carrie three hundred dollars' worth of flowers, with a note attached sending his love and promising her a part in his next movie. Outside the office, he heard two of the production assistants whispering.

"Three hundred dollars. Ah-*hah*. Think he's sleeping with her?"

He returned to the dining room, drank his cold coffee, and made soothing remarks to Ben, who was wringing his hands over what they were going to do for a female lead. Every day the crew was idle would cost them fifty grand.

It was a crisis, so Wilde became calm. In fact, he became so calm that Ben remarked acidly that if he mellowed out any more, he was likely to need CPR.

The calm lingered during the rushes until the final footage, when a girl in Amish clothing ran from the bushes, chasing his monster. He watched it to the end, and then spoke over his shoulder to the projectionist.

"Let me see it again."

"Maybe we can sell it to Monty Python," Dash said, sliding into the seat beside Alan as the scene began to flicker over the screen a second time. He removed the cigarillo from Alan's fingers, dragged on it, and put it back.

"Thought you'd quit," Dash said.

"I have. I'm just holding it."

"It's been in your mouth twice."

"Just keeping it lit."

Alan watched the girl run across the frame, and tried to assimilate the clamor she caused in his body. *What have we here? Love at first sight? Fascination with the exotic? Infatuation? Lust?* He knew himself fairly well, so he settled with resignation for lust.

His first thought was that she moved like a dancer. But he had lived with dancers, and he knew that when they weren't dancing they weren't always graceful. In this girl, every motion played with space, every line seemed merry, like a willow in the wind.

Film adored her face. She had amazing skin, the almost mythical ivory complexion of classic literature. An inner luminosity seemed to shine through the rich, pale color. Five or six freckles were scattered over a small, straight nose. And her mouth—Lord, that mouth. The lips were soft as a child's, the shape and color erotically evocative. He wanted to edge them with his thumb. He wanted to film her in a love scene, move in tight with a camera, cover a thirty-foot screen with her parted lips. Under escaping dark curls and black velvet brows, her eyes were sweetly brown, acorns with sparkles.

The scene changed. Wilde saw himself come into the upper-right-hand corner of the screen, looking half frozen, his ghost of a smile dripping patronage. *I should see myself on film more often. It reads me.*

He looked back at the girl in the film image as she gazed up at him. What eyes she had. He'd never seen eyes that embodied so much sensuality and reserve at the same time. Touch me, they whispered; don't touch me. Innocent, yet provocative. Cast the lady in a perfume commercial.

"Now, there's a mouth that would sell a lot of toothpaste," Dash said comfortably.

"Funny. I was just thinking perfume." Alan glanced sideways and saw Dash's smile. Reflected light from the screen fluttered over the old cowboy's weathered maze of smile lines and his thin mouth, and twinkled in his Newman-blue eyes.

"I figured out why she took out after me with a stick."
Dash straightened his long legs and crossed his lizard-skin
boots at the ankle. "She'd kinda appeared outta the blue,
and I was starin' at her, wonderin': What in the blazes . . . ?
Then it hit me that she was real scared, so I was about to
step out and tell her things were cool, when I tripped—
that damned costume. She must've got the idea I was goin'
for her."

"The woman must have the mental capacity of wilted
kelp." Ben sounded tense, querulous. "Sure, it's a very
sophisticated costume, but it's still obviously a costume.
Unless she thought we were under Martian attack."

Wilde was an open channel to the dark-haired girl on
the screen; half-attentive, he shaped the thought that Ben
was looking for an argument. Ben liked to fight when he
was nervous, and Wilde recognized his own sense of
obligation to give the man his cathartic hassle, and yet he
was strangely reluctant to make the dark-haired girl—God,
why couldn't he remember her name?—its subject. It was
an imprecise emotion. A protective shadow. *I want to
protect you, sweetheart. And I want to take you to bed. To see
your pretty eyes wide open with passion. To see your delicious
mouth wet from my kiss.*

Susan Peachey. Her name came to him suddenly.
Susan. It was prosaic, yet he liked it. It was simple. Clean.
Like her skin. He couldn't remember ever seeing skin
that looked so clean, so completely undefiled.

Wilde's attention drifted back to the conversation in
the room. Joan, conscientious as always, was giving Ben
his argument.

". . . So why would she have any way of knowing?
Believe me, I know a little something about them. I grew
up in Pennsylvania, quite near a large Amish colony. You
can't imagine the isolation of some of these people. Their
culture goes in an unbroken line back to the medieval
peasantry. Some groups are more liberal than others, but
you can bet that girl has never lived in a house with
electricity or running water. They don't own radios or
televisions, or even musical instruments. They don't use
buttons or zippers—too modern. Look on the screen! Can
you see how she's looking up at the camera—then she

turns and melts off into the trees with the children? That's because they don't believe in being photographed."

"I saw a group of them when we were driving through Greyling this afternoon. . . ." Max unburied himself from his handkerchief to speak, his sniffs punctuating his words like a tom-tom. "Very bizarre. The men had big black hats, and suspenders, and these huge beards like bushes growing out of their chins. Makes you think of Rip Van Winkle."

"It makes me think of Hobbits from Middle Earth." Ben hefted forward his chair with one hand, set it backward beside Wilde, and sat down facing the screen, with his arms folded on the chair rail. "When I look at a gorgeous lady like that, I only want to know one thing—does she get laid?"

Scattered laughter. The same question had been hovering in the back of Wilde's mind, but that made it no more acceptable to hear aloud. It seemed crude, and that amazed him. It had been many years since he could remember feeling distaste at a sexual reference—the long, hedonistic years had left him unshockable. Staring up at her face, the word "undefiled" came back to him. She was clean, and he wanted her. *Was this what happened to you when you became jaded enough? Did you begin to look around for some unspoiled being to corrupt? No. No. Dear God, don't let me have turned into that.*

Joan was answering Ben's speculation with some too-clever remark about the large size of Amish families, and Wilde interrupted in a tone that was light and free of emotion.

"No matter how enthusiastically they proliferate, those children can't all belong to her."

"No, I think she's a teacher," Joan said. "I've been taking County CC and Bridge Road out to the set instead of Highway 12—it's longer, but much prettier—and there's this little building that seems to be a one-room schoolhouse on a hill about a mile to the west. I think that's where they came from. That's why Security didn't run into her. They walked through the woods."

Ten minutes later, while he sat with Ben watching month-old screen tests, batting around ideas about who they could hire quickly to replace Carrie, Dash returned from a fast trip to the bar. Wilde looked up as the actor clapped him once on the shoulder and slid a piece of folded paper into his hand.

Wilde glanced down and saw it was a map.

"County CC," Dash said in a gentle drawl, and ruffled Alan's hair with an affectionate hand.

Alan Wilde watched screen tests until one in the morning. Again and again he saw the same scene, each time with a different woman. The heroine in the film was a logger's daughter called Polly Bates. The test was a short clip. Wilde never needed much to base a decision on. Polly tells a young suitor that she won't marry him and begins to walk away. She turns suddenly and says, "Good-bye, Mr. Burke." She walks on another few feet, then whirls and runs back to kiss him, crying out, "Yes! Oh, yes, Adam, I will!" Deathless prose.

He walked back to his room slowly, holding in his thoughts that image of one girl after another turning, whispering good-bye. He was stopped once in the hallway by Joan, who wanted to make sure he wasn't going to be alone tonight if he didn't want to be. Conscientious Joan. If the producer was edgy, she'd argue with him. If the D.P. caught a cold, she bought him time capsules. If the director was lonely, she'd sleep with him. Girl Scout and therapist, she kept the personnel content, and here Ben had only hired her because she was a former centerfold and he liked to look at her.

Wilde had just reassured her that he was all right, when he was stopped a second time by a supporting actress, a forthright and lovely California blonde. She wanted to replace Carrie. She was more than willing to sleep with him if that would help. At one time she had probably been an appealing person. Sometime in the future she would probably become one again. But at this stage of her life, aggressive ambition had blotted out all aspects of her character. For that, and because he wasn't going to give her the part, he felt sorry for her, so he kissed her once. It made frighteningly little impact on his senses and he opened the door to his room alone, hating the profession of acting, hating the desperation it could produce.

Susan Peachey's bonnet was on his bed.

For a blank moment, it seemed to him to have appeared there by some miracle. Then he remembered.

As she vanished into the woods, the bonnet had tumbled from her shiny curls. Someone had brought it to him and put it in his hand, and he had stood there looking after her like Cinderella's prince with the glass slipper in his palm. Unknowing, he must have held it through the rest of the afternoon, carried it back to the hotel, brought it to his bedroom. *It must have looked so lamblike of me. No wonder Dash gave me the map.*

He lifted the light, brimless bonnet. The fabric was pale ivory, delicately woven, with tiny tucks set in. It was almost weightless, and he could see his hand through it. Had she made it herself? He ran his finger slowly along the trailing ribbons that must have touched her neck.

It occurred to him to wonder if it carried her scent. Though he knew he was alone, he felt a little self-conscious as he brought it to his face and breathed in slowly. There was no trace of artifice or perfume, and yet the scent of her was so sweet that it ran through his body like the spill of a sparkling fountain.

All around him, the darkness seemed to recede.

Chapter 3

*A*h, the room was warm. So many bodies. The words of the sermon were sweet-flowing, like a lullaby sung ever more softly. The occasional rustling sounds of the worship-

ers around her fell into a contented hum, the colors before
her eyes becoming a blend of glassy patterns. Her eyelids
were sinking slowly. Moments passed, pleasantly heavy,
yet buoyant, and when images became clear for her again,
Susan found she was nesting her head on her mother's
shoulder.

Henry Zook, standing in the midst of two big rooms
of benches filled with more than two hundred of the
devout, was almost finished with his message. His hand
rested on the rail of a ladder-back chair; his other clasped
the white handkerchief, damp from the perspiration blotted
from his brow. A plate of crackers was being passed for
the children, and over in the men's benches, some of the
boys had begun to swing their heels, brushing them
against the hats that lay underneath like a field of flat
black flowers. Susan straightened, trying to close her
mouth around an unwanted yawn. She caught the eye of
her brother Daniel, and his grin, the one you got for
nodding off in service. There was a bit of mischief in
it.

Last night past midnight a playful breeze full of
springtime had tiptoed through her window, wakening her,
beckoning. In her nightgown and robe she'd gone out of
doors to lay her blanket on the picnic table, and curled up
there, watching the planets rise and set until she'd fallen
back to sleep. Daniel had found her when he went out to
milk. "We'll see if you can stay awake during sermon,"
he'd said. He knew her.

On her other side, her friend Fanny was trying to
appease her infant son, Jesse, letting him suckle a fingertip
in the pink bud of his tiny mouth. After giving the finger a
bit of a try, he cast it out with a howl that drew a smile
even from Henry Zook, who had been fairly wrapped up
in what he had to say. Fanny gave a rueful glance at Susan
and her mother, and over at her husband, Christ, and
carried Jesse off to the kitchen to nurse him.

A water glass began to circulate for the children, and
Susan dipped the corner of her handkerchief in it and held
it to her eyes, rousing herself to kneel and replenish her
spirit in the quiet ecstasy of prayer. She immersed her

heart in its soaring updraft until she was light, her soul outflung, bodiless.

After service, most stayed for pie and fellowship, and Susan spent some time in the kitchen cutting pie. She cherished the task, surrounded by the sweet berry fragrances and glossy colors. Point out a pie and she could tell you the woman who'd baked it. It was a remarkable thing, how each pie had its own personality imparted from its creator. There was her sister Anna's neat little fork pricks and the edges just so, everything orderly and quiet. Ruth Whetstone made a lattice on the top of her pie that, Susan realized, resembled the latticework around Ruth's porch where she grew the beautiful irises and herbs she was known for. Susan had a spearmint snip from her at home that was rooting in a glass on the windowsill. Sarah Beachy marked her pies with a carefree swirl that put Susan in mind of a musical note. They were great singers, the Beachys. Jake Beachy's bass sounded as though it came right out of the cellar.

And not much doubt about her mother-in-law's pie. Susan lifted Edna Peachey's pie, looking at it with affection. Custard again. It was the thing to do, to bring a two-crust pie. Everyone brought a two-crust pie except Edna, who did things a little differently. Edna said one crust was enough for any woman to make for each pie and that was all she was going to do, and let anyone who wanted to, tell her otherwise. Well, of course, no one ever did, though from time to time Susan had seen this one or that one glance at those custard pies just as they might look at a cuckoo in a nest. But they ate them all the same.

Susan took her own slice of pie and sat all in the corner with Fanny and Edna. Susan was hiding out a little, if the truth be known, even though it hardly seemed as if there could be one person left who hadn't asked her every question there was to ask about her brush with the monster. The kids had carried home a wild story or two, the littlest ones wilder stories yet. Their parents had started coming around to the farm soon after school, wanting to find out what really had happened. Karl Rader had even showed up with a deer rifle and his two grown sons, ready to hunt the thing. She had told her story maybe two hundred times. Some were disapproving; most thought it was funny. Since she'd played a pretty ridiculous part in the whole encounter, she'd gotten plenty of chances to laugh at herself. It seemed to her she'd laughed at herself enough by now to keep her for quite some time.

When Henry, a twinkle in his eyes, stroking his blond beard, stopped by their table she thought, here we go again, but he only said, "I saw I set you off to a wink of sleep this morning."

"No. I'll tell you what happened, Henry. I was so taken up in your testimony that I had to do some deep thinking on it."

"Oh, was that what it was, deep thinking?" He winked at Edna. "Well, I saw three or four deep thinkers out there today, including that husband of yours, Edna." He smiled and moved on, and Susan trailed him until she reached the spot where her grandmother was sitting.

After lunch on a Church Sunday like this one Grandma liked to go up to one of the bedrooms with old Mrs. Yoder and Ben Miller's Eleanor to reminisce about old times, or so they liked to say, but everyone knew it was to share a friendly pipe. Walking by the door, Susan could hear the creak of rocking chairs and catch the dry, ticklish scent of tobacco where it crept under the door. Since Grandma's sight had failed, Susan would walk with her grandmother up the stairs to sit after preaching service.

This time she led her grandma into quite a disturbance. One of the Yoder boys, Fanny's seven-year-old, Jonas, who was as wild as they came, had been pulling back the clothesline like a bow to shoot clothespins at the girls, and had smacked his sister Sadie a good one on the arm. Sadie went off to fetch her pop, and Jonas hurled himself inside and up the stairs and hid under one of the beds, and wouldn't budge even after his father arrived and yelled at him to come out. He was a tough one! Fanny tried to chase him out with a broom, so he shot out from the far side and climbed out the window into an old elm. Fanny was going to climb right out there after him—she didn't care, she'd been a tomboy—but Jonas yelled out, "Don't come up, Mom, or I'll jump." And he would have, too. He was a Yoder, and that was the way they were sometimes. Stubborn. So they left him to sit out there in the tree until he got tired of it.

Susan thought about how it was that way in her family. Dad didn't say much, but he had a way of looking at you that let you know he meant it, so all the children minded him good.

Susan spent a bit of time after that playing with Fanny's tiny daughter Lizbeth, whom she loved, and listening to people talk about Jonas, and how he would settle down when he got older, or how he wouldn't settle down when he got older if Fanny didn't take a firmer hand now. There was hardly a soul who didn't think they'd have Jonas straightened out quick if they had hold of him for a week or two. Of course, none of them offered to have him stay with them to try it, even though Fanny made the offer to let him visit with them if they wanted him.

The upshot of it all was that people had their minds off the movie company and the monster, which suited Susan just fine.

She walked home on the dirt road with her family, the sun falling on them like big, warm snowflakes through the leaves. All together like this with her brothers and sisters, and Mother and Pop and Aunt Mary and Grandma, they made four lines stretching across the road, boys together, girls together, because that was the way they always went walking. Near the lily pond and the fishing bridge she and Daniel would break off to go to chore at the small place they farmed together now, and her family would keep on to the big farm. Things didn't change much, except that they walked a bit more slowly since Grandma had turned ninety. And there was one less sister. Oh, but that was hard to think about.

"Were you up last night, Susan?" Grandma's arm, comfortable around her waist, gave a couple of soft, inquiring pats. "I woke up thinking about you late."

It was often that way between them. "I went out to see the sky."

"How is it for you, sleeping these days?"

"Better now."

"Having nice dreams sometimes?"

"A few. It's strange, you know. When I wake up I

forget what was in them, but I have this feeling something wonderful is about to happen to me."

"So it will. It may be that something's waiting for you just round the next bend."

Too bad that wasn't a prophesy. Right around the next bend they ran smack into Abraham Beachy, who had to be about the most cantankerous man in the county. He wasn't from the singing Beachys, but from the other branch, who didn't see the point in a tune. Abraham always had something figured out to be angry about—a neighbor who wouldn't keep up a fence; the county, which didn't make the shoulders of the road wide enough to pull a buggy onto; the state, for forcing Plain People to attach orange triangles for slow-moving vehicles to the buggy tails, so's they had to look worldly, like one of the High Amish churches that had slipped off from the old ways of thinking.

Today Susan had the feeling she was the one who was going to get it from Abraham, and she wasn't wrong.

Abraham didn't even bother to get down from his buggy. Instead, his beard bristling, he went right into how Susan shouldn't have been anywhere near where the English were making that movie. He didn't like his boy Elam exposed to it. Didn't Susan know what kind of people these were? Who could tell what could have happened? He ended up with: "I'd like to know what the die-hinker you were doing so far off from the schoolhouse, anyway, wandering around instead of having lessons. I'm gonna talk to the Bishop."

Susan could see her father had that pokery look he got when something rubbed him wrong. He spoke. "You can't keep children cooped up in a schoolhouse all day long. They have to spend some time out doors, stretching their legs."

Abraham made an angry gesture. "Letting them out is one thing; walking over on English land is another. And what does she teach them kids when they're supposed to be learning arithmetic? She's got them so boogered up you don't know what's in their heads. My Elam come home talking about this Poop Bear your daughter makes them read about."

"That's Winnie-the-Pooh, Mr. Beachy." You had to be

humble with Abraham and let him have his say or you'd hear about it all day. "I didn't see the harm in it."

"And I don't suppose you see the harm in Spiderman either. First he talks about this bear, then he goes out and buys himself a comic book and hides it in his room. What for kind of story book is that, about a man who makes like a spider?" Abraham's cheeks were turning ruddy. "It don't seem to me you have much of a proper idea about schoolteachering. I come riding by the schoolhouse last week and I see all the scholars laying *outside*, on the ground, on their stomachs! And there you are, there's the teacher right among 'em."

She tried not to have the thought, but it occurred to her to wonder if he'd turn purple right now if she smiled. "We were studying ants."

He fixed her for a minute with one of those stares that were supposed to make you feel beaten down. Her father came over beside her and said, "Susan is a fine teacher, Abraham. She does just right with those children."

"I'm going to speak with the Bishop," Abraham repeated impressively, like it was a great decision, and slapped the reins and left off with a nod.

"Let him go bother the Bishop," her mother said once the buggy was out of earshot.

"And make a pest of himself." Aunt Mary smiled fiercely. "Old sourpuss."

Susan got a squeeze from Grandma, who agreed. "Weaned on a pickle!"

Under the circumstances, anyone might think that Seth, who was Abraham's son and who'd been in the buggy and seen the whole thing, would have chosen not to leave his father's buggy by the pond, to wait and walk her and Daniel up the lane to their place. But there he was, tall, fair-haired, leaning on the fence post, with his hat forward shading his eyes, waiting for her after service, the way he'd done since the worst of winter was over.

She wished he wouldn't. She couldn't see him without calling up the face of her lost sister, because for years she had seen them together. It might be why he wanted to be here with them, to cling to some part of Rachel.

It was also hard to have Seth around because Daniel

didn't like him, even though they were much the same age, in their mid-twenties. Not that Daniel had ever said anything. He was like her parents and rarely spoke ill of anyone, but it was there. He let her see it in the expression on his face.

She knew she had to get the fight with Seth's father out of the way right off. "I guess your father doesn't think much of me."

"He doesn't mean anything by it." Seth gave her a flex of his lips that couldn't quite work up to a smile. "You didn't seem to take it too serious."

"Not too."

"You have to be careful, Susan. You don't know what it's like out there. You don't know what the English are like."

That was the way it was with Seth, the English this, the English that, as if all the evil in the world were out there past the county line, where the English houses started. He had run away from home as a teenager and lived in some big city in California for two years. She remembered how he'd looked when he'd come back, with hair so long it went right down his back. He had a tattoo as well. Her brother Levi had seen it when the boys were swimming, though he wouldn't say what it was. What had happened to Seth in those years, nobody knew, but it had to have been terrible, the way he'd talked about the English ever since then.

Seth had ways that were hard to understand. You never had the feeling you knew all there was to know about him. He kept something back. It might be the time in California that had done it to him. Or maybe it was living as he had, with his father and no mother. Maybe in a family like his one learned to keep things way back.

It had been her sister Rachel who had helped him put himself back together after he came home, and everybody said, "Isn't it something, the way that girl is so good to that poor troubled boy?" No one remembered now. Too much sadness had come after, and now Rachel was gone and there would be no more memories to make.

Susan snapped herself away from the unhappy thoughts

and stole Seth's hat to get him off the subject of the English, which it did, fast.

The warmth in the old barn was infinitely peaceful that night. Susan had shared the work in this barn and the acres beyond with her husband, John; now she shared it with her brother Daniel. Under a hissing Coleman lantern, she sat half-tucked beneath the wide girth of Muffin, one of their Brown Swiss cows, her forehead nestled against its flank.

"Have you been thinking you might have Seth?" Daniel's voice lifted from the shadowed box stall beyond, where he was teaching a heifer calf to take milk replacer from a pail.

The question came as a surprise. "Have him for what?"

"Anything."

She shook her head and smiled. "He hasn't asked for anything."

He let the subject drop. Then, "Did you get enough asked about your run-in with the movie business?"

She straightened, arching her back, running her hands underneath her shawl to find and press the hollow of her spine. Bending again, she said, "More than enough."

"Too bad. I was just working around to it myself."

She grinned. She'd known he would get around to it sooner or later. Daniel had a way with his teasing; never unkind, but always accurate. When he teased, it was like watching a sharpshooter pick off clay birds at a trap shoot. No one could match him. Tenacious, she thought, savoring the new word. Every day she tried to learn a new word and make use of it at least once. This morning her word had been "tenacious." Daniel is tenacious, she thought with pleasure, then with resignation.

She heard the click of tiny hooves, as the little heifer lost patience with its tedious new method of taking nourishment. Daniel spoke to the calf in a low tone, his murmur as dulcet as the rustle of the doves in the eaves and the faint brushing sounds from their contented animals. The aroma of warm, fresh milk drifted around her along with the fragrance of hay in the mow above.

She closed her eyes, letting scent and sound ply their magic. "What are they doing around here, anyway, do you know?"

"You remember how people were saying back in March about that group that was going to rent the historical buildings at Greyling? Said they were coming from California to make an educational movie about Wisconsin wild flowers in the spring? Turns out that was a false story they put about to keep away the crowds while they were shooting out of doors. That's why you ran into them without knowing. What they really are is a fancy Hollywood movie company. One of the fanciest. You'd think we'd have guessed, because they weren't likely to take rooms for a hundred people or lease huge sheds for their equipment just to take a few pictures of flowers." He chuckled, and in the pause she could hear the warm sound of splattering milk as he scooped thick handfuls to the calf's pink muzzle. "Innocents, aren't we? That seems to be why they chose this area. The story in the movie takes place more than a century ago. Hereabouts we don't have power lines and television antennas for them to worry about. They like having a few dirt roads, too."

From another Amish, such easy talk about the movie business would have sounded strange. But Daniel was different. For one thing, he had read a good deal of books one didn't find in Amish homes, and he had a good number of English friends. There wasn't much that their dad or the Bishop or anyone else could do about it, because Daniel hadn't taken the vows of baptism and joined the church, the way she and Rachel had at eighteen. In good conscience, he'd said, he could not. He had things to resolve in his own mind first. Well, you couldn't force a man to take vows to God he couldn't keep, but her parents used to do their share of pushing. They'd pushed, he'd pulled away more, and they'd quit their pushing fast. And Grandma recalled that their own dad had taken his vows late, too, at twenty-six. Baptized and married in the same year, he'd been, when he took a trip east to Pennsylvania and met Mother. In the Amish church there was no wedding without both members of the couple being baptized first. And since there was scarcely an unmarried girl in the county who wouldn't have Daniel in a minute if she could, her parents had a pretty good idea their son would succumb sooner or later.

Daniel could do things that would cause talk if done by other people. Even if he had some wildness in him, he was so full of love, he could get by with all manner of actions and talk. Even the Bishop said, "If the Lord takes anyone to Heaven, He'll take Daniel."

What the Bishop didn't know was that for more than a year Daniel had been in secret defiance of the order to shun their sister Rachel.

A sudden chill touched Susan's hands, and she warmed them in her skirts.

"Alan Wilde spoke to you." Daniel's voice sparkled with the teasing smile she couldn't see.

"Hardly at all."

"Think of the danger you were in!"

"What danger?"

"The magazines at the grocery store write about him often. He's lived unwed with some beautiful women—well-known ones, mostly."

"Has he? I suppose if I'd known that at the time, I'd have keeled over dead from the shock of it." There was humor in her voice, but an image of Wilde, of the light, clear eyes, the wide mouth, had remained with her, beckoning her to an odd restlessness as the night wind had done. How strange he was to her. It was beyond her power to imagine the part of life he must have tasted, and yet, almost as if those eyes had fed it to her, she sensed the depth of his experience and, somehow, its taint. Had this man's life begun to turn, twisting back like a venomous serpent in his hands until the days brought despair rather than peace? The child in him seemed to have died. Oh, yes, his eyes had summoned her, but they held no promises.

She compared Wilde's eyes to Seth's. Seth's were those of a disappointed boy, and Wilde's were more those of someone who had been forced to sup with the devil. And yet there had been laughter in his eyes, too.

It was hard to understand why Wilde's broken life fascinated her. She was no longer in her *rumspringa*, the time of running around, before marriage, when banned intimacies called like sirens. She remembered the vague longings. Then marriage had come . . . and quiet disappointment.

Daniel emerged from the stall and crossed his arms on Muffin's back, looking down at her. Mischief gleamed in his dark eyes. His broad hat angled forward over his long coal-black hair. "Think of all that sin coming in your direction." He wriggled his fingers drolly at her. "Did he look you all over in a wicked way?"

An unwilling grin broke over her face. "Go on. You'll make Muffin kick the pail."

"Answer. Did he?" Daniel ducked under the cow's neck, his face commanding her gaze with bright, humorous eyes.

She was disconcerted to find her grin widen, and warm dewdrops of color rose in her cheeks, because even though Alan Wilde had been far from giving her a wicked look, there was some guilty part of her that seemed to wish he had.

Daniel must have absorbed the unexpected intensity of her reaction. One black eyebrow swept up, and two dark eyes began to search hers. Daniel *was* tenacious, she thought, and this time amusement accompanied the insight. Resting her elbows on her knees, she tucked her chin into her curled fists and met his scrutiny with a candid stare.

"Speaking of sin . . ." she said, "I might have a question or two for you."

"Oh, you might, might you, now?" He took a seat on a pile of burlap feed sacks, his elbows propped behind him, his body comfortably stretched. His smile was faintly wary but not unwilling. The placid lamplight held them like a golden bowl, cupping them in its safe world. Delicious night murmured outside, inviting confidences.

"Have you ever seen a movie?" she asked, and held her breath, wondering if he would return with an answer or an evasion.

A pause. "Yes."

There was something nice between them—trust. They didn't speak this openly with frequency, but when it came, it was without the nervous qualifications: *Please don't mention this to anyone. Promise you won't repeat this.*

"Do they always have monsters?"

His involuntary smile told her she had asked an odd question. "No. They don't always have monsters."

"Were they . . . There've been a lot of them that you've seen? Tell me the name of one."

"Well . . . *Animal House.*"

"Oh. Was it about a zoo, then?"

He got that smile again. "No. College."

He stood up, ending the conversation, and she bent back to the milk pail, saying it was good that if he had to go and see movies, at least they were about such lofty things as college.

While she was pouring milk for the barn cats and laughing as she watched them come running on light feet with their tails upraised, she looked up to find Daniel still smiling at her.

"You know, Susan, if someone ever does look you over in a wicked way, there's a chance or two you just might not realize it." And then they were both laughing as he let her wrestle him to the straw to stuff a handful of hay down his shirt.

Chapter 4

Susan ran through the yellow light of dawn, the sun in front of her a halo on the horizon. The ground was cool. The meadow grass smelled like night and licked dew on the hem of her dress. The air shivered with birdsong.

Her donkey Clover was missing from her pasture this morning. In the evening, her little sisters had been to visit the donkey, and probably one of them had forgotten to latch the gate when they were leaving, and Clover was an opportunist. "Opportunist" was today's word. She stopped her search to grin and stretch in the middle of an open field. Today felt wonderful.

Like a cloud covering the sun, the brief unease following her run-in with the movie company had vanished. Summer was just around the corner, peeking like a child. The warming sun would bake well-being like syrup into a reluctant earth. Things would come right.

She drew her shawl more tightly around her against the morning nip, thinking how perfect it was to walk at this time of year before heat unshelled the swarms of summer insects. Bugs. She thought of them banging against her screen door on a hot evening, trying slyly to steal inside. Things of nature, yes, but a little hard to love. Except for ladybugs and fireflies . . . She spared a warm-hearted thought for fireflies. And who could be melancholy watching a butterfly lilt from petal to petal, or lying on a soft lawn observing ants in their sturdy industry?

But mosquitos were a mistake, Lord.

She could feel the flow of an infinite wisdom answering her with amusement. The emotion-rich flow became manifest in her thoughts. *You think so, do you, Susan Peachey?*

I do. She smiled, and felt the returning smile. Soon her garden would be filled with growing things. As the season advanced and the rains became fewer, there would be trip after trip from the pump to the garden, quenching thirsty tomato plants and beans. So many trips. She thought longingly about how nice it would be to have a hose, a good, long one stretching in a cool green strip across the wan dust behind the barn. But hoses were expensive, and every spare penny she had was going into the jar for Rachel. There'd be few enough pennies to spare soon, when school let out next week and the income from that was gone for the summer. She hoped that the Bishop would not say no if she wanted to find work cleaning at the nursing home. Even the money she earned there would barely scratch the surface of Rachel's need.

But hope sprinkled through the honeyed air of morning. *It will come out all right. It must.*

On the other side of the meadow she climbed a wooden stile over the barbed-wire fence, wound through a sun-speckled thicket, and came into the bright open stretch of freshly tilled earth, rich brown and fragrant.

She saw Clover near the far fence, the donkey's taffy-colored muzzle nosing in the hedgerow near the curving strip of dirt road. Susan felt no surprise. This had happened before. Freedom for Clover meant a chance to wander toward the home farm where she had been born and raised by Rachel's absent hands.

She felt no particular alarm as she began to cross the softly corrugated soil, clasping Clover's rope bridle. Then as she came closer, her sharpening view picked out the glinting strands of wire fencing that separated her from the small animal. Clover was on the wrong side. Somewhere a fence must be down.

Uneasily she quickened her pace. Four feet of sloping ditch were all that protected Clover from the road, and though traffic was infrequent, cars came fast around that curve.

Clover eyed her with interest as she approached the fence, speaking in an encouraging tone. With amusement and dismay, she could see mischief brewing in those great liquid eyes. Sure enough, as she parted the wire strands with care to crawl through, Clover skipped playfully up the embankment onto the road. At the same time, Susan heard the roar of a car engine fast approaching, made invisible by the curve. She hurled herself between the barbed-wire strands, her breath coming in a frenzy. Racing up the slope into the roadway, she was in time to chase Clover onto the far shoulder, though she barely escaped being struck herself. The churning wheels came close, spitting gravel across her skirts, sending vibrations from the roadbed up her legs. A push of after-draft flattened her clothing to her body.

She tumbled down the steep shoulder to where Clover stood amid a ramble of trees and the ribbon of a creek that trickled through a culvert underneath the road. She was breathing heavily as she slid the halter over the donkey's flossy nose. Shaken and only half-aware, she hardly noticed that the car had stopped not far up the road until she heard the gravel crunch under advancing footsteps.

"Gracious. What an exciting life you lead."

The words, spoken ever so softly, came from above her. She turned her head. Her startled gaze found Alan Wilde. He stood at his ease, his curving palms braced on the gray stone bridge that crowned the culvert. Morning breezes lifted tentatively at the deep burnished brown of his hair. His shoulders seemed perfectly relaxed under a supple leather jacket, but his light hypnotic eyes were vivid with his unknown thoughts.

Alan Wilde.

He moved away from the bridge and began to find his way down the embankment toward her. It became imperative that she collect her scattered wits—imperative, but impossible. "Gracious," he had said to her, "what an exciting life you lead." How odd it was that she knew the words were sardonic, though there had been no trace of that in his tone. For one thing, he was obviously the kind of man who didn't usually say "gracious."

He stood looking at her at the base of the hill, his silhouette sharply real against the slope of spring's uneven grass, raised in tufts. She had never thought of herself as timid, and yet she grew tremulous. Her throat became arid, her face tense. Her hands searched backward for support, coming to rest on Clover's neck, and the small of her back settled against the donkey's consoling warmth.

Wilde began to walk toward her. She assumed in her bewilderment that he would stop some feet away, but he came so close that she might have reached out with her hand to touch the enchanting upcurve of his elusive smile. She would have said something then, anything, but his gaze stopped her, holding her quiet and still and frightened.

He removed one glove and lifted that hand to her cheek. Very, very lightly she felt the back of his fingers brush her. A cold flutter tingled along her nerves as his hand skimmed slowly lower, following the meandering trail of her bonnet string over her jaw, her neck, her collarbone, her upper chest. And then the caress of his fingertip became a lazy glide following the gauze strand as it climbed her breast. The delicate pressure grazed her nipple, stroking her through the sudden tightness of her thin wool dress.

Holding onto Clover for dear life as his hand left her body, she gasped out the first words that came to her.

"Are you going to touch me again?"

"Do you want me to?" His eyes were full of secrets, his smile pagan.

"No."

"Why not?"

"I . . . I . . . Clover might get away."

He gave a soft laugh and stepped back, and she began to breathe again. Her thoughts were a quagmire, her senses prickling.

"Clover is the donkey's name?"

"Yes." Even the simple monosyllable stuck on her tongue as it became obvious to her that she ought to have protested. Somehow she'd been too aghast and now it was a bit belated. Too late, Susan. He's already *done* it. He had touched her in that terrible, throat-catching way, and then asked her calmly if Clover was her donkey's name. Trying to understand him, to clear her distracted thoughts, she looked down, lowering her chin. He lifted it on the arc of his finger, his light gaze examining her face.

Then she was released—and became more aghast when he uncurled her fingers, removing Clover's halter, tethering it to one of the posts of the sagging wire fence that looped along the tree-fringed field. Her eyes went wide as he peeled off his jacket and dropped it on a dry carpet of grass near a clump of cowslips. Taking her shoulders in a grip that frightened her thoroughly, he set her lightly down on his jacket. His shadow swept over her face as he sat beside her, his manner seasoned, his expression companionable. *Does he just want to converse with me?* she wondered. She stared down in embarrassment at her knees.

Breezes whirled across the hayfield before them, raising and smoothing the blue-green leafage like dappling velvet. Chilly water trickled in the creek. Birds sang with dizzying beauty, invading her senses. Sound became a physical presence around her, a comforting vapor. Behind her the bank rose more than ten feet, sheltering them from the road, and she had guilty gratitude for that, as though she were a child again and into mischief. Yet the feelings Alan Wilde aroused in her were far removed from childhood.

"Are you shy?" he asked softly.

She hesitated.

"If you could handle the monster, you can handle me," he said.

She had the impression that he was smiling. "Perhaps I'm tongue-tied. I don't know many English men."

"But I'm not English." His tone conveyed that he couldn't understand how she'd gotten such an idea.

"That's what we call . . . others. We call ourselves the Plain People, because that's what we are. Just plain people. We call you the English."

We call you the English. Alan Wilde felt a wave of elaborate delight. So English was the Amish word for honky. *But if there's anything you aren't, darling, it's plain.* She was wearing a sunbonnet today. Its heavy black brim projected forward, veiling her features. Only the tip of her nose was visible. *Here I am in Wisconsin trying to seduce Holly Hobby.*

"Tell me about your bonnet." He watched the patch of her nose, the tense perfection of her shoulders. "It covers you from the side, like blinders on a carriage horse. Is that why they make you wear it? Eyes forward, hands employed usefully, a life of duty, devotion, and submission?"

She turned, as he had hoped she would, and he bathed in the winsome pastels of her complexion. Her eyes held an expression that was closer to surprise than to offense; she sensed his irony, but found it alien, obscure.

"I wear it because it keeps the wind from my face. It's for protection, not restraint."

"And your clothes—long sleeves, long skirts—are they for restraint, or protection?"

She watched in fascination as the corners of his mouth curved upward like the tip of a cat's tail. The question was impossible. She couldn't begin to sort through his layers of meaning, and he was making it difficult to retreat. Could it be that in his unorthodox way he was simply trying to be friendly? Or perhaps he was interested in her way of life, as the tourists were. Curiosity about him was expanding inside her, an irresistible force that shoved against her will to deny it. The freedom he felt to question her was staggering, and far wider than she had been raised to believe was polite or proper, but the frank manners were intuitive and compelling.

"Are you working on your movie nearby?" she asked, finally desperate for a way to speak to him that was within the realm of her experience.

"Yes. But that's not why I'm here. I suspected you were an early riser, and I drove here hoping to see you," he said, and saw her receive the news with a jolt.

"You'd like me to pay for repairing the—"

"No. No, no . . ." He began to laugh, and the impulse nearly overcame him to drag her into his arms and hold her against him, kissing away her confusion. God, to be like her, that innocent again. The latent tenderness burned him briefly, and he regretted the poverty of conscience in him that led him to pursue her when he knew that it would have been in her best interest if he left her alone. He wasn't going to stop, and he knew it. The moment he'd touched her, he knew. It had become inevitable, established. He was going to take her to bed. But she was so naive that he was compelled to improve her odds against him, schizophrenic as that might sound. "I want you to understand, Susan. It's you. I came because I want to be with you. Don't invest it with hidden meaning. Don't paint it with elements it doesn't have."

She stared at him as if he'd slapped her.

If he meant what he seemed to mean . . . She felt white-hot shock. Was he saying . . . ? No. It couldn't be. Even in his world, this couldn't be how things were done. The light green-gray eyes were warm, his body relaxed, almost lazy, as he rested back on his elbows, looking at her. His peach-gold crew-neck sweater lifted color from the fragrant grass. His legs were outstretched, one knee flexed in worn jeans, the posture casually attractive. How natural he looked, how at ease. His expression was even rather sweet. It didn't seem possible that he could mean . . . There must be no one in the world who could meet someone once and decide right then and there that he wanted to be intimate with that person. She could feel the color building in her cheeks. He couldn't mean such a thing. She was giving his words hidden and shocking meanings, even as he had warned her not to do. Embarrassed, she tried to compose her expression, grateful that he couldn't know the trend of her thoughts. *I suppose I ought to remarry*, she thought desperately. *I'm becoming obsessed.*

"Why?" she asked.

Her brown eyes were inquiring, her head slightly tilted. It was a good question, but one that he pulled away from exploring, because he had no doubt that the answer would reveal an undertow in his character that he would rather store in his unconscious self. Her looks were almost incidental to his need for her, but that was the obvious explanation, and the safest.

"In part because you're one of the most beautiful women on God's green earth."

Her lips parted. She pulled a face and began to laugh. He could see clearly that there was no modesty in her response; it was simple oblivion. Her beauty, or her lack of beauty, if that had been the case, was not part of her value system. She didn't know. She didn't care. And she assumed he was teasing her, and that relieved her uncertainty. He could see that she seemed to have decided he was an eccentric but congenial stranger. For the first time he realized how separate she was from him. She came from a people that formed a little universe in and of themselves, different, apart. He had a nearly overwhelming compulsion to take her in his arms and bring her close. But he recognized now that she didn't understand the full implications of his interest in her, and wouldn't understand it unless he used very graphic language or laid her back in the grass and covered her with his body. Or gave her time.

She had stopped laughing, though her smile lingered. What a smile she had. He wanted to curl up inside it and sleep for a year.

I'll give you the time you need, Susan Peachey.

"Did anyone ever draw line pictures on your back?" he asked, slipping into the role she had cast him in.

Her nose crinkled. She looked curious, dubious, intrigued in spite of herself.

"I don't believe so."

He noted that her dialogue had expanded from monosyllables. There was no doubt she'd decided he was harmless. The internal tenderness nagged him again. He hadn't meant to leave her undefended, and some of the gentleness he felt went into the smile he sent her. "It's a game. I draw something on your back with my finger, and you guess what I've drawn. All right?"

"All right." She repeated the words, thinking how funny he was, how whimsical. He moved so quickly from one thing to the next that she could hardly follow him.

Earlier apprehension about his motives had fled, and she wondered if she hadn't listened one time too many to Aunt Mary's story about how she'd let her sister talk her into a covert visit to the fair where an English man in a fancy plaid jacket had offered to ride with her on the Ferris wheel and then forced a kiss on her mouth as they swung above the twinkling lights of the fairground. Daniel might say, "In my opinion, she loved every minute of it," but the story was supposed to be her warning about English wiles. It was hardly necessary. She'd had a few experiences of her own with English men—catcalls from passing cars, obscure innuendos from gangs of young men who lounged near the vending machine beside the grocery store.

Alan Wilde was another kind of man. There was a refined elegance to his manners, and there was humor, and those were qualities she couldn't imagine in association with ill intentions. Surely he was to be trusted.

It would be foolish to make too much of his touching her. The English were free and easy in that way. She had seen them holding hands in public, embracing with little reason. They saw nothing indecent in it, no shame. No need to read a meaning into it that was absent.

Watching him redirect his glamorous frame to her back, she had the slip of a notion that he wasn't as wealthy as she'd imagined. Those knees were one Monday wash away from needing a patch. The thought erased more of her caution, although it stabbed briefly when his arms rested lightly on her shoulders.

His fingers absorbed the tightening of her muscles. She turned to look up at him, her gaze anxious. She had amazing lashes. They swept downward, curving slightly with pliant silkiness. He reassured her with a smile. *Is it just shock, or are you responding to me, Susan?*

"It's a game, remember? You can't look."

She turned her face forward, looking at Clover nosing under the fence to prune the edges of the hayfield. She gazed at the distance and saw the same horizon, the same fields, heard the same sounds she had always known. Nothing had changed. Nothing altered. The material laws of the earth had not been transformed in the last ten minutes—yet there was this odd thing happening within her. She was becoming weak all over from the touch of this man's hands. Even as she recognized she should stop him, she couldn't pull away from his achingly pleasurable touch. Images came of nights in a warm bed with her husband, of the comfort of a strong body at her side. And of the times in recent months when loneliness overtook her and she would find herself half-weeping from the need to be touched, and she would pick up one of the babies at church and hold it, just hold it.

Capturing the upper edge of her shawl, he began to draw it gently lower. Again he felt her uncertain resistance.

"We have to give you a fair chance," he said. "How could you feel anything through this?"

She kept to herself a dismal revelation: She was feeling much too much already; he was touching someplace inside her that was desperately needy.

Wilde studied Susan Peachey from behind. Under the stark, simple lines of her dark azure gown, her back was straight, like a female gymnast's. Beneath her bonnet he could see the fine eggshell flesh of her nape, softened by a scattering of drifting midnight curls, and if he leaned over only a few inches, he could have stirred them with his breath.

"What's this?"

She followed the heart-lifting lazy path of his fingers. "A circle."

"Obviously it's a circle. But what object does it represent?"

"How could I know? So many things are circles."

"You're not getting into the spirit of the game," he observed.

She smiled at the gently chiding tone. "Well, then, it's a ball."

"Wrong."

"Is it the ring through a bull's nose?"

"Very creative. You're coming closer." Interesting. There was a Rorschach inkblot quality to this.

"Is it the nose plate on a water bowl?"

"Don't get technical. I'm not a farmer." He shifted to look around at her smile. "It was a wedding ring. You don't wear one."

"No. We don't wear jewelry."

Have we got a problem here, Susan? "Are you married?"

"I was. My husband was killed in an accident two years ago."

"I'm sorry." *Wilde, you incredible hypocrite.* "Any children?"

"No."

He was sensitive to the world of desolation in the single syllable. *Susan, Susan, what am I doing screwing around in your tender life?* His finger moved again on her back. "What's this?"

"Is it a pitcher?"

"No. A number."

"Is it a four?"

"No." He repeated the motion with the pleasure of touching her running in a thrill up his arm.

"Is it twenty-one?"

"Very good. Is that how old you are?"

Her chuckle sounded pleased. "I'm twenty-five."

"Ah. Aged." That produced another chuckle. He laid his palm on her back and began to massage her slowly. It occurred to him that he had expected her clothes to feel as archaic as he found her culture, but the cloth was soft, pleasantly saturated with her warmth. For the first time he was able to ascertain detail about the shape of her body.

"What are you doing?"

He didn't miss the breathless quality of her voice, the slight quiver. *Yes, darling. Respond to me. But don't give me too much too soon. My self-control is only so tempered.*

"I'm erasing the number."

He continued the game, and was able to discover by the same methods that she had twelve brothers and sisters, that her parents and most everyone else she knew was a farmer, except one uncle who made buggies; that a sixty-mile bus trip to the zoo in Madison was one of the biggest adventures of her life; that she taught seventeen Amish children in the one-room schoolhouse where she had attended school herself. He also accidentally discovered that she wasn't wearing a bra, and experienced a sharp chain reaction in his body. *Oh, Lord. I wish I hadn't found that out.*

"Is that a star?" she asked, enmeshed in her innocent involvement in the game.

"No. Those are letters." He made them again.

"Is it AW?"

"You're getting good at this. AW it was—my initials." He realigned himself to her side, smiling into her wondering eyes. He followed her hairline with one finger and said gently, "You've been branded."

She stared at him for what seemed like a very long time. Then her lashes fluttered and she looked down, tightening her shawl convulsively. Quickly and gracefully, she rose to her feet, murmuring that she didn't know what had gotten into her, she mustn't stay, there were chores, then school . . . While she untied the donkey, he had the impression she was trembling. He sat watching until he saw her stop, turning to face him as though it were something she couldn't prevent herself from doing.

"Good-bye, Mr. Wilde," she said.

And that brought everything together in his mind. A chain of girl after girl turning, whispering good-bye to an offscreen lover. It was so simple, so dramatically easy that he had almost overlooked it. And it was hard to remember that he actually had the power. All he needed were those great looks and great screams. It was too easy.

She had begun to walk away, leading the donkey.

"Susan?" She stopped. "Would you like to be in my movie?"

She turned, very, very slowly.

"I don't think I could have heard you correctly. . . ."

"Yes, you did. I asked if you'd like to be in the movie I'm making."

"Be in the movie..." She repeated the words as though she couldn't understand what they meant.

"As an actress."

"Actress. *Me?* I could never—"

"You could, or I wouldn't be asking. You don't have to know what you're doing. I do." He had never seen anyone look quite so stunned. "We can pay you thirty thousand."

She was so taken aback, because he seemed to be making the outrageous offer in all sincerity, that she heard herself say, "Thirty thousand...what?"

That made him smile. "Thirty thousand of whatever you want. It would probably be easiest for the accountants if it were dollars. Don't give me an answer now. Think about it. What time does school let out?"

"Two-thirty..."

"All right. I'll come by after that and we can talk. You're in the white clapboard building down the road, aren't you?" He rose to his feet, sweeping up his jacket with one hand, and joined her, climbing up the steep shoulder by her side.

She started to speak again. "I must not have properly understood—"

"You did. No answers until later."

Walking beside her, amused by her flabbergasted silence, they had just reached his car when he heard her murmur, "If I were to do that, I'd be an opportunist."

It was such an offbeat remark that he found himself asking, "What?"

"An opportunist." She gazed up at him, her air candid and instructive. "It means a person who takes advantage of an opportunity regardless of the consequences."

It had been a long time since he'd met anyone guileless enough to assume he needed the definition of a word. Quiet laughter rollicked through him. "I know what it means. Why did you choose it?"

"Why, because it was today's word."

Her eyes bade him farewell, and she left him, running

across the russet-brown face of a Wisconsin field. The donkey cantered at her side. Susan's heels caught her skirts, tossing them in an animated ruffle.

Alan Wilde stared after her, struck by the spontaneous rightness of his impulse. The haunting dove of a heroine in his movie did exist. Polly Bates was real. She was Susan Peachey.

Chapter 5

Alan Wilde anticipated a fight, and he got one. Those with any conceivable say in choosing Carrie's replacement were appalled at the introduction of Susan Peachey's name into the process. Wilde, they said, you can't be serious, and as soon as he heard that, he knew he was going to win. Can't. That word. He always won arguments that began with the phrase, "Wilde, you can't." It sharpened his appetite for victory. He had spent his adult life sating himself on the meeting and besting of challenges.

Often there was even a primitive pleasure in the industry dogfights, and in the exercise of examining and expanding the boundaries of his authority. One of his lovers had called it his "power-trip high," and it was not one of the qualities in himself he found particularly appealing. To ignore it, he had begun to try to separate his ego from the core of every dispute. The intense behind-the-scenes film-industry squabbles, the struggles over the fate of a million-dollar budget, were diminished in his mind to a cartoon fray, Tom and Jerry disappearing into a cloud of dust with arms and legs projecting from it.

Kay Lorine from wardrobe was his easiest victim. Her nervous blue eyes implored him from beneath the brown bangs that hid her eyebrows. When he picked up one of her hands to give it a friendly pat, he discovered that her palms were sweating.

"Alan, we have a fortune invested in Carrie's costumes," she said. "I mean—thirteen changes, Alan. Carrie is a size ten on top, a size six on the bottom. If you could just hire a girl with something like those proportions..."

The director as father figure. It was part of his responsibility to issue meaningless reassurances, so he did that while wondering silently what size Susan was. She looked like she could buy her clothes in the little boy's department.

Ben Rose was more interesting prey. Wilde made the announcement to him with careful simplicity.

"I want to hire Susan Peachey to replace Carrie." Nice. Dispassionate. As in, I want a Perrier with lime. I want to risk multiple millions of studio dollars on an inhibited Amish girl with no acting experience.,

Ben had enough innocence left in him to laugh. When he realized this was no joke, his brow tightened briefly like an angry jack-o'-lantern's before he relaxed into the authority figure that kept flamboyant young directors in line. He might be wearing a brown checked shirt, but Wilde could almost see the older man growing a smoking jacket and ascot, adopting the suave disgruntlement of a men's-club resident disturbed over his evening paper. Ben started with logic, his tone rational, if a little irritated.

Wilde settled back in his chair with a cigarillo in his mouth, listening with patience, letting his eyes communicate to Ben the futility of opposing him on casting Susan. Ben's face crumbled into frustration, then into fear and bullying, and finally into good, solid wrath. "Damn it, Wilde, quit your James Dean act and discipline your damned hormones. Where do you get the nerve to expect us to risk blowing this picture just to make sure you get laid?"

A roomful of bickering people fell into an interested

hush. Here it was: the secrets of the director's libido set up for display like sculpture on a pedestal in a gallery. Inside him, some remnant of sensitivity flinched. Outside, his expression remained flawlessly neutral.

He gave them nothing to fuel their arguments, and the vacuum of his poise caused embarrassed moisture to gather in Ben's eyes. Wilde prolonged the moment, waiting it out. Silence was one of the more practical forms of aggression. He could see Ben's determination beginning to wilt as the producer realized he had gone too far.

The older man crushed out his cigarette. He paced to the window and back.

"Can she act?" Ben snapped out finally, fighting for dignity.

"I don't know." Wilde focused on the small gesture that rid his cheroot of ash, wondering if he ever would be able to give up smoking completely. It was the symbolic capsule of every pleasure—quickly over, dissolving into a smear of carbon and smoke. It was good to remember. He wondered what Susan knew about pleasure. Anything at all? "She doesn't have to act. She can be herself."

Ben looked grim. "I suppose it would be heresy to suggest that *herself* might not have the kernel of an idea how to bring a character alive for the camera?"

So that was it. Wilde recognized the producer's defeat, the reduction of reasoned argument to baiting. They would give him what he wanted. Always. Ultimately, they'd have let him cast an elephant in the part if they'd thought it would make money for them. The native wisdom was to "give Wilde his head." His string of commercial successes had left his financiers with an almost superstitious reluctance to thwart his creative decisions. Susan was beautiful, and Wilde wanted her. It was that simple. Fortunately, these things had nothing to do with sanity.

In midafternoon that same day Alan left the set in the hands of his parade of assistants and went to find Susan.

He reached the tiny schoolhouse in time to see the children departing. Susan's children. There was a clear-eyed charm about them, the irresistible freshness of rural childhood. Smiling and unspoiled, isolated from the nether world of Saturday-morning cartoons, video games, and rock music, they piled out of the schoolhouse door, looking curiously sweet in their old-fashioned clothes. At the bend in the road he parked the Jaguar, watching the laughing schoolchildren gather among their engaging cluster of transportation, riding away through the long grass in many directions like expanding star points—boys on horseback with dangling shoelaces, four bonneted little girls bouncing in a pony cart, a brother and sister riding tandem and without a saddle on a mule, their bare toes trailing pink and dusty against the animal's rough belly. Barefoot. Was it that warm today? Strange to realize that he'd given up noticing the weather unless it annoyed him. What other major forces of nature had he stopped factoring into his life?

The children disappeared, leaving winsome, vulnerable images with him. He turned the car into a graveled drive. The school, and a stable behind, sat like a pair of toy houses on the rise of a wooded hillside. A truck tire hanging from a gnarled apple tree was the only play equipment in the wide mowed yard, but Wilde picked out the hopscotch patterns drawn in the dirt and the worn angles of a baseball diamond. Two sheds near the tree line confused him until he recognized with amusement that they must be outhouses.

Susan appeared in the frame of a front window, her eyes questioning. The sound of the car's motor must have drawn her. Again a shock made his senses jump. So beautiful. So damned beautiful. Like some overromantic establishing shot from a neo-Dickensian costume drama, she stood quite still, her posture perfect, her screen-goddess eyes lavish with curiosity. She gave him a tentative wave, and then watched openly as he crossed the yard. *An honest response. No games, then? You need more armor, Susan.* Caution was the one thing she was likely to learn at his hands. A painful thought, that he had the potential to harm this fragile person, but he held on to the feeling, letting himself experience it, letting it run like hot rain through his awareness. Pain, guilt, anything was better than the saline sterility of his inner life. The continued numbness had become unbearable.

Two scarred wooden steps led upward to a double screen door, its rusted mesh belled outward by small eager hands. The tired spring creaked a welcome.

Stepping inside was like entering a time warp. Half-forgotten incense of childhood assailed him—chalk dust, crayon, and strong hand soap. Diffuse light pearled through the windows, a honeyed softness glancing off varnished wood on the desks and floor, tinting the room in sepia hues so that everything looked as though it were trapped in an old photograph. He made himself see detail: the black-iron wood stove, low coat hooks, colorful alphabet letters and animal pictures ringing the walls, an aged set of World Book encyclopedias, and her desk, clustered with papers, an outdated globe, three apples, blue and gold wild flowers in a glass. The chamber was richly evocative for him, as though he had been here before, many times. But of course he never had, and he wondered if the one-room schoolhouse was a thought picture etched in the collective American memory.

Susan had remained by the window, too fascinated by him to think about moving. He had returned, as he'd promised, and this morning had really happened. With a suddenness that startled her, he stopped looking around the room and smiled directly at her.

"Hello, Amish."

There was a brief temptation to be affronted, but something in his knowledgeable smile would not allow it. She had a funny feeling inside, like a tickle, that made her smile back and say, "Hello, English."

As before, she had the sensation that he was too much to fathom at one time. Yet she could barely glimpse that thought before he spoke.

"Why did you say 'opportunist' was today's word?"

How quickly ideas came to him. Perhaps it tired him, the imaginative flow of his mind, like gazing too long into a bright flame. It must give him no quiet.

"Each day I try to learn a new word."

His pliant mouth crooked at the corners in a smile. His eyes beguiled. "You must know a lot of words, then." He relaxed against her desk, possessing it, his expression attentive. "How would you describe me?"

She had no understanding of how he achieved it, or even if the effect was deliberate, but she felt a lifting sensation in her chest, the curl of a response to him as a man. Her gaze made an involuntary traverse of his body, where supple muscles gave exquisite form to the jeans and sweater she had seen on him this morning. Since then, she had been shaky inside, filled with half-formed fleeting decisions and questions. Now he was here and very real and she was becoming preoccupied with the worry that he might touch her again. It amazed her that his smile could have such power to bite and enthrall at once.

"It would be difficult. . . . I've never known anyone like you, so interested in everything. I would say you seem to be a man who thinks well of himself." She watched the barb increase in his smile. "And that you're accustomed to having power over others . . . and you're very clever, more clever than most people. I should think that would be difficult, because you'd often be frustrated, or disappointed in those around you."

He flashed on an errant childhood memory of his father, the face scarred with fatigue and envy. *Kid, there are luxury cars with sticker prices lower than your IQ.* He remembered his own smothered impatience, the thing he had long since learned to control. Control. It was an area where he excelled, except that the threads of urgent desire spinning within him as he looked at Susan had no fiber that resembled control. She was much more awake to him than he'd assumed. And he wanted that, needed it; to wake her up, all over, all through her. "An interesting diagnosis," he said.

She watched him walk around the room touching things—the stove, the wall poster painted by the children that read "The Lord Is My Shepherd," a bat, glove, and ball on a low shelf—as though it helped him see them better.

"Conceit and disillusionment." His voice was light, enchantingly playful, as he ran firm, graceful fingers along the binding of a prayer book. "Can the patient be saved, doctor?"

The little-understood shaking inside her grew worse. "He can if he wills it so."

"Very practical. Though I'm afraid it's not what I had in mind." *You're so tender and earnest, darling.* The more he saw her, the more imaginary she seemed, like a fairy come to dance in his palm. *You need to be protected from me. But there's no one to do that, love. No one.* "Have you thought over my offer?"

"Oh, yes. I could hardly think of anything else. But if you could listen for a few minutes, there are some things I must tell you."

"Tell me, then."

It was a new experience, someone trying to talk him *out* of starring her in one of his films. She had no experience. She wouldn't be able to understand what he wanted of her. She had never even been to a movie. She didn't quite understand what they were. Was it like television? She had seen television once, when she had visited her sister in the hospital after a tonsillectomy. Her sister's roommate had a television, and Susan had seen a story about a street where people lived with a giant yellow bird and an angry monster whose home was a garbage can. Were movies different from that? She sat on a table as she spoke, her fingers curled around the edge beside her thighs, her expression sincere, the soft stretch of skin beneath her cheekbones carrying the misty flush of her hesitant excitement. Like many of the children, she was barefoot. Not quite touching the floor, her feet were long, straight, and lovely, the flesh clear and ivory under the deep blue of her skirt. Her delicate ankles and the vague outline of her slim legs under the fabric were sweetly stirring. She was as much myth to him as woman, exotic Americana. Becky Thatcher grown up. For all its fanatic excess, her culture was far from charmless. The notes pinned to her bulletin board had amused him.

The boys—Aaron and Elijah—may go barefooted today if they wish.

Mrs. Nisley

Our children have my permission to go barefoot today if it warms up like it did yest.

Fanny

These people have made themselves so damned innocent.

He answered her questions with care, subtly encouraging her confidences, taking care not to threaten her, assuring her that he wouldn't hire her if he had any concern that she wasn't able to handle everything he would require of her.

"Is it decent, Mr. Wilde?"

"Decent?"

Susan saw that he said the word almost as though he didn't know what it meant. He had been scanning her corkboard as he spoke to her, his attention casual, focused, it seemed to her, in a dozen directions at once. But her question drew his full attention back to her.

"We don't go so much for stories like yours, full of things that are not. Monsters, animals that talk." She remembered the Pooh Bear squabble. "Well, mostly no animals that talk. It isn't the kind of thing we like." She tried to search his bright, unfathomable eyes for answers. "In Exodus it says, 'Thou shalt not make unto thee any graven image, or any likeness of any thing that is in heaven above, or that is in the earth beneath.' We don't allow ourselves to be photographed, you see. Not at all. Even our books have no images of people in them. Would you care to look?"

She slid off the table, bringing him a reading book from her desk, and held it open with unsteady fingers, showing him, as though it might have some power to convince him, to make her world steady once more. "It's a good way, don't you think? To do what the Bible says?"

So Becky Thatcher grows up and begins to doubt. *Why don't you understand that I make a lousy Father Confessor, darling? We can hardly let a little thing like your moral integrity interfere with the things I want, can we?* He studied the illustrations, line drawings of a barn and pasture, a horse and buggy on a dirt lane, a bare kitchen. No people. No things that are not, no animals that talk. No Dr. Seuss, no Ezra Jack Keats, no Maurice Sendak. No photographs anywhere of Susan in diapers, riding her first bike, dressed for Halloween. He noted the soft heat of anger in his chest, liking it.

A seed-company calendar on the wall held a pedestrian photograph of a maple coming into leaf. He lifted the cardboard frame, gathering her attention to it.

"Is this evil?"

"You don't think so." Again there was an implied question in her words.

"No more than a reflection of a puddle. If it's a photograph, why are you allowed to have it?"

"It's on a useful thing, a calendar. It's not so bad to have a bit of that, just for pretty. The old farmers used to say it like this: *chust for pretty.*"

He smiled. "That's all a movie is, a string of pictures hooked together so they appear to move. It's not so bad; just the same as this calendar."

"I can't figure out why you think I'd suit."

The way he was smiling also was an enigma to her. He said, "Don't worry about it. You're exactly what I need. What did you mean when you asked me if the movie was decent?"

"You must have 'decent' out there in California."

"I suspect we have a different version of 'decent.'"

"Is there anything in it to make me ashamed?"

"I'm not sure. What sorts of things make you ashamed?"

She became embarrassed, the more so for his bright glance of inquiry. After a moment he laughed softly and said, "I see." His smile was burning and lazy. "Is this your first sin?"

She couldn't imagine why that irritated her, but it did. "Of course not."

"No?" He pretended to be aghast.

She thought. Then, with a grin, "When I was little, I dared my brother to lick a flyswatter."

"Did he do it?"

"You bet. It was a triple dog dare."

Then he said peacefully, "I triple-dog-dare you to accept my offer."

Her smile faded. Her thoughts whispered with the shock that she was really considering what he asked.

He came toward her, and she felt her heart compress in uneasy excitement with each step he took. He spread his arms, resting a hand on either side of her knees along the edge of the desk. She was inches from that engaging mouth, his voice intruding softly into her blank, chilly alarm.

"You want to do it," he said, letting the force of his will breathe conviction through her numb confusion. "I know you do. You're too honest to deny it, Susan. You want it. I promise there's nothing to make you afraid. Work with me. And I'll keep you safe."

It seemed like a long time before she felt herself nod. Filling up inside with the horror and wonder of what she was doing, she absorbed the light, seductive impact of his hand as it cupped the underside of her jaw.

"Don't look so worried, Amish." His wayward mouth held the trace of a self-mocking smile. "You might discover you like being a sinner."

Looking back on her conversation with Alan Wilde, Susan recognized two things: First, she'd never expected the devil to show up at her doorstep in dungarees, with wonderful eyes and a hypnotic smile. Secondly, she was going to be in his movie, although she knew it was wrong and ridiculous. She was going to do it, and then it would be over, and she could give the money to Rachel. So much money. She could hardly wrap her mind around the sum of it. For Rachel it would mean rest from the killing pace of college by day, working by night.

She had to do it.

An understanding of Alan Wilde for sure was hard to come by. He found her a curiosity, that much she knew, and she suspected he meant to give her some small task as one might do to employ a child, to give himself time to study her. It ought to offend her, she supposed, but how could it when she saw he had an irrepressible interest in all things? Rachel was like that, full of wonder, and Susan couldn't bring herself to believe there was anything guilty in that.

Do you like Alan Wilde, Lord?

Confirmation bathed her, soothing, bringing love and clean feelings.

But then, you love everyone, don't you?

Amused confirmation.

Is he a sinner, Lord?
Confirmation.
A bad one?
Confirmation. Then, *Stay close, Susan.*
I'll try.
Again the love and confirmation. *I know you'll try.*

Chapter 6

*S*usan reached her folks' farm that night in the deep dusk.
She could see a star through the blades of her dad's
windmill. They had lights on in the house, and in the
barn, and there was something especially cheery and inviting about a lit building this time of day. She liked the way
dim light came out the dusty barn windows onto the
cobble of smooth stones on the gravel drive and its fringe
of sweet clover. She could smell sorghum cookies baking in
the kitchen and fresh starch from the linens swaying on the
wash line.

Picking a clover and tasting the honey, she let herself
into the barn's side door. Her dad was inside, shoeing one
of their road horses, her brothers and sisters busy around
him in the shadowy spray of lantern light. Lamps brought
everybody close by night. Chester and Levi, straw hats
knocked awry, were pulling Whiskers out of his harness;
the little folks had got the goat cart out. Norman, just
turned five, was trying to teach his rollicking collie, Bess,
to play dead. Jacob lay on the feed sacks with two puppies

on his belly. Side by side on a straw pile, Freeman, Carolyn, and Mark were dreaming over a seed catalog, their dark hair tipped in golden light.

"Susan! My daughter who's a stranger! It's a good thing monsters chase you back from time to time or I'd only get a glimpse of you on Church Sunday." No matter how often she came, her father always said something like that. If she came every day, he would still tease her, that's what he'd do. She popped a kiss on his cheek.

"I'm here so much the path between our homes is worn to a trough. Anyway, I wouldn't miss today. Rumor has it Mom has made some gingerbread."

"You'd better eat some in a bit, then. Look how thin you've got, living on your own."

"Phoo."

"Thin enough to sleep in a straw." Glancing to the side, Dad observed one of his teenagers, Luke, carrying a shovel of feed. Luke wore his hat at a rakish angle, and her father tipped it straight as his son passed. To Freeman, munching raisins from a sticky palm, he said, "Hey, I told you there were Indians out tonight. Were you watching? Look, out the door! There goes one!"

Freeman looked quickly and Dad slyly stole a raisin. Secret smiles broke out on the faces of the other children.

In a minute or two, Dad halted work again. "There's another one!" He was able to steal another raisin. Jacob began to giggle.

After a bit, "There goes three of them!"

Instinct and the grins around him finally alerted Freeman, who pretended to check out the door, then swung back in time to catch his father in the act.

"Oh, Dad . . ."

Anna, who'd turned sixteen, and baby Katie ran in through the barn's back door with the wind fluttering in their skirts and their cheeks the color of strawberries.

"Susan! I didn't know you were coming tonight." Anna knelt and warmed her fingers in the collie's thick pelt. "I went to the marsh with Katie to show her the cowslips. I never saw so many, I'd guess! Did you happen to watch the sunset? There wasn't a cloud in the sky, and the sun sank so low, just like a ball of fire."

"Be sunshine tomorrow, then," Levi said, walking to the tack room with a goat harness slung over his shoulder.

"No. It's going to rain." Jacob caught Katie as she toddled by and scooped her up beside him, his grip strong and steady for a seven-year-old. "Mother said so. Tonight sparks clung to the bottom of her pot"—he grew offended when he saw the superior smiles of his older brothers and sisters—"and the fire roared in her oven." Seeing their smiles grow: "And her feet burned! That's a sure sign!" He gave up with a disgusted sigh at the burst of heretical laughter around him.

Dark eyes gazing like a scholar's from wire-frame glasses, Mark came matter-of-factly to the aid of his hot-tempered twin. "Mother always knows. Friday last the potatoes boiled dry, and Mother said we'd have rain, and that night came a storm."

"We'll settle it." Levi, buoyant and merry at fifteen, swung back into the room. "Come outside once and—Katie, you mustn't *knoatch* the puppy so. Touch it gently, not so roughly as you do. There, now . . . Let's go out and look for storm signs. A ring around the moon—"

"Or water beading on a pail," Freeman said, grinning.

"Or a heavy evening dew . . ." Chester tinged his voice with mystery.

A smile that became somehow painful hovered on Susan's lips as she watched them spill like moonbeams into the night.

Levi paused by the door. "Aren't you coming, Susan?"

"In a bit. Would you leave Katie?"

Alone with her father, holding Katie on her knee, Susan enjoyed the quiet in the barn. It was so still and peaceful that she could hear the splash near the back door of the house when her mother emptied the dishpan.

She nestled back comfortably into the straw, watching her father work. She had always loved to watch him. He seemed as tireless to her today as he had in the reaches of her childhood, when his deeply silver-threaded beard had been black and fleecy. His broad back was steady, each of his motions firm and economical. He had wonderful hands, big and sturdy, woven with a trellis of mature sinews and veins. She knew the strength in them. As though it were yesterday, she could remember how they had been able to toss her joyously in the air. These hands had been firm under hers, teaching her to drive his team of prize Belgians. These hands had grabbed the loose reins of the runaway hay wagon that carried her and Rachel, clinging until his daughters were safe, though the speed had thrown his body under the wagon and a metal-bound wheel had rolled over his back. These hands had lifted her young husband after his fall from the barn roof, cradling the slender broken body, surrounding him with loving arms.

"Pop?"

"Mm?" He might not sound like it, but she knew he was listening. Whenever one of his children was talking, you could bet he'd be listening good.

"School's out next week, you know? The kids will be helping in the fields, and there's no more teaching for me until fall. And, well, I thought I might take some extra work at Greyling." Her voice didn't tremble. A miracle. This would be the worst part, the half-lies. She had a vision of herself standing at the very edge of a plunging cliff, staring outward at the blackness.

He worked silently for a time before saying, "Why?"

"Got to shake the money tree, Pop."

"If you're hard up this month, Mother and I could—"

"No, please, Dad. Daniel and I still owe you on the vet bill for Muffin's milk fever." She was briefly queasy. It would be intolerable to siphon their money to Rachel without their knowing. "It'll be just temporary."

"You'd have yourself a savings if Daniel hadn't been so keen last spring to buy those registered heifers. No set of fancy papers ever made a cow a better milker."

Daniel's ambitions were her father's favorite old grumble. She let it pass. After a bit, he said, "Are you figuring to work and farm at the same time?"

"I do it while school's on. And Daniel will have Luke and Anna over to help out."

"So you go off to work for somebody else so's you can afford to hire someone else to come and work for you. That's real good sense."

He was assuming, of course, that she'd found some domestic work for a short time, as Amish girls did on occasion. It wasn't forbidden, but you sure couldn't say it was encouraged any, either. *Come ye out from among them and be ye separate . . .*

She put Katie on her hip and went to him, tugged gently on his beard. "You think I'll get myself in trouble in Greyling?"

"I just don't care to have you over there with the town slick with English. What about them from the movies, the monster men?"

"I don't suppose they'll be around long. They won't bother me any. And if they do, I'll jab them with a pitchfork."

"Oh, you will, will you?" He rubbed a hand through his beard. "See all the gray hairs I got here? This here's a special patch I got just from you."

She laughed. "Go on."

"Look here at the tip of my chin. That's where the first one came, about the time you was five years old. I come out and there you are way up in the catalpa tree with one end of a rope tied around your ankle and the other one around a tree branch, and you call out you're going to jump off to feel what it'd be like to fly like a bird. Three feet of girl, thirty foot of tree, and forty foot of rope."

She combed his beard with her fingers. "You've still got some dark hairs, though."

"Yep. I guess there's room for a few new gray ones." He worked quietly, then looked into her face. "Are you still having those sad days, Susan?"

"No. I'm pretty good, mostly."

"You're a little restless, maybe?"

"Maybe."

He formed a warm sphere around her hands with his own. "Then work in Greyling. Just temporary." He lifted one hand to gently pinch the tip of her nose, and everything inside her felt as if it had cooked down into one warm, hard knot.

By the end of the week, Wilde had flown in one of the best entertainment lawyers in the country to handle Susan Peachey's contract. Katelyn Fisher, attorney to the stars, entrepreneurial cavalier of the film-industry mega-projects, was eminently overqualified to handle Susan's relatively simple contract. Smooth, carefully charming, dressed to the teeth, Katelyn had given Alan her cool, Boston-bred smile and said, "I've worked out a nice little contract for her, Alan, if that makes you feel any better." She had walked toward the door and stopped. "Look, I know it's hardly politic to say anything—"

"I'd go with that instinct, Kate," he had said.

She had warily continued. "Strictly off the record, then. Friend to friend. She's a very bright girl, Alan, but she has only an eighth-grade education, thanks to her religion and the Supreme Court, which protects the right of these people to stunt their children. She hasn't got any idea of what it means to star in a movie. Do you know that before I explained it, she didn't understand that your film might be shown locally? She thought that because you were from Hollywood, the film would only show there. She didn't realize that it would be copied and distributed. Do you know what she makes teaching? Five bucks."

"An hour?"

"A day, Alan. Be very careful with this human being. She isn't like anyone you and I have ever met."

Chapter 7

"She's yours, Alan."

Kristi from wardrobe gestured in the grand manner toward the open trailer door where Susan stood framed by white corrugated siding. She looked like the engraving from *Godey's Lady's Book* that had given wardrobe the idea for her turquoise-blue gown. Even with a skirt tiered to the floor, bell sleeves that foamed lace, a ribbon-trimmed bonnet, still the eye was drawn straight to her face. Almost. Wilde corrected himself. There had been a slight detour over the tiny waist, the tender roundness of her breasts. *Halt the shooting schedule. The director wants to carry off the star and make love to her until they burn every thought from their minds.* Every thought...

She was thinking too much at the moment, that much he could see. Her dark-lashed eyes were magnificently bashful, doubt-ridden. One white-gloved hand made a fist that was pressing unknowingly into the flat part of her stomach as if to heal some suffering. There was something in the combination of her expression, her petrified stance, and the welter of antique detail that brought to mind a maiden missionary dropped into a cannibal's village.

"Hi again, Amish. What's today's word?"

She hesitated, obviously distracted, then said, "Growlery."

"Growlery?"

"It's jocularly meant as a place one goes to growl, some private spot."

"Ah. I can use a word like that. You look"—he considered her—"like a shot of sunlight. How do you feel?"

"Mr. Wilde..." Her tone was urgent. "You didn't tell me I couldn't wear my own clothing."

"Didn't I?" Add it to the growing list of the many things Susan didn't expect, that he hadn't anticipated. Something that obvious... "Gracious, I have been asleep at the wheel, haven't I? But if you think back, you might recall being measured. Do you remember the lady who came with the lawyer the day you signed your contract?"

"Well, yes. But I thought that was only for your—your records."

He wondered with amusement how the Screen Actor's Guild would react to a director who kept private files of his leading ladies' measurements. It spoke to the depths of illogic and obscurity his actions must have for her. "No. It was for costuming."

He could feel the thrash of interest in the busy set around them, the slightly turned heads. She'd met many of the crew early that morning, before Sandy had dragged her into makeup. He had thought, she'll smile at them, and they'll be captivated. She did, and they were. He wondered how long it would take them to adopt her and begin to give her an earful about him.

"Walk with me," he said. "You can tell me everything that's on your mind."

He was beginning to like Greyling. At first it had been no more to him than another set, a place to fill film, an outdoor sound stage that he saw frame by frame, the delicate shades of bark or brick rethought in Eastman Kodak Color Stock. But it had begun to invade his awareness as a place that was real, as something that had been here before him and that would have a life afterward, and not to be struck, dismantled, returned to a studio back lot. Its permanence, and the thought that it was not something he could make and unmake, pleased him.

He strolled beside Susan down the modern red-brick walk that led through a grassy stretch dotted with mobile units, crew, and the blizzard of technical equipment, forcing himself to think about the day's filming, systematically presolving the many small problems that would rain on him before evening, distracting himself from Susan's closeness until he could do it no longer. Then he gave up and turned to watch her, devouring her with his thoughts.

A crinoline spread her skirt, lightly teasing the fabric against the side of his leg. Sable curls escaped the delicate curve of her hairline, wreathing angst-paled cheeks that had the texture of glazed porcelain. Color was breathtaking against her ivory flesh: black satin brows and lashes, delicious orchid-colored mouth, smears of deep pink emotion underlaying her cheekbones. Each part of her made an impact on his senses like some sweet, heart-tripping melody.

But for her, the day was an assault. The newness of this, the rush of strangers, strange scents, strange voices, strange hands touching her made her feel odd and sensitive. Her body felt fragile, as though it might shatter if it were bumped too hard. And she was aware of Alan's silence, so different from any silence she had ever known.

It seemed to cut and soothe at once, to penetrate inside the overtender shell that he was examining so closely.

She made a soft "ahem," trying to anchor herself to a calm center somewhere inside. Glancing around, she allowed her curiosity to emerge, like a swimmer battling through sun-drenched water to an oxygen-rich surface.

"So many people. What are they all doing?"

He was growing more accustomed to the somewhat massive quality of her questions: Explain the operation of a large movie-production company in fifty words or less. "Nothing you have to worry about. They're preparing things . . . the set where we're going to film, the equipment that's going to catch your image and your voice. The better to see you with, my dear. The better to hear you." Rounding an electrical truck, stepping around a pile of cable, he recognized from her expression that she was finding him obscure again. "Are you acquainted with Little Red Riding Hood? No. I see. You don't have stories about animals that talk." Gazing into her upturned face, desire stung with fresh insistence within him, and he reached out to tap her cheek with a gentle finger. "Red Riding Hood is carrying a basketful of goodies to her grandmother, but, you see, to get to Grandmother's house, she has to walk through a dark woods—wolf-infested, on top of that. She stops on the way to talk to this wolf. Now the wolf knows where she's off to, so he runs ahead to Grandmother's house, stuffs Grandmother in the closet, and jumps into Grandmother's bed, wearing her spectacles and cap. Red Riding Hood shows up, and she notices there's something amiss, but she can't quite put her finger on it. She says, 'Grandmother, what big eyes you have!' And the wolf answers, 'All the better to see you with, my—' What's the matter?"

"It's foolish. Why would the wolf go to so much trouble? Why not eat her right there in the woods?"

"He never ate people in the woods. This wolf had class. Either he did the thing genteelly or he didn't do it at all."

He watched her stop, her chestnut-brown eyes searching his, the chimera of an intoxicating smile on her mouth.

"Anyway, even in spectacles and a cap, I would immediately know a wolf from my grandmother."

A cluster of trucks surrounded them like sheds, a pretense of seclusion. Smiling down at her lazily, with a pretense of menace, he backed her against a rental trailer, his palms resting on either side of her shoulders, the turquoise satin rubbing his inner wrists. She was half-laughing but very startled, her breath quickening in a series of bright little gasps that made his pulse race.

"Don't get cocky," he said, freeing one hand, running the back of his fingers lightly, lightly down the line of her throat. "Wolves can be clever."

Her eyes opened wide. Drawing a sharp breath, she gave him an inquiring look and said, "Which makes it all the more absurd that she would have been in a wolf-infested woods to begin with. Who would do such a—?" The word perished in her tightened throat. A bubbly sensation that she couldn't interpret quivered through her. "Is that what I'm doing, Mr. Wilde? Communing with wolves?"

With unhurried grace, he bent toward her, a long, sleepy motion. One of his knees was slightly flexed, his forearms eased upward to cradle her head, and the peculiar sensation inside her took on jewellike clarity. Heat spread in her, catching hurtfully in her stomach, prickling like the glowing quills of a sparkler. No more could she deny the strength of his physical image, of the gentle knowing movements of his hands as his thumbs followed the curve of her hairline, disturbing the scattered curls there. In all ways, he overwhelmed her: the suggestion in his hedonist's smile; the warm, fresh-bathed scent of him that drifted through the crisp fibers of his gray-flecked wool sweater; the water-brightness of his eyes, with their light, black-ringed irises.

"Yes." He said the word as a breath, bringing his body inch by inch against hers.

If it had been a game for her at first, it ceased to be one abruptly. She pressed herself backward against the trailer, trying to escape the coaxing presence of his thigh against her legs and the unexpected hardness of alien muscle against her stomach and breasts. His body felt so good, so unfamiliar and so lush with voluptuous promise, that she could feel pleasure tears behind her eyelids as they drifted closed. The warmth of tears and desire tickled through her until she was weak, light-headed, throbbing.

As slowly as he had given her the details of his body, he withdrew himself from her, and she stood breathing shakily, a captive in the circle of arms that no longer held her, but again were braced casually against the trailer. In the universe behind her closed eyes, she was aware of a curious instability in her legs. She fought it and her own sense of inner upheaval. Anger was rare for her, but she experienced it now, as in a dream, enveloping but vague.

He studied her, giving her time, and then spoke to her in a soft tone. "What was that like for you?"

She didn't answer him, so he waited, breathing in her scent and the fragrance of the cosmetics they had used so sparingly on her, a sophisticated scent out of place on the lilylike face below him.

When she opened her eyes, it was to show him the flame of her anger. Ducking under his arm, she walked quickly away from him with her hands clasped behind, her skirt floating like a bright wing over the bricks.

When he came beside her, she tilted her head to look at him, and the force with which she met his eyes surprised him. "You play with something that's holy with no more care than a child uses in playing with a toy."

"Not something holy. Something human. I wasn't playing. You were entitled to a warning. But that's probably the only one I'm going to give you."

Her flesh stung. She couldn't withdraw her gaze from his eyes, with their hints of disillusionment and remote kindness. "I see. You do a thing genteelly or not at all."

"Some variation of that." His expression was uncovered briefly, and what she saw beneath was stark, like pain but more bleak, as though he were investing her words with a lifetime of dark irony visible only to him. Torn from her anger, unstrung to her soul, she glimpsed the shadow of his sadness and its twisted complexity, the infinite path of empty mirrors reflecting one another into the void he saw within. *He thinks he's going to hurt me. He expects to. And he's deeply sorry.*

Then, in one of the abrupt shifts of subject that never failed to disconcert and fascinate her, he said, "If I were you, I wouldn't feel shy about the dress. You're very well covered up. You do have a body under all that?"

His question was absurd, the tone conveying a kind of sincere concern, as if it had just occurred to him that she might not, and the only conscientious thing to do was inquire.

Instead of running in the opposite direction as fast as her legs could carry her, which she knew she ought to do, she answered him, "I suppose I do. A body of sorts."

"Stomach? Thighs?"

"The whole catalog," she interrupted quickly.

He laid a hand on her shoulder and leaned closer. "Perfect. Where can I place an order?"

Warm sunshine struck her hot cheeks. They'd stepped from the area where the trailers lay like a mass of giant larvae and came into the crowded yard in front of the house where Alan had told her they would film today.

People swarmed around them, busy in strange ways, moving confidently and seemingly without direction through complex tasks that had no meaning for her. A young man in a baseball cap and frayed sneakers handed Wilde a cluttered clipboard that he studied and handed back. "Fine. But I still don't like the set. It's too"—glancing at the housefront—"well composed. Loosen it up a little. And get rid of that damned soldier marionette. Who put that thing in? The characters in this film have just come twelve hundred miles in a wagon. They didn't have room for four-foot puppets."

"Max likes the puppet." The young man looked nervous. "He says it has a surrealist thrust."

"Well, thrust it back whence it came. We're not submitting this to Cannes, so there's no point in trying to foist artsy conceits on an unsuspecting populace."

Though it was given with a smile, Wilde's order produced a flurry of response on the set. Strolling forward a couple of feet to watch the changes, his interest seemed so focused there that Susan didn't immediately realize his next words were directed at her.

"You didn't answer. What was that like for you?"

The voice compelled her like a gentle hand. She leaned on the white picket fence ringing the yard and pressed against it, wanting to force the tension from her body. Not looking at him, she said, "It was like being fed after years of starvation. But it was like being fed something bitter."

Of all things he had expected, it was not this insightful, articulate reply. Her words so touched his heart that he had to force himself to remember he didn't have one. What hidden thoughts were there still behind that expressive face? He had been seeing her in two dimensions, as a caricature, an extravagant beauty whom he would have given ten years from his life to possess. And here she was, being more, much more: intricate and appealing and fervent. A new emotion touched him, one that was incomprehensible and strangely unpleasant, and he tried to grasp it and hold on, but it slipped from him like sand running through his fingers, and he was left with the simple, unsatisfied shell of his need.

"They tell me you wouldn't look at yourself in the mirror this morning. Is that a sin too?"

"I don't know. Perhaps not, if you don't do it much. My mother doesn't care for them, though, so we never had one in our house. I believe she thinks they are . . . not modest."

"What about the English clothes you are wearing? Evil stuff, yes?"

She sighed. "I've gone against so many of our ways by working for you that I can't keep count. I had no idea—"

"That I was going to introduce you to debauchery beyond your wildest dreams?" Long, sensitive fingers gently applied themselves to her nape, the motion raking her spine with tiny shivers. "I've scared you, haven't I? I'm sorry." One finger traced a bewitching path up and down the hollow there. His voice seduced. "Poor lady. So tender. Never fear. You have only to survive this for six weeks."

"Six *weeks*!" She spun around to face him, her skirt billowing vigorously against his legs.

"Six weeks is the time we need to film."

"Oh, no, no—"

"Susan, Katelyn must have told you—"

She interrupted desperately. "She told me you were making a movie that was two hours long. Naturally, I knew it would take longer than two hours to complete, but I thought sure that in a day or two..."

"My dear beloved girl, one can hardly make a thirty-second commercial spot for television in a day or two. We're working with a hundred and twenty pages of script, of which we can shoot three, maybe four pages a day. For every foot of film I can use, I have to toss nine. Six weeks, Amish."

"But that's so long! Mr. Wilde... It would be impossible. Please understand. I can't."

Can't. Bad word, Susan. She was distraught, her brown eyes revealing the panic of a trapped animal, and he knew that if there was a speck of residual decency left in him he would let her go.

"I'm afraid it's too late to reconsider," he said. "You've signed a contract with us, and I'm sure you understand that's a legally binding agreement."

The color had disappeared from her cheeks, and she appeared aghast, as though she expected him to throw her in jail any minute, which revealed eloquently how little she knew about the legal system. Katelyn could have had her out of the contract in less time than it took to say *lex non scripta*.

Distress made her feel sticky and coldly sick to her stomach. Six weeks of lying to her neighbors and *freindschaft*. Six weeks of exhausting intimacy with English strangers and the affront of an unaccustomed culture. Six weeks of Alan Wilde. And she wanted it so much. She wanted it.

Ten minutes later Brian Randall, the young man with the clipboard, caught up with Max near the camera-dolly tracks. "Did you ask Wilde about the marionette?"

"Yeah."

"Well? What did the great man say?"

"He said—and I quote—'Get thee to a growlery.'"

Staring at Max's retreating back, Brian shoved his baseball cap to the back of his head and said, "Huh?"

Chapter 8

Alan's goal was to capture the love story with rich sweetness, to film it as though it were a beloved classic.

❧.

Polly Bates stands on the porch of a white clapboard house with a gabled roof. The building, lavishly trimmed with gingerbread, is painted white. A discreet sign by the door announces that it is an inn. Polly looks at the yard in front of her. It is littered with wooden chests and deerskin-covered trunks. The lids of many of the chests are open; some are half-unpacked to reveal silk-fringed lamps, a silver tea service, a gilt canary cage, delicate china. Rough men pass by the yard. Some guffaw at the sight of the refined housewares. Others sneer. A few direct sly glances at Polly, who does her best to ignore them. The clothing of the men and the tools they carry suggest they are loggers; the sad condition of the dirt track beyond the yard hints at just how primitive the village beyond may be. The household clutter in the chests and trunks suddenly seems poignantly out of place.

Tired but determined, Polly walks down the porch steps and over to a trunk. She kneels to withdraw a leather-bound law book. Ferns ring the base of the porch. The rich green of the plants is a perfect cinematic backdrop for Polly's beauty. The loose spiral of an escaped curl caresses the corner of her lips. She smiles slightly, as if it tickles her.

A man stops. He is young and darkly handsome, but hard experience has lent sharp edges to his features, and has cast mistrust into blue eyes that refract light like broken crystals. The hardness fades as he watches her. Longing takes its place.

She looks up into his eyes for the first time. The lens frames the two of them lovingly as the world fall to silence around them. The film captures one flawless moment . . . and the essence of a theatrical tradition many centuries old.

Polly's father calls to her from a third-story window. The spell is broken. She is flustered, and runs inside to join him. When she returns to the innyard, the young man has gone, but a spray of cherry blossoms rests on the books she was unpacking.

Tavern life has its disadvantages for Polly. She must avoid the barroom, where men brawl and drink. She appears startled when she has to step over a lolling drunk on the stairs to her third-floor bedchamber. Stagecoaches arrive at midnight, disturbing her sleep. When she complains to the proprietress that the linens are unclean, Polly is roundly informed that only the most gentlemanly patrons have used the napkins before her, and as for the towels, each one had been used by more than a hundred people since last washed and she is the first to complain.

She wakes to the soft light of morning. Against the rumpled bedclothes, she is a vision of loveliness, with dark tumbled curls and immaculate ivory flesh. On the pillow beside her she discovers a plume of cherry blossoms. Her surprise grows into alarm. She searches the room, her Victorian night-robe flowing like cream around her body. She is alone, the door locked from the inside. But lace curtains flutter around her open window. She is drawn there to gaze outward at the sky, saturated with the rosy blush of dawn. Unthinkingly, she touches the blossom to her cheek. The two fragile shades blend. A single petal slips innocently between her breathlessly parted lips.

*   *   *

After the scene played during that evening's rushes, Ben Rose made a joke of fanning himself vigorously, and one of the production assistants playfully dumped a cup of crushed ice over his own head. Wilde went alone to his suite to stand in front of an open window and let the cool night wind brush his face. He tasted the honey of a single petal on his tongue.

🐋

Polly wanders through a forest filled with luminous blue mist that swirls to the tops of the trees that tower above her. Drops of water cling to her dark curls and shimmer like jewels.

She enters a clearing beside a mill where a moss-hung wheel turns slowly in the silvery current of a stream. A small wooden footbridge arcs over the stream. Sound effects sweeten the voice of the water as Polly steps onto the bridge, whose entrance is draped with the fronds of a weeping willow.

The mist parts before her. Suddenly she sees him standing across the bridge, watching her. Him. The young man she has seen once in front of the inn. She is unsettled—she seems even to be considering flight, her face dramatically pale above the black velvet of the cloak she pulls protectively closer about her. Yet something she can't understand holds her as he makes his slow approach.

He is quite close before tension overcomes her, and she stands poised, like a wild creature assessing some unknown peril.

He speaks. "Would you like a kitten?"

Her face shows clearly this is not what she was expecting. "Have you one?"

He lifts a hand to show her the tiny black kitten curled into the bend of his arm. "We have too many cats in our stable. Some might go hungry if we don't get rid of a few of them." He looks down at the kitten. "She's healthy. Would you like her?"

She nods.

He starts to lift the kitten, which doesn't appreciate being disturbed. Its back arcs like a Halloween cat's, and it spits furiously. "Damn," he says.

"*Cut.*"

He starts to lift the kitten, but its small claws unfold, minute needles that cling like burrs to his jacket. Polly begins to laugh.

"*Cut!*"

He lifts the kitten and passes it into Polly's hands. She carries it to her cheek, where it fluffs itself softly against her clear skin.

The young man says, "My name is—"

She finishes for him. "Burke. I know. They talk about you at the inn."

"What do they say?"

"That your father is the richest man in the county. And that . . ."

It's clear that she can't continue, so he supplies the words for her. "That my mother was an Indian sorceress."

"Yes."

"Do you believe it?"

Polly is an educated young woman. She considers herself enlightened, beyond superstition. "Of course not." She looks straight into his eyes. Her own show the wealth of her spirit and strength. "But they also say you gamble and drink liquor."

"Which you do believe." The screen fills with her upturned face, and his, with its enigmatic smile, as he says, "I could change."

The offer shocks her with its implied promise of a future for them. This is going much too fast for her. She begins to walk quickly away. He joins her, keeping pace.

"Did you—" She cannot ask the question. Was it he who came into her bedroom and left cherry blossoms on her pillow while she slept? She begins to run, her cape flaring in a black wave behind her. This time he makes no move to follow.

After ten feet or so she swings around to walk back toward him, meeting his eyes.

"Thank you for the kitten." Again she turns to run, and vanishes like a sprite into the mist.

He stares after her, then looks downward. The camera

slowly travels lower, to his pocket, where there is a stem of cherry blossoms.

૪✦

She was not what Alan had anticipated.

She had no sense of "making an impression," so he had to learn her layer by layer, like uncovering an overwrapped gift.

The first day had been murderously difficult. Putting Susan behind cameras had made him feel as though he were raping her. The lights might have been emitting deadly secret rays, and the cameras might have been leaching out her soul, to judge from the way she stared at them. The technicians and actors intimidated her. And her trust in him had ebbed. He was afraid she was going to bolt. She was under too much pressure . . . the newness, the strangeness of it all, and part of it had come from him.

He used perceptiveness with her that he didn't know he possessed; he was gentle as he had never been. But he could not give her what she needed most—strength.

Then had come the surprise. Susan knew more about strength than he could have taught her in a lifetime. As Ben Rose said, it almost seemed as if the soundness of her mind couldn't tolerate the despair of chaos. By that evening, she had begun to heal. He saw the first evidence after the hours of careful tutoring when she had interrupted him, bending forward to sweep up a handful of grass and toss it at him like fragrant confetti.

"You don't have to tell me a thousand times," she had said, smiling at him like a street urchin, overpowering him with the surprise of it. "I can do it."

The funny thing was, she could. He had expected to pull an adequate performance from her through intuition, camera angles, and technique. He could have made any woman attractive on film; but a face like Susan's he could turn into a myth made flesh—which was more than enough for his purposes. He hadn't guessed that on film she would go far beyond it.

By the complex quirks of nature, she was wonderful on film. He had explained acting to her as a pretending game, not as an interpretive art. In some mysterious way, then it seemed natural to her. And, after he showed her a camera, took it apart, let her touch it, and detailed the way it worked, she began to lose her fear. In fact, after several days she was less self-conscious in front of a camera than anyone he'd ever worked with. She'd grown up without photographs and without physical vanity, so the cruel tricks of light and focus meant nothing to her.

Off camera, too, she was more than he'd imagined: livelier, more impetuous. Joyous, one cast member had called her.

She'd said, "I can do it." And she did it beautifully.

The other thing she did beautifully was physically complement her costar. David Thorne was playing Adam Burke. Watching them together was like seeing black swans pair in a mythical courtship rite.

In his mid-twenties, David's face had matured from the androgynous beauty of his teen years. He was the bad boy of a renowned British theatrical family, and had been brought up spouting Chekhov from his cradle. With one sibling in the Royal Shakespeare Company and another producing plays in Paris, David had taken off for Hong Kong, where he had made a series of remarkably bad Kung Fu movies that had made him both a strong international cult figure and rich enough to free-base. But he was worth the small fortune Wilde was paying him, because he was the best. He could dissect emotion into a thousand subtle shades, and by the slight alteration of facial muscles become plain or sensual. He could shed blackness over the lightest phrase or project warmth that could raise the temperature of a theater ten degrees.

In person he had an austere chic that couldn't be snuggled up to readily. If he liked someone, things tended to become warmer and warmer; if someone got off on the wrong foot with him, the relationship degenerated quickly because of David's acidly expressed intolerance. He had money invested in the movie, and he had not been pleased with the decision to sign Susan, though he was too seasoned either to bring his dissent to the set or to let Susan's inexperience disconcert him. He had confined his annoyance to asking several times, "What do you mean, she's Amish?" in a tone that was not cordial.

At the end of one day of working with her, he had appeared in the late evening in Wilde's suite, lounging with cultivated but effective movie-star grandeur in the doorway, and said, "Again we bow to the inimitable Wilde wisdom, and lie awake in our beds wondering whether you're brilliant beyond comprehension or simply damned lucky. Rumor, by the way, has it that you have carnal designs on that poor innocent. I had no idea you were so darkly romantic. Scratch a cynic, they say, and you'll find a raging sentimentalist."

Alan had been fighting a headache all evening, so patience became a conscious choice. Nothing short of disaster ever made him snap at actors, because, when it came right down to it, they needed every ounce of ego strength they could muster and he could encourage. Glancing up from the production board he'd been studying, he said, "If you want to talk about shoes and ships and sealing wax and cabbages and kings or any other reasonable subject, please come in. If you want to discuss my personal life, go away."

The young actor produced a more intimate replica of the smile so loved by the paparazzi. "What an attitude from a man whose personal life is the topic of the hour. Did you ever wonder why there's always such a wealth of people fighting for the chance to work with you? We're enthralled with the intricacies of your mind. Wouldn't it be touching if you turned out to be pure at heart?"

Each morning, Susan awoke early, as always, but disoriented. She would look around her familiar bedroom, then suddenly remember: *I'm in a movie. Today I'll be with Alan Wilde.*

None of it made any sense, and the longer she did it, the less it seemed possible that she was being paid a fantastic sum of money for doing almost nothing. He would say, "Kneel here, and lift this book. Then smile for me, just a little smile," and she would do it, and someone would call *Cut!* and everyone would seem absurdly pleased with her.

She liked to think of Wilde at dawn. She could see the complexity of his character reflected in the muted colors, sense the mysteries of his soul lurking in the purple shadows.

He had magic, that she knew. She'd felt it on the first day, when she had been half-crazed, a dreamer slipping into the bittersweet flicker of another reality. His will had surrounded her with gentle force, bringing her back to him, making her want to return. He showed her himself as a craftsman, a weaver of spells, and she felt herself becoming one more colorful thread in the tapestry of his imagination.

But she was aware every moment of the man too. If he stood silently behind her, she felt it. His presence brought her desperate happiness.

It was hard for her to believe she'd been at this five days.

She sat outside at lunch with others in the cast at a place where the red-brick walk widened into a circle. It was busy there, but pretty. Beside her the bricks opened into a planting of tall red tulips with a birdbath among them. There she had been resting her elbow and dipping her fingertips in the water.

The day was misty, and Alan didn't like it. He had needed the mist that morning for the bridge scene, but later in the day it would be in the way, and because it came from nature instead of one of his magic machines, he couldn't get rid of it. With amusement she had seen him frowning at it as if he believed he could find some way to make it go away, if only he thought it over an extra minute or two. Someone had handed him a sandwich and he'd eaten it slowly while he stood, talking to Max, the director of photography. He always ate over business, as though food were no more than a routine fuel to maintain his body, and he left most things unfinished, never seeming to taste them.

A production secretary had handed Wilde a stack of correspondence and he'd tossed the rest of his sandwich in a trash barrel and sat down in a canvas chair near Susan, relaxed in an earth-toned sweater that looked as though it would be nice to touch, linen pants, and soft leather shoes. Lean and elegant, poring over the pages, absorbing the barrage of stimulation with flawless calm, he was having an odd effect on her pulse. She wished she could get her mind off his hands, how his fingers were long and grace-ful, how they felt on her skin.

One of Wilde's assistants, walking by her, asked, "Get enough to eat, Susan?"

"Sure. I already had a handburger." She gasped. "A *ham*burger."

David Thorne gave her shoulder a squeeze. "We must examine the ecology of your id one day." He joined her, propping a chair close, but out of the way of the makeup artist who was retouching her hair with a curling iron plugged into a portable generator.

Avoiding looking in Alan's direction, she watched David stretch out his legs and take a sip from his wineglass.

David never ate lunch. He drank wine and took pills. It was hard to understand what kept him alive. She wondered what illness he had, to take so many pills. No one mentioned it. Although everyone treated him with great courtesy, or even awe, she had the feeling he wasn't much liked. That, at least, was no mystery. He looked at most people as if they were invisible.

She'd been an exception. On her first day here, he'd looked her over in a way that reminded her of a mother bird examining an orphan in her nest to decide whether she wanted to adopt it or peck it to death. She couldn't imagine what had made him lean to the former.

David said, "What did you think that was when you came across our monster in the forest?"

"I had no idea. Maybe . . . a bear with a skin disease."

That produced laughter, but Ben Rose looked pained. "After the money we've spent—"

"I guess the only other thing I could have thought was that it was the devil."

David smiled over his wineglass. "You'd better be careful. Maybe the devil doesn't look like that at all. Maybe he looks like Ben, here, or Alan."

The idea had occurred to her. Her throat started to get warm. She covered it with her hand. David said, "Do you worry a lot about the devil, Susan?"

"Not as much as I should, I guess. There's a lot of evil in the world."

"And it comes from the devil?"

"Where else would it come from?"

Joan arrived, friendly and vivid in a yellow wool jacket, in time to catch the last question. "I know where evil comes from. Testosterone."

Susan didn't know the word. Her expression must have showed it, because David supplied an explanation. "It's the male sex hormone."

"Oh." Susan grinned back at him. "That's probably right. Probably a lot of evil does come from that."

"That's it, Susan. Don't let them have it all their own way." Joan gave her a look of approval. "Has anyone seen Max? He's got a call from Japan that needs action."

"He was around a couple of minutes ago," the hairdresser said.

"He's in—the wardrobe trailer, I think. Sam mentioned it a while ago," Susan said.

Sam was eating a sandwich, sitting on a bundle beside the other cameraman. He gave her a look of surprise.

"Didn't you?" she asked.

"No."

"I'm sorry," she said. "I didn't hear right. I was so sure I heard you say after he left that you'd be glad when he came out of the closet."

Ben choked on his coffee. Everyone stared at Sam, who was red. Joan laughed. Mystified, Susan looked over at Alan, who glanced up from his papers and said, "And so a dozen people who consider themselves sophisticated—with varying degrees of justification—are stricken to silence. The next time any one of you says anything off-color around Susan, I'm going to force you to explain it to her." He smiled at her. "Never mind, Susan, nothing of importance has happened."

"So I'll go find him in the closet," said Joan, and walked off. Others left, went back to talking, worked on their lines.

"You're doing beautifully with Polly," David said to her. He crossed his dew-spotted boots at the ankle. "Nothing to it, is there? We're all actors."

"Why do you think so?"

"One learns young. What is growing up but learning to fake it? Don't you think so, Alan?"

Alan had gone back to his paper work, and Susan could hardly believe he'd been listening, but time and again she'd been amazed at his ability to concentrate on two tasks at once. Now he looked up and searched her face, and then directed a glance at the young man who was arranging her curls.

"Why aren't you working in the trailer?" he asked.

"We have a short in the wiring," the hairdresser answered. "Anderson is working on it."

Wilde dismissed the words with a nod. To David, he said, "It might be acting. Or it might be trying out different facets of ourselves."

The idea disturbed her. "Do you think people live in fragments, Alan?" It was not easy for her to call him by his Christian name, but she had learned she must. To call him Mr. Wilde was to be gently, though mockingly, corrected.

"Of course. That's what makes fiction appealing. We have some part of every character hidden inside. Take any story as an example. Take—"

"Red Riding Hood," she supplied, wondering at herself for the choice, wondering at the strange smile she could feel pressing at the corners of her mouth.

The smile he returned, showing that he appreciated her choice, left her breathless. "All right. Take Red Riding Hood. We're one part Red Riding Hood, walking into trouble we can't foresee. And we're one part wolf, ambitious and efficient predators. But the part of us that needs to be adored wants to be the woodcutter, who saves the day at the last minute. To make a successful film, we have to throw in characters to get all that across so those in the audience can experience all of themselves. Then they feel satisfied."

She wondered if there could be a predator in herself. Not much of one, she didn't think. Not according to his meaning of the word. *Maybe they think I'm incomplete. They respect the predator.* "What about the grandmother?"

She had spoken to Wilde, but David answered. "Grandma becomes the wolf, the loved ones we trust who'd like to eat us alive."

The queasy sense of being in a foreign land returned. They thought so differently. She wanted to dispute him somehow, but her thoughts were interrupted, as so many were on the set, from many directions at once. Apologizing for the interruption, David's private secretary arrived, urgently needing his signature on a pile of letters. Alan took a long-distance call on a portable telephone. The hairdresser asked her to shake her head. She obeyed, and let him tip her head forward to work on her nape, where the warmth of the curling iron felt pleasant on her skin.

Trucks roared into the compound behind her and she knew the second unit had returned from filming at another location. Voices of the arriving crew members floated through the fog. Their footsteps made scattered tapping sounds on the damp pavement. She looked up through her lashes to see the monster appear behind a veil of mist. She got a kick out of seeing it, now that she knew it was only Dash inside.

David gestured expressively at the monster. "There goes the neighborhood."

The monster was elaborately made, to allow it to express emotion, and now it registered offense. Massive and violent, it roamed forward, giant mouth agape, upraised iron claws closing around David's neck from the back, and the air shimmered with the eerie hiss of the creature's electronically enhanced inhalations. The hideous bared teeth opened over the young actor's throat. David planted a kiss on the monster's jaw and shoved it back.

"Don't touch my body," he said. "I charge for that."

"Who could afford it?"

Dash's chuckle resounded in the costume. He opened a claw in greeting to Susan. A mob of technicians in muddy sneakers had arrived with him, some umbilically connected to the monster by dangling wires that could help him move, grow distorted, change, light up.

Alan had risen; he handed his correspondence back to the production secretary with quick instructions and gave the telephone back to an assistant. He spoke to Dash and the technicians who had arrived in the monster's wake. "You're late. Problems?"

"*Problems?*" Tim, the second unit director, was striding by carrying a bullhorn. "The kid Jerry hired forgot to load film in the camera, the dolly tracks we rented are warped, and Dash is sweating to death in that suit. We had to put an extra hole in the head because his eyes were fogging and—damn!" His heel connected hard with the curling-iron cord, jerking it sharply from the hairdresser's hand.

Susan felt the iron skate a burn across her neck and saw it flip, sizzling, into the two inches of water in the birdbath. Registering it as a minor mishap, she started to reach out to retrieve it.

She had no idea that she was doing anything wrong, and the blaze of reaction around her was a horrible surprise. Alan's "Susan, *no!*" cut through startled shouts, and before she knew what was happening, Alan had grabbed her and dragged her out of the chair and away from the birdbath with such force that her chair went flying and fell cracking on the bricks. Her heart banged painfully against her ribs. She stared, astonished, into his eyes. A sickening weakness flooded her.

"What did I do wrong?"

He looked as though it were difficult for him to calm down enough to speak. Behind him Tim shouted, "Alan, it's okay. We've cut the power."

Alan glanced at him and accepted the words with a nod before his pained gaze sank into hers again. His soft voice was barely recognizable. "Susan, never, *never* put your hand into water if an electrical appliance is in it. Do you understand?"

Others had begun to join them, running up, asking what had happened. The excited conversation became a blur of sound. Embarrassment and confusion, thick as oil, rose in her cheeks. She hardly knew what she was saying.

"I beg your pardon. I had no idea . . . I didn't mean to cause any damage."

"Not damage." He was holding her tightly, as though he were afraid to let her go. His eyes were haunted. "Water conducts electricity. Reaching into it would have electrocuted you . . . killed you." His words were slow.

She felt only an overwhelming, disordered shame. Dimly she heard David's voice.

"Alan, under your fingers is human flesh."

Alan seemed to wake then. His hands went slack, and

Susan stepped away from him, murmuring an apology. She was not really thinking as she picked up the cloth bag she brought every morning from home and whispered, "Pardon me. I—I'll go for a walk. Excuse me."

But she walked only the first steps and then began to run, zigzagging between trailers, around equipment and startled crew members.

He found her in the mist-shrouded seclusion of the forest glen. She stood alone on the footbridge, her cape a black silhouette against the gray, lichen-covered wood. She watched the water beneath her, its surface silvery smooth except for patches where it purled over rocks in the stream bed.

He came closer, standing near the tall grasses on the embankment.

"I'm sorry, Amish."

She looked up and gave him a smile whose sweetness rippled through him.

"I know."

She seemed very alone to him suddenly, isolated in her scarred pride, and the distance between them became untenable. He rarely took his tension out on others, and she was surely the last one in the world he wanted to hurt. Even as he walked toward her, he could feel the insanity of what he was trying to do, and the insanity was intertwined in his mind with its inevitability as he crossed the bridge to her side. His overriding impulse was to hold her, just hold her.

"Peter thought he might have burned you when the iron flew out of his hand."

Her eyes told him it was unimportant. "Only a little."

"Show me."

She turned obediently, dipped her head, and brushed the curls on her neck upward. A small pink line streaked the tender flesh. In pity he bent to let his lips make the softest contact with her skin, just beneath the burn. He closed his eyes and willed her to heal, sorry that she'd come to harm at the hands of his culture. But it was a mistake. He could feel the deep warmth under the moist surface of her skin. He could taste her through his flesh. Her innocent fragrance flooded his senses, and desire spilled through him. His mouth moved higher, tasting her curls, her fingers, the curve of her neck, and his breath caught and hurt.

"Why do you do this to me?" she whispered.

"I'm not sure," he said softly, nuzzling her ear with his mouth. He could feel her breath quicken, but as his hands came around her to part the cloak and touch her body, she pulled away, turning toward him with passion-brightened eyes that raised the heat in his body like a tide.

"I've brought you a present." Her words seemed random, whimsically sincere, and they made him smile. The cape fell in a black halo around her as she knelt by her cloth bag. He watched curiously as she drew out a dark object half-hidden by her hands. "No," she said, dissatisfied. "You should see it in the right way." She went to a small apple tree on the far side of the bridge, arranging the object in the crook of a low branch heavy with blossoms. He saw then that it was a nest, with red and yellow ribbons woven gaily into the twigs.

"One year when I was very young, we had a different teacher, not an Amish one, and she wore colored ribbons in her hair. That spring she lost a blue ribbon outside, and a month later my sister and I came across it woven into a bird's nest." She stood utterly still while she spoke, though her eyes were vividly expressive. "We wondered after that if the birds had only used it because it seemed practical or if they might have enjoyed the pretty color. So the next year, Rachel"—she paused, finding the word difficult— "made ribbons from cloth scraps and hid them in the forest, and sometimes we found them later in nests. But this one was special. Robins built it in the maple tree outside my window, and I watched the eggs hatch and the tiny nestlings grow and finally fly away. One day the robins abandoned the nest, and a breeze came in late summer and blew the nest inside my open window while I was sleeping." She was smiling as she let out a soft breath on the ribbons, sending them fluttering, but the smile faded as she faced him again. "At the time I thought it had great significance, and that it meant a wonderful thing was going to happen to me."

He could see her as she had been, an eager, lively child

with eyes full of hope as she knelt at dawn on a braided rug, lifting the nest. He started to go to her, but she shook her head and looked frightened.

"Alan, you have to understand. It can't be. For us, it's like the birds. We nest with our own kind. I know—I think I know—that you want something less. But what you want is impossible."

The fog began to penetrate his sweater, and he was chilled inside and out. "Why do you let them do that to you?"

Anger shone in her nut-brown eyes. "There are no 'them' who make me do things."

Something came into his chest, a gentle emotion, and it struck him that he was experiencing feeling, and that it was real, and now senses long dormant, unfamiliar, began to be kindled inside him. He was aware of the aged softness of the wood under his feet, the cool air on his face, the vibrant rhythm of his heartbeat. He wanted to be able to let her go, but his need was more potent than anything he had ever known. And it must have been the same for her, because the strength seemed to leave her suddenly, and she covered her face briefly with her hands and then ran back toward him, halting at the end of the bridge, her eyes wide and panicked.

"What would you have done if I hadn't stopped you?" The words were forced from her. She turned away from him, clutching the handrail on the bridge. Her thoughts were poor, storm-tossed things, consumed in the wonder that his mouth had created in her.

"I would have touched you, Susan, just kept touching you."

"Then touch me," she whispered.

A new, more violent flame seared his heart. Very gently, he said, "It isn't easy for me to touch you and stop."

Helplessly, so softly he could barely hear her, she whispered again. "Do it. Quickly."

He came behind her and buried his face in her fragrant curls while his arms came around her, dragging her back against the scorching hunger of his body. His hands parted the cloak, desperately seeking, and discovered the thin muslin cloth and her delicious warmth beneath. He felt her gasp as he covered her belly with slow erotic strokes, lightly contouring the taut flesh. Ruffling soft kisses along her hairline, below her ear, along the curve of her neck, he let his hands climb her body. With his fingers resting upon her quick-rising chest, his thumbs came gently to brush the sides of her breasts, making long, sensitive passages until he felt her skin grow hot. Her hair was a cloud of midnight on his mouth. He filled his palms with her breasts, softly kneading, entranced by the rapid patter of her heart.

"I go halfway to heaven with you in my arms." His whisper was thick, fervid. "I want you so badly. If you don't want me in return, God knows what will happen to me."

She pulled around then, in the shelter of his arms, and took his hands in hers, holding them to her throat. "I was in a field once when a tree was struck by lightning, and just before, the space around me was filled with crackling air, and I felt like I was one with it, and in that moment my soul seemed to dissolve and reappear, and I could feel life within every cell of my body. And that's how I feel when you touch me." She raised his warm, knowing hands to her lips and kissed them. "I don't know what I'm going to do," she whispered, and then left him, disappearing into the mist.

But he remained there, and Dash found him an hour later, standing under the spreading boughs of an apple tree, holding an empty bird's nest.

The mist thickened, and they quit working outside three hours early and shot interiors. Because none of those scenes involved her, Susan left, taking a new path along the stream toward the east gate.

She saw a silver trailer parked under a willow. Lanky, muscular Dash lay in front, his bulk bowing out the aluminum frame of a web-work lawn chair. He appeared to be sleeping. His eyes were hidden under the brim of a battered Stetson.

She tried to pass quietly, so as not to disturb him, but his slow drawl halted her.

"Howdy." He pushed the Stetson up with one finger.

"Howdy."

"I'm just havin' me a little siesta. They let you escape for the day? Then how'd you like to set a spell? C'mon in."

Inside, the trailer was built along massive lines, with size-and-a-half armchairs and a little extra headroom for the doors. One wall was covered with oil paintings of two beautiful Arabian stallions and a mare. Susan sat on a brown leather couch. Dash pushed buttons to turn on lights and to open the wall to cupboards and a refrigerator. She just stared.

"This is where you live?"

"Only while I'm making movies. I have a farm in Arizona. Look yonder. That's my family." Another section of wall opened to expose shelves of books and photographs.

There were eight children, some of them of different races. All adopted, Dash explained. In one photograph he sat on a corral fence bear-hugging a grinning woman with straw in her hair. His wife. Beside that one was another photograph of a young cowboy, solid on a rearing palomino. Dash himself in his twenties, he said, when he was King of the West. The studio had picked him off the rodeo circuit.

"Got my start in B movies."

"Bee movies?"

"Yup."

She learned also that Dash had helped to pay for Alan's earliest movies. He had his ranch and didn't need to work, but he kept up the acting for the fun of it and to spend time with Alan, whom he'd known since Alan was knee-high to a steer.

He held up a bottle. "How about a whiskey?" He laughed at her expression. "Nah, I'm pullin' your leg. I know little gals like you don't drink whiskey."

"I'm not so little."

"Darlin', I got socks older than you are. Your religion got anything against soda pop?"

"No. I've never had it, though. It's too expensive."

"Splurge, then." He poured some into a glass and handed it to her. "It's on me."

He sat on the arm of a chair and smiled at her. His expression was both tender and rueful, and she was afraid he might mention Alan, but he only said, "Tell you what.

You're going to be in a movie, you'd better have a look at one."

He worked briefly with a machine that was a box on a box with a screen—a television. A moving picture began to form on what had been vacant.

Dawn on a prairie farm and a slim boy moves about his chores, hauling water buckets and scattering feed to chickens.

She felt an immediate sense of recognition, and her first thought was that she owed that to her own farm background, but in a moment she realized more was familiar to her than the setting. The camera showed the handsome boy in close-up, the face bright and forbearing, half-quizzical, half-detached. The eyes were light blue-green.

A pleasant something stirred inside her. "It's Alan, isn't it? Alan as a child! Was he a—what do you call it? A star?"

"Susan, honey, a star ain't nothin' but a ball of hot gas floatin' in a vacuum."

She strained forward, fascinated by this magic window that held Alan in it, partly formed, becoming himself. "He was blond then."

"His hair's gotten darker over the years."

The story was gripping, shocking her with its tenderness, its brutality. The boy loses his parents and is blinded when rustlers burn his home. Ill and dispirited, hardly alive, the orphan is taken in reluctantly by his uncle, a gruff, aging gunslinger played by Dash. First to reduce the boy's dependence on him, later out of concern, and finally out of love, with inventive humor and patience, the gunman teaches the boy to live with his handicap, to sustain himself, even to ride.

"Is that Alan in the saddle?"

"No. A stunt double. Insurance companies wouldn't let him ride. Poor kid wasn't even allowed to ride a bicycle."

The blindness disturbed her. It was too real, especially in the end. Dash has been shot trying to protect the boy from one of his parents' killers, who has the mistaken belief that the boy can identify him. Despairing and alone, the child nurses the dying gunfighter. When he has done all he can, the boy goes outside and stands under a low red sun, gold-streaked hair falling over his forehead and in his eyes, some strands brushing the unblinking irises, the sun-tipped lashes darkening with tears. All the world's sorrow was in that young face.

Dash lived. The film ended. She kept the grief like a stone in her stomach.

"How could he do that?"

"Nobody understood it," Dash said. "Even most adult actors can't play blind. They want to stumble around like a stick with arms, knocking into furniture. And here Alan made it look so natural, dignified. I don't know how he did it. Genius, maybe, like they say."

"I didn't mean the blindness. I meant the tears. How could he cry like that?"

There was silence, made profound by the fresh absence of movie sound, and she turned from the dead screen to find Dash watching her, his expression friendly, even admiring. Yet she had the feeling he was holding something back.

"His parents weren't the best there was . . . I guess he had a cry or two in him, saved up." Then, "I ain't too worried about you making your way around the movie world. You were raised on a farm. I got a feeling you'll know bullshit when you see it."

Chapter 9

On Sunday the preaching service was at the home of Susan's parents. For her those many hours of worship were filled with awe and reverence. She was whole, completed by God and her community, profoundly in harmony with things that could only be felt, not seen or explained. It was a mystery planted in her earliest memories, ripened throughout her life, brought to mature flower when she had requested her adult baptism with the traditional words: *It is my desire to be at peace with God and the church.* In the slow hymns, the sermons, the stretches of time spent kneeling in silent prayer on warm aromatic floors of polished hardwood, she found strength and renewal. And even now, rest.

By dusk more than fifty neighbors and relatives had gathered there for the evening meal. Susan had spent the afternoon at her own farm and returned to find her mother's kitchen cozily hectic and filled with her female relatives.

Anna was putting glasses of milk on a tray. Aunt Mary was mashing potatoes, and a cloud of steam rose to her elbows. Fanny was arranging pickled beets on a plate. Off to one side, Grandma was in her rocker with Katie on her knee and Fanny's Lizbeth next to her, the girl's hands and tiny nose resting on the chair arm. Grandma's aged, yet still clever hands entertained the children, folding a handkerchief into twins in a hammock, into mice.

Susan's mother was wending her way through the group of women, carrying a heavy enamel coffeepot. Her apron was wrapped around the handle, protecting her hands. She was an even-tempered woman, without big surprises, but with small, delightful ones. In last winter's cold snap, she had knitted red wool caps for the horses. She wasn't a disciplinarian, or a teacher except by example. There was no cunning in her, no competitiveness.

There wasn't much to distract from the personality of an Amish woman; not the differences in dress, decoration, and habit that were precious to the English. Nothing outward separated one woman from another or severed the invisible thread that bound them in faith. Where everyone was the same in appearance, the nuances of each spirit were revealed rather than hidden.

Susan hung on the edge of the scene, basking in it. After a week of the exotic, this was comforting. Here were things she knew, the big bowls for mixing, the wooden spoons for licking, the pathways worn in the varnish on the floor, from the front of the stove to the counter to the table. Here were the scents she'd grown up on: chicken in the oven, corn boiling above, allspice from the mincemeat, cinnamon from the orange cake, molasses from the taffy.

The bonnets and swaying skirts and cooking scents were part of a life she loved all the more as she spent time away from it. She wished to be folded into the scene as if it were a thick quilt on a cold winter night, then to fall into a deep, protected sleep.

Come winter, this was the warmest room. You could soak in its heat, and it would stay right in your bones. You could set your coat and boots by the stove so they'd be toasty-warm around you when you went out. Tonight she needed that.

She reached a finger into the mashed potatoes as she walked by, and Aunt Mary tried to bat her hand away. She nipped a slice of pickled beet from Fanny's carefully arranged platter, causing her friend to grin and wave her fork indignantly. Then she picked up a chocolate cake, platter and all, and made a show of making off with it. Amid laughter and commotion, she was surrounded by cousins trying to get the cake back, and by Carolyn and Anna flocking to the rescue.

"Susan must be here," said Grandma, shaking her head and smiling, rocking faster.

"It's me, Grandma." She hoisted the platter over her head. "And I've got the chocolate cake. You and I and the little ones are going to carry it off to eat it."

"That's what the commotion is about," said Grandma. Smile lines wrinkled the corners of her eyes. Wisps of white hair curled out from her *kapp*. "You're up to your tricks."

Susan surrendered the cake with a precarious swoop that had them all gasping, and pulled up a kitchen chair close to her grandmother. She took hold of the gnarled old hands and rested their clasped hands on her grandma's knees. Touch had become more important to her grandmother, with her sight gone.

"Here we thought that when school let out we'd have

you with us more, but it turns out we've got you less." Her grandmother's smile held the richness and subtlety of a lifetime of memories. "It's something, the way you keep yourself busy. You don't have to help with spring planting like your little scholars do."

"You've sure had no time to *dopple*, Susan," her mother agreed. "Esther's Joshua saw you out Wednesday night hanging wash by flashlight."

"It was only ten-thirty. Anyway, I was out of bleach and didn't dare put it out by day. Not with Fanny up the road and her sheets so white. She shows me up something fierce."

"Such a one you are!" Grandma said. "You'll get too tired out!"

"It was a wonderful night for shooting stars, Grandma. Do you mind how we always watched the stars together?"

"Why, sure, I do." Grandma's voice had a soft, dry rustle like pages of an old, much-loved letter. "That was back when we shared a room after Grandpa died. Most nights you'd wait up until I came to bed. I'd come into the room and see your little eyes shining in the dark, and your head would pop right up. We'd sit by the window together and look at those stars."

"We used to talk about everything."

"Yes, we did. One time, after we was done talking, you were quiet for a minute, looking at the sky, and you said, 'Grandma, I wish I were a star and could shine on the world.'"

That night came back to her. Grandma could so easily bring a memory from the past into the present: the deep blackness of the sky, the stars like heavy silver dust, and above all the feelings of that moment, the yearning, the smallness of the body, the largeness of the wish, the growing of the mind.

"That's one thing I won't do, get too busy to look at the stars," Susan said. Then, to Fanny, "What's there on your arm?"

Fanny pulled up her sleeve. "Stung my arm with a couple of wasps. We've got a mess of wasps under the corncrib."

"Those are bad ones." Susan's mother bent over the afflicted arm. "Wasps have a case on you girls. This is the fourth year in a row one or the other of you got stung."

"That was the best time I had last year," Fanny said to Susan, "the day you and I got chased by hornets out on the melon patch. There you were, tearing off with a gunny sack of melons on your back. Pretty soon goes the sack flying and there's melons smashed everywhere, and I couldn't walk for laughing. . . ."

"So you sat down and ate yourself full," Susan's mother said. "I remember that, you out-to-here pregnant at the time. What a pair."

"I haven't been able to look a melon in the face since," Susan said.

"Do you work much longer, Susan?" The question came from Edna, John's mother.

"No, just part—another four, five weeks."

"You're not the only one from the church working over to Greyling now, did you know? There's Sadie Yoder, too. Seth's driving her. She's out on Third Street a little piece, cleaning house and watching kids for an English family."

Anna was bending over the chicken in front of the open oven. She said over her shoulder, "Does she like it?"

"She likes it fine, but she wouldn't want to be at it long. She says they eat their supper in front of the television and watch it so they don't hardly visit with each other. She says it gets her disturbed, some of the things they watch. She has to go in another room."

Different ones shook their heads, feeling sorry for the English having to watch that horrible box. But Susan had seen another side of that box: a rich and compelling story with Alan as a child. She wanted to tell them. It gave her a feeling of unutterable loneliness not to be able to do so. The rightness of the day faded.

"You're working up to the old buildings, I hear, Susan," her cousin Priscilla said. "In the coach-house kitchens, I suppose?"

She felt hateful to deceive them, just hateful. The outright lie would not come. "I do this and that, whatever they need."

"You don't see those from California, though, do you?"

"They're around. I don't let it concern me. They keep themselves pretty busy." The half-truths were bitter on her tongue.

"I imagine they do," her mother said, looking as if she could barely imagine them at all, much less imagine their doing anything.

"There was a big write-up in this week's Greyling paper about that one that's head of it all, that one, what do they call him . . . Mr. Wolf—"

"Wilde."

"It was wrote up how he went to some swell university, and how he's had books written about him, and how he's traveled to far-off places and won all these honors, and I don't know what all," Priscilla said.

"He must be real interesting to talk to," her mother said.

Priscilla got a smile on her face that made Susan wonder if she had been reading those grocery-store magazines Daniel had mentioned.

"Wasn't it Alan Wilde you met in the woods with the monster?" Edna asked.

"Yes."

"What sort of man is he, did you think?"

After a pause, she said, "I wouldn't think he'd make much of a farmer."

They laughed. He was of the city, of the world, different and far away from them, and, they imagined, from her too. So they allowed the subject to drop, because what was outside was not part of them. They were pilgrims in a sinful world. Separate. The Plain People.

What sort of man is he? How full of that question she was herself. She had wakened at dawn, thinking of Polly finding cherry blossoms on her pillow, half-expecting to find them on her own. But there had been only the warm impression where her head had been and the fresh, whispering memory of his caress. She had pressed her eyes closed; tentatively, fearfully had retraced the path of his hands with her own, moving her palms lightly over her breasts. Her whole body wore the burning imprint of his closeness. He had carried her too far . . . too far. What was the antidote to this sweet poison of his that made her feel so sleepy and full of nothing but him?

On the bridge he had said he wanted her. She remembered the shock of it, the honest surprise that he could say it so bluntly, so openly. As disturbed by it as she had been, she had still let him draw her inexorably toward him.

And true to his own peculiar sense of integrity, he had warned her on her first day on the movie set. Only, she had failed to absorb the reality of it. It had been one of too many curiosities coming quickly, and with so much competing for her awe, the impact had faded.

What sort of man was he? Intricate and clever, with a strictly controlled surface and light-filled eyes and beautifully made mouth that hinted at the wildness inside him. One sure thing about him—he was too much man for Susan Peachey.

Before she left for home that evening, Fanny called out, "Wait once, Susan, I'll walk with you. The kids'll go home with Christ in the buggy."

They took the long way. It wasn't a walk to Fanny if she didn't get to climb a fence or two. Making their way across a hayfield, catching the damp of evening on their skirts, Susan said, "Christ was in high spirits tonight, I thought."

"I'm about done weaning Jesse."

"Oh?"

"I've had Christ sleeping downstairs. I told him, no more babies until Jesse's weaned."

"Does he mind?"

"He don't say anything, but he sure looks long-faced when I go upstairs to bed."

They laughed and then there was quiet, just their skirts brushing the pasture grass, and the frogs singing. Then Fanny said, "I sat by your Grandma at dinner."

"I saw you did."

"She leaned over to me and said, didn't I think you got awful quiet when the talk got to Greyling."

Susan's footsteps slowed. "Don't notice so much, please."

"That'll be some kind of day, when you look troubled and I don't notice."

"I can't bring you into this."

"Why not?"

"To know and keep secret, you would have to break your vows to the church."

Fanny stopped walking. She looked small in the evening light. "You must be in bad trouble, then."

"You can't help me, Fan. Not now."

"Don't shut the door in my face, Susan."

"I don't want to. I've seen so much, I've felt so much . . . but I can't tell you until it's over and I've put myself right with the church."

"Don't wait. Share it with me now."

"I care for you too much for that. If I had typhus, I wouldn't come over to share it with you either."

"If you had typhus, I'd be there looking after you."

"When it's over and I tell the Bishop and don't feel so good, then you can come by, and bring me a pie and hold my shoulders."

There was a shaky silence. They began to walk, and Fanny slipped her arm around Susan. In a scared and unfamiliar voice, Fanny said, "I don't have to wait to hold your shoulders."

Waiting, changing buses, walking the stretches in between, Daniel made his way to Chicago. Passing through the green of the suburbs and coming into the city was like descending into a concrete vault. The noise always hit him first. He could almost see it, like black scars everywhere in the air that left the taste of metal on the tongue. Acre after acre of good farm land buried under blacktop and steel. If they kept doing this, where were they going to grow what it took to feed all those people?

And people were everywhere. He could hardly take a step without bumping into someone. In the country, people always seemed to him like healthy, growing things, but in the city they were like an infection. He was xenophobic, he supposed. Rachel thought he was. She'd taught him the word.

"They do that to you, Daniel," she'd told him once.

"How many times have you seen an Amish mother or father say to a child when English are around, 'Hush! Don't speak!' They make you feel like something's wrong."

Don't look at city people in a mass, she'd said. Look at each one individually, because that's how they look at themselves. And she was right. Individually they were fascinating.

Rachel lived within walking distance of the university. She'd had to ride the bus from her first apartment. Now she only had to take a bus at night, to the nursing home where she worked. It was that bus ride that bothered Susan more than anything. Him, too, after what he'd heard about crime in the city streets.

Rachel's apartment building must once have been elegant, but it was shabby now. Soot had worked its way deep into the architectural embellishments, a brave weed or two struggled up through cracks in the front walkway, and here and there someone had spray-painted a four-letter word—slogans of the decay.

"I like it here," Rachel had told him. "It has atmosphere."

He had written last week, and as soon as he pushed the buzzer in her lobby and said his name, she was running down the inner steps, throwing the door open, and wrapping him tightly in her arms.

He pulled back to look at her. Her eyes brimmed, but she would not cry, he knew. She was too obstinate. Her tears would come after he left.

Small, mannish, and strong, she looked out from soft eyes, moved with clean motions. Her face was angular, ascetic, like a monk's face, a saint's face. It was not pretty, but with makeup it might have been striking. He wondered if she'd tried it.

Though she no longer dressed Amish, she wore simple clothes. Today a pair of jeans, an undecorated white shirt. But each time he saw her she seemed a little further from him and the girl she once had been. She was wearing a necklace, he noticed; it was the first time he'd seen her do it. It was simple, too, a pewter ornament. A gift, perhaps, from the man in her life, an artist who worked in acrylics, she'd said.

She took both his hands, pulling him up the steps. "Come on! I'll go crazy if you don't see this right away!"

Her second-floor apartment was full of plain, sunny spaces, and it struck him with a pang how her Amishness showed here too—except that everywhere there were books. She picked one up and handed it to him, then stood back smiling.

Her book.

He had been expecting to see it any time, but the first sight of it had an immense impact on him. He read the cover. *Woodsmoke in Winter: Memories of an Amish Girlhood*, by Rachel Hostetler.

He opened the cover, smelled the tangy new-paper fragrance, read the title page, the name of the university press publisher, the inscription she had written to him and Susan. He opened the book at random and read.

> If there weren't so much to do, my mother would have sat in one spot all her years and watched the moon rise and the sun set and the changing face of the meadows. She loves the world and her place in it.
>
> My father is more restive. There are times when I think he's not so sure of things as he wants to seem. He's careful; careful of his feelings, careful of others.
>
> The younger children are a meld. The images of my parents are less clear in them, but the three of us who are oldest seem like mirrors of our seed. Daniel has the serenity of our mother. I am restless like our father. Susan has both the peace and the haste. We found roles. Daniel became the peacemaker, I the chronicler, Susan the poet.
>
> It is the hardest for Susan. The world to her is an ingenious puzzle she believes she will never understand. My grandmother used to say that Susan has two gears: all out or full stop. Moods hit her in turns, each one so deep, so convincing, yet different. Two strains, two temperaments, compete in her, and that is one of the things, I

think, that draws people to her. She is exciting, and in her own way unpredictable. Although I was taught that envy is a sin, all my life I have admired Susan and envied her. For her serenity. For her ability to bring sunlight into moments of shadow.

Daniel closed the book and took Rachel in his arms, holding her again, the book between them.

"I'm going to come to the farm one day," she said. "I won't stay. I'm just going to give the book to Pop, try to explain, and leave."

They talked and had a beer together. They'd often had beer as teenagers . . . the drinking was a small secret expression of their rebellion, childish perhaps, but something they did.

He asked, "What do you know about Alan Wilde?"

"You mean the movie director, or producer—whatever he is?"

"That one."

She shrugged. "Just what everyone else knows, I guess. The wonder boy of American films. Former child star. Handsome, and rich as the Pope. What about him?"

"He's making a movie on location in Greyling."

"You're kidding. I heard they were filming in Wisconsin, but I had no idea it was practically in our—in your backyard. Caused much excitement?"

He was quiet for a moment. Then he took the crumpled envelope out of his back pocket and gave it to her.

"What's this?" She studied it, turning it over. Then she tore it open. And was still. When she spoke her voice was thick with the pain she would not shed as tears. "Do you know what this is?"

"Yes." He had seen it, the check for ten thousand dollars endorsed over to Rachel. And he'd seen Susan's note, which read only, "So you don't need to work. So you can go to school and write. I love you. Susan."

"Dear God, has she sold the farm?"

"No. We don't have that kind of equity in it."

"Then where—"

"She's working for Alan Wilde."

It took her a very long time to assimilate it. He understood. It was impossible to accept the reality of it.

"As what?"

"She says he gave her a part in the movie."

She slapped the check into his hand, her eyes hot. "Give it back to her, please, and tell her to stop being nuts."

"She has a contract."

"So what? Surely under the circumstances it can be broken. She couldn't have had any idea what she was signing."

"She didn't. But they'd already filmed a week and a half before she told me. You can understand the kind of financial commitment it is for them. If she made them lose that kind of money they might come after her in court. I don't know what they could do to her." He took her hand and slowly uncurled her fingers, then put the envelope in it. "You have to keep it, you know, or she will have done it for nothing."

They stayed like that for a while, hands together, not speaking. Then Rachel began to laugh, a strange, painful laugh.

"Oh, Susan, Susan," she said, and laid her head down on his knees. "Did you see? She didn't even think to take money out of it for income tax."

Chapter 10

*O*n Monday morning Susan cried for no reason while they were putting on her makeup. Like a sun-shower, it was over before Alan heard about it and came.

He was his public self, all polished charm and professionalism. No references, however oblique, were made to their heart-catching moments on the bridge. There was no visible display of more than friendly interest or directorial concern.

"Are you nervous about today's shooting?"

"No. It was just silly."

But something had changed between them. Under the polite manners, the spark glowed more hotly. Together they were an island of warmth and light in the crowded trailer. Her senses were restive. Where there had been tears, laughter came. For no reason.

"You may film me. You may take movies of me. You may even process and print me, but you may not *shoot* me. And it's no wonder that I'm nervous. You only give me the script a bit at a time. I don't know from one day to the next if you'll have that monster make a meal of me."

"I give you the script a piece at a time so that you won't be intimidated by the size of it. The monster won't eat you. I won't shoot you. I promise."

Over the next days, the new feelings multiplied, growing with a strength that was beyond Susan's power to understand, beyond Alan's ability to absorb. Whatever her accomplishments in front of the camera or his behind it, their greatest performances came when they were together. He tried not to scare her. She tried not to scare herself.

The time limit comforted her. In a matter of weeks he would be gone, and that meant her control need not last forever. In the meantime, the feelings were too rich to withstand.

Friendship was the one acceptable path for her. She tried to push her volatile emotions into that category, where all her familiar rules would apply. He watched her efforts to become his friend, his chum, with something akin to awe. It was an illusion so transparent and helpless that even his ingrained cynicism was no match against being moved by it.

He began to know her better.

Susan had no concept of "work." To her, work was

play, and play work. A gentle fancy invaded everything she did. When he explained a scene to her, fathoms deep in technicalities, she had a dozen ways to draw him away from it.

Once she deposited a caterpillar on his shirt. As the insect made its bumpy way along the cloth, she gazed up at him with bright eyes and said, "He likes you. He's measuring you for a new suit."

She spent an afternoon break by the stream with him, washing pebbles, showing him the vivid colors they became when they were wet. Another time she brought him a jar of her homemade strawberry jam and held it toward the sun to let him see how the light came inside and made it a jewel. Hardly knowing it, he began to learn about the definitions of wealth and beauty in her world. Vitality began to seep, via him, into the love story between Polly and Adam that he'd written to be no more than a token subplot. Viewing the dailies was becoming an event.

❧

Adam continues his courtship of Polly, but Polly's father, disillusioned by his own marriage, has decreed that the couple must have a long engagement to be sure they both know their own minds. Polly is making a decorative wreath of feathers, an elaborate Victorian ornament. Each time Adam visits, he may give her one feather. When the wreath is completed, they may wed.

Short takes. Polly is framed in the moody light of a rain-streaked window, adding a feather. She adds another on a sunlit afternoon, the kitten cuddled against her cheek. Another, then, in her shadowed bedroom, the candlelight gleaming in the loose waves of her hair.

Then—a shift to a farmhouse. Adam steps from his front door and a barnyard of geese and chickens explodes into panicked flight.

❧

Laughter hummed through the screening room.

"When'd you film that?" Ben Rose asked.

"While everyone was at lunch," Joan said. "It was just

David, Pete, Susan, and me. Pete ran the camera. It was Susan's idea. We thought it'd give you people a chuckle."

❧

Adam's impatience erupts. He slices into the mattress on his bed, scoops up an armful of feathers, and rushes to the inn. Polly is on the porch, enjoying a summery evening with her father, and Adam casts the fluffy mountain on the wooden steps. Polly runs to him, her skirts sweeping the feathers into a hurricane. The stern father's heart melts at the ardency of young love, and he gives his final nod of approval. In an arbor of feathers that swirls around them like apple blossoms, Adam catches Polly to him in an exuberant embrace, lifting her at the waist, and she is laughing, laughing, the expression on her face heart-robbing in its beauty.

❧

David had been pacing restlessly around the screening room, cocaine singing arias in his blood. "Is it love, or is it confusion?" he murmured, subjecting the screen to a jaundiced study.

From the back, Max spoke sleepily. "Love—that which impels you to scratch your initials with hers on a bathroom wall. Valium for the masses." He stretched and strolled forward to examine the screen in closer detail. "Damn, that woman is gorgeous. We get ten thousand volts in every closeup."

"She has a European kind of look, don't you think? So much done with the eyes." Joan took a swallow of Scotch. "She makes you think of Isabelle Adjani. The face stays with you."

"Yeah." Ben Rose put his feet up. "It has the classical dialectic: arousing but innocent. Not quite virginal, though."

"I know what you mean," Max said. "Fragility marked by experience. She looks like a woman who's been with a man. But only *one* man. A grand passion that's left her wounded, and now every man who looks at her wants to take her to bed and heal the scars. You do a great job with her, David."

"Thank you. I didn't have any choice. Besides, I think she's going to be a star."

"Not according to her," Joan said. "She swears up and down this is the one and only movie in her life."

Ben laughed. "That'll change as soon as she gets an idea of the bucks coming her way. By the way, what did you decide to do with the bedroom scene, Alan? Is she going to play the whole thing by herself?"

"No. We've hired a double."

"What a headache that was." Joan let Max take a sip of her Scotch. "Susan has these incredible proportions—tiny, but with long legs. That's why when you look at her on film without a point of reference, she looks tall. Casting finally put their hands on a runway model who does petite fashions. The features don't match, but *c'est la vie*." She frowned. "By the way, has Susan been told?"

David rested his palms on Joan's shoulders, absently massaging them. "It hardly matters, does it?"

"Of course it doesn't matter," Ben said irritably. "Fortunately, there isn't a damn thing she can do about it. If she doesn't like it, she can count herself lucky we had the sensitivity not to make her do it." He glanced sideways. "You off to bed, Alan?"

"To sleep, perchance to dream. Good night."

But he was still awake at midnight. When Joan and David wandered along a red-brick path through the back garden of daffodils and red tulips, they could hear the majestic passages from his piano. Brilliantly played, the music sank from Wilde's windows and lay like a sorcerer's mist along the cozy walkways.

"Always the Mozart," David said.

"Mmmm. Sounds marvelous. Is it live or is it—"

"That's him, all right. Fabulous technique."

Joan gazed up at one of his windows. "Everyone says he's good enough to be a concert pianist."

"No question."

"I wonder why he never pursued it." Then, "Why was that funny?"

"He could never do it. He'd go mad from boredom in

a month. He doesn't compose, he can only interpret. For Alan to devote himself full time to the piano he would have to write the music, play it, and build the whole damned piano himself. If he were still acting, he'd be commanding over a million a picture. So why does he direct? He needs the autonomy."

The music stopped, the cessation abrupt, in mid-bar. The garden fell into eerie silence.

Joan's voice lowered reflexively. "What do you think that was about?"

"The Amish. How can you doubt it? Probably he's just contemplating our—what did Ben call it?—our sensitivity."

They had accurately predicted her conservatism. But they had not come within ten miles of gauging the depth of it.

Susan took the script for Polly's wedding night to read over lunch. Alan found her later sitting by herself near the stream under a sky whipped with mare's tails. Her Victorian-era gown matched the sky, and was beautiful next to the deep tone of her hair, but she had treated the lustrous billows of cloth with scant respect, pulling them up to uncover her bare legs to the knees, her toes plunged into the rippling water. The pages were crushed urgently to her chest.

He came to her side and sat down. She tapped the pages with her fist. "Have you read this?"

"I wrote it."

"*You* wrote it?"

"Guilty."

"But why?"

"Because if someone else writes the screenplay, they get paid for it. If I write the screenplay, I get paid for it. And if I hire a writer, it breaks a heart when I make a change. I'd as soon film my fatuity as anyone else's."

The simple statement seemed to deprive her of her powers of speech. Finally she said, "I can hardly believe you've done a single fatuous thing in your life. It's a pity, because I think a bit of foolishness does everyone good. But that isn't what I meant." She riffled through the pages and pointed.

70. INT. BEDROOM. NIGHT.
    HIGH ANGLE SHOT SHOWING POLLY AND ADAM,
    CAMERA PANS DOWN ON ADAM AS HE APPROACHES
    HER.
71. CLOSE ON POLLY'S FACE. ADAM KISSES HER. SHE
    RESPONDS.
72. ANGLE. TIGHT ON ADAM AND POLLY AS HE CAR-
    RIES HER TO BED.

A cloud of pink color was spreading over Susan's cheeks. He had the strong impression that she had the idea she'd been looking at some pretty graphic material. Enchanted totally, he tensed his muscles, disciplining the arms that begged to surround her body. "It *is* their wedding night."

"I can't see where that makes a bit of difference. I'm not married to David, and even if I were, I'd hardly be having a camera fixed on our marriage bed. What can you be thinking of?"

You. Holding you. "We want to let the audience know how much Polly and Adam care for each other."

With great earnestness, she said, "Alan, no one's going to come to a theater to watch two strangers kissing. They'll be disgusted. You won't sell any tickets to your movie."

He searched her eyes to see if there was any chance she was kidding. No. The dark, lovely eyes flooded him with sincerity. He put the gentleness he felt into his voice. "It's very common for lovers to kiss in movies."

"Not near a bed!"

"Near beds—and in beds."

She looked taken aback by so much vice. "No wonder people sit in the dark to watch them." She stared, appalled, at the pages in her hands. "Does David know about—this?"

"Sure, he does. It's part of the profession. He does it all the time. Don't worry. Just put yourself into his hands."

With a distraught moan, she buried her face in her skirts. One of her curls tumbled from her shoulder and fell, loose and sun-warmed, on his hand. A sensual thrill twisted through his nerves and he lifted his hand, playing against the silky column of hair, letting it caress the skin on his inner wrist. "Susan?"

She looked up to see him carry one dark lock to his

mouth and lightly kiss it. His expression shook her. She'd expected to find a reassuringly humorous facade. Instead she intercepted a startling moment of naked longing, a glimpse beneath the casual sexuality and studied indifference. She wondered, shaken, if he knew it was there himself. It was like watching wind move on water, breaking the surface into a thousand reflective points before the water goes still and the hidden depths become sharp and clear.

"If you wrote the movie, Alan, then you must have Polly Bates inside you. It makes me wonder whom else you have inside you."

"I thought you knew." He released her curl. "Monsters."

The wedding set was beautiful, complex, authentic to period. His crew became so carried away that Alan had to make them redo the bedroom set three times, simplifying. He spoke patiently to his set designer. "This is not the Americanization of *Fanny and Alexander*. I'm not Ingmar Bergman. I'm not Federico Fellini. I want to excite people, and scare them, and entertain them. I do *not* want to make them think. I make a movie. It has a monster. It eats people. Very basic. Please don't give me art."

But it was difficult to remember when he saw the bedroom in its final form. Polished woodwork absorbed the subdued saffron lighting. Transparent draperies fluttered around an open window.

≥♠

Polly sits in a golden aura, her hair falling in loose, shining waves to the floorboards. She is examining her reflection in a mirror. She touches her cheek hesitantly. What appears to be Polly's poignant reverie is only Susan, baffled by an image of herself that is strange to her.

When Adam enters with his shirt open, her wide-eyed look is more subtly humorous than she can know.

She stands jerkily, and he approaches, speaking softly.

David was in his element. There had been a thousand women, a thousand bedrooms on- and offscreen. Tough and experienced, he was perfectly relaxed, concentrating on hitting his marks and developing the much-photographed facade of moody sensuality that had brought him a small fortune in poster residuals.

He took her in his arms. A look of sheer terror came over her face. Even for an actor with David's insouciance, it must have taken considerable nerve to persist in the face of her inappropriate bridal response, but David's theatrical background was the finest, and he invariably tried to give some form of life to the most moribund scene. He took Susan's adorably stiff face between his hands with a credible show of *savoir-faire* and brought his lips down to hers. They met empty air. Susan had vacated his arms and was clinging to the bedpost for dear life.

❧

The crew looked numb with suppressed ecstasy. Seeing David lose was not a routine event. Max murmured, "Sensational. For a Lavoris commercial."

Susan didn't need to see the assortment of smirks around her to know that she had erred grievously. David's face was calm, but she was not deceived. If his eyes were sparks, she'd be on fire. Nervously she watched Alan emerge from the line of lights and cameras, his expression cheerful and encouraging, soft-pedaling the disaster.

"That was nice. I like what you're working on, Susan," he said, as if she'd thought up something really clever. "It had . . . drama. David, I wouldn't change a thing about what you're doing. Very sexy. I like your instincts."

He knew David well. Alan's absurdity and his congratulatory tone drew a reluctant smile from the actor. "If she does that to me once more, my instinct will be to tie her wrists to the bedposts."

"My fault," Alan said. "A couple of rehearsals will smooth it out. Let's take ten and bring back something fresh."

He stayed behind with her until they were alone on the dim, deserted set. She hadn't moved.

He said, "I wouldn't have kissed him either."

She found his voice both soothing and exciting. "No?"

"No. Too much Brando." Realizing she made nothing of that, he said, "He can't help it. His fans want him sultry."

He brought two canvas chairs and sat on one. When he smiled at her expectantly, she sat in the other, staring at her knees.

After a short pause, he asked, "What was your husband's name?"

She'd expected him to talk about David, the scene—anything but this gentle inquiry. She felt strangely uncomfortable, as if there weren't enough air in the room.

"His name was John."

"What was he like?" Then, "Why did that make you smile?"

"Yesterday I got asked the same about you, by some people I know. Some Amish."

"And you told them?"

"As little as I could get by with."

The way he smiled, she could tell he was used to getting talked about. "Tell me about John."

"Well... He was good with horses."

He waited. When it was evident she had nothing to add to that, he said, "That doesn't tell me very much."

To her surprise, she could see that it had not. "I don't have the knack of describing people. I haven't had to do it. Everyone I know knows everyone else." The jumpiness in her refused to dissipate. "John had a pony trained to throw bad boys, he said. The kids used to love it. They'd climb on its back just to see if it would throw them. Of course, John gave the pony a signal, but the kids didn't know that. He was lively that way. He... What I mean to say is that—John was good with horses like Dash is good with horses. They have the same manner, a little bit. They're practical, but they like to see the best part of a person."

Clearly, it wasn't what he wanted to hear. "He must have been a paragon. How did you spend your evenings together?"

"Sometimes after milking we'd go visiting family or friends and maybe stay on to sing hymns. If we were at home, we might do a puzzle or play games—Scrabble and so on. Or we'd sit on the porch to watch the sun set, and plan what we were going to do the next day. In good weather we'd walk out to hear the birds. Just country things."

"Was he good to you?"

"Yes."

"Always?"

"Yes, always." Kay, from wardrobe, had wrapped a large shawl around her as soon as the big lights went out. She toyed with its fringe. "We wanted the same things. He was contented, not hard to understand, never full of ideas. Not like you. Well, maybe in one way. He always wanted to do the right thing."

Trust Alan Wilde to take that as an insult. She saw, fascinated, that his eyes held a vivid gleam.

"I don't always want to do the right thing."

"It seems that you do."

He launched himself from his chair and crossed the short space between them, placing his palms flat on the arms of her chair. His voice was quiet. "Susan, I don't try to do the right thing. I do whatever suits me. Believe it."

He waited a minute, making sure the message stuck, before he moved back. She stood, too, smiling into the deep storm of his eyes. "Even now—did you notice?—you tried to do the right thing by being honest."

That checked him. She could see him examining her, examining the statement, trying to find a way around it. She knew that a disbelief in the goodness of human nature, his own in particular, was an important part of what he registered as clear thinking.

"I don't know what I can do to make it plainer," he said, and Susan knew the subject was closed. "Can we talk about the kiss?"

"If we have to."

"What made you slip away from him?"

"Aside from having a roomful of people and cameras watching me?"

"Aside from that."

"I didn't know what he was going to do to me."

"Just kiss you. Or I would have dropped a boom on his head."

"Maybe what I mean by a kiss isn't the same as what you mean. I'd thought . . . it would be just a little smack, but then I saw it was going to be more than that. I didn't know what to do. I haven't seen much kissing."

"All those brothers and sisters and you didn't see your parents kissing?"

"Ho! That'd be the day. Never."

"Why not?"

"They just wouldn't. They'd think it was—"

"What?"

"Showing off, I guess. Or setting a bad example. I don't know. It just isn't something they'd think was right. Did your parents kiss in front of you?"

"God, yes. They never hid a thing, so I could grow up complete"—the fine mouth shaped itself into a smile—"and without hangups."

His tone suggested ironic amusement rather than bitterness. Still she caught the echoes of a bleaker emotion long ago put away. He didn't feel complete. He didn't feel that it was possible to become complete. She could tell that he accepted this about himself, that he felt the journey through life was ultimately solitary, with all men and women orphans under the sun. How desolate that must feel, not to live within a community of the spirit. It was not easy to turn her back and say, ah, well, that's the way it is for him, and leave him to the emptiness. Yet it was surely impossible to change him. Mature, sophisticated, she saw no evidence that he was in any way malleable. But he was not corrupt. Whatever he might think of himself, she couldn't believe he was bad. He might be a sinner, but there was much good in him.

Dismissing what he seemed to consider the unrewarding topic of his early life, he began to pace the set, viewing it in different ways.

"Let's figure out a kiss you can live with. Would it help if the scene began with David already in the room?"

"But the script—"

"Doesn't matter. It wasn't written in stone. Ben calls it one hundred twenty pages of typing. I've told you. If I were an author, I'd live in Vermont and write novels. You've probably noticed that the rest of the cast regards the screenplay's dialogue as no more than a polite suggestion. I don't think David's said a single line straight since page one. What do you think Polly would be doing on her wedding night?"

She cuddled more deeply into the shawl. "I think it would make more sense for her to wait for her husband in bed."

"Why?"

"Because she would. If it's Wisconsin, and springtime, and you live in a house without central heating, the evenings are chilly, and when you get into your nightclothes, you get right into bed. It's just what you do. And I don't think she'd be so comfortable having him see her in a nightdress, either. If she were in bed, she could pull the bedclothes around her."

He appeared to consider her words. Then he asked, "Is that what you did?"

"When?"

"On the night you were married."

He had asked so gently, it touched her, though her cheeks colored. "I don't remember."

Again, with great gentleness, "Were you afraid?"

"How could I have been afraid? It was the right thing to do to make a family."

"Were you shy?"

She stared at her toes. "Not the way I am with you."

"Susan . . ."

She met his gaze with difficulty. He had come to a stop beside the bed.

"Teach me," he said. He drew back the covers and ran his hand back and forth across the bedsheets. "I'll warm it up for you." His soft gaze pulled her closer. "Teach me how it is with you."

Her knees were up to mischief. They felt slack, light as two reeds. "How it is with Polly," she corrected.

"How it is with Polly."

So his mouth said. But the strict professional distance had vanished from his eyes, and it became hard to know if he was talking to Polly or Susan. There wasn't a bit of doubt in her as to who was responding. She took one step toward him, and it was like stepping into a dream. Even the air seemed different. It began to caress her skin. She could feel the narrowing of her perceptions until they took in only the scent of poplar wood, the ivory bed linens, the closeness of him. As in his films, this was a place of the imagination, potent with secrets and new laws. And the sense of release she had not felt with David, or even with gentle, inhibited John, came to her now as it had on the bridge.

He moved, or she might have, and he took her hands, nesting them between his palms.

"Cold hands," he murmured, and carried them to his mouth. His breath and the pattern of his lips began to imprint warmth, touching her fingertips once, then the base of her hand where it met her inner wrist, presently the plumpness beneath her thumb. He was no longer smiling.

His eyes had become brighter and more diffuse, and his fingers traced hers with exquisite care, imparting deep-traveling sensations.

Cradling her two hands in one of his, he held them against his chest. His other hand stroked her hair with hypnotic slowness, alternating with his palm and the back of his hand. At length he spread his fingers, supporting her while he tipped her head back. With the sleepy eroticism of a dream, his mouth descended toward hers.

"You're always too far away," he whispered.

His lips touched the curve of one cheek, of the other, then came to her mouth, feather-light. Her breath caught in her throat, tightening against the light, quick beat of her pulse. Firm as his mouth appeared to her, she was unprepared for the softness of his lips, unprepared for the rush of feeling that ran to the depths of her body as his mouth kept up its slightly brushing exploration. His thumb did the same to her palm, making a circle there.

He lifted her to the bed, his arms strong under her, and covered her legs with the bedclothes. Then he sat beside her in the half-world where wan lights and sightless cameras surrounded them like a fairy ring. His hands were braced on the bedcover at either side of her hips, and the sheet pulled at the quivering sensitivity of her thighs.

He softly kissed her nose at the tip. Clean and mint-scented, his hair skimmed the edge of her face, tickling her hairline. "So far, Susan . . ." His mouth dragged over her lips, back and forth, a gently questing pressure that left her mouth tingling and unbearably excited. The room around her was falling away and she was tumbling, tumbling into his kiss. Her hands sought and held on to his waist. Under his shirt, she could feel the detail of him, the warm, lean skin, the solid motif of muscle and bone.

The full sleeves of her gown ended in a cuff at her

wrists, but an open top seam bound in satin ribbon ran from wrist to shoulder, exposing glimpses of her flesh. One by one his fingers discovered and released the slippery bows, and the fabric slid away to bare her arms. His hands came to her unclad arms, moving gently up and down, and the rhythmic caress heated her blood.

His breath came more rapidly and mingled with hers, and his mouth came to hers again, fuller this time, more searching, his tongue delicately touching her to openness. His fingertips curving under her chin gently altered the tilt of her head, deepening his access until she could only hold onto him tightly to experience over and over the sensitivity of his mouth. Urgency sang its hard, bright notes in her blood. The surface of her skin burned. She found herself twisting closer, seeking the sating hardness of him.

His arms prevented her. "Not here, Susan." She could hear the unsteadiness in his breath, feel the unsteadiness in his hands where they curved around her naked shoulders. *Not here.* Her drifting descent ended in a soft jolt. Not here, not here...not ever in this life. A shudder passed through her, thrumming like light fingers in her middle, a cool spot in the heat of her desire. Gazing into the pagan iridescence of his eyes, she reached up a shaking hand to thread her fingers wonderingly through his hair, feeling the fine silk stream like spring water against the inside of her fingers.

"Tonight, Amish?"

She couldn't answer him, because none of the bewilderment in her mind could take form in words. And so quickly it became too late for answers, for she heard the others begin to return.

Her confusion was obvious as she stared at him, as though the enormity of his question might eat her alive. She didn't have to give him an answer; he knew it would have been no. He knew also that each time she told him no, she faltered more.

Not tonight. But soon.

He hadn't planned the kiss, and he swiftly came to regret it, because it left them both raw and in the worst possible state to film a love scene. Susan was shaky and stoic, flushing when David curled one of her untied satin bows around his little finger and looked askance at her. And Wilde had to regear himself so dramatically to tease her into relaxing for the camera that he did a poor job of burying his own unsteady emotions, which kept resurfacing. Four times, and for trivial reasons, he interrupted the scene just before David could kiss her. The fifth time, he realized what he was doing, and saw by the quizzical glances and astonished silence around him that others did also. David, clearly, had had about as much as he could take. The actor's eyes promised retribution.

And later, when an excruciating headache came, Alan had no choice but to retire to his suite. He could barely see. Feeling like an idiot, he was sunk in a chair by an open window, with his forehead buried in an ice pack Joan had discovered for him in the prop room. David came in without knocking. Alan looked up at him, wondering with the detachment of agony whether or not he was going to be able to placate the actor, when he saw the harsh temper lines around David's mouth begin to loosen. Another minute of the star's hawklike scrutiny and the mouth relaxed totally.

"So how do you feel?"

"Like someone's tried to flambé my skull."

"You look like bloody hell. You know, don't you—that thing isn't going to do you a bit of good." David's smile touched on the ice bag. "Because you've got it stuck on the wrong part of your body."

Chapter 11

*A*fter three hours he was able to work, which was a relief and an escape for him.

Joan came much later. Finding him at his word processor, she slapped her cheek in mock despair, stored his text, and switched off the power. Bending over to shake his shoulders, half-smiling, she said, "Rest, Alan. *Rest*." She poured him a glass of Chivas Regal and slid it into his tense fingers. "Have you had dinner? You know, food? It's not just for breakfast anymore."

He had no memory of whether he'd eaten, so, shaking her head affectionately, she phoned in an order for him. Putting down the receiver, she said, "There you are, wunderkind. Let the brain waves wane. Go to your piano and play. When your food comes, consume it."

"If you leave a schedule taped to the mirror, I'll do my best." He was less than his most pleasant self because although he had the vague instinct that she was right, it was often tearingly hard for him to stop working. He tended to resist the moment of letting it go. Typical compulsive personality trait.

Joan's smile said she wasn't intimidated. "The body parts aren't bionic, Alan. Feed them. Refresh them." Before she left, she wrapped him in her arms and held him very tightly, as if she were trying to protect him from something.

Alone, he played the piano, drinking, hearing his own errors, substituting one task for another until his food came, another duty.

He had just begun to eat when the first scatter of sound hit his window. Rain? The sky had been clear earlier. He hadn't noticed it himself, but Dash had remarked on it. The showering sound was repeated several times before it occurred to him that someone was throwing gravel against his window. He didn't react immediately, because he registered it as a minor detail and he was used to having assistants deal with such things: *Get me some black-and-whites to preview the shots; backlight the monster; find out who's throwing gravel at my window.* After a second or two of hesitation, he went to the window, opened it, and looked outside.

There was nothing to see. Leaving the window open, he went back to eating. When something round flew into his wooden salad bowl with enough force to scatter its contents, he jumped. Scraps of lettuce littered the white tablecloth.

"Okay. Tossed salad." He picked a sliver of cucumber out of his hair and then peered under the overturned bowl. A softball with a message tied to it. Sense of humor piqued, he unwrapped the note, and between the vinegar spots he read, "Alan, I must speak with you. Please come outside. Susan."

He felt momentary disbelief before he recognized her handwriting. He had seen it on the notes she made so conscientiously on her script.

Smiling, he experienced a thrill of feeling, although he knew it was a bad sign that she had not come to his room. Juliet awaited him without, and with winsome hesitation. Go out, Wilde, and get another headache.

Susan saw him approach from where she knelt beside a lilac bush. He was tossing the softball slowly in his hand, and when he was close enough to speak, he said cheerfully, "I'm sure it would have been immoral for you to have used the phone."

"I don't have one. Besides, I didn't know which numbers were yours."

Adoring the originality of her self-expression, he knew his eyes were soft with it. He put down a hand to help her to her feet. "We get high marks for discretion, at least. Don't worry. Your message will self-destruct in ten seconds."

"Pardon?"

She felt a little shaky about the whole venture, and it didn't help when he pulled her into his arms, fitting their bodies with disturbing accuracy so that she could feel all of him against all of her and she couldn't think straight for how good and hard and warm he felt. His mouth arrived on the base of her throat, pressing softly, and made an upward path to her ear.

"Our images are all different, have you noticed?" he asked. "We don't think in a common cultural dialect. Do you know Yoda?"

"Who?" His whisper traced tingling, exciting patterns

on her skin. Her respiration came quick and light.

"As I thought. Know Garp?"

"No. Alan—" She took a sharp breath as he laid a hand on her side, and moved it gently up and down.

"Carl Bernstein . . . ? Valium . . . ? George Carlin . . . ?"

Exquisite searching kisses made slow strokes on her ear, then just below it, tenderly marking each question, and she said no, no, no, and finally, "Alan, *no.*" Shaking with unwilling laughter and from the stimulation of what he was doing to her, she put him from her with a reluctance she could hardly admit to herself. "Alan, I came here to say—"

"Sigmund Freud?"

She picked up his hand and held it between both of hers to halt its unsettling massage of her waist. "No."

"I was afraid of that. We may have to go back to the Enlightenment and start there." His fingertips rubbed lightly on the inside of her wrist. "Would you tell me, Susan Peachey, just what was the point of having the twentieth century if you don't even know about it?"

She withdrew her grasp from his hand, feeling breathless, trying to ignore the temptation of his beautiful mouth, with its charming contours and tender corners. His eyes, in the soft light from the distant window, were bright, coaxing, promising pleasure beyond her imagination. She gazed wistfully into them for a minute and then said, "You've been drinking?"

"For medicinal purposes only." The hand that had been so light and knowing at her waist drew invisible bisecting lines on his own chest. "Cross my heart."

"Don't." She caught up his hand, stilling the long, aesthete's fingers. "I don't want you to forswear yourself to me. Oaths are serious things." This time instead of releasing his hand, she wove their fingers together. "Come with me." Tugging gently, "A walk will clear your head, and we can talk then."

Her touch did many things for him, but clearing his head was not one of them. Her small, boyish hand clasped his firmly, and he strolled beside her, their footsteps whispers in the grass.

"Curiouser and curiouser," he said presently. "Is there any way for us to make sense of each other? I come from a place where they paint the white roses red and you can only see cats by their grins. Have you read *Through the Looking Glass*?"

Her sigh said, Oh, this game again, but she was smiling and unembarrassed as she shook her head.

"For God's sake, give me something. Kermit the Frog? Louis L'Amour? The Mahara Ji?"

Dropping his hand, she covered her face with her hands. Laughter made her voice delicious to him as she said, "You want proof, I suppose, that we come from the same planet?"

"Does physical evidence exist? You see, I'd like the chance to be something besides strangers with you."

She spun to face him, stepping backward on the black, starlit lawn, and gave him that smile again, the one he never quite expected from her features no matter how often he saw it. She had a smile that didn't understand its own power, and he was unaccustomed to beauty that made no attempt to charm. The humorous opening of her eyes and slight tuck of her lower lip cast off the classic look her features had in repose and made her smile puckish.

"How about Laura Ingalls Wilder?" she asked.

An unfamiliar sensation was building in his chest, a kind of skipping delight in her, in everything about her. "I'd call that a nice, sound start. I was afraid we might have to rewind to Eden, but if we're already up to the pioneers—"

"Spiderman!"

"*Spiderman!* Then we're practically blood br—take a hard right or you'll plant yourself into a tree trunk—blood brothers. I like this track. Twentieth century with a vengeance, and very funky."

She halted, glanced furtively from side to side, testing the air for invisible spies, and whispered, "Winnie-the-Pooh."

They had arrived at a high wooden fence where she

had tethered her Belgian mare. Gently forestalling his attempt to take her again into his arms, she said, "So you see, it's hopeless. We're hopeless, you and I. Our ideas were shaped so differently."

"You'd be astonished how many profound relationships are based wholly on Spiderman and Winnie-the-Pooh."

"I could give you a dozen others I've heard since coming here that I don't know."

"I triple-dog-dare you to."

"Gatsby, Gucci, Spencer Tracy, post-Vietnam syndrome, Mr. Greenjeans, rolfing, middlebrow, Wagnerian, okay kemosabe . . ."

"That was only nine."

"Argyle socks."

"I'll never wear them again."

"And there's all those initials you use, like it's too much trouble to say out a whole word: SAG, NOW, TLC—"

He smiled encouragingly. "TNT."

That word she knew, and if she hadn't, she'd have been able to make a good guess from the way he was looking at her. "It's not good for you, to stay in your room having drinks instead of being out in the fresh air. You'll ruin your disposition."

Disposition. He liked the word—funny, old-fashioned, practical. He spoke softly. "If you're interested in helping my disposition, I can think of something right now that would do me a wealth of good."

"I don't know what shocks me more—the things you say or the fact that I'm beginning to understand what they mean. And I don't think it would do your disposition or any other part of you a bit of good for us to have carnal knowledge of each other."

Another old-fashioned phrase, but he found this one a lot less charming. "Make love."

She shrugged with fair-minded indifference. "Changing the word doesn't change the—"

"I didn't grow up with sin and Satan hung like gall and wormwood over my head, so please coddle me. The words are 'make love.'"

His abruptness and the intensity of his tone made her smile. "You use the words that are right for you and I'll use the words that are—"

"No." He took hold of her shoulders. "I want you to say it. Say, 'make love.'"

She cast a droll glance heavenward.

Very softly: "Susan, say it."

"All right, then." Her level voice sounded loud in the hush of night. "Make love." The wide, haunting eyes narrowed enchantingly, and she said more loudly, "Make love." Curving her flexed palms around her mouth megaphone-style, she said very, very loudly, "Make love. Ma—"

He stopped her with the light pressure of his hand on her mouth. His palm caught the last stir of her lips as an inadvertent caress, marking his skin with her warmth and softness, igniting his senses.

"I'm sorry, Alan. The guards will come."

"I don't think so. They know I'm here. I told them I'd forgotten something on the set."

He was amused, because he couldn't help it, but his body was serious, so serious that wanting her was stinging him everywhere and the fingers he had loosened to let her speak drifted upward, following her cheekbone. Reaching her temple, he put one fingertip under the rim of her bonnet. Slowly he slipped his finger deeper under the bonnet and around, tracing the edge of her hairline. Soft, soft . . .

"Let me take this off you, Susan," he whispered.

She put her hands flat on his chest, shaking her bent head. In a light, endearing gesture, she rested her brow against his chest, rubbing her face against his sweater, the gesture unconsciously sexy, affectionate.

Her lifted face then was poignantly optimistic. "I think it would do us both good to get some exercise. Fresh air and exercise."

He bypassed the easy, juvenile comment on what kind of exercise he thought they needed, only pointing out mildly that they'd already had plenty of fresh air.

"We need *more* fresh air."

This time the determination in her voice made him laugh. But the side of his thumb continued to stroke her ear. "Maybe, then," he murmured smiling, "we should try breathing faster."

That was too risqué for her, and she didn't want to smile at it. He could see the *didn't want to*, could see her shut her eyes and tense her facial muscles, fighting the pull of her lips; and he encouraged the smile, the lightness, with the gentlest of sweeping caresses, toying with her ear, lightly tugging on the corners of her mouth with his thumbs, and this time he said, "What we need is to make love to each other."

"There are other things, you know." Her words were arrhythmic because of her uneven breath. Her unwilling smile hovered, wary and appealing.

Amusement coursed through him. *Are you trying to distract me, Susan?* "What others?"

"Riding is good. Do you go horseback riding?"

As he watched, her smile fixed itself and tried to become sensibly encouraging, as though that overcame the mist of yearning in her eyes. Such wonderful eyes. Her emotions found graphic expression in them. Unknowingly they pleaded. Unknowingly they touched him. It was a temporary reprieve only, but he allowed the distraction.

"I've suffered the experience. Dash has a stable in Arizona of pampered Arabian horses who live better than I do and are probably worth a lot more. Once upon a time he convinced himself that it would do me good to get out in the country and have the healthful and spiritually uplifting experience of galloping across the majestic desert sands with the wind in my hair. I got on one of his overpedigreed animals and it brushed me off under the first tree limb."

"You should have gotten right back on again!"

"So Dash said. I did, and the beast threw me off into a saguaro. I had one broken ankle, two cracked ribs, a sunburn, and thirty-seven puncture wounds."

"It happens that way when you start riding. You've got to take a knock or two."

So Dash had said also. He put a hand on her shoulder

and leaned forward confidingly. "Susan, I don't know how to tell you this, but I don't like animals."

She smiled, not believing him. "See, Alan—these great, soft eyes . . ."

He had been politely ignoring the Belgian, but now he gave the animal a studious once-over. "Are you sure it's a horse? I thought it was a dinosaur."

She was too honest and straightforward to see the trap, the conscious challenge; when she volunteered to take him riding here and now, she had no more on her mind than to soften what she had come to say with an act of kindness and friendship, and perhaps to bring some fun into what she saw as his sterile existence. He resisted, though he fully intended to go with her, because her efforts to urge him into it were delightful. But when she finally was convinced she'd talked him into it, and linked her fingers to make a stirrup and cheerfully offered it to help him, he began to laugh.

"Thanks. But I think I can manage. Please, after you."

It had a strange, fairy-tale feel, watching her take a handhold in the dense mane and clamber onto the mammoth back, extending a hand to help him on behind her. Loose bonnet ribbons made pale tracks upon her breast. Distant light formed soft tails of muted brightness on her bare feet and legs, where her dark gown rode back to expose her flexed knees.

Behind her on the horse's broad back, he rode over gravel paths and starlit grassy slopes to the front gate of Greyling. A fascinated security guard let them out, watching them with benevolent interest, storing the anecdote.

Past the gate lights, the night fell into barbaric darkness, black edged against blacker still. The sky was refracted with brilliant stars over a horizon busy with trees.

In spite of Alan's protests, she was not surprised at the ease with which he'd leaped behind her onto Belle, moving in a single flood of clean motion. Logic might hint that people who lived without physical labor were soft, but she'd already learned during their closeness on the bridge that Alan's muscles had steel. They felt like her father's might, or her brother's, except that Alan's arms had the power to make her feel alive in a way no man's had before. And that was no simple thing to ignore.

They rode for a while in silence, joyously together and alone for once. One mile, maybe two, passed before she directed Belle off the shoulder, down the shallow slope of a ditch, and up the steeper rise into a sweep of wooded parkland. Gravity jostled her, tossing her back until she was brought up short by his hard, warm body behind her, and sudden thrilling wings of heat fluttered inside her. *Alive . . . so alive . . .*

Alan was forecasting another night of headaches. She was enticingly near, a silhouette picked out in stardust. He could see the luster of her hair beneath the translucent bonnet. The breeze caught her skirts, making them move up and down his legs in a caress. Above them, the high, parted branches exuded a pleasant coolness, heightening the sensation of warmth he received from her body and the massive Belgian beneath. The lane was a ribbon of starlight, and the horse stretched itself into a canter.

He gently laid his hand on her waist, curving his palm to her shapely flesh, catching the swing of her body elegantly matching the horse's rhythm. *So much delight . . .* "Would you be interested in hearing my theory about young women who enjoy spending so much time on horseback?"

She knew him well enough by now to spend a moment or two looking below the surface of that one, innocent though his voice had been. She glanced back at his shadowed features, then looked quickly forward again, swallowing shocked laughter. "I'd better take to riding sidesaddle, then, so you'll have no more grist to make theories of." The hand poised delicately at her side tightened, a brief acknowledging pressure that became softly kneading, and her breath caught, her hands began instinctively to slow Belle, her eyes closed briefly. "Please, Alan . . ." The touch left her obediently, but then the back of one finger came to rub lightly, comfortingly on her cheek. A small turn of her head and she might have pressed her lips against his hand, she might have learned the texture of the firm, clean-scented skin. She held her breath, concentrating until the temptation was withdrawn, though her heart continued to hammer uncomfortably.

"I'm of two minds deciding how you see me," she said. Holding aside a low-hanging bough, she brought them from the main path into a woodland corridor, where mossy scents made each breath delicious. "Sometimes it seems like you think you have me all figured out: a country mouse, primitive but healthy—"

"Definitely healthy."

She smiled at the provocative tone, and in a moment he prompted, "And other times?"

"At other times you seem to make me up as you go along. David says—"

"What?"

"That you'd like to make me into Polly Bates."

"No." It would be simpler, perhaps, for him to see her as Polly: Polly, who lived in a context of his design; Polly, whom he could direct, his own invention, his toy. But Susan was so much more. Reared in the lost paradise of Los Angeles, self-contained, and spiritually malnourished in a pop-culture environment he could never have created a character with Susan's contradictions and color and passionate observation of the earth, whose jubilant emotional life challenged and fed limitless inner serenity. "I don't want you to disappear back into my unconscious."

Belle had ambled to a halt. Without the friendly thud of hoofbeats, the forest sounds swelled. Flitting shadows danced on his legs, on her back, on the Belgian's mane. Beyond that, his vision was useless. Ink.

"What's an unconscious?"

The darkest ink. He'd never been anywhere with such a complete absence of light. "The part of your mind that operates without your control."

She paused, seeming to think it over. "I don't have one of those."

Her tone was good-naturedly scoffing. He understood. Another one of his wrong-minded secular concepts. Ordinarily he would have enjoyed jousting the issue with her. Now his city-dweller's paranoia had begun to function. He was not afraid of the dark. In fact, he found it comforting—but within the confines of his own security system.

She sat in silence, waiting for an answer, and when it didn't come she clucked once or twice to the horse, applying the sides of her feet to the great belly, sending her skirts in a flying caress over Alan's lower legs.

The animal trotted into the swallowing darkness. Pebbles scattered; twigs snapped, crackling under the weight of the hoofs.

"It's dark," he said.

She interrupted the pretty tune she was humming under her breath. "Very dark."

"Do you know this area well?"

"I could ride it with a blindfold."

"I'm glad. We seem to be doing the equivalent."

"Don't worry. We haven't far to go. I know a nice spot where we can talk. When I was little we ran all over these woods, playing Anabaptist."

"How do you play Anabaptist?"

"You make teams, half Anabaptists, half persecutors, and the persecutors chase the Anabaptists and torture them. Well, pretend to torture them. That's how it was for us in Europe. Before we were Amish, we were Anabaptists. I had a grandfather, I don't know how many times great, who had his eyes gouged out." She paused and said good-naturedly, "It's better for us in America."

"I'm glad to hear that."

"When you think of it, if we'd met a couple of centuries ago, you'd have likely been tying me to a rack, or something."

He tickled her nape with a tender finger. "I would have tied you real loose."

Her nearness and the forest played with his senses. What a crazy place this was . . . gnarled blackness and a wizard's cauldron of scent. Her fragrance was more subtle here, a siren's whisper against a dampness that carried the animal tang of the horse and forest humus. No color shone through the absent light, but he could smell green everywhere. The black boughs above them dripped with it. Everywhere he could sense new life and decay. Snow White's forest. What kind of animals hunted in these woods? He could sense them crouching, invisible in the shadows, taking the scent of humans and horse from the air: *Is it good to eat? Yes, it's good to eat.*

A shriek exploded from the web-work of blackness in front of them.

"What in the name of—"

"Spooky, isn't it?" Her voice was a sudden whisper. "That was two branches scratching against each other."

A breeze licked the treetops, and leaves spoke in different voices, like whispering strangers. The darkness moved in broken quadrants. In the distance an abstract shadow sprang, glinting, on the right.

"What was that!"

"What? Where?" she returned in a quick whisper. "Did you see something?"

"To the right. Something moved behind the trees." Amazing. His pulse had begun to accelerate.

"Not . . . to the right?" she said in a little voice.

"Yes. Why? What's to the right?"

"Oh—nothing." The little voice tried to sound airy. His pulse. Oh, his pulse. "Susan—"

"Well, if you must know, it's the . . ." She swallowed. "It's the swamp. I think I may have lost my way."

"But you just said you could find your way blindfolded."

"I *thought* I could. Some dead trees have fallen in odd ways since the last time I was here and . . . I'm not completely certain . . ." Her voice became even smaller and more anxious. "To be one hundred percent honest, I don't like to go near the swamp at night. There are some strange things that—Never mind."

Prickles ascended his spine. "What things?"

Her voice was shaky. "We used to hear this . . . I don't know. A scream, you might call it. We used to get together on our porch and listen, and in the morning we'd find the tracks of a big animal. At least, it must have been an animal. No one could tell. That's why when I saw Dash made up to be a—" The words had hardly passed her lips when she swung fully around and laid a quivering hand over his mouth.

"What the—"

"Shh!" Her cool, strong fingers pressed more urgently.

Her whisper became an eerie strand of breath. "I saw it too. Oh, Alan..."

He could dimly see the sheen of her fear-widened eyes, and that fear sparked in him a potent instinct of tenderness and protection. It flared in his mind: Women. Night. Attacks that had nothing to do with the supernatural. Swiftly and gently disengaging her fingers, he whispered, "Let's go."

She was perfectly still, a dusky statue. Terror seemed to have suspended her very breath. Then, startlingly, her posture alerted, tensed. One quick, frightened shake of her head and she slid from the horse, a streak of shadow.

"I have to look," came her soft voice, hoarse and impulsive. She spun in the black daisy of her skirts and vanished into a thicket alive with shadows.

He reacted quickly. He had to. His mind exploded with images of her frightened, injured, harmed.... *She had ran at Dash, instead of away.* Whipping off the horse, calling her, running, he had only the muffled crash of her footsteps in the dry leaves to guide him. But it was not quite as dark as he'd thought, after all. Space opened; trees and branches were bold strokes against the sky. And then the forest burst wide into a star-flecked glade.

Her voice streamed back to him like a banner of fear from the dappled shadows. "Alan!" A sepulchral voice rasped through the night air. "It...is...a...werewolf." A small body bent like a witch's emerged from the black shadow of a gnarled oak. Two arms were outstretched in amateurish menace. "You...have...disturbed...its... *slumber!*"

Her words dissolved into a carol of bright, clear laughter. There must have been something in his face.... When she was close enough to see, the laughter doubled in intensity, until she buckled at the waist, hands knit in the lap of her skirts, giving herself up completely to the emotion.

When she could speak, she gasped out, "Have I the knack of it, do you think? Can I scare people? I remembered that you said fear was in the mind—leaping images, imagination, surprise..."

Again, looking up into his face, laughter overtook her.

His own heart rate had barely begun the process of recovery, and there was nothing to do but stand and laugh with her and let his senses absorb her. That laughter. Nothing was held back; there were no inhibitions, only complete release, the way an infant might surrender to tears. Only the healthiest and most unconstrained temperament could have abandoned itself so totally to the moment. He had never laughed that way in his life.

Made silvery in the starlight, she stood upright as the laughs wound down into a graceless pattern of husky coughs. By now his eyes had adjusted to the darkness and he could see her grin and the apology in her eyes. Her shoulders and breathing were relaxed, her posture supple and undefended. Somehow, he could see, scaring him had lowered her guard. She'd liked it. It had confirmed the idea she clung to that he was harmless. Under the wariness, she still possessed the ironclad determination to believe in his essential goodness.

As before, something stirred within him, a fleeting knowledge of his own slain innocence, a wondering pleasure in hers. In twenty-five years, nothing had defiled her charity or destroyed her trust. She was whole.

The claws poised before him again, scratching exuberantly at the fresh night air. Her brow was a happy questioning arch. "Did I give you the willies?"

"I passed into the outer limits of human anguish." He put an overdose of sincerity and enthusiasm into his voice, and she responded with a smile.

"You didn't, I know. But I think you got just a *little* nervous." She leaned forward and laid her fingers confidingly on his arm. "Do you know why I brought you here?"

"I have dozens of optimistic fantasies."

She sighed. Her fine eyes chided, and then began to sparkle at him. "I brought you to see the stars."

"Stars?"

For Susan, the ticklish feeling persisted. From the first, she'd watched him view the world through a screen of sardonic indifference, the smile self-mocking and aware but distant. Here was something new. An edge was gone. She had just seen, quite clearly, that he had the potential to laugh at himself. He wanted to live with more freedom and more heart. She could *feel* it. She could feel the part of him that was wistful, reaching out, wanting to be part of her play but not quite knowing how it was done. An image half-formed in her mind of a crippled child hanging back in the quarantine of his crutches, watching the running, the shouts, the comradeship. Except that Alan was no child.

She knew she should behave more cautiously with him. Her conscience whispered and prodded, but she found it difficult to listen, because even now the fascination of being in his company was dancing throughout her body.

She saw that he looked surprised. Stars? He might well not have realized they were up there. When he gazed up into the magnificence of heaven, it was to check how its brightness registered on his light meter.

"Come with me." She took his hand, leading him to the forest's edge, their footsteps bringing up long crackles from the pillowy dry leaves.

In the meadow she found a patch of new grass, sweet-scented from sunlight, dry from yesterday's breeze, soft from the earth's riches. She sat down in it, then stretched out on her back, her hands crossed behind her head. His shadowed expression wasn't visible above her, but he must be doubtful, she supposed. Flopping full length on the ground was probably not something he was used to doing. So she patted the grass at her side invitingly.

"You'll like it," she said. "It's warm."

He came beside her, his legs graceful and coltish in silhouette, his body brushing soft sounds from the grass.

Above them the sky spread out like a brilliant diadem. She took a deep breath, letting the peace of it drift through her, hoping he could see, could feel the glory of it. Around them the meadow spoke in placid murmurs, in the scent of pasture grass and new clover.

"Look at all those stars," she said presently.

"There are so many of them."

His voice had a dreamy quality that stirred her, and she lowered her own voice to match his mood. "Guess how many."

"Maybe a billion?"

"Maybe. But not that we can see. On a clear, dark night, with an unaided eye, you're looking at . . . oh, say, twenty-five hundred stars."

"Is that all? It looks like more." His leg dragged against her as he sat up, gazing skyward as though the thought amazed and stimulated him.

But she hadn't meant to prick his intellectual curiosity. She wanted to give it a rest and let something deeper come forth. "You might get a sore neck, leaning back like that."

Starlight picked out the vigorous lines of his smile. "I'm not used to relaxing."

"I know."

It seemed utterly natural to be here with him, alone on the rim of the universe, restful as she might have felt with a friend, a sister, or brother, though the faint erotic pressure of his thigh against hers reminded her of the dangerous and powerful pull of the land beyond friendship. Feeling his quizzical regard, she gazed up into it, knowing the darkness was hiding the sudden heat in her cheeks, knowing that he would be aware of it anyway.

The experienced eyes searched hers, grew gentle. "You know more than I realized." He settled back beside her in a fluid motion, folding his hands under his head.

She paused in pleasure, studying him. "The stars have names, like people do. Did you know?"

"I seem to have that fact stored away somewhere." His gaze strayed back to the sky, and for a long time they stared upward together at the serene starlight, drinking its beauty. "Is that the North Star?" He pointed.

"No. There. Can you see? It isn't the brightest star—only second magnitude. But it's the only star that's constant. Everything else moves while Polaris makes a nest in the northern sky."

"Where are the planets?"

"In the constellations of the zodiac that ring the earth in a giant band. There's Saturn, in Taurus. The bright yellow spark—there—that's Mars. The earth is passing between it and the sun. Imagine these immense stately bodies drifting through the chill of space. But it has such order. In each season you see a different sky in a cycle without end."

The earth had a rich, licheny scent. Grass tickled their legs and caressed their cheeks.

"I'm looking for the Milky Way," he said.

"In springtime it's low on the horizon, and you can't see it for the ground haze. It'll be back before summer. When I was small my grandmother told me that if I made a friend of the stars I'd never want for companions, because they'd be back faithfully year after year."

"Did your grandmother teach you about the stars?"

"My father did some, but mostly it was Grandma." A memory returned, making a warm flash in her heart. "She used to say that if I knew my way around up there, I'd have a head start when I got to heaven."

"Is that where heaven is—up there?" His voice held the gentlest amusement.

"That's where it is. And when I die, I'm going to go up·there and fly around until I've seen everything—the gold rings of Saturn, the great comets, the most distant galaxies."

"It'll be some adventure. Will you have wings?"

"No wings. I won't need wings." Tender blades flickered between her toes as she dug them into the grass. "I'm going to explore one end of the universe to the other and then—"

"What?"

"Then I'll be meeting my grandmother. We have a star all picked out."

Quiet. Then, "Which one?"

"Arcturus. It's in the Herdsman, east some from the Great Bear's nose. This time of year it's the first star of evening, glowing like a marigold. It's one of the brightest stars in the heavens, first magnitude, and there aren't more than fifteen of those."

"It should be easy to find, then."

She smiled. "Yes. And it's convenient to Earth, too. Only thirty-two light years." That date and another clicked pleasantly together in her mind. "The light we're seeing tonight was made the year you were born. Imagine that now we can see it together, like a birthday present."

After another pause his voice returned, a murmur. "Susan, let's have a star together."

Waves of sudden and unexpected shyness began inside her. "I don't know . . ."

"One star, Susan. Don't you think in all the universe there could be just one star for us?"

Shyness persisted, but it was a dim voice, the vapor of her conscience. Stars seemed to drift down, surrounding her, surrounding him.

"Choose one."

"It has to be bright." He thought, and then pointed. "Like that one."

She followed the line of his arm. "That's Deneb. In the constellation of the Swan. She flies toward the constellation of the Eagle."

"That sounds good. How bright is it?"

"First magnitude. It's a beautiful star, one of my favorites."

"Is it close to the earth?"

"No," she said. "That's the hitch. It's very far."

"Thank God. Then it's perfect." The humor in his voice made her laugh before they were silent again together, admiring the Swan, flying with it.

"You know," she said, "maybe we shouldn't have such a famous star."

"That's what I was thinking."

"How about—the little one that's a bit north of Deneb—there. Such a merry little flicker in the darkness . . ."

"Just for us . . ."

"Just for us . . ."

Then, because it seemed the most natural thing in the world, he rolled over and kissed her. At first, the touch of his lips was no deeper than the starlight. His kiss stroked her mouth gently, learning again the shape, the unique contours, the flow of her breath. Slowly he developed the contact until her mouth began to stir under his.

His body shifted slightly, half-covering hers, and fear sparked with pleasure all down her body, as though the star points had suddenly come inside. His chest made a careful caressing weight on her breasts. His hips pressed against hers with sweet strength. Questing against her mouth, his lips urged hers into moist and softened openness. His tongue touched the inside of her mouth.

He lifted his head, holding her star-tipped face in a gentle, exploring gaze.

"Yes?" he whispered.

"No."

His parted lips lowered toward hers. "Yes."

Her fingertips stopped his mouth. The innocent fingers, slightly spread on his lower lip, had a powerful effect on his inflamed senses. She was like an unfamiliar delicacy beneath him, exotically fragrant, deeply inviting, deeply desired. Easing his mouth against her fingertips, he pressed the kiss there that he would have delivered to her lips.

Her breath wavered. Starlight accented the simplicity of her expression and the dark, startled quality of her eyes as she withdrew her hand and held it to her chest, then lifted it urgently to her own mouth, tasting his kiss. Then she lowered her hand and was still a long time before speaking, while he listened to the meadow and the beating of his heart.

"I encourage it, don't I?" she asked finally. "I don't understand why. I'm like a child playing on the edge of a cliff."

The print of her fingers remained with his mouth, an incredibly sweet sensation, a gift, in its way. Her confusion moved him, but his need was strong, so strong. Gathering her face in his palms, caressing her cheekbones with the sides of his thumbs, he spoke quietly.

"Your body wants me, Susan."

His gaze followed the light where it showed the curve of her cheek, the crisp linen of her *kapp*, the shine of her eyes. He felt the long stroke of her exhalation under his chest.

"I can't seem to help that." Her eyes became rueful. "I am resolute, you know, in my mind at least, even though sometimes the other parts of me aren't so sure."

"Is that what you came to tell me tonight?"

"Yes."

If some parts of her were vacillating, his had no doubts at all. His pulse hadn't slackened its leaping rhythm, and his skin surfaces felt as if they'd been too close to a torch. His blood was eighty-proof adrenaline. If any chance existed that he could control the urgency of his need, he would have stayed where he was, coaxing her gently with humor until she became as ready as he was himself. But he was too close to the borderline. Even during the insanity of adolescence, he'd never experienced anything this intense, and for all he knew there might be a point beyond which he would not be able to hear her say no.

Separating their bodies and sitting up took an effort that made his head swim. The alcohol in his system obviously wasn't helping. He sat still, not touching her, and counted to ten. Thirty times.

When he had his body back in some semblance of order, he stretched out near her on his side, supporting himself on his forearm. "You are one naive lady," he said with feeling.

She was sitting upright, hugging her tucked legs, her cheek resting on one of her bent knees. "When John and I were courting, nothing like this happened. It wasn't to be thought of."

Not to be thought of. To him, she was the victim of brainwashing on a profound, intimate level. *You might not have thought of it, but I'll bet points on my next picture that Johnny-boy thought about it plenty*.

Her eyes remained solemn. Plucking a stem of tufted grass, he tickled it over her bare toes to make her smile. "No shoes."

"I'd never have them if I didn't have to. Barefoot is the nicest feeling."

"Almost."

She smiled a little. "Part of the problem is that no one has ever tried to seduce me before. I don't have my fences ready. I would suppose . . . you do this often?"

"It varies. I try to seduce . . . say, six, maybe seven a month."

The smile grew. "Then this month you're running behind."

He made his expression sorrowful. "If things don't happen pretty soon between you and me, I may end up having to seduce the whole bunch on the last day of the month."

Her head came right up and she laughed. But then, "Not really?"

"I've never seduced anyone in my life."

"Pshaw."

"Amish, the date of the last recorded seduction was 1903. As a social convention, it's been extinct since the demise of the secluded alcove. Now when two people discover they want to love each other, they do."

"Strange world, English."

"Freedom, Amish."

Immersed in the agony of a headache on the ride back to Greyling, he said, "You know what they say about the wisdom of Solomon. And he was a strong believer in the pleasures of love."

"You've read the Bible!" Her voice was surprised and gratified.

"I saw the movie," he corrected. He watched her shake her head and heard her laugh, amused by his incorrigibility but trusting him still, trusting her own resolve and his capacity to understand it.

His capacity to understand her resolve was greater than she anticipated. He understood, as she did not, how close he was to breaking it.

Chapter 12

*I*f this were Baton Rouge instead of Greyling, Wisconsin, they'd call this place a honky-tonk, Joan decided with a certain artistic satisfaction. She sniffed the air, redolent with cigarette smoke, sweat, cologne, and beer.

Inveterate party types from the movie company rocked with the locals on a strobe-lit dance floor. Joan had a good view of Max, slicked up in his khaki safari outfit. He looked sort of like a collapsed pup tent.

Having danced with everyone from the lighting director to the bartenders and fielded a number of single-entendres, she had a sense of having discharged her responsibility to the male sex. Contentedly seated by herself at a pine table surrounded by a clutter of deserted chairs and half-empty bottles of light beer, she was soaking up atmosphere for her novel—a roman à clef about the movie business—"the business," they called it in L.A., as though there existed no other businesses that mattered. Marvelous to be here in Wisconsin in a tavern with cheap paneling and bad paintings of mallards and stags. Even the neon sculpture on the roof—a bubbling blue highball—seemed wholesome.

Let's face it, girl. You're licking your wounds from last night. No, actually, the night had been magnificent, a sensual free fall. But it wasn't worth the aftermath. The funny thing was, she had no one to blame but herself. She knew David's reputation; who didn't? And Alan, who had a policy of complete noninterference in anyone else's life, had observed the sway of David's libido in her direction and had actually gone so far as to look straight at her over a clipboard last week and say, "If I were you, I wouldn't."

If she'd had a quark of sense, she'd have listened. But no. It might have been the residue of a star-struck adolescence. Or it might have been that ridiculous vow she'd made, over birthday candles and her first bottle of wine, when she'd turned eighteen that some day she was going to sleep with David Thorne, Robert Redford, or a *Time* magazine Man of the Year. What was that platitude about the gods making your dreams come true when they really wanted to make you suffer?

She'd waked after a night of fantasy in David's bed and discovered that the eyes that were as luminous as searchlights on the wide screen were looking at her with a certain abhorrence, as though she were laundry he'd left on the floor, looking at her as though he couldn't understand why she hadn't had the tact to sneak back to her own room before he woke up. He had been perfectly polite, noblesse oblige, but distant, and she was probably lucky he hadn't stuck a couple of fifties in her purse. It was quite clear that that was about the value he put on the experience.

This morning she hadn't seen the humor, just felt a fierce mortification and anger at herself for being another easy mark for a selfish movie star. And there was queasiness, and the frustrating realization that if she told him what she thought of him, it might be the last time she ever worked in "the business." He was perfectly capable of getting her fired, maybe blacklisted. Yep, that's the way it is in the big, bad world, Virginia. Big fish gobble up little fish.

She took a long sip from her glass. She enjoyed the mellow malty flavor of the beer, the pleasant funky rhythms of the band, the answering tangle of dancers. Funny that she never realized she was a little fish until she got to California. Back in Pittsburgh, she had parents who owned a small string of supermarkets and called her Princess and had raised her on the philosophy that she could grow up to be anything she put her mind to. And there had been the miracle of the summer she turned thirteen when she'd had fun with her mom's makeup and gone out for a walk in short shorts and her first halter top. Two teenaged boys in their father's Lincoln had driven over the curb looking at her, turning a fire hydrant into a geyser, and she'd learned she was beautiful. For years she'd reveled in the male attention lavished on her for the Barbie-doll face and figure, the hair she was accustomed to hearing described as leonine.

And then one fine evening, one of those rare ones spent at home, she'd flipped on the tube and watched Marilyn Monroe going through her paces in *How to Marry a Millionaire*. She remembered laughing right along until, for no reason she could understand, the armor of her complacency had buckled and she had realized in one sickened moment that she was looking at a self-portrait. Men found her lovable, perhaps even soulful, but there wasn't much doubt that her mission in life was to be a hormonal stimulant. The rest of her wasn't anything to take too seriously.

After that, none of the adoration had seemed quite as wonderful.

Somewhere around that time had come the friendly, funny affair with Ben Rose that had led to the studio job, and two years later the opportunity of getting to work for prestigious Alan Wilde.

Aside from her dad, one ninth-grade algebra teacher, and the well-mannered teenaged boys who'd tucked her into rides at Disneyland, Alan was the only man since puberty who had failed to define her in terms of her anatomy. That first interview was to be etched forever in her memory—those far-seeing eyes had never strayed downward from her face, the compassionate smile didn't know how to become a leer, the dispassionate voice carried no trace of an innuendo. This, even though on the employment application where it had said "Sex," she had crossed out "Male" and "Female" and written "*Yes.*" She'd come away thinking of him as a brilliant android, C3PO repackaged in a captivating and glamorous facade.

Months elapsed, and she discovered she couldn't have been more wrong. Legend didn't lie entirely. He did keep people at arm's length. You had to wait for him to make the overtures toward friendship, and those were rare. There wasn't a flicker of doubt in her mind that the "daddy dearest" horror stories about his life as a child star were true. He carried the telltale caution of someone who'd had his heart and soul worked over at an early age.

In spite of that, he was a magical companion: brilliant, generous, vital, entirely without airs, and, unique among her acquaintances, he had not once referred to her never-to-be-sufficiently-rued centerfold sprawl. She would have gone to bed on barbed wire for him.

Alan's own involvements were conducted with so much old-school discretion that one didn't know a thing about them beyond what one read in print—gossip never confirmed by Alan, always claimed as true by the other party. In the last year there had been a network correspondent to the White House, that Japanese avant-garde artist whose name she never could pronounce, a literary critic . . . People were going to be puzzled about just where Susan Peachey fit into that up-scale lineup. Very weird. It was becoming emotionally wrenching to watch.

At least Susan had the good sense to recoil from kissing David. God, why hadn't she had the same sense? She should have listened to Alan about David. Damn. Stupid, stupid, stupid . . . Why did these things always have to hurt so much? How come it never got any easier to take? *Maybe I should enter a convent, or a school for overly friendly girls. My epitaph is probably going to read: Slaughtered in the sexual revolution. She gave her all.*

The germ of a smile teased at her mouth. She dug into her red leather clutch for her gold cigarette case, a birthday present from Ben. Her lips had that itchy feeling of wanting a cigarette. God, she loved the things, bad as they were for you. Horrendous. Maybe they should start making them out of broccoli or something. Feeling in her purse for the matching lighter, she was lifting the cigarette to her lips with her other hand, when a lighted match arrived under her nose, the flame wavering in the hollow of strong masculine palms. Incredible hands. The thought popped into her head that each one could hold a whole breast. She looked up.

And saw suspenders. She'd noticed the young man come in; there'd been no missing him. Even if she'd missed his melting, dark good looks, he would have drawn her attention because he was the only Amish man in the place. The rowdy cluster in baseball caps at the bar had greeted him with surprise and bonhomie, offering him drinks, which he rejected, stealing his hat briefly to pass it around. Obviously, he was popular.

Physiques like this didn't come along daily. The body was a cross between that of a soccer player and a surfer; the shoulders went on forever. The face could have been plucked from the painting of an angel in a sixteenth-century Florentine chapel, and there was no doubt that the smile he was beginning would have passed and exceeded USRDA standards as a nutritional supplement.

The match had burned short. Clear, rosy light swept over his lips as he put the flame to his mouth and extinguished it with a breath before discarding it in the punched-aluminum ashtray. His finger ran over the remaining matches as if he were counting them. "We've got another fourteen left, so don't worry. You can have as long as you like to make up your mind."

He offered a second lit match, and this time she jarred her gaze loose from his sparkling eyes to accept it. Unexpected electricity flicked through her senses at having those broad hands close to her face. She took startled pleasure in the rough, steady coolness of his palm brushing her hand as he tilted the match for her.

He dropped the match in the ashtray and extended his hand to her in a friendly way. She accepted it, noting that he had the kind of skin that tanned to a rich, coppery brown, that the callused hand felt like a brick but that its control was ever so gentle as it closed around hers.

"Daniel," he said.

"Joan." She copied the laconic manner, letting her eyes tease.

"I know. The others told me." He inclined his head toward the kids wearing UW-Platteville T-shirts, seated at a table near the door. She'd danced with several of them, slow with one of them, keeping his eager, dazzled smile at arm's length. Only a sip apiece, boys. What else had they told him? Amusement flickered in his dusky eyes—perhaps too much amusement. She experienced a sudden sense of exposure, as though she'd caught him at her desk reading some sentimental entry in her private journal. Did he find her faintly ridiculous, vamping callow college boys with her off-the-shoulder blouse and slit skirt? A painful memory returned of David in her room two nights ago, glancing at her Laura Ashley catalog, knowing condescension adding a sharp twist to his smile. "How sweet," he'd said.

She was sick to death of being judged by men. *All right, sonny, I've got to take it from David Thorne, but I'll be damned if I'm going to take it from a country bumpkin in a felt hat.* She cooled the smile that she realized with a pang must have looked unutterably coy.

"Nice of them to tell you," she said icily. She couldn't quite believe it when, instead of retreating with tail tucked, he said, "My first time. Would you mind if I joined you?"

"Would I mind? Daniel in the lion's den..."

The dark eyes were fairly burning with amusement. "Why? Do you bite?"

"Apparently not hard enough." Grasping her purse, she would have snapped out of her seat if he hadn't stopped her with the gentle pressure of his powerful hand on her tense one.

"Don't. Please don't," he said, and while she sat there with every stereotype of shy and gawky country boys and bromidic Amish men exploding in her mind, he let go her hand, leaving hot spots that could have registered on a Geiger counter. "You don't need to run away. All you need to do is tell me to go and I will. Is that what you want?"

And she saw suddenly the thing she had not noticed before in the strong, wind-burned face. Kindness.

Alan greeted with resignation and courtesy the intelligence that Joan had become infatuated with an Amish boy who had invited her to meet him in the morning at an auction on a local farm. He had politely rejected her surprisingly intense request for his company. More surprisingly, especially for Joan, she wasn't accepting his firm "no."

"Alan, think it over a little. We'll just go for a short time and check it out. Who knows? Apparently they're selling off a lot of antiques, so we might find something great for a prop. It'd be good for us to see something besides the inside of a rented room and a closed set. I'd like you to meet Daniel. I mean, you should see this man. He's just so... You can imagine him in a suit of armor, know what I mean? And he has eyes..."

When the rest of the sentence disappeared into a rapturous pause he murmured agreeably, "Glad to hear it."

"... Eyes like Jesus. They have these beautiful crow's-feet at the corners like Dash has, the kind you get from being out of doors most of the time. I really don't know why you're smiling like that. I thought you, of all people, would understand."

The smile perished. Rather gently he said, "Oh, I understand very well. And it's not an experience I'd wish on a dog."

"Alan, I'm not talking about falling in love. Merely a little civilized lust."

He slapped the stack of papers he held onto the crowded desk. Paper clips ricocheted off the wall. "Take it from a beleaguered initiate. There's no such thing as civilized lust. It reduces an ordinary mortal to the approximate social level of an amoeba. If you want to retain any feeling whatsoever of yourself as a humane individual, don't develop intricate fantasies about boys or girls with eyes like Jesus. And I'd like to know what makes you think I'm in love."

A self-mocking flex in the long stretch of his mouth and the soft, ironic voice robbed each word of its importance. He didn't want to show it—he didn't want to show anything—but Joan had the eerie sense of having stumbled into the unquiet privacy of his extraordinary, tangled soul. It was a little too much like putting your foot through a da Vinci.

She touched his sleeve. "Are you?"

There was a moment of puzzled silence that felt terribly long to her. Then the austerity of his expression softened, and he gave her a smile of breathtaking sweetness.

"I don't know." Again a silence. "I don't know." His return to the paper work on the desk was automatic, self-protective. She thought about the golden eagles, who never seem to be at peace unless they are drifting, suspended on a stream of air. After a moment he spoke absently. "Have fun, then. You won't have any trouble finding someone else to go along with you. I'm not the logical choice."

She couldn't wait half an hour and try him again. By then he'd be deep into work intoxification. He went on line like a megacomputer.

"Still, I think you ought to be there."

"Thank you, but no."

Alan's final "no." Everyone who had worked long with him knew it; anyone who didn't learn to recognize it quickly had a brief tenure in his world. So, having almost failed, she'd come with a brickbat.

"Alan, I think the boy I met last night is Susan's brother."

He stopped, a page half-turned in his hand. "Why?"

"He has the same coloring. And the same . . . well, the same eyes. And he made a point of finding out that I was with the movie company before he approached me."

"You're hesitating. Is there one more 'and'?"

"And, in the most respectful way possible, he spent the better part of an hour grilling me about you."

"So." The page drifted from his fingers as they went lax.

"So?"

"So . . ."

He stood. "I'll get my car keys."

Chapter 13

*I*n a yard of pebbles and trampled weeds, with a trim white farmhouse and dark red barn and outbuildings in the background, a large and intriguingly varied crowd had gathered. Parking on the stubble of a cornfield, Alan had the first taste of it—a Porsche with Illinois plates beside an Amish buggy beside a rusty Chevy. It was easy to spot the antique dealers from the cities, the families from the small towns—and the Amish, exotic in their plainness.

It was the kind of crowd scene Alan usually avoided. He'd always been a celebrity whose life was of interest to strangers. In spite of that, he was uncomfortable under public scrutiny. The balance of the world shifted at such times, and the people who stared and asked for autographs and were in turn worshiping or critical of his films seemed real, and he was an exhibit, a preconceived fragment in someone else's real life. Dash had another explanation for it. He had no memory of it himself, but Dash said that Alan's parents had been terrified he might be kidnapped and had overdone the lessons of caution.

Strangely, he felt relaxed here. Sunlight fell heavily on his shoulders, warming his hair. This sun meant business. Here was the willful fertility that could pull the thick weight of a corn stalk from the earth in a single summer, and he could feel its ability to grow and nourish. It was the same force he could feel flowing from Susan.

"Good Christians, the Amish. I can't complain about them myself." Under the faded peppermint-striped awning of a 4-H concession trailer, Alan had struck up a conversation with a man the size of Eddie Arcaro who was up to his elbows in a vat spinning clouds of pink cotton candy. "You never saw anything like how they stick together. Run their own schools, care for their own old folks, help out the widows—they take care of their own. If one family has a barn fire, the whole community'll get together and have a new barn raised before the ashes cool. And I'll tell you what else—they can *work*. You got work for hire, take on an Amish kid if his parents'll let you. You'll get your money's worth. Most people today"—the woeful shake of the head included the better part of the modern generation— "they're waiting to win it in a lottery, know what I mean? Say, you want to know about the Amish, you ought to talk to Ben Hosely over here. He's got a farm up by Hostetlers and he's real tight with them—goes to their weddings and everything, and that's unusual. They don't mix much, you see. Hey, Ben!"

A little banty rooster of a man in a new-from-the-package white undershirt, heavy denim trousers, and work boots turned and identified with clear pleasure the man who'd called him.

"Charley! How you been?"

"Pretty fair. How come we haven't seen you in a while?"

"Plantin' corn. Didn't you run into Mary last week down to the drugstore?"

"Yep." In a spirit of innuendo, he added, "Asked after you and she told us what we need to know."

Ben grinned. "And then some, I'll bet."

"You bet. Ben, here's someone interested in the Amish. I'd like you to meet—"

"Alan Wilde!" The farmer extended a sun-infused hand that closed around Alan's like a clamp. "Ain't that something! We've never missed a one of your pictures. My kids must have gone to see *Star Wars* four times. That was some movie!"

Alan felt a spark of real amusement. "It was. But I'm afraid I had nothing to do with it. You may be thinking of George Lucas."

"I may," Ben conceded, perplexed. "Then how about that picture about the archaeologist who tries to get the ark away from those Nazis? *That's* the one you directed, wasn't it?"

"Sorry. Spielberg."

A little crestfallen, Ben took the disappointment in stride. "How about that? I could have sworn . . ." He took off his cap, smoothed back his hair. "So you're interested in the Amish? The things I know about them, *I* could make a movie. I wouldn't, though. They wouldn't care for it. I think the world of those people." He set the cap placed on the counter, beside Ben's crossed forearms. "We live neighbors to an Amish family—thirteen kids he's raising on that little place. Those kids are something else. You never saw anything like the way they bring up kids. A honey, each one of 'em. Last week I was up there after I got this new hat from AMPI, and the kids came over to fool with me and rassle, and one of 'em got the hat off my head. So I said, 'Say what? I'd like you to keep it.' But do you think he would? No chance. He draws himself up so straight and proud and puts the hat right back in my hand and says to me, 'I don't want it. I want to look Amish.' Think of that. Just ten years old and dedicated heart and soul to his people."

That was altogether too sanguine for Wilde. "It can't be that surprising. He's never been exposed to anything else."

Charley straightened up from handing a puff of spun

candy to a child in pigtails. "True enough. They don't mix. And there's some wouldn't care to mix with 'em, either."

Ben nodded. "Pacifists, the Amish. They won't take up arms against their fellow man. You study their history, you see how way back when they had to flee from one country in Europe to the next. They were tortured, jailed, killed, but it's against the way they believe, to fight back. And don't think for a minute that those little Amish kids don't know that part of their history. They learn it from the cradle. Well, how do you think it went down around here during the Vietnam War when the Amish boys wouldn't take up arms for their country?"

Wilde could imagine it: an isolated rural community, burning under the tension of the draft and a divided national conscience. "There must have been some resentment."

"Plenty. Young fellow from here in town died during the Tet. Fine boy, Doc Mason's son. Group of his friends egged a couple of Amish houses and set fire to a shed. And later, after they got themselves good and drunk, they caught one of the little Amish girls bringing cows in from the pasture and attacked her. Spit on her, pushed her to the ground, I don't know what all they done. Don't know if she ever quite got over it. Of course, not one of them boys was punished for it, because the Amish don't believe in taking an oath in court and her parents wouldn't have her testify against them."

It had happened a long time ago, and in a community this size, the odds were against it having been Susan. But he still felt a fierce tightening in his chest. What year was Tet anyway? 'Sixty-eight? Yet the farmer told the story with a sense of immediacy. The past was that real to these people. Time and events wouldn't pass into the shadows, and they would remember him and his presence here today. *That was the year that movie fellow came to the county. Met him at the Hosely auction. Fellow name of—Mary, what was his name?* Because of that, he disciplined the impulse to make sure that the little girl wasn't one who had grown up to become his—God knew what—his obsession.

So instead of asking the question that would link Susan's

name in county history with that of a Hollywood movie director, he returned a remark that was quietly sympathetic, carefully appropriate. A mask.

And the conversation became lighter, touching on the diversity of people passing by. Alan listened like an outsider, encouraging Ben and Charley to talk about their families, the crops, the weather, the history of the region, all the time noting gestures, body language, dialect, with the artist's acute, alienating need for observation that he could rarely turn off.

Suddenly Charley's gaze took note of a distant figure and froze on him.

"Well, I'll be . . . Ain't that Amos Yoder? I didn't know he came among 'em."

"Not often." Ben was staring too. He shook his head solemnly. "See there, Mr. Wilde? There walks a man without a friend in this world. Been cast out like dirty water."

It was easy to spot him. Gaunt, bespectacled, his face underlined with the red bramble of a full beard, he was dressed Amish. He had just made a purchase, a leather harness, weighty and awkward to carry, and he stood like a sentinel, gazing across the yard to the folding table where he would have to go to pay for the item. It was an open face, as undefended as Susan's was, and the fear there and in the posture of his body was nakedly, helplessly legible. Then he put his head down, his eyes fixed on the ocher dirt in front of his feet, and began the long march through the Amish throng.

In a yard of smiled greetings and chatter, not one of the men, women, or children he passed either spoke to him, looked at his face, or acknowledged his existence. Yet they knew he was there. They were aware.

"What did he do?"

"Heretic. Went to a meeting with some traveling evangelist and got slain in the spirit, so he claims. Since then, he come back preaching like the Charismatics, going against the sayings of their church, and when he wouldn't give it up, the Amish community put him out. Shunned him. Not even his kin will speak to him. Has to take meals in the basement of his own home, and his wife told him

she can't have relations with him. It's a hard lot Amos has
took."

Wilde saw it. The steady, lonely figure with the
loose harness slapping his knees, walking through rejection—
the skirt yanked swiftly back, the averted gaze, the turned
shoulder. Silent, effective, shaming. Complete.

"The man's lucky the auctioneer ain't Amish." Charley
leaned over the counter. "Plain folk won't do business with
him. Let me tell you, they take their beliefs serious."

Wilde watched the painful journey until the purchase
was made and the shunned man vanished behind the barn
in the direction of the parking field. "Yes," he said without
warmth. "Righteous, aren't they?"

Joan came soon after, across a trampled lawn strewn
with metal tables sparkling with depression glass, old
kitchenware, and a typhoon of knickknacks. She paused to
flirt with Ben and Charley and two others who happened
to be nearby and tucked her arm in Alan's to stroll away
with him, leaving behind her a miniature dominion of
awed admirers.

"So many men," Alan murmured cheerfully, "so little
time."

"Just fine-tuning the wiles." She gave him a glance
that said Harlow. "Sorry I took so long. I became en-
grossed in an ice-cream mold, then a ceramic frog on a
mushroom. I hope you didn't need rescuing."

"Don't fret. I know how to extricate myself if I have
to."

"You modern, independent males. Seen your Amish
yet?"

"No. Seen yours?"

"Not so much as a suspender. Shall we sally forth to
peer under bonnets and black felt hats with our pulses
doing the funky chicken?"

"Impossible." He felt the pressure of a ridiculous
smile. "My heart only plays classical—presto, prestissimo,
allegro, scherzo . . ."

And the auctioneer bellowed away like a flugelhorn
trolling pig Latin. Broad and sweating under a Panama
hat, with a wicker fan and shirt buttons that barely met in
the middle, he was more *African Queen* than *Little House on*

the Prairie. His assistant Oliver—as in "Okay, Oliver, what've we got now?"—was skinny and beaked in a shiny black suit, his springy hair standing up to show through sweat and sunlight. His falsetto phrases ricocheted off the end of the auctioneer's chant like exclamation marks.

"Pair o' matching whale-oil lamps, *matching* lamps, *guaranteed* sandwich glass, heart and thumbprint pattern, pewter collars, pewter burners, pewter pewter, twin oil spouts in each, two rare and terrific antique lamps today." The auctioneer stopped, wiped his brow, and fanned himself.

Oliver hoisted the lamps. "Mighty fine lamps!"

"There you heard it! Who'll take these beauties home today? Who'll give me one-fifty? One hundred fifty dolla, who'll gimme, who'll gimme . . ."

Joan squeezed Alan's arm. "Alan, there he is."

He followed the direction of her gaze, upward to the high open windows of the barn, where young men, mostly Amish, leaned out, watching the crowd below. One man was separating himself from the others. At a wide double doorway fringed with hay, he leaned over the sharp drop and grabbed a rope suspended from an old hayfork track just beneath the gabled roof. Clenching the rope in sturdy fists, he jumped into space and let himself down rapidly, hand over hand, his heels releasing a golden spill of glittering straw.

Joan's cheeks picked up color. "Me Jane," she murmured.

"If I were you, I wouldn't count on it," said Alan, admiring the young man's fluid descent. An experienced stunt man couldn't have made it look easier. Fifteen feet from the ground, the strong young hands discarded the rope, and he landed gracefully on his feet in the packed dust. With no hesitation, his attention centered on Wilde, and for the first time Alan could see his eyes. They were Susan's.

It was one thing for Alan to know she was part of this harsh, sequestered world, another to step through the looking glass into the sanctum. Her life, like a fragile cloth, would be a visible thing laid before him, and no longer just the bare threads spun in his imagination.

He was accustomed to good-looking people. He found most human beings attractive in one way or another; his aesthetic sense was more elastic than convention or fashion. He liked the human body, the inner brightness of the eye, the soft texture of skin, the underpattern of bone, the striking individuality of external structure. Years in front of the camera and behind it had long since shorn beauty of any mystique; it became less enveloping with the realization that it was a combination of sculpture, confidence, and care. He looked for other things in faces, intangible things, the qualities he needed to complete himself. He saw them in Susan. Now he saw them in Daniel.

The steady brown gaze altered, holding Joan with its warmth.

Joan had simple and devastating methods of flirtation. When the young man stopped in front of them, she looked at him cheerfully and said, "When you smile like that, I want to kiss your teeth."

The poise never faltered. The smile grew. After a glance at Alan, Daniel leaned forward to say something for Joan's ear alone, something effective, judging by her reaction. Her eyes gathered light like new pennies. Alan watched their glances mesh, the exchange eloquent, laced either with elemental, intuitive understanding or a misunderstanding of cosmic proportions. Alan couldn't decide which. It was a little like having his face rammed in a mirror. These two were simply having fun; there was none of the darkness and sunlight that passed between him and Susan. Even on their level, however, the basic insanity of the mixed relationship was too apparent.

Daniel's brown eyes remained eloquent as they returned to Alan, but the humor was starkly absent. It was impossible to assess how much the Amishman knew or had guessed at, but pretense was unpalatable. Alan said, "Are you a Peachey?"

The young man didn't pretend either. "I'm a Hostetler. Peachey is her married name. I'm glad you could come."

As though I'd received a personal invitation to show up and be scrutinized. "I don't think so. Your young face is amassing dismay like a thunderhead."

"Not because you're here. It's just that you're not what I'd hoped."

"No?"

"I had hopes you might be . . ." The dark eyes transferred their gaze to the sky, seeming to hunt for the correct adjective, before they returned to Wilde. "That you'd be tawdry. She'd see through that."

"All right. Having given you the opportunity to assess my facade, is there anything else I can do for you?"

The young man thrust his hands into his pockets and took two steps backward, rocking fractionally, studying Alan with eyes that were hard. "I doubt it would do much good to ask you to let Susan be."

Anger kept on, pricking like cold needles. Who was this kid? His conscience, arriving fully fleshed. "Susan is an adult, with free will. If anyone's attempted to erode that, it's you and yours, not me. No, it won't do much good to tell me to let Susan be. You can live like a Trappist if that's what you want, but don't try to strut into my life sowing dogma."

"You know, Mr. Wilde, I have a choice thing or two I'd like to say to you, too, but I don't know that this is the place."

"I don't give a damn what you want to tell me or where you say it. Do you understand?"

The pause simmered with crowd noise and with Wilde's awareness that the face before him seemed suddenly youthful and anxious. *He loves her. He wants to keep her safe. He and Susan are like children and I'm hurting them.* The needles turned hot from cold as they changed from anger to those of conscience and confusion. He tried to let them exist, to be integrated and speak, but they became virulent. He could feel with despair the denial flooding him, numbing him just as it had his whole adult life. The meticulous defenses that had once been his immunity to feeling were now his enemy.

Joan, who knew very well when not to speak and as well when to do so, came politely into the moment, her voice light and refreshing. "Is your family here today, Daniel?"

"Yes. Haven't you seen Susan? She's back around by the fence watching the bidding. The others are here and there in the crowd, watching us."

"They don't know Susan's working with us?"

Daniel shook his head. "They won't understand what it means when they find out. Not at first."

"I imagine when they find out it will raise some eyebrows?"

Daniel's hands disappeared into his side pockets. He looked directly down at the earth at his feet, up into the opaque blueness of the sky, back at Joan. He seemed to be torn between distress and the strong desire to laugh. "It'll raise some eyebrows, all right." His tone was kinder when he said, "Have you been enjoying our simple pleasures?"

"As a matter of fact, it's been interesting," Alan replied.

"See a movie in it?"

"Several. Amos Yoder, for instance."

The shadowed laughter vanished. "You don't have rejection in your culture?"

"Not as an institution."

"Then perhaps it would be interesting for you to discover more about what it is that we're trying so hard to preserve." Then Daniel smiled, really smiled, and Alan found out why Joan had told him this man had eyes like Jesus.

Wilde's worst nightmares had never included meeting Susan's mother, her father, her blind grandmother, several aunts, her uncle, and the flower garden of her brothers and sisters, in bonnets and straw hats that wreathed their faces like pansy petals. But then, no one had claimed that the rehabilitation of one's soul was painless. The Dickensian quality of it was strangely appealing to him. Wilde as Scrooge . . . presented with haunting phantoms conjuring days past and days yet to come. *Here we learn to keep the fires of Christmas burning all through the year*, he thought.

Susan's grandmother, the aged lady who had taught

Susan to find pathways in the stars, was the hardest spirit for him to understand. Her face carried beautiful seams of age, wonderful and soft and engaging, like a lovingly carved apple-head doll. She had a warmth that he found almost frightening, asking him with charm how he found Wisconsin, the weather here, if he lived near the ocean in California, and what the sea looked like in a storm.

It was during these moments that the auctioneer changed location to auction a miscellany of farm goods on a hay wagon, and as the crowd shifted, Alan saw Susan.

Seated on a wooden fence in a gown the color of cherry syrup, she was surrounded by other Amish—friends, judging by the intimacy of their postures and smiles. Details sprinkled on him like a sunshower. Her head was slightly bent as she spoke to a tall girl in pale green standing beside the fence, and he marveled at how still Susan could be when she talked, the animation of a strong body diverted into the expressive features, the vivid eyes. Under a translucent bonnet, her hair glowed like moon shadows, the dark tone coming to life again in the arch of her eyebrows and lashes that made drama on her bisque skin. Her breasts pressed against the wear-softened fabric, which draped downward at her waist, defining her thighs where they parted slightly. Her smile was as charming as an old-fashioned ornament.

Now he knew the taste of that mouth. On his tongue, it was a piquant sensual memory. He felt the percussion of his heartbeat in his throat. Prestissimo.

Someone in the crowd bumped the fence and she wavered, keeping her balance. In that unsettled moment, she saw Alan. He had expected . . . He wasn't certain what he had expected. Not to have her smile at him as though he were a field of sunflowers. *Dear God, she's so open. Anyone looking will know.* Her arm extended straight upward and she gave him a wave that, from the summit of Everest, could have flagged down a Sherpa at its base. He lifted his own hand to wave back.

"*Sold!*" The auctioneer's gavel clacked once, and sharp-pitched feedback crackled through the dusty sound system. "To the illustrious visitor from Hollywood, California."

The many fascinated glances that had been focused on him began to multiply, and he realized that he'd just bought something, and for a disordered second he lived the fantasy that it was Susan. Getting himself together under the curiosity of the large crowd, he slipped into the plastic shell of celebrity and smiled like a publicist. He raised his voice so the auctioneer could hear him. "What am I the proud owner of?"

Oliver hefted something that looked like a transistor radio. "Joltin' Johnny," he said, igniting laughter in the crowd. "'Lectric prod. Sez on it, 'Make That Hog Move.'"

"We're joshin' you, Mr. Wilde." The auctioneer was grinning widely. "We knew you were only wavin'. It's a big day for us having you here, and that's just our way of saying hello."

There was more laughter, scattered friendly applause, and a certain amount of puzzlement among the Amish. He didn't know what the damn thing was, only that his priority was to remove himself from the stern glare of the spotlight in any way that was quick and unspectacular. "I'll take it anyway."

Laughter. Cheers. So much appreciation for so small a gesture. He knew from experience that once he was singled out in public, the awareness of him became more overt and he seemed more approachable, which meant that he would be approached often and his sense of discomfort would become acute. The auction resumed, dragging only a portion of interest away from him, and through the broken weave of people he saw Susan coming toward him at a run, her skirts tossing gaily, her smile sending fresh adrenaline to his heart.

"Alan, hello! Grandma, have you met my friend Alan?"

Others had been standing on the edge of Susan's family group; three Amishmen of various ages, all with eyes only for Susan. Suitors, he realized by intuition. His competition.

One in particular Wilde had noticed, a man somewhere in his twenties, clean-shaven, very blond, with angry, pale-lashed eyes that had observed with acid hostility Alan's acquaintance with Susan's family. Suddenly the blond man spoke.

"Is he your friend, Susan? I thought he was Daniel's friend."

Her color wavered. Even such a small deception was clearly beyond her. Her eyes became stricken as she came to the belated realization that she had said too much. Wilde watched the blond man register and draw ineffable pleasure from her distress. He knew. *What is this, little one? Have you an enemy?*

He would have rescued her himself, but Joan had already moved into check.

"We met Susan a while ago when she had the bad luck to stumble into an area where we were filming. How are you, Susan? No bad dreams, I hope."

"No. I—didn't think to see you here today."

"It's a wonder we are. Alan's terrible in crowds. We can never get him near them. The frustration is too immense for him. He wants to direct them. Right now he's probably thinking, 'That group is walking too fast. Tell them to stroll. Where's a dog? The scene needs a dog. Get me a mongrel with a black spot on one eye. Put that toddler in the shot, the one who just dropped ice cream on her sundress. Have her do it again.'"

How things moved from there to being invited home to eat with Susan's family, he wasn't quite sure, except that the inspiration came from Daniel. Under the circumstances, it was appalling to accept their hospitality. But there was a gauntlet thrown from Daniel to pick up. *Come and look closely at the life you're trying to pluck away.* None of it could make him want her less, nor was one afternoon likely to alter the reflexes of a lifetime. But he'd go anyway and try to discover if the spirits could put Christmas in his heart instead of what had always been in there before— Halloween.

Leaving the sale, clustered among the Amish, he saw Ben, the farmer, waving at him from the concession stand.

"Hey, Mr. Wilde! What was it like, anyway, working with Harrison Ford?"

Alan surrendered with a smile. "Great, Ben. Just great. He's a heck of a fella."

Chapter 14

*S*usan was different here in this house where she was born. Like a pearl in a perfect setting, she shone more brightly. Her gestures were broader, her smile stronger. Seated at a table behind her, Alan could see her sturdy shoulders, the ivory fragility of her neck, the lively motion of her head and arms as she talked. Here she was one of them, not a gypsy on his home ground.

The house was so simple, so plain that it seemed elegant to Alan. The furniture was stark, the wide-planked oak floors uneven. The main room was full of light coming through the many wide windows on the barren walls. The homey scent was compounded of wax, cooking odors, flowers.

Even their clothes smelled different. Hung on lines to blow dry in the sun and the wind, they caught and kept the breeze and the fragrance of green leaves and pollen. Hand scrubbing made them soft, utterly clean, and faintly battered. And each garment showed the flaws and strengths of the human hands that had cut and stitched and pressed it.

Alan realized that Susan's father had caught him taking an inventory of the long rows of happy children. "Big family," he commented.

The Amishman's eyes sparkled with droll understanding. "We can't seem to figure out what's causing it."

The meal was a game. Susan's mother called it a mystery dinner, which meant that one's food and cutlery had to be ordered from a menu of disguised items. "Cow juice" meant milk, a "drip dryer" was a napkin. Before he and Joan learned that smoked squeal was ham, not a hybrid of squid and eel, and cooked ear was corn, they ended up with a collection of plates and silverware and no food.

The adults were having as much fun as the children, and Alan participated with good nature, but it tired him quickly. Prepared for today by neither his experience nor his imagination, he found it jarring to be in a minority in this atmosphere of naive exuberance. The pleasures here were strange to a spiritual orphan. *We lost beings don't take well to this. The level of simple happiness here is intolerable.*

Susan's mother was round and pretty, like a panda, and her father was lively and strong, with his massive beard, thick forearms, and fond, clever eyes. Both were warm to him, and yet there were barriers, nothing Alan could put his finger on, nothing as concrete as standoffishness. They could be friendly, but they were separate—different from him. That was understood. It struck him as dignified and unaffectedly honest. If there were sycophants in the world, they wouldn't be Amish.

They asked him about his family and he answered politely, but evasively. They asked him about his movies and listened carefully to his reply, trying to keep it from becoming obvious that they couldn't understand why anyone would want to see a movie with monsters in it. And then, clearly wanting to return to familiar ground, they asked him about his family again.

He never would have admitted he had no family if he'd known how it was going to affect them. Better a lie than the startling compassion in their gazes. He tried to correct their counterfeit impression, but it stuck like glue. Susan swung around with a grin, watching her aunt Mary ply him with food.

"Well, mercy, no wonder you're so slim, with no one around to feed you. You've got no more meat on you than a darning needle. Anna, *kumm mol haer.* Make Mr. Wilde another plate. He don't eat enough to keep a hen alive."

He'd never seen farmers eat before, huge amounts grown in their own gardens, different, better than what the caterers brought for the movie company. Supermarket vegetables. David called them *légumes fatigués*.

Eating was always difficult for him. He didn't seem to have what other people called appetite, and he rarely ate much at one time or his body began to tense, resisting the process. Nice and neurotic. It was a favorite topic for the amateur psychoanalysts among his past lovers. He was preparing to be firm about the refilled plate when Susan's small sister Carolyn smote the half-organized thought to amused silence by asking him frankly, "Mr. Wilde, why haven't you any wife?"

Amos Hostetler's brow descended in his daughter's direction and he delivered a curt sentence to the child in dialectical German.

"Why, I just thought how he must be so lonesome," the child persisted, tiny and maladroit and earnest in her *kapp*. "Did your mother and dad have no brothers and sisters for you?"

"Nope. My parents took one look at me and said, 'Never again.'"

The tyke returned a disbelieving smile, and Anna leaned over the table on her elbows to glare menacingly at the child. "I, for one, could do with fewer brothers and sisters sometimes."

The unswerving, wide-eyed childish gaze never dropped from his face. "But there must have been no one to play with."

"And no one to have to share toys with and fight with and tease 'til they cry." Susan stopped as she passed with a basket of bread to gently nip her sister's nose with her fingers.

"You mean these angelic children fight? I can't believe it." Joan was smiling. Amos looked up and chuckled through his beard.

"Not big fights so often," Chester said cheerfully, "but once in a while, look out."

"The shingles come off the house," Daniel said.

Susan's mother clapped her hands over her ears. "You can imagine all these kids, all screaming."

"Daniel, I thought you said there were thirteen of you," Joan said. "With so many, do you lose count?"

The room held an instant odd silence, like a film where the sound track has been magnetically erased. Even two of the children who had been assembling a puzzle in the corner stopped and looked up. The other children had gone still as well, listening fawns in an adult forest. The mother's gaze flew downward to her hands. Susan's aunt turned her face away. Hemmed in by the vigor of his full beard that concentrated each emotion, Amos Hostetler's features carried a deep, recessed chill. He broke the silence.

"No longer are there thirteen children." The strongly formed hand came palm down, once, on the table, a jarring crash. "No more."

Alan's gaze rested on Susan's grandmother. Staring toward the window as though the light there formed a bright spot in her world of darkness, tears came in a soft bloom to the sightless eyes and were slowly blinked away.

Amos's chair scratched the floor as he thrust himself upright. "I've got to go down by the creek and make fence." His good-byes were brief if not unkind, and when the front door closed behind him Joan said, "Mrs. Hostetler, I apologize if I've said anything—"

"No. No, of course not." She looked up.

"I understand you've lost a child?" Joan's voice was gentle.

"A daughter. Rachel." The words were produced with painful dignity.

Susan's Rachel, then. The one who wanted to embroider bird nests with colored ribbon. So sad. So inexpressibly sad. Alan saw Susan standing motionless as glass beside the kitchen, her hand gripping the doorframe, her gaze following her father's retreating back. But there was no sorrow in her eyes. There was wrath.

Banished outdoors while the table was being cleared, Alan was put in the charge of Susan's sixteen-year-old brother Luke after Mrs. Hostetler had made the hopeful suggestion, "Mr. Wilde might like to see the turkeys."

Clean and dramatic, sunlight bounced off the white barn lofting above the outbuildings like a giant ark. Sounds had a midafternoon mute on them, the wind tickling the leaves, the lethargic stirrings of napping animals. Soft scents meandered from the downy sawdust scattered near the woodpile.

Luke endeared himself to Alan immediately by slamming his finger in the yard gate and snapping out a distinct expletive. He glanced quickly at Alan and said, "Sorry."

"Don't be sorry."

Luke cheered him up even more by saying firmly, "You don't want to see the turkeys."

"You have something more exciting in mind?"

"Well . . . I have to breed a pair of my rabbits. Want to watch?"

Alan found himself starting to grin. "This is a spectator sport?"

"Don't expect much. You put them in a hutch together and it's all over before you can get the latch fastened."

This proved to be no exaggeration. If Alan had blinked he might have missed it, and then the little buck collapsed on his side into an exhausted heap of gasping bunny fur.

"Dear me. Is he all right?"

"He's fine. They usually fall over like that. It means that he's—"

"Right. Right. I get the picture." Wilde was increasingly amused by Luke's farm-boy cool. "You realize if we put this in a movie, you wouldn't be old enough to be allowed in to see it. Why are you taking him out of the cage?"

"You have to separate them afterward, or half the time they get into a fight."

"There's one thing the species have in common."

He got back a lopsided grin that reminded him a lot more of Holden Caulfield than John-boy Walton. As the boy sat down on the sun-speckled floorboards of the shed with the rabbit on his lap. "How'd you like to hold one? Pick one out."

Alan was not especially fond of cute things with fur, but for some crazy reason he wasn't averse to these rabbits. He glanced down the row of hutches, at white-and-black-spotted rabbits, and then went to a cage that held a small rabbit sitting hunched down in the fluff of a sleek chocolate-

brown coat. Instead of having ears that poked up like a
Beatrix Potter bunny, this rabbit's ears hung downward,
giving his bright little face a doleful air.

"What's the matter with his ears?"

"Nothing. It's in his breeding to be lop-eared. His ears
are fine. It's the other parts of him that give me trouble.
Go on, take him out. He's very gentle."

Alan gingerly withdrew the rabbit. "What's the trouble, then?"

"I've got to cull him." The boy glanced up as Daniel
entered the shed with Carolyn on his shoulders, bending
under the low doorway.

Daniel swung the child to the floor. "You haven't had
any luck with the Lop?"

"It's hopeless."

Wilde made himself comfortable on the clean floorboards and set the Lop on his knees. "What's so hopeless
about him?"

"He took sick the first week I had him, and Anna
brought him into the house to nurse him. She litter-trained
him, and he got to be kind of a pet. Maybe it was the
babying, maybe it was being sick, but when I brought him
back out..." Luke shrugged. "He won't cover a doe."

Alan watched the rabbit drop its chin and gaze up at
him in a woebegone manner. The glum expression had to
be rank anthropomorphism and a trick of the preposterous
ears. The thing looked like a basset hound. "What does
'cull' mean?"

"Rabbit stew."

"You intend to *eat* this bunny?"

"Not me. I'm too attached. I'm going to sell him to
the Zooks, down the way, and they'll, er..." Luke settled
his spotted rabbit back in its hutch. "The thing is, you'd
like to take pity, but on a farm you can't be feeding animals
who don't earn their keep, or pretty soon you'll find
yourself out of business. He's either breeding stock or
stew."

Daniel hunkered down beside Alan and scratched the
Lop behind the ears with some expertise. "Have you tried
switching him cage to cage with a doe?"

"Time after time. Nothing."

"Have you tried setting him on her back?"

"He climbs off and sits in the corner."

"Are you sure he's a male?"

Luke gave his older brother a look that was heavily sardonic.

Daniel took his hand off the rabbit. "No help for it, then."

"Are you sure you don't want to think this over?" Alan said. "Impotence shouldn't be a capital offense."

Alan's voice filtered out the uncovered window to Susan and Joan as they strolled through the sunlight toward the shed. Joan leaned closer, on the verge of laughter, and spoke sotto voce. "What on earth do you think he's talking about?"

"One of Luke's rabbits, I guess." Susan felt her own smile fluttering upward from deep within. "Have you ever noticed? It's so funny, the way Alan is with children."

"Are you kidding? We see it all the time when he works with child actors. It's a total stitch. He's wonderful. He absolutely doesn't adapt."

"I know. He talks to children as though they were adults. He doesn't seem to have the first idea he's doing it, either. It's so . . ." A strand from Susan's *kapp* veered in the breeze, rubbing the side of her neck. She swept it aside with her finger. "It's so charming. He has such patience. He'll be a wonderful father."

"If the thought ever occurs to him to become one."

"Why wouldn't it?"

"Because that's not the image Alan has of Alan."

From the shed, Susan heard her little sister's voice. "You should have him, Mr. Wilde. He'd be good company to you."

Resting her elbows on the sill, she was in time to see Alan with an armful of rabbit, and the admonition she'd prepared for Carolyn, to tell her not to tease Mr. Wilde because he didn't like animals, became a forgotten echo. He was holding the tiny buck improperly, his grasp rather awkward, as though he couldn't figure out the logical way to support the plump belly and dangling legs. But even in his inexperience his grip was trying to accommodate it with a tentative gentleness.

He wants to be more than he is. He wants so much more. . . .
Susan saw him shake his head at her sister, smiling a little,
handing the rabbit back to Luke, tactfully rejecting Luke's
endorsement of the offer. Alan looked different today, in
jeans and a loose cotton shirt, nearer to simple, less
confined in elegance. He looked, for once, like someone
who could get dirty. Darned if she wasn't going to try.

And it became swiftly apparent to her that he was
willing. For one thing, he let Luke talk him into learning
how to milk.

He was something to see, with his long, well-made
proportions folded up on a milking stool under a huge
Holstein, half a dozen cats coiled expectantly around his
ankles.

"Does she kick?"

"She never kicks," Luke splashed out the sudsy water
he'd used to wash the Holstein's udder. The scent of the
foamy soap mingled in the barn with that of wet cow and
alfalfa. "Unless you put cold hands on her bag in the
winter. Tell you what, Alan. You won't get far that way.
You've got to take a good hold on her tits, like I told you."

To the interest of his large, encouraging audience,
Alan made a better showing, though he said, "I thought
they were called teats."

Studying Alan's shaky technique, Luke said, "Nah.
Just call 'em tits."

Incredulous delight seized Susan when she saw Alan's
color fluctuate. "Please, Luke, you're making Mr. Wilde
blush."

"I've led a sheltered life," Alan said meekly, and then
looked up at her with a direct smile. She felt her own color
rise.

"He has." Joan stood to the lee of the stanchion, her
arms full of cat, with the cow's head in the manger at her
feet, placidly chewing, chewing. "Thirty-two years of age
and I'll bet he's never been in a K-Mart."

"What's a K-Mart?" said Alan and Susan almost
simultaneously. Joan's answering smile was full of mystery.

Luke bent down, giving Alan a bracing nudge. "There
you are. Getting a nice rhythm on her"—he grinned—"how
about we call it her bosom?"

Clever, cosmopolitan, and hardly sheltered, Alan gazed at the healthy pink flesh squeezed between his fingers. "Please. My sensibilities."

Afterward they walked and sat down by the creek, Susan and Alan, Joan and Daniel, under the cool awning of an oak. Nearby, Anna had her feet in the water while she made Joan a maple-leaf crown, overlapping leaves and using the stems to pin them together. They could see in the distance a haze from disc plows, and the spring leaves were a mist in many shades of green. A robin was singing somewhere, an afternoon melody that became part of the air. The children searched for gelatinous strands of frog eggs in the cattails, their feet wavering images under the clear stream. Carolyn lay on her stomach on a warm flat rock, blowing bubbles in the water through a dandelion stem. Far off in the hedgerow, Jacob and Mark were collecting asparagus in a reed basket, small figures under a stretching sky. The sun's rays were slanting in, moving across the landscape like golden fingers caressing the earth.

Alan lay against a fallen black oak, one knee bent, one arm resting on the dark trunk. Susan watched him uncover an oblong of soil under the rich mixture of leaf litter, scooping up a handful to study. He didn't sniff it, as a farmer would have. It wouldn't be his instinct, and yet there was something in his half-experience that frustrated her. *Smell it*, she thought, sending the message with her eyes even though he wasn't looking at her. *Smell it.* When he did not, she stood and went over to kneel beside him, pushing his wrist upward so the soil was near his face.

"Does it smell good to you?" she asked.

His expression was curious as he thought it over. He's deciding what I want to hear, she thought. "Be honest. How is it?"

His eyes took in light as though he'd caught her thought. "Like dead leaves."

She sat up on the log. "I remember when this oak fell. It came down one year in a spring windstorm, and I saw it the next day when I was walking with my grandmother. There it lay, the roots ripped from the ground, some of them clutching rocks as if they'd tried to cling there. And I said to my grandmother, 'Poor tree.' And she said, no, the tree was just coming home." Running her hand over the fissured bark, over the spring frosting of bright moss, she found a soft place in the wood where the timber had become red ocher meal. Leaning forward, she showed him, and then showed him too how the same deep red dust was in the scattered bits of soil in his hand. " 'See,' she told me. 'See how nature takes back the trees.' "

Tomorrow . . . Things that would one day pass away . . . She could feel his resistance to the idea. Like the images he captured, frozen in his films, he lived in a present that he willed to be eternal. What did it matter, to cling so hard to this world, when the next one would be so much better? But she knew without being told that Alan didn't believe in better worlds. If you can hardly see the virtues in this life, it must be impossible to imagine the perfection of a future one. She wanted to take off his blinders and let him see.

Tilting her hand above his, she let the red wood spill from her palm to his and watched him close his fingers slowly around it. *He wants to touch me.* So strong was the impression that it caught like a trapped breath in her throat.

He never made the move she could feel he so desired. Aware as he was that they were not alone, he stared at his hand for a brief time before glancing up and around and finally smiling into her face.

"Does this little creek have a name?"

"Government Crick."

"Why do you call it that?"

"I don't know. That's just what they call it."

"Susan, you know better than that," Daniel said. "You know. It's Government Crick because it goes by Government Tree."

"Oh, yes, I didn't think about it." To Alan, "Far down the crick there, see the giant elder tree that stands against the sky? Hereabout, they call that the Government Tree."

"Is that just what they call it?" Alan's smile teased.

At moments like this, she wondered if in a hundred years there'd ever be a way to become immune to that smile. "The old folks say they call it the Government Tree because every branch is crooked."

"Social comment." There was a thread of laughter in his voice. "I'm horrified."

Anna stared at him. She appeared to be caught up in his wayward charm, the aura that was gentle and slightly dissipated. "Do you put social comment in your movies, Mr. Wilde?"

"It shows up as a subtext. The reviewers think so anyway, even when you try to be consciously apolitical."

Anna twirled a leaf by the stem. "What's a subtext?"

"A message. A philosophy. The thing you say while you're pretending to say something else. Take a soft-drink ad. They show you a group of people, young, beautiful, having a great time, drinking from these cans of carbonated chemicals. The surface message is that the stuff tastes good. The subtext is that if you drink the stuff you'll be young, beautiful, and have a million friends. You look doubtful. You don't believe it?"

Anna was grinning. "No one could be that stupid, to think that drinking some kind of soda pop would do all that."

"True. That's why you can't tell them directly. You have to pin it underneath."

"And what's the philosophy you pin under your stories?" Susan began to brush the wood dust from her palm.

"That life is like a war where you don't get any medals."

"What a thing to say!" He'd meant to provoke her, and she knew it. Laughing as much about his unruly intellect as she was at his words, she whipped off Daniel's hat and stuck it on Alan's head, then pulled it down over his face. "Too bad you aren't Amish. We'd fix you up quick."

"Fix him up anyway." Joan tossed over the jacket Daniel had discarded on a low branch. "Let's see what he'd look like Amish."

So Susan pushed Alan to the ground, stuffing him into the jacket, making him laugh, making the children laugh. He made it hard for her, too, struggling enough to prolong the contact between them, and she wanted him to, taking guilty pleasure in each touch, each unguarded brush of his body against her hands and arms. Charming to her in the hat, the jacket, she imagined him Amish, how he'd be so good-looking and vital, how he'd wait for her under the moonlight in a buggy and she would run outside after milking and ride with him. What riches she would have had then.

She hopped to her feet, pacing quickly backward to see if he was going to chase her to retaliate. She saw he was, and ran from him, letting him catch only the trail of her mirth as she plunged toward the stream and into the water.

"A creek race!" the kids shouted, bounding after her, and then it was all of them and Alan, too, racing along the creek bed in cool, crisp water halfway knee-high, laughing at the bristling silliness of it. The creek became vast splashes, silver curtains that surrounded them as they ran with the current under willow boughs that grazed their bodies with wet, glossy leaves as they passed. A pasture of Holstein heifers stared at them in astonishment and then bolted away through a woodland carpeted in the curled furry heads of infant ferns.

They threw themselves down to rest on the grass near the schoolhouse, letting the sun paint dry spots on their clothing. Susan made the outline of a smile on Alan's shirt with sandburrs.

Strolling along the shoreline, Alan picked up a sharp stone, and when they looked it over and said yes, it was an Indian arrowhead, he examined it as though a childhood dream had come real for him.

They had stick races on the culvert, tossing twigs off one side, watching the other side to see whose twig the water carried through first.

"Funny idea," Alan said.

"We borrowed it from Winnie-the-Pooh," Susan told him. "When I was little we used to do Winnie-the-Pooh things."

"Such as?"

"We used to be the Pooh Corner animals. Anna was a little chubby, so she was Piglet. Luke was Tigger, always bouncing. Daniel was Christopher Robin, because we went to him when things went wrong."

"Your sister Rachel?" His soft voice became softer. He

wasn't aware, of course, only perhaps that something was terribly awry here, a blank mark of sorrow in her family. It was soothing in a very intimate way to hear him speak openly about her sister, making her real again.

"Rachel was Owl, since she loved to use big words, but she usually said them wrong."

Alan gave her *kapp* string a tug. "I'll bet you were Pooh Bear."

"As a matter of fact, I was. You know how Pooh had adventures and then made a poem about them? I made up poems about the things we did. Sometimes I made up a Hum. Then you can hum the words, and every line ends with Tiddly Pom. Now, what on earth have I said to set you off laughing like that?"

"I don't know." He could hardly say the words, he was so wrapped up in his laughter. "I don't know. It's being with you."

The visitors from California were a lot scruffier than they'd been when the day began, Joan with a laurel of maple leaves and Alan's damp jeans finding the shape of his long, handsome legs.

In the fading daylight, they played Auntie-I-Over around the schoolhouse, teaching Joan and Alan the simple rules: two teams, one on either side of the school; one team threw the ball over the roof. The other team members tried to catch it, and if they succeeded, they could dart around the building and try to tag out those on the other team. Susan remembered Rachel's saying that it was a dying game because there were so few country schools left and in the city the schools were too big, and that was sad. Her grandmother had played it as a girl and recalled the fun of it, the excitement of the ball rumbling over the shingles, of not knowing when it was coming or where it would appear. And there was no way to know if the other team had caught it and was sneaking around the corner silently to burst out into the open and chase you while you ran screaming.

Alan, as captain of the other team, proved to be a subtle and crafty strategist, full of spunk and derring-do. And gallantry, too, Susan discovered, watching him give chase to Carolyn, seeing Alan pretend she was too fast for him, seeing her sister's delight.

The setting sun poured fiery reds over them, a translucent glow that rose in a sky streaked with bold crimson and delicate pinks. Hurtling around the corner, trying to nab Luke, she ran smack into Alan.

He steadied her. The others ran on, and they were briefly alone. Smiling, she tried to pull loose, but he held her hard against his body.

"For a minute. Please."

Her smile was gone, forgotten in the stress of feeling all of him pressed to her. The sounds of exuberant play became distant, and she heard nothing beyond the unsettled patter of her breath. Sunset tinted him, gold on his skin, red-gold in his hair, warm tones, coming warm inside her, then shudderingly warm as his hands on her back made her closer in clever ways. His clothing carried to her the scents of the meadow and the golden sunlight, and beneath, his body was solid and delicious. So male. And she needed that so.

The door he had opened for her would not close again, and the wanting came not as a shower, but in a storm, and if there was resistance in her, this time it was helpless. Her passion came in a clear voice, hiding nothing. She wanted him, wanted to be under him, to feel the goodness of him, with his thighs making a cradle against hers, his chest in a caress against her breasts. She needed him to take her mouth in long, melting kisses and come inside her and ease this intense, angry aching. Graphic and controlled, unexpected, the thoughts flooded from the depths of her with such speed that she could not stop herself from yearning against him, tightening the contact, her mouth dry, merciless desire grabbing at her throat.

How was this happening?

He held her close to him for another moment and then she was gently released. She wondered if he could see that she had begun to tremble. The failing light shadowed the expression in his eyes as he said, "Let's do something wonderful and write a poem about it." The corners of his mouth tucked in a charming smile. He walked his fingers lightly up her arm. "Tiddly pom?" Then, with great gentleness, "Don't be ashamed, Susan. It's good."

Prickles of sensation continued to shiver through her limbs. "It comes all at once."

He touched her face. "It's been building for so many weeks, we can uncover it quickly."

"What you mean is, you know how to uncover it quickly."

"Yes," he said quietly.

Hardly thinking, not thinking at all, she came back into his arms, holding on, her cheek pressed against his rapid heartbeat. She whispered fiercely, "This is crazy."

"No. Everything else is crazy. This is the only thing that makes sense."

Walking back to the farm beneath the first sprinkle of starlight in the animated cluster of her family, she found herself looking upward, searching out the little star that rode the northern sky above the Swan.

Alan's car departed the Hostetler farm, but stopped partway down the country lane and backed into the farm driveway, where he spoke out of the window to Luke.

"Are you really going to cook that bunny?"

"Well . . . the Zooks'll cook him."

"Let them eat cake. I'll buy him."

The image had the power to make Susan smile all evening, of Alan, worldly and discriminating, holding the brown, long-eared rabbit, rubbing the tip of one long finger over its nose.

Past bedtime she sat alone, balanced on her porch railing, her arms around the big square oak corner pillar, leaning her face into the cool wood. A big, old moon was on a slow rise. It glowed on her bare toes, rimmed her arms in white luster, and made shiny reflections in the dark windows. Down in the marsh, the bullfrogs kept up their ticklish-belly bass, like the distant plucking of wide red rubber bands. Minty resins from the spruce she'd planted with John made the air a bouquet.

Home. Her home. She'd never wanted anything more. Never before.

Lord, twenty-five years I pray to you, lead me not into temptation. And now this.

A breeze moved through the grass in quizzical whispers. *Am I leading now, Susan, or are you?*

She smiled in acknowledgment, and then the smile faded and a memory tore at her, instant, sharp, of Alan's body coming against hers. Each hard plane, each warm sinew came alive again down the front of her, gripping her with agonizing need. She closed her eyes and pressed her forehead against the pillar, her body aching.

Chapter 15

&

Something is terribly wrong.

It is night. Polly searches through a cranberry bog, searches for her husband. Around her, twisted vegetation takes on an iridescent blue glow in the mist. Her cape flares behind her. Her hair is dark and streaming. Will-o'-the-wisps ignite near her skirts, throwing light on her face, which is white with fear . . . and stunningly, heartbreakingly beautiful.

&

The scene had the quality of a hallucination, the poetry of an Arthur Rackham drawing for a fairy tale.

Filmed in a large shed near the hotel, the scene was the product of crude but dramatic special effects—a fog machine, sodium lights. .Alan had placed Susan on a treadmill in front of a huge screen onto which footage of fantastic foliage had been projected from the rear. And he'd found it easy to get a good performance from Susan. She was frightened by the equipment, the exhausting repetition.

It was not so simple, however, for Alan to help her with the scene that came next—Polly seeing her husband turn into a monster.

Alan had directed this sequence of sophisticated special effects back in California at the Lucasfilm facility. In it David's body decayed in a slow, horrific explosion from which the monster emerged like a giant larva, metamorphosing by degrees into its new form. In his time, Alan had seen some brilliant cinematic wizardry, but this was in a class by itself. During a screening of it for the crew the night before, everyone who had been eating stopped abruptly. One of the cameramen had dropped his head between his knees, and a grip had run from the room.

"Maybe it's a bit much," Alan had said to his visual-effects supervisor. And they'd both grinned.

Susan's job was to show such horror, such terror, that she established the credibility of the transformation scene in the viewer's mind.

Alan had allowed David on the set—a bad decision, probably—but David had done such a superb job with Susan so far that it seemed appropriate. He hadn't quite anticipated the intensity that David would bring to this sequence. There were reasons for it, of course. Scenes like this could make a movie or ruin it. At present it wouldn't even get into the movie. Susan, reacting to nothing but a yardstick held up to give her a focus point and David's coaching, had dissolved into helpless laughter in every take.

They took a short break in late afternoon while Susan was having her makeup restored for the fourth time. Consulting briefly with Tim from the second unit, Wilde was interrupted by David, who snapped, "It isn't coming, Alan."

"It will."

"Not at this rate. Her head's in the wrong place.

You've got to show her the footage of the transformation so she has some idea of what she's supposed to be reacting to."

"David, that isn't pretty stuff, and this is the lady who hasn't even paid a visit to 'Mr. Rogers' Neighborhood.' It might end up having a terrible impact on her. Anyway, we've already suggested it to her and she says emphatically that she doesn't want to see it."

"Make her."

Wilde felt a strong academic curiosity about how fully his internal recoil expressed itself outwardly. "No."

"It's her bloody professional responsibility to look at it."

"She isn't a bloody professional."

"Alan, maybe you haven't realized what you've been putting in the can. This is going to be an incredible picture once you finish massaging it together in editing. It's going to do for fantasy what *Gone with the Wind* did for the Civil War. Let's don't fade on the home stretch because you've let your personal appetite cloud your judgment."

His patience kicked into third gear. David needed Susan's performance to make himself look good. Perfectly understandable. The bigger the picture threatened to be, the greater the panic. Again understandable. The personal reference he let slide. David was prone to that sort of thing.

Alan had no sense of making a mistake when he put his hand on David's shoulder and summoned up what Joan called his father-figure stance.

"I'll make it work, David. It's taking her a little time to give us what we want, but I never thought it wouldn't. Don't bring your frustration into this. Take off, have some fun. Leave Polly to me."

Distracted by a quick conference over lighting, keeping his finger on the pulse of production in a mosaic of areas, he was vaguely aware that David had gone back to Susan and was talking to her, making explanations. She was listening intelligently, nodding often. Her voice, with its neat sibilants and friendly intonation, came to him across the noisy clatter and conversation on the set.

"It's no use. I can't be afraid of a yardstick."

Speaking to Tim, his gaze strayed reflexively to Susan.
He saw David take her hand, turn up the small palm, and
strike her hard there with the yardstick.

"Are you afraid of it now?" David asked.

She had not cried out. Her eyes were open and
incredulous, then irritated. *"No."*

He struck her again. *"Now?"*

Alan couldn't even feel himself moving; he experienced a sensation like flight: his body high and light,
suspended. He didn't know he was going to hit David,
didn't feel the pressure of the impact, only saw David fly
backward, trying for a fraction of a second to find his
balance. The actor seemed to realize it was impossible and
then abandoned himself to the momentum, expertly lax,
tumbling for what seemed like a long time. A chair fell, a
lamp. Crew members were turning, staring. Some obviously hadn't seen David strike Susan and were finding it
difficult to believe that the director had just punched out
the leading man.

David ended the fall in a roll and came to his feet,
wild with fury. Everyone within reach who wasn't frozen
with surprise launched forward to stop him.

"David, use your head. Not here . . ."

"Enough, already. Are you both nuts?"

Joan said, sounding scared, trying to humor him,
"David, we all know you could kill him, but please don't.
Can you imagine what it would take to replace him? We'd
go another week off schedule."

Wilde could see the others were looking to him,
expecting even now that he would pull it all together,
snatching calm and certainty from chaos. But his mind
continued to dissociate from the act, the emotion that had
provoked it. He was detached and languorous, as if he'd
barely waked from a long sleep.

David, shedding restraint, had to bring his breath
under control to speak. "You consummate maniac. It isn't
my fault you've spent your life in some kind of flagellant's
coma. I've had it, do you understand? Don't act out with
me because someone fed you cleaning fluid to make you
cry in a movie when you were a kid."

To Susan, watching, the air had a terrible weight.

Silence came, the silence within a silence of an empty room, made violent by David's erratic breathing. Nothing so formed as thought came to her, only a desperate distaste, because she couldn't understand David's words. They were some English insult with images unknown to her. Then she looked at Alan. And she knew the insult had not been random. It had struck at the soul, caused deep agony in a brilliant human being who valued above all things the privacy of his spirit.

Later she would learn the story wasn't a secret, that it had, in fact, appeared in a major newsweekly. Though no one had ever discussed it with Alan, there wasn't anyone in the room who hadn't heard it—repeated it, in fact.

None of this she knew, but she could feel the guilt and the embarrassment. The air became stale with it. There was only that, and her crushing sense of Alan's isolation. The whole world might have withdrawn from him, he seemed that alone, his face shorn of feeling, and she had the sense of him by himself in some vast space, on the endless reaches of a deserted planet. She wanted to go to him and touch him, but the sphere he built around himself had already been so violated that she held back, sick with hurting.

Seconds passed. The haze seemed to leave Alan's eyes. "It wasn't cleaning fluid," he said in that mild way he had, as if it were something that needed to be said. And then he stood there, as if he didn't know what to do next.

"Alan?" Ben Rose stepped closer, his exasperated expression imperfectly concealing his deep affection and concern. The tension in his face heightened when Alan turned slightly to face him. "For God's sake, Alan, go take a break. Just . . . take a break for a while, will you?"

After a short pause Alan nodded. Susan watched him half-turn, this time toward her. He smiled gently at her. His expression carried a faint hint of apology and something else, an inscrutable emotion that was too fragile to be named. Though she couldn't name it, it took her breath away.

He said softly, "Are you all right?"

"Yes."

In the same disturbingly passionless tone he spoke to

David. "Don't hurt her again! Do you understand? Nothing here is worth that."

Then he walked off the set. She stared at the open doorway after he went through it. The edge of her gaze caught Joan. The red-haired woman stood to the side, gazing sightlessly after Alan, her posture composed, one arm loose at her side, the other crossing her chest in a horizontal bar. The skin over her high-boned cheeks looked ashen.

There was a numb pause, and then Ben Rose rounded on David. "You're an uncivilized son of a bitch and I don't care if you walk the picture."

"I'm tired of pretending I don't know what's happening here," he said simply. He looked at Susan. "Well, Ben, look at her face now. You may not like my methods, but never say they don't work. Let's film."

And because in this world time meant money and money was all, they did.

David disappeared before they finished, and Susan had to seek him out. She knew more than she had at first, whom to ask to find his entourage, then whom in the entourage to ask.

David had gone to his luxurious suite, which rambled over the full upper story of the main guest house. There were hints, strong ones, that she shouldn't penetrate the stronghold.

She walked in anyway and found him half-reclining on a canework silk couch, with the curtains drawn over the late-afternoon sunlight. He had one heel braced on a vast exquisite carpet from the Orient, the other leg sharply bent at the knee. His rough-textured black shirt was sleeveless. One bare arm rested against his thigh, his fist clenched, the graceful sinews rigid. Rubber tubing strangled the youthful flesh of his forearm. He was injecting something into a vein in his wrist with a hypodermic needle.

She might have made a sound, she wasn't sure, or he might simply have sensed her presence. He looked up at her, his eyes widening.

"Of all the damn things," he murmured, emptying the needle, withdrawing it. His eyelids clamped down. He set his teeth and gasped out, "In a minute." Pushing his shoulders back into the cushions, he lay prone, one foot flat on the rug.

The ornately cut cheekbones seemed more sharply defined. Once, his breath became uneasy and he restlessly arched his back, dragging up his shirt impatiently, uncovering his chest. One of his hands remained limp against the carpet's subdued sheen, compulsively clasping the syringe, his thumb lazily caressing the plastic barrel.

He turned his head slowly, studying her, then said thickly, "If you'd looked the way you do right now for the camera, I wouldn't have had to hurt you."

The indistinct focus of his eyes brightened with amusement. He opened his hand around the syringe, offering it. "I ought to do it for you. Then you'd understand how good it is."

He continued to search her eyes. After an extended time, he sat up, using the strength of his arms, dropping the syringe on a glass side table, shaking his hand before he recaptured her with his shrouded gaze.

"Come in. There's no need for you to stand huddled by the door. I'll try not to eat you. I can see you're good and harrowed, but it's too late for either of us to do anything about that now." He paused. "You do understand what you're seeing?"

She had come another foot or two into the room, grasping the back of a chair with moist, shaking fingers. "You've . . . put something into your blood."

"Synthetic euphoria. Tell Alan I've allowed you to see what you just saw and he may feel compelled to drive a fist into the other side of my jaw. You should have knocked."

"I know that now. I'm not in the way of it. We don't—"

"Don't what?"

"Have doors that need knocking on. Not in daylight."

"Admirable," he continued to regard her with half-opened eyes. "I suppose you've come to ask me about Alan."

"Yes."

"No one would talk to you, would they? His friends are too discreet. The others know you're close to him. They don't want it to get back that they were setting themselves up as experts on his joyous childhood." He'd been pulling off his shirt over his head while he spoke, the shapely muscles taut, rippling with small tremors. "I'm not especially disposed to elaborate myself."

"Why aren't you?"

"He wouldn't want you to know. He doesn't seem to recognize his early existence as part of himself. He's disowned it. Too maudlin. Or maybe just too crazy for others to come to terms with. I don't know. How much do you want me to tell you?"

"Enough to understand."

"I owe you that, I suppose." He rubbed his face in the folds of the black shirt and emerged with reddened eyes. "Sit down. There's no reason to look so distraught. The one thing you're feeling bad about happened years ago; the other isn't the tragedy you're innocently interpreting it to be. You've heard about the Oscar that found its way into Alan's pocket."

She sat stiffly. "That's some kind of tribute, isn't it?"

"Yes. Some kind of tribute." Even though his words were slurred, the dryness of his tone came through clearly.

"Dash showed me the movie."

"To gently clue you in, I imagine. It was an important picture for its time. Hot young director. A couple of aging stars. Floundering studio. A lot of people needed the film. Alan's old man needed it too. He'd run into debt getting Alan the right kind of exposure. They started filming. He'd already done five pictures, so it wasn't anything new for him. Alan was fabulous. The script was fabulous. Word of mouth on the rushes was sensational. Alan was totally unlike any child anyone had ever worked with. He had incredible personal charm, immense poise, creative maturity beyond his years. Did everything he was told the first time he was told to do it. Never showed he was tired. Never complained. He was nine and the tutors were giving him college-level work. Great expectations were building around this kid. He was going to sell the film that would make Empire Studios solvent. All right. You look mystified. Where did I lose you?"

"How old did you say he was?"

"Nine years old."

"He was only a little boy!"

"He wasn't *a* little boy. He was *the* little boy. Physically arresting, and he could act. Then comes the big scene.
Alan is supposed to find Dash dying, then breaks down.
But he can't. The kid has probably never cried in his life.
He's too self-contained. They try everything to get the kid
to cry. He can't do it. They experiment with rewrites
where Alan doesn't have to cry. The film falls flat. They
need this scene. Okay, says the director. He doesn't cry—
he's off the picture. He'll cry, says Alan's father. He hauls
Alan off alone, and when they come back, Alan has no
color in his face. He'll give you what you want, his dad
says. And damn, does he ever. Then the rumors start. A
year later there was another picture, another scene with
emotion, another rumor. He'd had this pet, some kind of a
pet Dash had given him. Then he didn't have it anymore.
One version has it that his parents destroyed it. The other
story is that there were only threats, and that when he
made a charity appearance at an orphanage a couple of
days later, he gave it away. Too dangerous to keep living
things around his parents. There were other episodes."

She was silent so long that he reclined onto the couch
and lapsed into a dreamlike state that was not sleep,
making sporadic aimless movements.

"Was there no one to intervene?" she asked.

"Someone did intervene. When he was fourteen years
old, the state took him away from his parents."

This second silence was deeper, stretching like the
milk-white bands of light that broke through the drapery
folds. Dun shadows divided the brightness, ringing him in
bowed bars, fanning in flat petals on the carpet. When she
thought of it, she searched out a clean handkerchief and
blew her nose. Getting to her feet, she went to the glass
table, lifting the syringe. She turned it over, a glinting dart
in her palm. It was nearly weightless, the surfaces arctic
and unfriendly. Withdrawing the plunger slightly, she sniffed
the minute fluid residue and then touched the tip of the
needle, trying to imagine the rupture of spirit it would take
to make human beings drive such a thing into their own
flesh. She saw him watching her and set it down.

"If you could learn how it is to have Jesus in your

heart, you could feel this way all the time, without drugs," she said. It was no surprise to her that he laughed. It would be that way, the Bible said. In their pride, they would mock.

"Why is it, Susan, that every time I begin to foster the idea that we might be able to connect on some rational level, you say something like that? If you're around long enough to need it, come to me and I'll give you one hundred fifty milligrams of the best Jesus you ever had."

Steadfastly neutral, if skeptical, in spiritual matters, it was neither mockery nor reverence that led Alan to choose "Jesu, Joy Of Man's Desiring." It was simply a piece of music that he was familiar with, and though he didn't play Bach often, the melody had come to him when he walked into his room and saw the late-afternoon sunlight on the piano. So he played it. It wasn't particularly to his taste. It was the kind of thing he kept for people who said, *can you play anything off the* White Album? *What do you know by Van Morrison? I don't like classical music.* When he played the Bach, they would listen and say it was pretty, and ask what it was called again, and then forget. Except for Joan, who called it "that thing about desiring." Next time they wanted to hear it they'd ask him to play *that* piece, you know, *that* one, and try to hum a few bars as if it were a lick from "Yellow Submarine."

The piano sounded especially nice. There were days when the piano sounded nice; other days it wasn't as nice, and he was never sure if it was him, the air temperature, the humidity, an imperceptible glitch in the tuning, or a combination of factors human and atmospheric. There was always a secret dimension in music.

It was unusual too for him to look around the room while he played, but today he did, and his gaze fell on that absurd rabbit. He interrupted the Bach abruptly and played the opening bars of "Here Comes Peter Cottontail." The rabbit stared at him.

"I see you haven't figured it out. Confusing, isn't it?" Alan gestured learnedly at the piano. "You have before you a quadripedal creature of questionable zoological origin, possibly order Atiodactyla. Caveat: Don't copy that pronunciation; I'm not sure it's correct. So what is this? It has a complex and highly variable vocalization, but it neither eats nor sleeps nor walks around." He stood and ran his hand over the gleaming woodwork. "At least I've never seen it walk around. When I'm gone, who knows?" He smiled and tapped the piano decisively. "Maybe it's stuffed."

He poured some red wine, taking his time, thinking to open the window, to take off his shoes and socks and toss them in the bedroom, concentrating on preserving his emotional poise, as he had since leaving the set two hours before. One had to face these things with aplomb. Yes, he'd said on the phone to L.A. I hit him. If you want to replace me, fair enough. There had to be concern in the voice, enough to let them know he was still rational. But there had to be confidence there, too, and the whisper of a threat. Ride me about this and I may decide I don't want this picture that badly, and then what would you do? Wilde playing the role of the indispensable director, messages weighed to the last dram, never overplayed. Never waffle. Bluff and die with your boots on. He'd learned to play poker from Dash. You're going to need this, boy, Dash had said. . . .

He wandered back to the hutch, the goblet loosely clasped in his hand, and gazed down at the rabbit. "You might remember that you were recommended to me as good company. Can we be frank? As company I'm afraid you rank right up there with a house fern." The rabbit put its head to the side to deal with an apparent itch in one droopy silky ear. "Heavens! Signs of life. I stand corrected. Oh, are you going to wriggle your nose?" He dropped his voice. "That's cute. That is so damn . . ." He watched for a while before getting down on his knees to open the hutch, scratching the furry creature behind its lop ears. Then he relaxed on the carpet on his back, his knees bent, the wineglass by his hip, the rabbit on his chest regarding him thoughtfully as he stroked it. "I don't know if anyone's told you this before," he said softly, "but it was a very bad choice to be a bunny. You should have been something else. Maybe an astronaut, or an accountant. If I hadn't come along, you just might have been eaten." He ran a fingertip down one of the long ears. "Do you fully realize how sick it is to be raised by one's predators?"

Perhaps five minutes passed before someone knocked on the door. Whom would they send? Not Joan. There was protocol involved. This was important—the first person to speak with him *after*. It would be Ben, probably, apologetic, bustling, stern if he thought he could get away with it, and trying to give no appearance of being comforting, which might be badly received. He must look a little deranged in this posture. Should he put the rabbit away? No. Give Ben a good scare. He smiled.

"Come in and join us for a glass of wine."

He heard the door open. Then, "I wouldn't care for wine. Will you have me anyway?" Susan.

Her voice, unexpected, intimate in tone, went through him like flickering heat.

Coming in, she couldn't help but smile, seeing him there cozy on the floor with a rabbit on him, the informality unlike him. He got a lopsided grin. His grin grew; so did hers.

"I'd have you under any circumstances," he said calmly. "I've had a hard day, running amok."

She could hardly think of a single reason to keep up the smile, much less laugh, but she did both, and he did, too, though it wasn't easy, lying on his back. Reasons for things weren't easy for her to see anymore. The air was too filled with feelings, bright, demanding feelings that she could almost see, biting into the very oxygen she was trying to breathe.

He was laughing as if he weren't going to quit soon, the rabbit jouncing with the rhythm of his chest, and he had to put it down to the floor. When he could, he said, "Do you think I've taken a step or two toward ruining my reputation as a model of composure?"

"You did real good on that."

"He's a martial-arts expert. I never could have landed that punch if he'd been expecting it."

"I don't know about that. I think you could give a pretty good account of yourself in a ruckus." Getting back to reasons, there wasn't a reason on earth for that to set them off again, but it did. Sometime in the middle of it all, he gasped out, "I never forgot my professional responsibilities for a minute. I want you to know that the last thing that went through my mind before I hit him was, Oh, no, I shouldn't hit him in the face. I need his face in a closeup in the next scene." They laughed at that until they had tears in their eyes and their stomachs were hurting—at least hers was; they were laughing as if they'd run out of sense, out of ways to make sense out of anything.

When it was over she was dizzy and breathless, and the way he was looking at her made her breathless too. The air was still thick with feelings, different ones now. And there wasn't a thing either of them could do about it anymore. Laughter remained with him like the whispered fragrance of a sachet, but his eyes revealed his curiosity.

"When I called the office they said you'd gone home."

"No," she said. "I went to see David. I thought you might like to know—he did apologize, after a fashion."

He got that objective look of his, the one that covered up his thoughts. After a short pause he said, "I can imagine the fashion."

"He said it was nothing personal."

"It never is, these days. They get themselves wired and run over you in a car, it's nothing personal. They bomb your village, it's nothing personal. I'd like to know what ever happened to old-fashioned, honest malice."

"I guess the devil got a lot smarter."

He smiled, the corners of his mouth stretching into their charming tucks, and it occurred to her that he didn't believe in the devil. She'd bet the devil would get good and frustrated trying to get some respect out of Alan. He conjured his own devils on film, where they could be captured and controlled.

He was starting to get up, she wasn't sure why. Maybe it didn't suit his notion of being mannerly, to be on the floor like that and have company.

She put out her hand. "Just stay. You look comfortable. I'd only planned to put my head in the door for a minute. If you're resting, I don't want to interrupt."

His smile became inviting, his eyes more so. It was the expression she could never get away from in her mind.

"Rest with me," he said.

She was torn for a moment. She wanted to stay with him; she wanted to escape to the security and peace of her own home. His smile gave her no peace, not anymore. She couldn't remember the last time she'd been able to look at him without the inside of her heart twisting in all directions.

Her whole body prickled like awakening flesh as she sat beside him, facing him, settling her violet skirt around her knees. He looked too tempting this way, nice and clean and a bit golden in the slanting sunlight. It hadn't surprised her particularly that he didn't look upset. It wasn't his way to show such a thing. Alan was that way to an extreme degree. She was glad his eyes had lost the sleepy look they'd had on the set after he'd hit David. Enraptured pain, Joan had called it. Now his eyes were light with introspective humor. He seemed to be deriving some amusement from the way she was looking around his room. She had never seen it before, and though it was pretty and full of luxury, she'd as soon have had it plain.

In the center was the piano. Though musical instruments were not things they had, she'd seen one before when she'd delivered eggs at the home of an English neighbor. She remembered it as warm and homey, like an old cabinet, much different from the magnificent one before her, its wide polished surfaces gleaming in the sun-wash. She saw the keyboard was uncovered.

"Have you been playing?"

"I was awhile ago. Then you know what happened? I had this scrap of a memory. A dream I had when I was a kid, about my piano."

"What happened in the dream?"

"The piano used to come into my bedroom and look at me while I was sleeping. It'd be wandering through the house looking for me, and there'd always be this one funny part when it found my bedroom door. To get through the door, it had to stand upright on its spindly hind legs and edge in sideways. Then it tiptoed over to the bed and it would just kind of watch over me while I slept, until it grew tired too. And then it crouched down on the rug by the bed, and the keyboard turned up in a smile, and it went to sleep. . . ." His voice became suddenly tight, soft. "Don't do that, Susan. Please. Don't do it."

She had wanted desperately to hide it, staring down at her clasped hands, concentrating, trying to crowd her mind with everyday matters. A tear had fallen anyway, striking her wrist. It was a large tear, big enough to be embarrassing, falling with a splash, fracturing into fragments as chaotic as the hot commotion inside her.

"You're wrong to think it's pity." Her voice was warm and thick and strange. "The sadness isn't for you. The sadness is for the little boy you were."

She had been half-expecting him to touch her. Instead he seemed to avoid it. He stood up after a moment and went to the piano. When she looked up, he was seated on the piano bench, regarding her steadily. The blue-green eyes had become friendly and sustaining, all traces of the earlier momentary panic neatly erased.

"I'm sorry, Amish. I can't permit you to feel sad. Consider it a forbidden emotion. For one thing, when you're sad, I can't think straight."

A second swift tear streaked backward across her cheek, marking a damp spot in the hair over her ear.

More gently still, he said, "Everyone has something. Everyone. It's not so terrible. I had more armor than you imagine. Don't let knowing about those years affect how you feel about me. It wouldn't be fair to you. It's over. It's been over for a long time. I was unhappy for a while, but even that gets to be a way of life. You lift yourself out of it in stages. You get used to it. Things go on. You get up, go to work, go to school, do whatever you have to. You have a place in those things. You have that structure, even when you start wondering who you are. In time, your personality starts coming back. It's a miracle. Same you. Same sense of humor. Same values. Same intellect. Except that it's you without emotions. You don't feel anything anymore. There's no pain. The nerves are cauterized. It's a relief."

In his way, he meant to comfort her, she knew, but she could only listen with horror to his objective description of the slow destruction of his human responses. He had learned to cope with it in the only way he knew.

They sat and looked at each other, in tension for a time, and then the tension passed, and they were content

to sit like that together with each other, to hold each other
in sight.

Not knowing why, she said, "I wish I could feel what
you feel."

"No. It wouldn't be good for you."

"I wish it anyway."

"Everything?"

"Everything."

The uncanny tension crept back in a new form, one
she couldn't quite understand. Her muscles felt tender and
alert, and there was a sting of warm blood in her throat.
To distract herself, she gestured toward the piano.

"I'd like to hear how it sounds."

"All right." He rose and went to the piano, looking
down toward his slightly cupped palms, studying and
flexing his fingers before he laid them on the keys. When
the first notes came, she started, unprepared for the piano's life, its resonance, unprepared for how he would
look, his face captivating in its prayerlike concentration.
His long-boned, tanned bare foot worked the pedals; his
fingers moved with grace over the keyboard, calling up
dazzling, unfamiliar tones that shocked her with their
beauty. When they stopped, the room fell into a hush.

He looked back at her, his gaze whimsical, but without ambiguity, and her heart began to beat quickly, like a
gosling's.

"Again I have to apologize, Susan. I don't seem to be
able to go on like this indefinitely. I've got to carry you
into the bedroom and make love to you. Or else I have to
take you home."

She didn't say anything. Words couldn't get hold of
her thoughts or her feelings. Nothing seemed to exist in
the world beyond her need to have his body close to her
and his hands stroking over the warm places on her skin.
So she said nothing at all, only sat and threw the whole
thing in his lap, although she knew it was unwise, and not
very kind or practical.

He waited with that otherworldly patience he had.
And when he realized at length that she would not speak,
he slowly closed the lid of the piano, smiled at her with

such gentleness that it drew a third silent tear from her, and drove her home.

Chapter 16

*I*t was the first time she'd allowed him to do this, to take her up in his car, even though he always offered. For one thing, the community would have raised hob if she'd been seen zipping here and there in a car with an English bachelor. Another thing was, she liked the independence of coming and going on her own. She took the buggy sometimes, or she walked or rode, becoming part of the sunshine, or the pearly gray of cloudy days. She could hear the birds in the morning and again in the evening, and how the wind changed. You couldn't hear much in a car, only road noise and the engine. "The hum of the engine" was the phrase she'd read in books. She told him it didn't sound like a hum to her, more like a roar, and he gave her back a comical look, the kind he gave to tease her when he thought she was being kind of out-of-date.

The discomfort persisted in her muscles, though she tried to make it leave, but she and Alan could still talk together pretty well. She worked to let friendly words cover the urgent needs and unsteadiness that lashed at her continually inside. His inner struggles were hidden under the flawless polish of his manners. Knowing him better now, she could see some evidence of strain. It was impossible to figure out how much it cost him to keep the facade intact, but she sensed he'd do it as long as he was able. That was the thing. She wasn't sure anymore what was going on in his mind. She could only see shadows and guess at substance.

She could have asked him what he was thinking, but the idea of laying too much in the open disturbed her. Even the thought of asking him was an English one, something she'd learned from them. On the set she had heard Alan say to this one or that one: "Are we communicating?" It meant, saying things right out. They had great trust in words. That was the hard thing to understand. On the one hand, they believed words had a tremendous power to solve problems, that somewhere there were the right words, almost like a spell, to make any two people get along and understand each other. On the other hand, they were careless with words, throwing out anything in anger, using harmful words without a thought. Words were nothing, words were everything.

It wasn't the way she'd been brought up. There was a lot in her family that was never put into words. Many things. She thought about the times when there was a break in the harmony between her mother and Aunt Mary. It only happened maybe once a year, at most, because her mother was easygoing, but there were times when Aunt Mary would want to do things her way, or she'd be fussy about this or the other, and Mother would put her foot down. There was no yelling, and no harsh words were spoken; her mother just said how she wanted it to be and that was that. Then they'd both be quiet for a couple of days, not talking much to each other, and before long it would blow over and they'd be friends again, back to getting along and enjoying each other and sharing things. But while they weren't on good terms, no one said they should sit down and talk it all out. They wouldn't have done that. There were things they just didn't say. It must have bothered Aunt Mary sometimes that she lived as part of a household where another woman, no matter how goodnatured, would always govern. But she never said so. It didn't sit very well with Mother that Mary had to have things just so, and that when she was out of sorts she got sharp with the children. But Mother kept that to herself. It was hard to believe that if they talked things out, things would change for better. They'd both have the same natures afterward. They'd both carry on with things the same as they always had, except that, if they'd talked about it, they'd have hard words and hard feelings to get over. Her mother and Aunt Mary didn't complain or try to change each other; they only let be.

Maybe now, with Alan, she should let be.

The funny thing was that as soon as she was done figuring it out, Alan said, "All of a sudden you're quiet. What are you thinking about?"

"I was deciding not to ask you what you had on your mind."

After an amused pause he said, "That's probably wise. Which way should I turn at the crossroads?"

"It doesn't matter. Right'll get you there. So will left."

She could see he had a little trouble accepting that. Daniel had said once it was that way for city people. They thought about directions in right angles. Going from one place to another was following set after set of ninety-degree turns. Around here, the roads curved, hopped over little hillocks, scooped down knolls, coiled along the crest of puffy ridges like a stripe down the back of a grass snake.

"Which is quicker?"

"Right."

So he took the left fork. They went slowly, and she started to tell him how this family lived in that farm, that family in this one, and a little about them, some of the funny things, some of the sad ones. Dusk gathered in the eastern sky, making shadows grow together, strengthening her sense of being close to him. The cool, fading light was good to her eyes, which were itchy from a day of bright lights, makeup, smoke, and tears held back.

He noticed aloud that one of the farms had electricity. She told him it was an English neighbor, Ben Hosely, and that Ben and Mary his wife milked at noon and midnight, unusual hours, because they liked to go into town and polka two nights a week when a band came to the tavern. She pointed out their new house, just up two years, and told him about how fancy it was inside, how they had a matching gold-colored stove and refrigerator in the kitchen and how the bathroom had paper on the walls with flying ducks on it, with the same color carried on in the fixtures. Alan had that smile, the delighted one, as if he were enjoying what she was saying out of proportion to how interesting it was. She was wondering if there was something humorous to him about her notion of what was fancy, when the smile left his eyes.

If something was wrong, he didn't say. Only, "I met Ben at the auction."

Her own home lay in darkness. Gloom clouded the partly open barn door, dusting the threshing floor.

She couldn't figure out the car door, but sat pressing and pulling on parts of it while he came around the other side and held it open for her. Standing by him, she called out, "Daniel?" A bit louder, "Luke, you here? Anna?"

She listened to sleepy cluckings from the hen house and the murmuring cattle sounds from the barn. Beyond that, even the wind was quiet.

"The young folks must have gone on home. I guess Daniel is out." She ought to say good night. She formed the words in her mind. Good night, Alan. It wasn't so easy to tell him good night, because it wasn't what she wanted. It might be the right thing, but it was hard to think of Alan in terms of right and wrong. She was charmed by the way he was looking around, interested and awake, as though every detail of her home were important to him.

Not planning it or talking about it, they began to walk together, on the slope of her yard. There were a good two acres of lawn around the farmhouse. To him there was a storybook quality in the rural images: the strawberry beds mulched in straw, poplars skirting the dark sparkle of a brook on the side of the property, the weedy, dry ditch in front, the heavily crowned shade trees. It had a free-spirit country look, kept up, but not tutored into submission. Clover made a fleece of white tufts through the spring grass, which sent up its own fragrance, ripe and organic.

More often than not when he thought about Susan, he placed her here, not on the set, and though this was not the same place his imagination had conjured, it was near enough to lend it the quality of a daydream. Quiet excitement passed through him, something gentle and rapturous. Emotions were no longer segregated into orderly regions for him, some cerebral, some physical. He wanted her with his body; he wanted her with his being.

Walking at his side, she seemed to him unusually slight, uncertain, defying the uncertainty. Here were the results of his careful, careless cultivation of her ambivalence. He had taught her to want him, and now she did. Her body was new and alien to her. Desires resided there that she could neither quench nor control. He could see too much in the way she carried herself, each step exact, with a barely perceptible stiffness, as if her flesh were infinitely fragile and it would hurt to move the wrong way. Her smiles were restless, full of ardent whimsy and alarm.

The tautness in his body answered hers; his own stark hunger driving him. He needed to have her. Now.

On the north side of the house she grew wild flowers, transplanted from her parents' woods, where they grew in abundance, she told him. He bent down, cupping a yellow blossom in his hand. "What is it?"

She knelt beside him. "Lady's slipper." He gave a slight smile, taking pleasure in her. She misinterpreted the source of his smile, for she said, "I'm glad you like it. My mother used to say men ought to enjoy flowers. She raised the boys that way. We all had our own part of the garden when we were old enough. We could grow vegetables, but we had to grow flowers, too, boys and girls. Some of the neighbors thought it was strange, that boys shouldn't care about those things, the way girls should, but that didn't worry my mother."

He had plucked a buttercup near the pump, spinning the stem absently between his fingers. Smiling a little, he brought it up to stroke it gently under her chin, the gesture testing, curious. She had no resistance to it. None at all. He could see it in her eyes. Susan, utterly vulnerable to him, undefended.

He stood first, breaking the tenuous contact.

She joined him. "It frustrates me, not to know how the world looks through your eyes. It must be another earth."

"Not one you'd think was friendly." In the dying light

he saw the airy shadows her lashes cast on her tense, pale cheeks.

"What do you make of this?" She swept her hand to the side.

"Your home?"

"Yes."

"It seems like an imaginary place. Can you show me inside?" Her eyes held for a moment a saint's longing, a saint's despair, along with, unexpectedly, some self-mockery and humor, and it struck him inside. Amish boys and girls with eyes like Jesus. *So you intend to take the lady, Wilde, take her into her modest little house, take off her handmade clothes . . .*

"If you'd like. There isn't much to see. . . . I have some quilts I could show you."

"Quilts?"

Under the rose-tipped sun flush, another, deeper band of color marked her cheeks. She put one hand there, stroking the spot as if she didn't understand it. "That's what we usually show English visitors. They always want to see the quilts. We're known for them, I guess."

Her front porch was deep, with a swing hanging in cottony grays. Inside the house it was warmer, darker, with the closed-in scent of warm woodwork and a faint ethery tang from the mint plant in her window box. She seemed closer to him indoors, enclosed in a hushed crucible with their unresolved passion.

"You don't lock the door?"

She didn't look at him. "We never have. What have we got to steal?" Flame from a match head made a blue streak in the dimness as she lit a propane lantern, flooding her half-turned face with smoky light. "What's the matter? Does it worry you? There's no one to bother us out here in the country."

He said nothing. She seemed more fragile now, more restive. Stretching her arm, she settled the lantern on a ceiling hook. Honey-colored light swept over her and spread in an expanding circle, not reaching into the corners. She looked around in it, bewildered, as though she'd entered a strange land.

He wanted to say the right thing to her, but his thoughts began to have a way of evaporating under the pressure of wanting to take her in his arms, bring her close, closer . . . He gave himself a minute, walking around touching the plain furnishings: the cupboard, with its few pieces of decorated china, the splash of bright colors of preserved goods in the Mason jars on her counter, the straight-backed chairs around a table with a faded red-and-white-checked cloth.

She roused herself, going to the cupboard and lifting out a cardboard box, and took a handmade puppet from the box, an Amish girl with embroidered eyes and a miniature *kapp*. Slipping her hand inside, she said, "From Daniel's sock. I made it for the little ones at school."

Her dark eyes were fierce with panic, though she was smiling. He was acutely conscious of that smile, that mouth, of the shape and color of her lips, how they would have the taste of damp satin under his, damp satin and panic.

The puppet was perusing him curiously, its head tilted. He had to smile at it. While she was sliding it back in the box he noticed the pile of blank report cards, and took one to look at.

"Is it like yours?" she asked.

"Only in the basics—arithmetic, geography, spelling. Maybe we don't call it geography anymore; maybe it's social studies now. I like these . . ." He read aloud, "Singing, deportment, poetry, inclined to mischief, comes poorly prepared. Shows courage . . . Does it frustrate you to see them drop out in the eighth grade?"

She seemed to sense the judgment he'd been careful to keep out of his voice. "Some aren't too fond of school. They'd as soon be out."

"And others?"

She stepped backward. "What's there for them to go on to study? English culture. English ideas. English literature, English music, English painting . . ."

"Agriculture—"

"How to grow a tomato with no taste to it."

"Law?"

"Writ after writ of it, and what's it given anyone? In the Bible there are only ten, and people can't even abide by those."

"Susan—"

"Maybe things should stay mysterious. Why do people have this urge to learn and learn and learn? No one can learn all there is to know anyway. In all the universities in the world, is there anyone who knows everything? No one can change the weather, or stop war, or make life come from dust. People are still hungry and fighting, and frightened . . ."

A moment of quiet passed before he spoke, very gently. "Are you frightened now?"

"Yes." The brown eyes held fast to his. "I never thought I'd come to like it so well."

He felt a chill of desire and sympathy, hot sparks, cold prickles in his blood. She stirred fitfully, her eyes unconsciously wooing him. She didn't know how to begin what she was desperate to have begin. Not seeming to know that he could see, she put her hand on his forearm, rubbing him. Modest and needful, the gesture erased all but the heat.

He took the ribbon trails of her *kapp*, one in each hand, and followed them down until they were stretched taut, with his fingers barely above her breasts. His smile was soft.

"Where are your quilts?"

Her bedroom was at the top of a steep stairway. The aged wood was springy underfoot, mewing and creaking, reanimating images from children's poetry for him, A. A. Milne and Robert Louis Stevenson, children on their way to bed wearing pajamas with feet and carrying glass-chimney lamps. When you lived the classics maybe it became less important to study them.

There were no closets in her room. Her few garments hung from hooks behind a single bed and table. She set down the lantern and knelt on a braided rug before an oak chest.

"My father made this." Her hand swept lovingly over the lemon-colored lid before she hauled it open. She tipped her head forward, looking inside, and his attention fastened on her neck, its gracious curve, the uncovered skin of her nape, the subdued shine of a few escaping tendrils of hair. Lightly he touched his knuckles to the hollow of her neck, moving up and down, letting his fingers drift just under her gown. She drew a single, sharp breath, her shoulders quite still, almost rigid.

"Lovely neck."

Her mouth quirked at the corner, doubting it. He came down beside her, and touched her cheek with the back of his hand.

"Your skin feels cold," he said.

"It does that sometimes. It can change in a minute, hot to cold, cold to hot. It's in the family. Some of my aunts have it too." She was pulling out the quilt, her hands tense from the weight of it. "My grandmother worked this one when she was a young girl. We call it the Diamond. The quilting around the edge here, she calls the pattern 'feathers and leaves,' see..." Spread outward, the massive central diamond took shape on the floor, royal purple on crimson, the colors brilliant, almost neon, like op art.

"It's beautiful," he said. "The colors are striking."

"You know why that is? I read once in a book about our quilts by an English woman that we like to use bright colors because our lives are so dull out on the farm." The satin mouth developed a fascinating, sardonic curl. He could see she thought it was pretty funny that the English had the idea their own lives were richer and more exciting than Amish lives.

"And this..." A second quilt floated in undulating coils over the first. Warm air puffed against one strand of her hair, lifting it prettily, dropping it where it could tease her collarbone. "My mother made each of us a quilt to take to our new homes when we married. It's a—I don't know how you'd say it. A bridal quilt? She made one for me when I married John. When he died, she made another one, this one. We call the design Sunshine and Shadow. See how the colors are the shadows of one another. I think she was trying to tell me: Remember, after a dark time, the sun will come out again. It's part of life, the dark and the light."

In the small pause that followed, she was thinking, *What nice silences we have.* Enclosing her hand in both of his, he carried it to his mouth, his own palms open as they would have been if he were to sip water from a stream. His breath came, blowing gently, warming her hand and then touching her thumbnail, the inside of her wrist, and, moving her thumb gently, in the scoop between it and her first finger. With his lips he repeated the pattern, and each stroke marred the rhythm of her breath.

She whispered, "You touch things. Things and people. I've noticed it before. Why do you like to do that?"

He was absorbed in her hand, following the contours with his fingers. His voice was soft, as hers had been. "A habit. I have a visual sensory prejudice. Maybe from the years of taking moving pictures of things. Appearance is the only thing that matters, not taste, not scent, only visual texture and moving colored light. I don't know why I touch. Maybe to remember that things have substance. Maybe it's a habit I started as a child. I did a lot of magical thinking."

He had gotten the relaxed smile she loved, the one with the parenthetic marks snuggled close to the corners of his mouth. There was humor, too, in the fierce desire in his gaze.

"What's magical thinking?"

"The little spells you concoct when you're a kid. Not all children do it. 'If I walk through the field, I'll make a new friend. If I run my hand along this picket fence, my parents will forget to make me practice my violin.' I never used to ask for anything specific, only that something good would happen. And if I touch here"—one long finger considered the undercurve of her chin—"and here . . ." His fingers spread slightly, palm upward, and made fractional contact with the base of her breast, caressing from side to side, moving slowly upward while he watched her eyes. "Something good . . ." His voice was more than a breath, less than a whisper.

His mouth tipped her nose with a play kiss before it descended, bypassing her mouth, and he leaned forward, nuzzling the underside of her chin with his face, then lower. Her smile tightened and her breath became quick, like his, jumping in meter, a rapid, feverish sound. One of his hands continued to clasp hers, massaging her fingers, the sensitive skin between them. The other pressed gently against her breast in different places. She shivered when his lips found her nipple, caressing it through the fabric.

"Are you still cold?" He brought the quilt around her like a cloak, covering even her hair, settling it in tender, uneven movements. But the shivering went on, coming in waves.

"I had a special way to touch things when I was little too," she whispered. "I never could feel enough through my fingers. I always wanted to put things next to my lips." His hand had grasped the quilt near her throat, and she dipped her head to stroke with her mouth across the heel of his hand, where the skin was tight and fragrant, a light, pithy sweetness from his hand soap and his cotton shirt. She put her mouth there, then her cheek, and then tried to find all the ways she could fit against his skin, every variation in form against form, warm, curving flesh, startling humanness. First he moved not at all. Then he began to help her, putting his hand this way and that against her face, giving her his wrist, then his fingers, and, when she parted her lips, letting them come barely inside, where they tasted dry and sweet to her.

He drew her to him slowly, his hands on the quilt, the quilt dragging her closer like a seine until her breath came quickly on his mouth in a motionless kiss. His grip began to shift on the quilt, pulling one side, then the other, varying the kiss in texture and pressure. Flesh slipped against flesh, into flesh, becoming moist. His hands through the quilt made yearning motions behind her, kneading her shoulders, the small of her back, below. Saying her name as if it were a sonnet, he brought them together so that she was enclosed in a cocoon of warmth, his body in front caressing her chest and belly, the fabric behind veiling her from sound and ambient sensation, and all she knew were his hands, his mouth, his exhalations making delicate motifs on her flushed skin.

Too strong, he thought. This is too strong, like a drug anyone would have to be insane to experiment with. No matter how close he pulled her, he couldn't stop the pain of wanting her in his muscles. The sheen of the lantern reflected off her lips, made her skin look hot and golden to him. He was unaccustomed to the light. It seemed special, elfin party light, shed of the weary, purposeful romanticism of candlelight, retaining the splendor of day, the mystery of night. Glint by glint, he wanted to lick it from her lips.

She had begun to laugh, the sound like many quick sighs, her eyes closed, rubbing his cheek with her nose, her lips trembling against the side of his jaw. "This is the only thing that makes sense, you said. But I feel crazy when I'm with you."

He touched his mouth to her underlip to catch the tremors of her laughter. "I feel crazy too."

"Good crazy?"

"Very good—but very crazy." His spread fingers made a nest that cradled her head; his forearm supported the arch of her back as he lowered her, lying her on the welcoming field of fine rose wool that was the quilt's backing. Her breast brushed his chest as he followed, and he pulled impatiently at his shirt, and his inhalation divided into two sharp parts when his nakedness touched her there. His mouth found hers again with urgent heat, and his soft words were also urgent. "Susan, I can't wait anymore. I've got to have you, darling."

Flying inside, passing into the turbulent universe where only he could bring her, she drove her hands into his hair, clinging to the kiss. When he drew her hem upward, she wanted only for it to happen faster. She received his knee between her thighs, fascinated by its exquisite inquiring pressure, then frantic from it. He slipped a hand beneath her thigh, trailed it higher, making entrance under the final layer of cloth, his palm sweet on her bare bottom, holding her against him, holding them together where they both stung for each other, her skirts in a drift over his thighs and pelvis.

She was deaf to her own whisper, but he heard the repeated words clearly. "Please, Alan. Please . . ." He shuddered with arousal, scattering her face with kisses, tracing the shell curves of her ear with his open mouth, finding and lightly, shakily massaging her pulse points with his fingers. Her skin had grown warm, silken in tone, as it might have during a fever. He had to look down at her face one more time before he undressed her. Pulling back, he gazed down through the gauzy mist that was the creation of his desire, loving with his eyes the deep passion marks of color on her cheekbones, the shiny distended smile, and her eyes, overbright, brown as wet cinnamon, direct in their trust.

Then he felt it. His blood stilled like ice in his veins as he felt the frosty tentacles of despair curling up through the thousand empty places in his spirit. The act he had contemplated so long with her was never going to be enough.

The desire that gave him no peace remained, pitiless in its heat, and a now-forgotten nerve command led his hand to her bodice to open it. His abstractedly searching fingers discovered no buttons, no zippers—she used straight pins to bind her clothing. He knew, but had forgotten. The Amishness of it struck him as it never had before. How separate she was from him. One by one he could remove each innocent pin, and bury himself in the heat of her innocent body. . . .

Despair had risen higher, shoving at his throat. He was never going to get close enough to her, not even through physical penetration. He was never going to know how to protect her enough. He had chosen all the wrong goals.

Too late, he understood. He wanted what he couldn't have. He wanted to be with her a lifetime.

His thoughts were in no way rational, but even then, far inside, he knew he had made mistakes there would be no way of righting. He had done her terrible intrinsic damage, something he could never wash away or heal, or even palliate. It gave him strength to pull himself away from her, to sit up nearby, facing slightly away, his knee up, one arm straight to the ground, the other balanced on his kneecap. His pulse ran with fury, questioning the decision. Fresh shudders began in his spine, radiating outward, making his shoulders ache, forcing his lungs hard against his rib cage. Shock set in, a kind of resounding surprise with himself that after everything, after all this time, he would not carry her this last step. The reawakened life inside him was like a stranger he was meeting for the first time. Why couldn't he have foreseen this moment?

In time he completed the painful process of bringing himself under control, and when it was done, he could look at her again. She had drawn herself together, her knees up and close to her body, with her skirts organized to cover them, her arms tight around her shins. She looked small and battered, like a sick wren ruffled into its feathers. His heart seemed to leave his body.

"Love, what's going to happen to you?"

"Apparently not what I thought." She was trying to sound brave.

"Susan—"

"When? What will happen to me when?"

"After the movie goes into general release."

"Oh."

"People will find out. Do you understand that? Even your people. Even Amish. They'll know you've been with us and that we've—that we've filmed you."

"Oh. Oh, then."

"You told me once that your community is very conservative, even for Amish. You've broken—what's the word?"

"*Ordnung?*"

"Yes. What will they do?"

She shrugged. A little smile passed over her mouth. "I'm too old for the buggy whip."

"What instead?"

"They'll think I was a pretty big dope, I guess. Maybe they'll say something like: 'What for did you do that, Susan? You're such a *schussel*. Do you have it so in the head? Your feet haven't touched the ground since the day you were born.' Something like that."

"Love, the truth."

She sighed. Her cheek dropped to her forearm. "Some I care for will be hurt. That I dread."

He dealt in a practical way with his increasing nausea, closing his eyes, correcting his internal balance, taking an iron hand to his biochemistry.

He heard her say, "Don't be so guilty. I wanted your money."

The room around him was redolent with her scent. It clung to his clothes, his hands, surrounding him. "I wish to God I'd just given it to you. You don't understand what it will be like. When you star in a movie, people become interested in you. Nice people, not-so-nice people . . ."

He opened his eyes again and saw she hadn't moved. The compulsion to take her in his arms was too powerful to be trusted, but he knew she needed to be touched. Moving closer, he stroked her hair slowly with his palm, every cell of him alive to detail, to the way each hair shaft swelled against his hand. Damp wisps on her brow brushed the side of his thumb. He removed his hand and said softly, "I apologize deeply to you for the defects in my conscience. Don't be afraid. I know it doesn't solve errors to compound them."

Her head lifted, and she stared at him curiously. "Don't be afraid. . . . And me like a jelly jar all set to go out of a canning bath, and here there isn't a strawberry left in the house . . ." She blushed, laughed painfully, briefly dipped her hot cheeks between her knees. He was forced to savage himself inside, to smother his violent yearning for her.

"What changed in your mind?" she asked.

She was hurting, he could see that. It made it much, much worse for him. "One night wouldn't be enough. I'm not sure that all the nights in my life would be enough. I know now that from the beginning I wanted more from you than—I can't believe I'm saying this—more than love-making. I'm so sorry. . . . Even in an amoral world, some people have to be exempt from pursuit. The sexually innocent, the sexually inexperienced—"

"Which am I, do you figure?"

Her *kapp* had fallen earlier. He picked it up, trailing the strings through his fingers. "For me to love you now would be . . ." All the wrong adjectives sprang to his mind. God, how he wanted to hold her. "Everything I've done with you has been wrong. Because of who you are. You see? You have to watch out for people like me in the world. There's a lot of bad out there. 'E-vil,' as they say on 'Dr. Who.'"

"Dr. *Who?*"

His smile burned the tense muscles in his jaw. "I can't have you. I can't. If I did, that would make me . . ." More inappropriate adjectives. "God knows. A sidewinding four-flusher."

"What's a four-flusher?"

"I don't know. Worse than a three-flusher."

"Twice as bad as a two-flusher."

For a moment, he listened to the night song from the window, the rhythm of her breath, the whisper of his heartbeat. He lifted her hand, found the streak on her palm where David had struck her, a faint smear like a grape stain. There he placed a kiss, with all the new, brilliant tenderness in his soul. "Poor little hand."

She had been watching his face closely. When he released her hand and began to stand up, she said, "What's the matter?"

"Headache. I get them."

"Then I'll pray for you. It will be better by the time you get home."

He smiled. In the doorway he stopped, facing her. He touched his heart, then extended his palms in a miming gesture, offering it to her. She extended her two palms in acceptance, drew them close, bending her head to place a kiss in the air above them.

But it wasn't until he was outside and alone that he said, "I love you."

Stepping from the car in the deserted garden near his room, he realized that his headache was gone. Puzzled, he looked into the sky. Windstrewn clouds stretched out under the stars. In one place they were rent, torn like woven fabric into a network of shimmering threads, with the moon immense and yellow as a jonquil behind.

Is something up there? He was not expecting an answer, and none came.

From his desk he phoned the cinematographer. "Max, can you go out and get me a shot of the moon?"

Pause. Then, "You want the moon, Alan?"

"I want the moon."

Chapter 17

*F*or once, she'd beaten Daniel out of bed. Most of the
night she'd been awake, sitting in the darkness on her
bedroom floor, gazing at the stars through her window,
wrapped in the quilt, her finger tracing the patterns of
stitchery, tulips in baskets, eight-pointed stars, hearts.

Sometime in the starlight she'd gone to the barn for
Daniel's old bicycle and ridden into town to the public
telephone by the slow-pitch park. Her skirts dark and
heavy with dew, her black shawl around her shoulders gave
her a pleasant feeling of freedom, one dark, invisible object
in an ocean of indifferent darkness. She tried to place a call
to Alan, picking out the numbers, as he'd coached her once.

Like most mechanical contrivances, the telephone was
touchy and erratic. She got Joan instead, groggy but
patient, diagnosing that the reason they couldn't hear each
other very well was that Susan was speaking into the
receiver. Susan hadn't realized it made any difference
which end she spoke into.

Joan explained that Alan wasn't there anyway; he'd
taken a late flight to Los Angeles, something to do with
soothing the investors. A story had appeared on a television news show that Alan and his star were coming to
blows on the set. He'd return soon, in a day or two. Less,
maybe. He'd probably call. Was there a message?

"Would you please tell him that I said I think he's only about a one-flusher?"

"Tell Alan about Juan Fletcher?" Joan sounded as if she were talking with her eyes closed. "Won flesher? Unflush her?"

"About a one-flusher."

"Oh. Got you. Right. Susan, is something going on? You sound like you're excited about something."

"It's going to be a beautiful morning, Joan. Fresh. I can feel it. The air feels like it was drawn from God's first breath."

"Susan, where are you? I'm coming to pick you up. You need to talk to someone."

"I've got someone to talk to. If I let loose of the earth, I could soar like a swallow. I'm fine. I feel . . . full up with myself."

"I think you've been full up with Alan."

"No. Remember."

After a murmur of bedclothes, Joan's voice came stronger, as if she'd sat up. "He's only about a one-flusher?"

"Yes. And now I think he knows it."

Back in her kitchen, Susan made oatmeal, doing everything without light, all by touch, sound, and memory, pretending she was sightless, like Grandmother, sharing the void.

She ate the oatmeal on her porch swing, one leg tucked under her, the other cold on the spongy dampness of the wood floor, setting the swing into motion when she felt the need to be rocked. The ceramic bowl was warm in her palm. She watched a horizon appear, lightening tones of gray from crepe-paper black. When it was pale light all around, she stretched, arching, greeting the day.

The back of the spoon was warm and sweet from oatmeal and brown sugar. She licked it, then rubbed it against her lips in circle after circle, thinking about Alan's mouth.

Her stomach got hot. She sat back down on the swing.

A cat jumped into her lap. Whiskers skimmed her arm. A tail flicked her earlobe.

Footsteps upstairs. Daniel was getting up.

She took off toward the barn, thinking to surprise him, as a joke, by getting started on things. Some steps she was running; others were flying skips over grass weighted to the ground with dew and slick stones. Passing the peony bush, she grabbed off one of the huge blowsy blossoms.

The barn door was open, clanking in the unpredictable rhythm of the breeze. She had left it hooked, the bike inside. And Daniel was upstairs. She stopped.

"Hello? Who's there?"

The dogs came milling around her, happy tails working the air like reed grass. They must have been out for an early gallop. Their panting droned under the early birdsong and the clamor from the barn, where the calves had begun to wake up and bawl. One-Ear, Daniel's old tomcat, arrived like a shadow to make her an offering of a field mouse, depositing it with finicky precision on her bare toes.

So normal. Yet she knew it was not. Instinct scratched a warning.

This was her home, a place of cordial spirits and rest, not omens and foreboding, and any one of a hundred friendly faces might await her inside. Why was the barn suddenly so full of menace?

She picked up One-Ear, stepping inside the vaulted blackness with the cat's purr thrumming through her chest.

The animals stared back at her, their eyes flickering spots in the dimness. Beyond them, she was alone.

Another spot glistened farther in, high, out of place. Coming closer, she saw that it was a piece of paper, no bigger than a dinner plate, curled in upon its shiny inner surface. It had been speared on the lantern hook with some force. The hook jutted like a tusk through a jagged, star-shaped rip.

"What is it?" She spoke aloud, hearing herself form the words in German. One-Ear twisted in her arms, impatient with being held. She released the cat and unhooked the paper.

A photograph. A girl's photograph. Across the print in rough capital letters was scrawled a word.

Standing near the window, she watched the dull silver light make the image plain.

The girl's dark hair was curled, her dress in the

antique English style. Her expression was sober. That expression—they'd had to work some for that. Alan's voice came back to her: *Susan, don't smile for this one . . . just let your mouth relax. Okay, it's coming. Susan, give me this with your mouth, like this . . . That's it. Nice. God, that's nice.*

The girl in the photograph was herself.

And the single scrawled word was ADULTERESS.

Sadly she said, "Oh, boy."

In the farthest corner of the haymow she hid, clasping the picture, holding the peony to her face, the petals growing wetter and wetter.

Though she was perfectly silent, Daniel found her. He knew her places and he knew her ways, how she could be outflung one moment, throwing herself to the world, and the next be drawn in like a flower that folds itself back into a bud when the sky grows storm clouds.

Cold and desolate, she was crouched under a straw stack. Descending draperies of light came through the cracks in the barn walls in layer upon layer, and behind the many transparent folds she seemed to have no more substance than a spirit. Seeing her there, he had a stray memory of Rachel; once he had found a secret book of hers, by an English philosopher, and when he asked her what it said, she had thought it over and replied, "It says that God is a sadist."

He wondered if Susan knew the word. When he wiped her face with his hand, bruised petals clung like wet feathers to his fingers. He held her face.

"You saw Alan's car last night," she said.

"And the light from the window. I waited in the barn."

She nodded, her eyes helpless. "I thought you must have. You came in so soon after he left."

"I should have brought the shotgun."

"That would have been something." She slid her arms around his chest and laid her head down there. "It wasn't needed."

"I know. Or he wouldn't have left you so early."

She twined her fingers in his, getting his smeared by

the moisture as well. "If you get after Alan with the shotgun, I suppose I'd better get after Joan too."

"Do you mean because I had her out for a buggy ride, showing her around last week Wednesday?"

"Last week Wednesday, last week Friday . . . She must be shown around so good by now, she has the county memorized. What do you do when you're together?"

"Mostly be surprised we don't run out of things to talk about. Susan?" He felt her brace herself because of his tone of voice. "I had to tell Luke and Anna that you were in the movie."

"Oh, Daniel, no. I wanted them to know last, so they wouldn't have to lie."

"I didn't have any choice. They were going to come into Greyling and bring you lunch for a surprise with Mother yesterday. I had to tell them so they could help me keep her away. The two of them took it pretty well. You'd be surprised. It made them feel important to be told. You know how kids are, prone to admire anything involving risk. Luke said that he thought Dad and Mother would be secretly relieved that Rachel had money, even if they could never admit it."

She squeezed his hand and relaxed against him. "You know what?" she asked. "These are the only times I feel safe."

His throat hurt with the force of his frustration. "Why don't you let me help you more?"

"Too much needs doing. Too many bits and pieces."

"Piece by piece, I'll help you."

"No one can help. It's come to be like a rock high up on a mountain that's begun to roll. Nothing can stop it, and it's just going to roll until it rolls itself out."

Was this how it would be? he wondered. You grow up, then older, and watch the people you love slipping away like wind taking the topsoil.

Regaining her poise took a long time, but she allowed it to happen as it would in its natural span. Later she washed her face in the cold creek water, holding her head under as long as her lungs would stand it, the ribbons of her *kapp* stretching in the drift of the current. She let the sun dry her skin.

Alive again, she walked around the long way to visit Fanny and Christ. The breeze picked at her hair and drove the clouds in fast fleecy herds through a bluebell sky.

Passing the home of Seth's father, she saw he had the grandchildren for a visit, running here and there, playing Red Rover. She hunkered down to talk to tiny Abraham, who was sitting with his legs apart in a bare spot near the road, spooning dirt on his trousers with elaborate care. When Seth appeared from the house she smiled and waved.

Seth ignored her, frowning at his nephew. "What have you done to yourself? Your mother has better things to do than wash your clothes. Go on in now and get a fresh trouser. We're going to visit Auntie Wilma." Setting the toddler on his feet, he sent him off toward the house with a kindly scoot.

When Seth looked grave, it was her habit to tease him out of it. "Not too long back, I remember there were days when you looked about the same. Like a dusty little shake rag."

His glance was as clear and cold as autumn rainwater. "It's no surprise to me you'd like to see a child at play in the dirt. You do it yourself."

It felt as if a fleeting cloud were crossing the sun. The world turned darker. "Best you don't talk so loud when you want to spread hate, Seth. You don't want to give Satan too much of a voice."

"And you, Susan? You've given him your whole body."

Today, she thought as she turned from Seth and walked quickly away. *It will happen today*.

But Fanny and her husband, Christ, were, as ever, happy to see her, with no trace of distance in their manner. There were new puppies from the setter to show her. Fanny was talking about the twelve quarts of sausage she'd canned with her pressure cooker.

Christ had the carriage in for work on the brakes, so they rode in the smaller open buggy to visit the Raders, happily snug together, Fanny on Christ's lap while he watched the road and handled the reins, Susan holding

Jesse and Lizbeth, while Sadie and Jonas trailed behind on their Shetland ponies. Christ had to joke about how it was just like when they were all courting, and to Susan that time seemed like yesterday—Christ, with his yellow duck's-down hair and eyes ripe with merry devils; John, sun-browned, making plans. How much running around had they done crammed tight together on the narrow seat, cozy and excited? The boys liked to drive down by the dam to look for berries, they said, but the truth was that they wanted to smooch, until the township put up a sign that read "No Parking" and, below that, "No Buggies."

Time passed pleasantly at the Raders'. Susan was pretending nothing had happened that morning. Acting.

Then they were on the way home and a family of English tourists taking pictures of the rolling scenery turned to aim their camera at the buggy. Christ put his hat between himself and the camera, Fanny put her two hands like a shield to block her face, and Susan realized she had no impulse anymore to protect herself from cameras. But no one noticed. Christ flipped his hat back on and said it had been as bad as Pennsylvania around here lately; he'd be glad when the movie company left and there weren't so many English tourists coming around trying to have a look.

They had a good rousing sing the rest of the way home, timed to the percussion of hoofbeats. More than ever, Susan valued what she had, the fresh air, the friends, the belonging. She tried to cling to each minute, to understand its perfection.

They let her down at her parents' farm, waving broadly as they drove away.

The house was quiet. Leaves bobbed in the breeze, painting the grass with dancing shadows. Four cats made plump mounds where they slept on the sunny porch rail. There was no one in the yard, no sound from the barn, no one visiting except Daniel. His buggy stood near the house.

But something separated this quiet from the reverent peace she'd always known of the long afternoons on off-Sundays when there was no Church. On this nice day, there should have been children outside in their Sunday clothes sitting on a blanket cracking nuts or pushing each other in the tire swing. Someone should have heard the buggy and be calling to her from the window. The empty yard looked desolate.

They know, she thought. Her legs refused to function, and then they carried her forward quickly, her heart battering at the walls of her chest.

Lady, the retriever, was scratching by the kitchen door, unusual behavior in an outside dog. She hadn't been quite right since Rachel left. She'd been Rachel's purebred dog, a gift from Seth so extravagant that Susan could remember her parents thinking over for a few days whether or not Rachel would be allowed to accept it. Rachel had never trained her, just loved her up, and when Rachel did her chores, Lady used to follow her, never underfoot, faithful, a beautiful, silent golden wraith.

As Susan approached the door, Lady turned, agitation in her eyes, tail wagging wildly.

Rachel's dog. Rachel.

She tore open the screen door, calling out, "Mother? Grandma?" to an empty kitchen. Tasks had been left half-done. On the stove a pot had cooked dry. She took it off the heat.

Voices drew her to the living room.

Her family clustered there, bleak disbelief in their faces, making them look like bewildered survivors of a calamity. Some were missing, out visiting, but her mother was here, flour dusting her chin, her hands twisted in her apron, her eyes blighted and longing. Grandma was in her rocking chair, with the square of a handkerchief pressed to her cheek. Behind her stood Aunt Mary and Luke, both of them hiding sensitivity under hunched shoulders, Luke glancing in a strained way at Daniel, searching for cues. The open window backlit her older brother. He held his hat loosely, turning it around and around by the brim, his face still; his deep, field-work tan the color of fine wood, all lines clean and clear, his eyes watchful, angry, loving them all.

Most pitiful were the children, Anna and Carolyn, their lips trembling, Norman's face pink and puckered from crying, Katie pulling at her mother's skirts for attention.

Only on two faces was there certainty. As in the deadly calm within a hurricane, her father stood like an aged and wrathful Moses, facing the lone child he said he had severed thoroughly from his heart. And here was Rachel, eerily present like one who had died and been reborn, re-formed in another incarnation. Too painfully familiar was the thorny dignity, the sense of great leashed emotions; too shocking was the alteration in her appearance. She wore English garments, a red dress with a woman's black suit jacket over it. The hair that had hung past her knees, that Susan had so often washed for her, was cropped short, English-style, so that she looked like a shorn lamb. It made her eyes larger, her face thinner, more worn.

Rachel's gaze lifted, hit hers, held there, gripped like a vise before slipping away to become part of a rueful smile, a slow headshake. Susan moved like a sleepwalker to that lonely soul, put her arms around her, and pulled her close. She felt as if she were choking on her own breath.

"Enough!" Rarely as her father raised his voice, it fell around them like a thunderclap. "Is that why you came today? To make like a wedge in this family?"

The words were for Rachel. He wouldn't say her name aloud. Rachel's back became rock-hard; her arm muscles quivered. She drew away from Susan in a strong movement, as though she were abandoning a weakness.

She pulled a book from a black clutch purse. "This is mine. I would like you please to read it."

"So. This is how you are, coming to us swollen in your pride, showing off this thing you have done."

She held it out, her calm beginning pathetically to slip. "This is me. This is my body."

He made no move to take it. She set it on a bench, and made her back straight again. Her eyes fogged. "I love you."

"I've learned real good about your kind of love. Sometimes I wake up at night and hear your mother crying for you in her sleep. Where is your love then? For one year the little ones ask for you again and again, the little ones, who don't understand what you've done. You should have been here to see their hurt. Is that love, that brings such hurt? You left Seth like a man with a snake in his belly."

"Should I have married him and spent the rest of my life with a snake in mine?"

"Who was it picked Seth? You chose, not me." His hand slashed the empty air, an impotent reflex. "You didn't leave because of Seth. You left for this—" he sought the word, his palm savagely indicting the book, "this pride. You say you love. I think it's yourself you love."

The effort at control had drained color from her cheeks. "Dad, why is it that you won't ever let me explain things to you? Maybe if I did, you could understand—"

"What could I understand? Right now I understand already. Before from you I've heard this explanation. Here you can't thrive. You don't fit. You have to go out there, in the world. This I don't want to listen to again. What kind of talk is this: I should live this way, I should live that way? Who are you to say how you should live? Are you smarter than God?" He took the German Bible from the mantel, his hands clumsy in his rage. "Here's what God has written about how you should live: 'Be not unequally yoked with unbelievers. Love not the world, neither the things that are in the world. If any man love the world, the love of the Father is not in him.' That's the kind of talk I want to hear in this house. That's the only kind of talk I want to hear in front of my family."

It had become too hurtful to look at her father. Instead Susan stared at the hat in Daniel's hands, seeing that it had gone still.

"Dad, it wasn't easy for her to come," Daniel said. "She didn't have to. Can't you give her anything back?"

Susan looked up. The face of each person in the room was too ravaged to look at. Staring fixedly at the floorboards, she didn't see her father grab Rachel's book from the bench and hurl it through the open window. Flying pages smacked the air like the helpless, flapping wings of an injured bird.

"It is for the father to govern the son. Never for the son to govern the father." Her father's voice belonged to an ill man. His blunt shadow fell across Rachel's feet. "No more bending. You understand? First I bent when you were reading a book instead of doing your chores. I knew where you were, yes, up alone in the attic. But I thought, what harm can there be? I bent when you sent your stories to those magazines, press of this, press of that, English publishers. You think I didn't know why you were restless before the postman came, why you were first to the mailbox? I turned my head away from how you were so clever. I took pride in it. It was my pride, my sin. I think how you have a wonderful gift. But I was wrong. It was a temptation. Mine. Yours."

Susan's gaze traveled upward. She watched her father's rough hands fasten on Rachel's upper arms. He was looking at Rachel as he would have looked into a cradle. "Whatever it is that you think you've discovered, it could never be so great that it would be worth throwing away your hope of salvation."

A flush had begun to streak Rachel's cheeks like slap marks. "Maybe some of the things you think come from the Devil come from God."

His arms fell to his sides. Rachel stepped back, hesitated before speaking again. "And maybe some of the things you think come from God come from the Devil."

He half-turned from her then and spoke to the window, his face as empty and leached as the sun-washed pane. "We have no welcome for you in this home. If you are hungry, you may eat alone in the basement. If you have no roof, a bed will be brought for you there. But no member of this household will keep company with you. To me you are dead."

As much as he, she had become immobile, clinging to the tattered cloth of her defiance, making it a shield. Then, with no warning, the facade broke. "Dad," she whispered, and like spilling water she put herself against her father's chest, her pale knuckles on his coat, her posture crumpled, her face hidden in his shirt. Her short hair caught like dark satin threads in the bristles of his beard. Open-eyed, he watched the window. His body gave her nothing, the chill of winter, a stone.

In the end, she did what was necessary herself. Humiliation in her eyes, she made herself separate from him, straightened, picked up the clutch purse. She spoke to her father's profile.

"Unless someone stops me, I intend to kiss the rest of you good-bye."

She put her arms around her mother's stiff form, kissed the unmoving cheek. Equally brief, equally soft, her parched lips touched Anna, Luke, Carolyn, and brushed like raw cotton on Susan's cheek. Aunt Mary rebuffed her with a turned head. Grandmother received her into her arms, taking the burden of the shorn head on one delicate shoulder, rocking her to the same slow rhythm they had each learned as infants. Then, moving half-blindly, Rachel knelt before Norman and Katie. Their unformed baby faces were slippery with tears, a pair of tiny blemished Hummels.

"Don't you remember me, Normie?" She put out her hand to stroke his, but he pulled back, his sobs keening. Katie tried to run, and fell backward in her skirts, yelling in fear.

After everything, Rachel could not seem to take this last, grim rejection. She had been at both their births. She stayed as she was until Daniel came, his hands on her as they might have been on a newborn life, telling her to come, he would drive her back in to the bus. They left, Daniel taking her through the front door, the door that company used.

Stress spun through the room, worse now, a desolate web-work of consequences. Her father remained in wordless communication with the window, his arms rigid at his sides. Then, flat-voiced, he said, "There's cows need milking," and stalked out. Susan's mother watched him pass, her eyes darkening over the last spark of hope. The kitchen door slammed.

Susan rushed to the window. There was only one sensible path from house to barn: along the cement walk, through the white picket gate, across the gravel yard, where Rachel was climbing into the buggy. In long, unshaken strides, her father followed that path, coming within feet of Rachel, but not once did he look toward her.

Their mother fled the room. Luke was sitting, his hat dipped forward on his brow, staring hard at his fingers. Anna was holding Katie—they were a skein of wool, wound together. The others were the same as when she'd entered, bereft, in postures of barren formality.

"Susan?" Grandmother was standing. "I'd like to have that book. Will you get it for me?"

"Yes." Her hoarse voice made only a fragment of the syllable.

Outside the sun struck her, made her cold, and she

realized she had been sweating lightly. If there was mercy anywhere in the situation, it was that the buggy was gone, with Lady frantically chasing behind.

The book had landed on its back in the grass, the pages open and tumbling in the breeze. She heard her sister's words in her mind, *This is my body*, and lifted it with care, squeezing it to her chest.

At once, all the bitterness in the world seemed to coalesce inside her, the anger she had kept in and kept down, the urgency about her sister's life she had tried foolishly to solve with money.

"It doesn't have to be this way," she heard her own voice ring out.

He would read the book or word by word she would read it to him. Scorched in hatred, she ran toward the barn, after the flinty tyrant who had stopped listening far too soon.

Soft sounds halted her at the threshold. She stepped inside quietly. Herbal scents assailed her, with the chitter of sparrows in the eaves, the peaceful blurred light. Her father sat on a hay bale, his back bent, his broad shoulders bowed, elbows on his knees, his face in his hands, his fingers spread like stars. And he was weeping.

Chapter 18

*I*n the past twenty-four hours, Alan Wilde had sustained eight hours of meetings, interviews with two major news magazines, a network morning news show, and a late-night talk show that was taped in the afternoon. Having assured the continental United States that he and David had never been closer, he planted careful seeds to awaken box-office interest in the film, and sidestepped questions about whether the unknown local girl he had hired to replace Carrie was really Amish. Up to his neck with production and self-discovery in Wisconsin, he'd had no idea how widespread the rumor had become. It was only a matter of time before someone pursued it seriously.

Wedged in between, there had been briefings on the movie he'd done before this, the movie he planned to do next, an appointment with his lawyer, another with his manager, drinks with an old lover he accidentally called Susan. So much for picking up the threads of a former life.

If every day had a theme, today's was the evil attendant on having one's name appear on a best-dressed list.

"Sexy Alan Wilde, the khan of horror films, is forever haunting. His style is loose and artsy, and he carries casual chic to its spine-tingling nadir. From his scuffed docksiders to his breeze-weight linen pullovers, he drapes his thoroughbred lines in a gorgeous mongrel assortment, looking both pulled together and pulled at random from his drawers. And we'd love to have a chance at those drawers." Plenty there to live down.

He arrived back in Wisconsin tired of himself, exhausted by triviality, tense from the effort of projecting blasé good nature about a subject that embarrassed him. He spent some time in the producer's room, explaining the trip to Ben, David, Dash, the others, watched himself as the laid-back director on a late-night talk show, drank a brandy, and retired gracefully to his suite.

Someone had aired the large front room. It was full of garden smells and moonlight. He flipped on the light, killing the romance of it, walked into the semidarkness of the bedroom and opened the closet door, flung in his jacket, closed it.

His mind froze on a picture of Susan, huddled on his closet floor, arms wrapped around her knees.

His thoughts often conjured Susan. It took a second to distinguish the reality from a wishful thought. Light-headed, he opened the door again.

She was there. The jacket had landed full on her, draping her chest and shoulders. Above, her eyes shone like a doe's, startled, twilit.

He had prepared himself carefully for the moment when he would see her again, though he hadn't expected it to come by surprise, at a time when he was tired and low on resources. He must do this right. He took a breath and steadied himself.

"Good thing it wasn't my suitcase."

"I'm sorry," she said. "I heard someone outside and I thought it might be the cleaning woman coming back." Her tone was surprisingly prosaic. She started to get up. He backed away from her and turned on one of the bedroom lamps.

"Has something happened?" he said.

"Something happens all the time." She was putting her arms through the sleeves of his jacket, cocooning herself in the soft gray leather, not zipping it, drawing it tight around her. The satin lining must have contained the heat of his body as it slid against her skin; his warmth upon hers. He felt with panic the delicious response that thought gave him.

She went to the lamp he'd just put on, studying it, then put it out, staring at it as if it were a miracle. In the other room she did the same, her gaze rapt, amused by the game.

In front of one of the long windows was a silver branch of candles, never used, and she lit them. Tiny flames appeared like golden cherries reflected below her face in the window glass, making one bright strand across her breasts. Her reflected gaze lifted into his. "I hope you don't mind. The electric light hurts my eyes." She became motionless in that way she had. "You know why I've come?"

It was worse than he'd imagined, a thousand times worse, his mind a cacophony of trip-hammering emotion. Gently he said, "I know."

"But it doesn't please you." She turned.

He looked, not at her, but at her reflected back, at the flame beads strung from arm to arm, wreathing her like a chain. "It isn't a matter of what pleases me." His heart was in his smile. He could feel it. "But you have to go home just now. I'll call someone to drive you."

She rocked up on her toes, and back down. "Will you call someone to carry me out too?"

His gaze snapped to her fine-boned features, and this time he saw clearly what he'd missed in the smog of his fatigue and shock. She was dedicated. Like an apostle, she had consecrated herself to this night with him. Chills became steel threads in his nerves.

"Why are you doing this?"

Her hands moved impatiently, swathing herself more tightly in his jacket. "Don't try to figure things out. It's no good doing that. You can figure everything out just perfectly and things happen anyway."

"What's been happening to you that I don't know about?" His voice matched hers in softness and intensity. "Who's been cruel to you—besides me?"

She withdrew deeper into the jacket, as if she were cold, considering him. A sudden smile swept over her face. She lifted her hands to the heavy coil of hair under her *kapp* and one by one pulled at the pins, dropping them on the Oriental carpet.

He felt the blood rise in his cheeks. "Susan—don't do this."

She kept on. "Help me."

Her youth and optimism were enough to break his heart. Her wildness was a siren's voice. He went to the wall and flipped on a light, to a lamp and snapped on another. It was a mistake. Fuller light detailed her face in its innocent hunger, detailed the tender roundness of her breasts pushing against her gown where his jacket swung open.

Pouring himself Scotch, he stopped asking of himself that he do this right—*Lord, only let me do it at all*. His will was drifting from him like sand in an hourglass.

"You have to leave. It's that simple."

She tossed down another hairpin.

"Amish, don't force me to say things that will hurt you."

This time she tossed the hairpin at him. It landed near his foot. "Go ahead." Her smile cut to the depths of him. "Let's see how you do. Hurt me."

The level of her incaution frightened him.

"All this has been a fantasy for both of us," he said. "You were curious. I used your curiosity. That's all you and I ever were to each other. That was our history. This is the time to end it. Now. So we can part friends."

She ripped out a hairpin and chucked it through the bedroom door. Every nerve in his body felt as if it were beginning to fray.

"Susan, every qualm you had about me in the beginning was correct. I stripped each one of those qualms from you deliberately. I became what you wanted. I do that—I change. There are a hundred different people in me. And not one of them is good for you."

"You know what? You start with the wrong assumptions." She passed her finger through the yellow spear of a candle flame. "Did you see? It's fire. But I haven't been burned."

"Hold it there a minute or two and you might change your mind."

Defiant, fluent with the power of her own inventiveness, her small figure dramatic against the vast black gleam of the window, of the goblin blackness beyond, she moved to obey him.

Stress brought him half out of his chair. "That's enough, damn it. The point of the exercise is to spare you the lesson."

A smooth undulation of her shoulders sent the gray jacket slithering to her feet. Hypnotic as the flame, she released the final hairpin. In the astral darkness of the glass, he saw her hair tumble, uncoiling in a shining spiral until it caressed, through her skirt, the back of her thighs. He tried to think. Nothing came. Disorder. Nothing lived beyond the ravaged plane of his desire and his need to harbor her from it.

"You have to leave, Susan. I didn't want to tell you, but you haven't left me any choice. This afternoon in Los Angeles I met an old friend, a woman I was very close to once. She's coming in tonight on a late flight. She'll be here in about an hour."

She had no reaction, except that the dark, splendid eyes opened wide in thought. "I wonder what that means."

"It means that you have to go home. Unless you want to try being three in a bed." Less weary, he would have known better. There could have been no worse choice. This was Susan, uncorrupted, clear-sighted. She stared. She stepped back. She fought for control. Her control gave way, and mirth sprang into her eyes, making them like jewels. She began to laugh out loud, the music of it merry, chiding, shocked, gemmed with relief. Breathless, she collapsed on her knees among the scattered hairpins, dragging the soft jacket around her rib cage. When her eyes became clear enough, she saw that he'd propped his elbow on the chair arm, his brow resting in his hand.

"I lie well," he said.

"I know," she said kindly. *But you're no good at being crude*, she thought. *You'd never bring another woman here when you had nothing to give her.* Recovering from the laughter, she was no less breathless. Her smile felt as if it were becoming permanent. "Now you've got me curious. Have you really been three in a bed?"

He didn't move. "I've had to put up in some crowded hotels." After a pause, "If I told you I had, would that make you go?"

"No. If this is the best you can do for a display of vices . . . I can't for the life of me think what there is for a third person to do."

His observant blue-green gaze rose to meet hers, and took on the faintest edge of amusement.

Am I breaking through to him? She wondered. What must I do? Must I undress for him? This was hard for her, almost too hard, to offer herself this way. If there were subtler ways, she didn't know them. And, because the force of his will was so strong, subtler ways might not have succeeded. Inside she felt like broken china and soap bubbles, and jumpy from the explicit voice within her that demanded she give herself to him, the voice she had gone beyond knowing how to control. Only her unrelenting need for the comfort of his words and his body could have brought her this far. If she paused to think about how she was acting, her nerve would falter.

She stood and picked out a distraction at random, a machine on a table by the wall, one of those many sleek boxes of various functions English people filled their rooms with.

"Is that a computer?" she asked. "Why are you smiling?"

"Whenever you see an electronic appliance, you ask if it's a computer. It's a stereo."

"Stereo?"

"A record player."

He apparently decided her nod betokened recognition, because he added, "Try it. It's one of our more harmless inventions, I promise. Touch the button on the far left."

She saw with amusement that the button was marked "power." Not "on-off." "Power." So typical that they would have boxes with buttons called "power." She pressed. The box came alive with red and green lights.

"Oh. Very pretty." She looked for a way to turn it off.

"There's more to it. If you lift the cover of the turntable—to the right. That's it. Is there a record on it? The black disc. All right. You see the s-shaped metal arm?" She pointed. "That's it. Lift up the end nearest you and set it on the disc. Anywhere. It doesn't matter."

The disc began to rotate, the shiny black lines orbiting a silver center. She watched it politely, nodding. "It's nice. But wouldn't it get a little tiresome after a while?"

"Without the volume, yes. Try it with sound. The dial on the amplifier—the other thing."

Reared apart from volts and current and the vagaries of wattage, she approached the volume without hesitation. Like an infant, she immediately flipped the volume three hundred and sixty degrees. Sound attacked her from the wall, excruciating, roaring, undifferentiated noise. She shot back, helplessly trying to protect her ears. As quickly as he moved, it was an eternity of agony before he brought the room back to silence.

She forced a flickering smile and slapped her forehead. "Susan Peachey, that's a poor thing you've got for a brain."

"I thought it was harmless," he said. His hands came gently to enclose the sides of her face, his fingertips skimming the outer rim of her ear, and in that touch there was more sweetness than she could have explained in a lifetime. He had briefly forgotten his intention to send her away, that she could see. She became caught up in his eyes, the color of them clean and transparent. His thumbs lightly followed the crescents of her cheekbones.

Suddenly his hands left her. He crossed the room to the piano and pressed his fists on the lacquered hardwood, one knee slightly flexed, his shoulders taut with strain. In each tract of long, graceful muscle she could see the sharp effort at control.

"Please go, Susan," he said. "Please, little love."

She went to him, swathing his waist in her arms, rubbing her smile in the hollow of his spine. For a long time they stood so, she nestled to him, and at last the resistance shattered inside him and he began to accept that it would happen. He came with innocence, with gratitude, into the peculiar universe of peace and mystery they made together.

She sank against him, a slight erotic weight on the back of his thighs, her skirt enfolding his knees, her flat belly and breasts distracting sculpture against his back.

"What a warrior you are," he said.

"I was brought up to be that. Our ways aren't easy."

"I should make you go."

"Your shoulds. Your darned old shoulds."

He turned, taking hold of her upper arms, the heels of his palms moving in slow, shaken circles there.

"My darned old shoulds," he said, and drew her close.

"I know you're afraid I'll be hurt. I'd choose that over a lifetime of never knowing how it would feel to be a part of you. I need one warm hour to cling to."

"I need that too." One hand cradled her head, tucking her close; the other lovingly stroked her back. They stood that way, sharing the moment, the joy that they would be together. Holding each other was everything, unlike anything she'd experienced before him, unlike anything he'd experienced before her.

He made the box play, and sat with her on the carpet to listen, holding her from the back, closing her in the shelter of his thighs, his head on her shoulder, his lips soft upon the powdery warmth of her neck, his forearms crossed on her chest. Her hair fell in a swag of smooth filaments on his cheek and throat.

And the music . . . It came like something made on a late-spring afternoon, when the greens are at their richest, seen as they are at no other time of the day or year. Dulcet and stately, the notes came together like ribbons in the air. Among passages of spiraling tenderness, he turned her in his arms and placed his mouth very lightly on hers. He lifted his head. Close above her, she saw his face in a new way, eyes transformed by passion, the straight, dark lashes bright against his skin, the lines on either side of his face supple and smile-softened.

"Would you like to know how the music feels? I can show you."

Beside her at the piano, he took her hands, curving them over his, making from their four hands two. He began to play, the long, musician's fingers calling up sounds not of this world, carols to God. The pleasure of his fingers beneath her palms was heady, and she began to understand the startling strength there, the sensitivity, the subtle flex of bone and tendon, her hands floating as his above the keys, clad in rhythm and grandeur. He spoke to her in a language more perfect than words, more articulate, and they shared one vision, like a dreamer.

But then his hands left the keys and with the same sensitivity held her for his kiss. Cool and soft, their mouths moved against each other's, creating slight patterns, bolder patterns, silly, dizzy ones, their hands playful emissaries, sharing the wonder.

Rose-cheeked, breathless, she rode in his arms to his bed, covering his jaw in a mist of kisses, her hair flooding down his back. For the first time, they had set themselves free, to touch, to taste, to tumble like kittens. They didn't think to undress, to lie down. Happy and artless, he pulled her onto his lap, and she made a closed circle around his hips with her legs, awe whispering through her body at the joy of holding him so. Rocking together, they kissed until their breathing came in hard shocks, and then he laid her back in the magnificent halo of her hair and filled his mouth with the tip of her breast, his hand running up and down her sides.

Falling backward, he pulled her with him, spreading her over him, her hair toppling like a sparkling curtain around his head. Massaging, lifting the fragrant sliding mass, he dragged her mouth closer, kissing her to openness, to moisture, until her tongue was honeyed and seeking in his mouth. His hands stroked down her back, tracing the dip, rising on her buttocks, making kneading circles, drawing her skirt upward to follow the curve of her bare legs up, onto the pliant cotton of her underpants, under them, surrounding the warm flesh, sliding her against his hips.

She gasped, took a breath, murmuring, "I've wished for this, and wished . . ."

"If only I could have been there, inside those wishes."

Holding onto him with her gaze, she put her hands on her gown to unbind the pins. His hands covered hers, warm as mittens.

"No. Let me. Teach me how."

She touched, showed him, again, again, his hands gentle and intimate on her clothing, her flesh. He had seen her only in the concealing dress of her culture, in the Victorian film costuming. He hadn't seen her arms, her shoulders, the strong classic beauty of her legs, the way her skin drank light like the undercolor of a pearl, every inch of pale skin a revelation.

Beneath she wore a white petticoat in soft cotton, the curved neckline laced in a dainty hand-crocheted edging.

Kneeling before her as she knelt also, he ran his finger along it, feeling both pattern and skin. His fingers spread out on her rib cage, swept upward to cover her breasts, lifting them under the fabric, lightly squeezing, and he bent to kiss the soft cleft he had made. His lower lip caught the edging, and in one breath he tasted her skin, the texture of cotton, the clean, crisp, faintly spicy scent feeding his senses as flame. He looked up. "Your eyes shine like the cup of a poppy, and I'm so lost in them."

They kissed in lost ways, on their own path, as though this were a thing no one had taught them, that they had not experienced before. There was no one to be now. She had no cares. He had no identity except as her lover. They were too joy-filled to be proficient; too much in love to notice. She didn't care where she gave kisses or where she received them. It was enough to become shivery under the stroking of his mouth. She welcomed the harder strokes, the deeper ones, his tongue massaging her lips, filling her. She welcomed his hands on her, under her, his fingers hooked under the straps of her petticoat, drawing them lower, uncovering her shoulders for his mouth, his hair catching hers. No thought entered her mind to have him turn out the light. Eager as he, she opened his shirt, discovering how he was naked, how beautiful, how vulnerable, bone knit just so with hard muscle, rich, vibrant skin, satin in places.

Her own hands eased her petticoat lower until the edging was just below her breasts, tickling the uprise. Many pulses fluttered in her throat and chest; her respiration and his came in hectic, rapid sighs. A flush of love heat flared like a sun mark on his nose and cheeks, touching his eyes, making them brilliant, rapturous. So gently, his breath breaking often, he lifted her, lying her down on her back. His mouth dipped to her repeatedly, tasting and kissing the erect nipples, pink as the chalice of a shell. Her fair skin colored unevenly, in bright fever spots, and he followed them downward with his mouth, only that part of himself on her, and his hair, teasing her nipples, brushed the underside of her breasts, her belly, her thighs, starting tremors, cool on the hot places.

In the delirium of passion they spoke to each other,

incoherent, guileless words, half-sentences, elated phrases, the thoughts pouring out between gasping breaths.

"Susan, Susan, you have the sweetest skin . . . the *sweetest*, sweetest hair . . . wrap me in it . . . wrap me in you. I love you so much," he whispered. "I love you so much. . . ." Slowly, slowly, by exquisite half-inches, blindly euphoric, he sank himself into her body.

He could hardly see her. She was wreathed in star points, her hair limned in silver light, and he wanted only to be one being with her, surrounding her, surrounded by her. *How deep can I get inside you?* he wondered, and had no idea he'd said the words aloud, until the lustrously shimmering mouth below his curled up in a hazy smile.

Huskily she murmured, "This would be about it, I guess."

He gazed down at her, and then began to laugh, and so did she, the flutter of her breath, her muscles, sending pleasure shudders through him.

She brought the back of her hand to her cheek. "I'm so hot."

She was. Burning up, feverish. He touched his own face. "Me too." He kissed her soft, swollen mouth. On one final strand of breath he whispered, "I can't think what we're doing now. Could it be making love? It was love already."

He had come to her as one goes to Lourdes, expecting miracles. And in her, he found them. Trapped in a streaming universe of rapture, he watched her reach her summit. And when that moment came for him, it was so complete that he died in it and came back reborn.

"Hello, world," he whispered to the air.

It came slowly back to her: the warm, disturbed bedding beneath her, the shelter of her lover, his arms holding onto her hard, the bewitching tangle of their legs. His breath was soft in her hair, softer on her scalp. The backs of his fingers lay on her cheek.

He knew when her eyes opened. Her lashes stroked the side of his thumb. Leaning on his forearm, he pulled away to look down at her face. Her hair clung damply to her shoulders, spreading in a shimmering web-work that melted into the dense pool of her curls. Framed in the night shadows of her hair, in the black brows, her skin was very light, the few freckles across her nose standing out in an intense, creamy field, her lips wet, stung, the color of a tea rose. She was older than her years in some ways, in others much younger. It was the youth he saw now, so undefended it wrung his heart. Gazing into the tender depths of her eyes, he said again, "Hello, world."

He stroked her hair, his hand unsteady, continuing many minutes before he spoke gently. "Do you regret this, Amish?"

"No."

"If it were possible to die one more time, I would have done it if you'd said yes."

She laid her palm on his chest. "In my heart, you are my husband."

"You are my wife, my parent, my child..." He gathered her close, loving her so, and was silent, holding her.

Presently he tipped back her head and brushed her mouth with his, and then drew back to pass his fingertip over the distended fullness of her lips. She closed her eyes and parted her lips at his touch.

"Do you think we can set our hearts to beat together?" she whispered. "We can be like two clocks in time to each other, no matter what happens. Let's try."

He rubbed her breathtaking smile at the corners with his thumb. "It won't work; I'm already too fast."

"I'm fast too." She arched, her hands winnowed his hair, and her body aligned itself to his. She whispered, "Make me faster."

He had read once about fireflies in Thailand that gather in great numbers in trees upon a shoreline, spreading light like a galaxy. Thus was this night, with delight. For them, love was not an art, or a science, or even a feast of the senses. It was two souls coming home together at last.

It was much later that she lay in his arms, listening to his murmured love words, profoundly at peace. Candlelight draped the room in delicate shadows and gave their flushed skin the color of warm cider. The earth had a great quietude.

She felt him stir. His hands tightened around her. He put his cheek on her hair. *He's trying to figure things out again*, she thought. In time, he spoke.

"Is there a chance we could make them understand?" he asked.

"My 'them'?"

"Your 'them.'"

"No." A pause. "My dad's changed. It's not like it used to be when I was little. Used to be he'd put on his glasses in the evening and sit down with a storybook and read out loud to us—to Daniel and Rachel and me."

"What kind of storybooks?"

"The one about Pooh. I've told you about that, I guess. There was one about four sisters who called their mother Marmee. We thought that was so funny—'Marmee.' One of the sisters, Jo, wanted to be a writer. She was Rachel's favorite of the sisters...." Presently, "Another story that struck me particularly was *The Count of Monte Cristo*. Do you know of that one?"

"Yes."

"Dad and Daniel got so excited about that story that they ran out to the woods and picked up branches for a sword fight. We used to have more fun.... Another time Daniel told me about, when he and Rachel were too young for school yet, Dad took them to town with him to go by the feed store. That Saturday, musicians from the high school were playing in the band shell at the south park and Dad pretended to stop so that Rachel could swing, but Daniel says he could tell Dad just wanted to hear the music. After he said, 'Don't tell your mother we stayed. Such foolishness, she'll think.' Today if music were playing, Dad would drive right by, I'll bet. My younger brothers and sisters, they don't know that side of him."

"What made him change?"

"It's hard to say. Maybe getting older. There was another thing, too, a bad thing that happened...done to one of my family by English. After that, he wasn't so easy about English things."

With infinite tenderness, he stroked the side of her

face. "Your neighbor Ben told me that an Amish girl here was—I'm not sure what—beaten up, harassed, raped . . . during the Vietnam War."

A violent chill seized her fingers. "My sister Rachel."

He knew. Somehow he knew in the second's hesitation before she spoke. "Were you close to her?"

"Never. But we were entwined. Sometimes it was thorny between us."

He waited for her to speak again. When she didn't, he asked, "Who's Seth?"

"A neighbor."

"Is he in love with you?"

"I don't think so." Her hands were beginning to ache. A smile hovered, uncertain. She pressed her lips to his throat. "One auction and you're ready to write my biography."

He rolled on his side to touch her lips with his, not in a kiss, only the gentlest nestling, and then pulled back, loving her with his eyes, loving her, his heart aching with it. Then very softly, he said, "Have you had a child, Susan?"

"Yes." The word was a whisper, a depthless sorrow.

"You didn't tell me."

"I knew it would make you sad. You see, she couldn't live."

She had turned her head. His hand became unsteady against the soft flesh of her cheek. "You had a little girl?"

"Yes. She came early, and she had that . . . like the Kennedy baby. . . . So many early babies have . . ."

"Hyaline membrane disease?"

"That was it. They did what they could at the hospital, but she was just so small." Her face tensed, and she was hardly able to whisper, "Her tiny little hands were as small as acorns."

The air against his eyes became painful. He shut them, and enclosed her in his arms and didn't speak, because he could not. Many minutes passed before she drew away to look at him, and he smoothed back her hair and said, "I would like to write your biography. Everything from this moment on. My name on every page."

*   *   *

She dressed by touch in the predawn darkness, as she had done much of her life. He slept, and she didn't wake him. Partings were things she had learned to dislike.

Outside it was coming to be light, violet-gray, with a clean-swept feel. Chilly air bit her warm skin.

On the path home through the woods, she met Daniel. Unsmiling, he stood under a birch, stark in the graying light against the veins of white bark. She stopped twenty feet from him, jelly in her middle. He gazed back, silent.

"I'm not ashamed," she said.

She'd never seen his eyes look darker or more kind. He shook his head. "Do you think that's going to make a difference?"

"No. Nothing will make a difference."

"And what will you do when he leaves?"

She started to walk again, shivering under her shawl, looking down at the damp sponge of forest litter. "I'll remember him."

Chapter 19

Alan was facing the demolition of a lifetime's assumptions about love and romance. He needed a card reading, "Be Gentle: I'm Newborn." Daylight was painfully bright to his eyes. Colors exploded at him in new hues. His body seemed not to be bound by the law of gravity. His nerves were raw from the assault of sensation. From more than a hundred voices on the set, he could pick out hers at any second and center there.

No less meticulous about their work than they'd ever been, they met the complicated round of their daily obligations with concentration. But the real part of their lives was spent together, pretending time didn't exist. The force of their love felt like magic. Perhaps they were waiting for it to create magic, a waiting not acknowledged, never forgotten. She'd been reared to love, not to fall in love. He'd been reared to do neither. Surely there would be more miracles.

For her it was easier. She lived by the moment. He planned. He solved problems. That was what he did best, his raison d'être—or it had always been before. Here was the problem of problems, the Grand-Slam Problem of a Lifetime, and he was wandering around in it blind. *God, this was so fragile.* But solvable. It had to be solvable. Everything bent to logic—so Alan told himself again and again, by the half-minute.

Alone with each other, they were intoxicated, exultant. Kids prancing in the moonlight. Kittens with yarn. Crickets in the cool grass. She taught him German songs; he taught her English ones. They made up songs of their own. She told him Amish stories, he read her poetry; they wrote each other sonnets. They gave each other flowers, tucked them into each other's hair, lay for hours enfolded together, caressing each other through their clothes, whispering. For intimacy, they invented their own language, exotic and sublime, like the Latin name for a flower. Smiling, they let the hours unfold. There were so few of them now.

Time withheld the miracle. Someone handed Alan an itinerary his secretary had prepared. In three days he was to return to Los Angeles; a raft of appointments was listed for each of the following several days. He was stunned by the reality proclaimed by the itinerary, and that same afternoon, he filmed Susan for the last time. Afterward, in front of everyone, he said, "Susan, I'd like to see you for a minute." And he took her to his room, where they made love with desperation—damp, shivering, making each other wild, exhausted.

He drove her home in the middle of the night. Holding her close in the starry darkness in front of her house, he whispered, "You're part of me now." Then he left. Somehow he would solve it.

She didn't make it to the house. After the car lights faded, she collapsed in the sweet grass, her hands behind her head, and gazed up at the low-flying moon and the vast bead-point necklace of stars. Deliciously relaxed, suspended, she tugged a handful of grass and sprinkled it like sugar over her chest and face, her eyes closed, glorying in the ticklish flickers on her skin, throat, and cheeks, the pungent fragrance.

Brushing the grass from her face, she tried to re-create Alan's touch and imprint it in her mind. Her forearm dropped across her face, and she could catch the faint freshness of his scent on her skin. Heady memories tickled as though the blades of grass had slipped through her skin.

Gathering energy, she sat up, stood, and began walking toward the house. The lemony light behind a kitchen window and the scrape of a chair inside told her that Daniel was home, back from the cattle auction. The porch swing creaked under the stir of a subtle breeze. The night sounds chimed. This was her home, her place in creation, and when she opened the door, she looked forward to the soft light, the serenity, the simplicity.

Defilement hit her like an open fist. Urine and pig excrement made a cloud of suffocating odor. She flinched violently and choked.

"Daniel?"

Hogs were in her kitchen. Her voice made them riot. Bewildered, vicious with fright, snarling and squealing, their trotters slipped in the filth that covered the floor. They had rooted into the flour. Her own raspberry jam had been smashed on the floor, clotted and blood-red like a small animal had been torn apart.

She twisted away, her fist on her stomach.

These were strange animals, not hers, a boar, four sows. This was not an accident. This was hate. "Who has *done* this?" she gasped. Wilting inside like a poisoned reed, she watched the porch ceiling begin a slow reel. She clutched the doorframe for balance, holding up her body, though her soul was shrinking and withering. *Take this cup from me, oh Lord.*

It had begun. The paying. She shut her mouth on the nausea, the horror. She didn't hide her face until she found her bed filled with baby pigs.

In Anna's dream she was a child in a button-back dress. The aurora borealis filled the northern sky, a monumental haze in the shape of a giant ghostly sea gull, the wings slowly beating, stars showing through. Her sister Rachel watched it from the porch, closed up, as if it were carrying her a message. But Susan swung around and called out, "Quick, Anna! Get the others! You've the loudest voice!"

And then she was sixteen again, in her bed, with Daniel bending over her in the dark, his hair gleaming like a starling as he spoke hushed words.

"Dress right away and come outside. Don't wake the others."

When he took his hand from her mouth, she whispered, "Is this real?"

He said, yes, it was real. But it didn't seem real when she followed him to the other farm and found Susan being sick in the outhouse, and the house with the stench of a dirty barn. Help Susan clean it up, Daniel said. Hogs had got in the house. But if that was all, why did Susan hold onto Daniel's arm when he said he was off to check on the heifers in the back field, shaking her head, her eyes pleading? He left them, though, and soon after, Susan said, "I don't know what's going to happen, but I don't want you to see any more of this," rubbed her gently between the shoulder blades, and firmly sent her home.

Halfway there, she'd put it all together, and was back in a nightmare. Seth's name had been mentioned by Daniel, and Susan had gasped, "No." Daniel had gone to confront Seth. These terrible things to Susan . . . and she knew why! The sky landed with all its weight on her shoulders. When she was running again, it was toward Greyling.

She asked for Mr. Wilde at the high barred gate, dwarfed by it, alarmed at having to talk to the uniformed guard. How could Susan come here every day? Guards and uniforms always made her think about how it'd been in Europe, where secular princes sent out spies to capture and torture the righteous. They'd played that game when they were little, hiding secret notes under their clothes and inside baskets of baked goods, being imprisoned in the corncrib, going bravely to the pyre. Here she was, living the game, but it had twisted, as the dream had.

The guard talked to the telephone. She was given permission to enter when she explained she was Susan's sister, though no one knew where to find Mr. Wilde. They offered to drive her to the buildings, but she'd never been in an automobile before and she was afraid to try it, especially sitting beside a uniformed stranger. Armed with vague directions, she followed a long paved drive under electric lights that buzzed angrily and ruined her night vision, making what was beyond into a solid, formless black. She knew perfectly well the monster was only a man in a costume. In spite of that, the sick suspicion remained that it was here somewhere, crouched in a cavern strewn with bones.

She'd thought it all out, about moving pictures, staring at the picture of grazing cows on the barn calendar, trying to imagine how it would be if some part of it would start moving. It wasn't natural. It made her feel queasy. Out there, the world was getting stranger.

Tonight the movie people were having a party to celebrate reaching the end of their work here. Strings of tiny lights were twined in the maple branches. Laughter and music filled the paved gardens. For the first time she heard music without words. To her it sounded empty and cold.

No bacchanal, this party barely made it to PG13. Alan had been to many worse. When he saw Susan's little sister coming toward him with David's guiding hand on her back, he only thought, *What's happened?*

Willowy, tear runners on her creamy cheeks, Anna was ethereal in her distress, a shocking reminder of the innocent lives he'd accidentally trapped in his web. After several failed attempts to speak, she was able to gasp out,

"I couldn't go to my dad. He doesn't know about the movie. There wasn't anyone else..."

Then she told him, her words halting and quaint. In those few minutes, Alan understood at last that he had ruined Susan.

Alan was everything Anna had hoped: calm and kind, someone she could trust. He assured her he didn't think Daniel and Seth would kill each other, but he'd go and make sure. He'd do everything he could for Susan. He put his hands on her arms, squeezing a little, and her stomach did a flip-flop, the way it had last winter by the skating pond when Isaac, godlike at twenty-two, had taken up her hands, kissed her cold mouth, smiled, and said, "I've been trying to court you, silly." It was disconcerting to think this even more godlike being—and English, to boot—could do the same thing. But she was glad she'd come. There had to be a way to mend this. This was *Susan*. People would understand.

They found Seth and Daniel at Christ Yoder's farm, and, as Anna clambered from the car, what she saw wasn't understanding. Seth was up against the chicken house, brushing his forearm across his nose, his coat sleeve coming back slick with a line of blood. And Daniel, the sanest, the most insightful of men, had his jacket torn and covered with dust. He was advancing toward Seth, speaking harshly. Christ was standing in front of him, pushing hard on his chest.

There were others there too. Fanny stood by the fence in her nightdress and shawl, with a lantern at her feet, and others from the young folks—one of the Rader boys; Sol Whetstone, who was a best friend to Luke; and two of Susan's brothers-in-law, Dan and Isaac. Seeing them all made Anna realize that Seth couldn't have done it alone. Her old playmates and one budding love, friends she had trusted since infancy, had dealt her sweet, fanciful older sister an unforgivable blow. She sought the comfort of Alan's gentle grip, Alan, a man she barely knew.

Alan received her in his arms, and held her tight although he saw the Amish had frozen in the bright funnel of his headlights. They were staring at Anna with him, and it was clear that none of them liked the combination.

Handsome eyes alight, tawny in the lamplight, a young man stepped toward Alan. "You'd better take your hands off her. Anna—"

"Don't say my name!" Clasped in Alan's nerveless grip, Anna had become rigid. "Don't you stand there and say my name, Isaac! Were you with Seth in this?"

In love himself, Alan was sensitive to it in others. He saw it in the face before him. The tall boy was hating this moment, hating her pain, hating his own. He made no attempt to speak.

"There's my answer. You've made yourself nothing to me. Less than nothing. Never speak to me again. Never come up to my house." Increasingly frantic, Anna turned to the young woman by the lantern. "Fanny, have you heard what they did?"

"I heard about it. Left some of their relatives in Susan's house, then come here trying to spread more dirt. Well, they can go off with their nasty talk about Susan. We don't listen to such here." They were firm words, but Fanny's eyes were frightened, her voice shaking.

"You think I wanted to believe it?" Isaac walked closer, speaking to Anna. "Do you think I get joy from this? I've seen proof. I went with Seth to talk to the guards at Greyling and they sold us a photograph for ten dollars. Susan in the arms of a man, an actor, and her dressed in some kind of fancy"—a slow twist of his hand revealed the revulsion his words couldn't articulate—"*paint* on her face, her hair uncovered and curled . . ." He grabbed a breath, spoke through it. "That's the way she keeps my brother's memory."

"And this is how you keep it." Still jittery, Daniel had brought himself under control. "Don't put John's name behind your tricks. He never did a thing in his life but to love and honor her."

Isaac ripped a folded paper from his pocket, opened it, and thrust it into the hand of the bearded man, Christ, who'd been restraining Daniel. The man tried to shove it away, but Isaac grabbed his hand a second time and slapped the paper into it. Unwillingly, unhappily, the bearded man's eyes were drawn to the paper. It was a photograph of Susan, a large glossy, soaking up lantern light like Turkish copper.

Christ pushed back the photograph as if he couldn't wait to get it out of his hands. "Take it and get off my farm. We don't want your proof. For Susan to do this, she must have had a reason. I know what Susan is."

"You know what Susan was." Seth's voice was muted behind his forearm, applying pressure to his bleeding nose. "You don't know what she is."

Rage gave a white-hot edge to Alan's thoughts and feelings of pain, but he denied himself the relief of expression. Protecting Susan mattered. That was all. Rarely in his life had he raised his voice. He did not do so now. "You want me, not Susan."

He could see they found his presence among them so alien and embarrassing that they scarcely could acknowledge it. Preoccupied with their own misery, it was almost beyond them to deal with his connection with Susan. It was nothing they wanted to think about, or be conscious of.

"Don't blame her," Alan said. He caught Seth's gaze, held it without relenting. "She agreed to work for me without any real understanding of what I wanted her to do. Once she did understand, she held to her commitment because I wouldn't release her from it, and again, she didn't know how to make me."

They stared at him as though he were on the other side of a plate-glass window, as though they couldn't hear him or see him very well or didn't even care much about what he was saying.

"No. She wanted to do it. To give money to Rachel." Anna's wide-spaced, honest eyes focused on Seth, became rapt. "Susan didn't want Rachel to fail and have to come back to marry you. You violated Susan's house to get back at Rachel."

Naively she had chosen the weapon. In one stroke she had done the thing Daniel and Alan had been avoiding, each in his own way, by holding fiercely to the ragged edges of their self-control. Striking blindly, Anna had pushed Seth past the threshold.

"*He* violated your house. Your English friend." From the lantern came a gloaming shade of gold, marking highlights on Seth, glittering in his eyes. "Wilde used your sister for more than you know. He's had her for a whore."

Only Isaac had heard the accusation before. For the others, it was like being splattered with poison.

Anna stared at him. "You're a filthy, dirty liar, Seth Yoder," she shouted, "and you're going to hell for it. Just because he's her friend. Daniel—"

"Don't put out your hands to Daniel," Seth said tersely. "Your dear brother's laid his blessing on it. Ask him. Go on—ask him. No? Then you might ask Wilde...."

She swung back to Alan, trusting and fiery, confident of his denial, and he became blind to everything but her face. He heard Daniel's voice, low and neutral.

"There's nothing you can do, Mr. Wilde. Susan will be asked. She won't lie."

Seth's expression was savage. "Maybe he doesn't answer because we're not using his language. Ask him this way, Anna: 'Did you screw my sister?' Or try 'Did you fuck—'"

"Shut your filthy mouth in front of my wife," Christ yelled, then, "Wilde, no! No more here."

Magnified a thousand times, Alan reexperienced the emotion that had made him plant a fist in David Thorne's face. Christ's grip on Wilde's arms was anything but gentle.

"You're stupid, all of you," Seth said. "I know the English. Those are their words—in their books, every two minutes in their movies. That's how they think about women. That's the word you use, isn't it?"

Alan's answer was soft. "Never, *never* about Susan."

"You're no mystery to me, Wilde. I know how it is with men like you. You have woman after woman and despise us because we love God and choose one woman to care for until death, and raise how many children the Lord gives us."

His body weighted with rage, Alan shrugged out of Christ's slack grip. "You don't have to lecture me on the way you care for women. Down the road there's a young widow, and tonight she walked into a house you made into a sewer. And that's all I want to know about the way you 'care' for women." Seth's hat was laying in the dust. Wilde swept it up and said, "Here." He shoved it hard against the the younger man's chest. "You've done what you've set out to do. Go home."

The Amishman's hostile gaze remained steadily on his. "Time will have the last word," Seth said. "We'll see if she hurts longer from what I did to her . . . or from what you did to her." He stared at Alan another minute, then swung around, walked to his horse, and mounted.

Distantly, Alan was aware that Fanny's husband was ordering off the others.

Beside him Daniel was stroking his sister's hair. His other hand held and gently lifted her chin. "You should have done as I told you, Anna. I told you to stay with Susan, and you should have done that. I don't give orders often. When I do, you should listen. You didn't listen and you were hurt. Don't forget another time. Now I'm asking you to go on home." He placed his index finger over her mouth when she started to speak. "Listen now. When you get home, wake up Luke quietly and tell him. Then when Dad get up to milk, you and Luke meet him in the barn and say what happened here." Stilling a second protest, he said, "*Listen*. Tell him everything that happened tonight just as it happened. It would be bad if he found out you knew and kept it back. Tell him please not to come and see Susan. I'll bring her come morning. It's better he doesn't see her until he's had some time. . . ." He laid his hands on her cheeks and kissed her brow. "Go on."

He withdrew his hands and they came away glistening with her tears. She left quickly. Isaac had lingered. Achingly, he tried to touch her back, a gesture of compassion, but she flinched from him, and he didn't try again.

Alan realized he had been staring abstractedly at Daniel's hands. He heard himself say, "You're bleeding." He put his hand on Daniel's arm. The fabric was spongy with fresh blood.

"Daniel, you said it was nothing," Fanny said sharply, bringing the lantern.

"It is nothing. I have to get back to Susan."

"I'll go to Susan. You—" She'd uncovered the wound,

and sucked in her breath, appalled. "You get yourself to the doctor. This wants stitching." She looked up at Alan. "Would you take him? My son Jonas left the pitchfork out and Daniel fell on it while he was fighting with Seth."

Alan must have nodded. She looked away and moved to wrap the arm in a shawl.

"No." Daniel handed her his handkerchief. "Use this. You can go, Mr. Wilde. I have to get home. I'll go in later if it bothers me."

"So your uncle said, and lost his hand." Fanny was bent over Daniel's arm. "Christ, talk sense to him."

"Get yourself stitched." Christ held up the lantern, throwing light on the blood-saturated arm. "I'll milk for you. Fanny'll stand by Susan. We won't let anyone near her, don't worry."

Alan pulled open the passenger door of his car. When Fanny raised her face to him again, her eyes were so misted with unshed tears that she must have been hardly able to see him. Yet when she spoke, her gaze was direct and icy.

"You take him to the doctor and then home. And after that, don't come back. Ever."

She watched them leave, standing straight, but Alan saw her in the rearview mirror, a wisp of yellow in the oil light, going like a broken puppet into her husband's arms.

Beside him, Daniel stirred.

"Don't talk," Alan said. He still felt the stress in Anna's thin arms, saw Isaac's white, drawn mouth, the heartsick loyalty of Susan's friend Fanny, clasping her shawl with cold knuckles. And Susan's last smile when he'd left her . . . His worry for her was a barbarous emotion, tormenting him. He couldn't think. *Susan, Susan . . .*

He had to steady himself enough to drive; he shoved a tape in the cassette player. The car filled with Mozart. Miles passed. Daniel leaned forward, touching the speaker.

"That's very nice. Why do you like it?"

Alan stared at the twisting path created by the headlights. "It has purity, clarity, and order. And it's beautiful. I don't want to talk."

They passed slumbering farmyards, some lit by high

yard lamps that hung like yellow stars above the drowsy buildings.

Daniel rested his head against the seat. "I'm bleeding all over your car."

"Very appropriate."

"Sorry. I thought it was a safe subject."

"Dear God. Safe." Then, "For a couple of pacifists, you two did a fair job on each other. Why are you trying to make me talk?"

"You don't seem to breathe otherwise."

The headlights picked out a sign bedded in crisp fern fronds. "Caution: Horse-Drawn Vehicles." Alan slowed the car. Under his palms, the wheel felt slippery, as if it were melting. He remembered a dream he used to have, that he was in a car speeding somewhere, with a feeling of urgency, and then the dream showed him the car from outside and it was empty. He spoke. "You said she'll be asked. By whom?"

"My father. The Bishop. Maybe some of the ministers."

"They'll ask if she's been my lover?"

"Yes. And she'll say she has."

"Why wouldn't it work if I went to them first and took responsibility? If they knew she was intimidated— why doesn't that make a difference?"

"You aren't responsible to the community for your behavior. We don't attempt to punish outsiders, or convert them. You aren't accountable to the community, but Susan is. Anyway, she'll contradict your story."

"What if I told them I want to marry her?"

Daniel let out his breath in a soft sound and looked out the opaque shield of the window. "Put it out of your head."

"Why?"

"If she goes to your bed, that's a sin. She can be reclaimed from that. If she marries you—"

"What?"

"She's damned."

It was a long time before Alan spoke again.

"What did Anna mean when she said Susan did it for Rachel?"

"Rachel was excommunicated from the church, charged with heresy. She lives in Chicago. She writes and studies."

His hands became tighter on the wheel. It was something, at least, to hold on to. Daniel added, "Susan saw the money as security for Rachel."

"When that's known, will it help Susan?"

"No," Daniel said, grim.

They crossed a bridge framed in metal scaffolds, the tires plucking musical vibrations from the steel, trickling with little shocks through Alan's rigidly clenched sinews.

"Last weekend when Susan came to you, it was after Rachel was to visit my parents." Daniel was lower in the seat, his eyes closed. "Rachel didn't stay long. But it was painful."

When Alan spoke, the motion of air in his throat was agonizing. "Susan's sister—"

"Susan's twin."

After a pause, Daniel sat up and looked at him, then said gently, "Wilde, pull over and rest. It's all right."

He didn't respond to the directive. He hardly heard it. "Rachel is Susan's twin?"

"Not identical. The other kind."

"They're different?"

"Yes. But not as different as they think they are."

Condensation on the fences reflected pewtery starlight, streaking the night in sorrow. Very quietly Alan asked, "What will they do to Susan?"

"They, they." Daniel's mouth quirked into a brief smile. "Susan told me you say that."

"Consistency is my only virtue. What will they do to her?"

"You shouldn't know. It would be better."

"I love her. Tell me."

"To be forgiven, she'll have to go on her knees before the church and confess her sin with you."

For what remained of the ride, Daniel watched him. But he did not try again to make him talk.

Chapter 20

A deep prairie sunrise spread over a field of hay. Before it, Susan's house looked small and rugged, every window open wide, sucking in the warming air. To one side, Susan's grandmother was hanging out wash as a barefoot child in a lilac dress handed her things. The sheets snapped and settled in the breeze, throwing off faint bleachy whiffs.

The car's wood paneling and leather upholstery were stained with Daniel's blood. Earlier, climbing out of the car in front of the small town hospital, they'd seen the mess for the first time. Punchy, distraught, they'd both laughed until they'd made themselves light-headed. Now, watching Daniel walk toward his grandmother, Alan tried to remember why it had been funny.

Daniel spent several minutes with her and returned. "Christ brought Grandma over. She's sent the others away. There's coffee and jelly bread inside. You should come in and have some."

Alan shook his head. "Where's Susan?"

"In the barn, up in the mow. She likes to go up there. Carolyn went to check on her a few minutes ago, and she had gone to sleep."

After a tense pause, Alan got out of the car and began to walk toward the barn. Behind him, Daniel said, "Be careful what you do. That was what people in the olden days used to call torture—pulling people in different directions."

She slept among the hillocks of hay fair skin and dark hair against a cardinal-red wool quilt.

For a long while he sat, gazing at her, breathing in the scent of her and the sweet-smelling hay. The experiences of the night had left no signs on her face. He had expected that she might look drawn, her cheeks silvered with dry tears. Instead her skin looked clean and soft. Her expression was intent, as though she had to concentrate to sleep. Nor did her soft breath fall into rhythmic patterns. The cadence of her respiration would break sometimes into sighs, quick catches, and moments came when she breathed so subtly that he could hardly detect that she did so at all. He did not touch her. Last night's anger died in him. Only one thing held any importance. Whatever he could, whatever she wanted, he must give to her.

Life teemed around them. Shafts of light from known and unknown sources speared through the worn timbers of the barn walls, golden roads with depth and dimension paved with dancing motes of grain dust. Flittering barn swallows punctuated the murmur of pigeons nesting under the eaves. In the far corner, a mother cat tended her kittens.

Suddenly Susan awoke, not moving, blinking in the white sunlight until she saw him. And he found in her wide eyes the wounds missing from her sleeping face.

For a long time communication between them took place in silence.

Then, remembering, she said, "Daniel—"

"He's fine. He's in the house."

She must have been relieved, yet her expression didn't alter.

He said, "Fanny told you about what happened on her farm?"

She nodded. After a pause she sighed, rolled on her back with her hands behind her head, and gazed upward at the far vault of the ceiling. Her lips relaxed in a smile that was hardly a smile.

"You should see how it is in here come winter. Hay goes clear to the ceiling, and frost settles on it until you can see every piece of it. Frost makes on the cobwebs, too, and they hang down like sugar candy. We clean it all up in the spring with willow boughs; we have to put handker-chiefs over our noses." She sat up, looking around, seeming to see things invisible to him. "Summers we used to like to sleep up here, while rain pattered on the roof. If John was away at a cattle auction or somesuch, I'd have my sisters with me, Fanny sometimes, and we'd be talking until all hours. Dad used to fool with us, tossing rocks up on the roof, running by the windows with a sheet over his head, and we would get so worked up, chasing around . . ." She walked to the open hay door, limned in colorless light, and beyond her was a field cut with the claw marks of a plow. "I came to watch our star last night and found it all covered with a cloud."

He went to her, standing close, resting his hands lightly on her shoulders, his thumbs penetrating beneath her collar to find the soft skin at the base of her neck. She shivered under his touch.

"I have to tell you good-bye," she said.

"No."

"I have to. My parents might come, or ministers from the church. If they find you here, it could be bad."

"I can't leave you."

"Please."

"I can't leave you, not to this."

"*This*, you say. But this is my home."

"Make a new home with me. You'll like California." His voice was low, close to her ear. "It's warm there all the time. Camelias bloom in January. I have a house on the beach, and at sunset the water turns colors you only see in dreams."

She was shaking her head already.

"Susan . . . You can do anything you want, be anything you want—"

She turned in his arms, her face tight against his chest, her hands holding him tight, and he was hurting so badly, every cell in his body alive and burning, he couldn't seem to think.

"I'm not separate like you." Her breath was quick and frightened, caressing his chest in a spot of sensuous warmth. "I'm one limb of another body. I've always known what my life would be." Not a hard life, but one that would be intimate and tender. She would know what her husband would be to her, who would cherish her children and teach them with a parent's care. She knew what work would fill her hours. Loving and familiar hands would care for her when she grew old, and comfort her final hours; and when she was gone, no stranger would touch her—no one but her family would make her ready for burial in reverence and love.

With all he had, he never had more to offer her than himself. Long before she knew who he was, she had become everything she wanted to be.

He drew back her *kapp*, tasting her hair inside his mouth—it was the most perfect taste, perfect in infinite ways, past the power of his imagination to grasp how perfect. He closed his eyes, and the bright image of the hay door blazed on his retinas like black fire. "I want to stay with you today."

But she shook her head once more. "Go quickly." Her whisper was like his, only she was gasping. "This is too hard."

"I love you so much, Amish."

"Don't love me."

"Ask my heart to stop beating; that would be easier...." Holding her, just holding her... "I feel like it's some horrible cosmic error that we should be apart for even one second."

But she pushed his chest with the flat of her hand. He drew back, blind; no light seeming to be getting into his eyes, no air into his lungs, but he could smell the loft around him, grainy, musty. Afterward he was never sure how he found his way home.

Afterward she baked. *Home* was here, intangible in the yeasty puffs of bread rising on her kitchen sill, in the scents of spice and cream and a hot oven, in the sticky mystery of uncooked dough licked from her fingers. Everything pleased the surface of her mind, the delicate strengths and textures, egg shells and pastry, foam candy and cornmeal.

She took what she made herself to neighbors and family, not saying much, but in each drop of syrup and molasses was the sweetness of her affection; in every grain of salt, her sorrow that any act of hers had caused them to be angry at or ashamed of her.

She would have liked to cling to that, the joy in simple things. But her stomach never felt good, and her thoughts were jumping, jumping. Every second held a terrible feeling of anticipation—anything might happen, anything would happen.

There's a blankness, missing him.

Her body was a clumsy shell, as if she'd grown it new and couldn't get used to it. Daniel came up behind her once and touched her arm, and she dropped a plate of ginger cookies. After that, he spoke first when he came in.

Panic is in me here, always....

Alan had been to see her father. She'd had a good account of it from Luke, who'd been with Dad by the forge, sharpening corn shovels. Dad hadn't raised his face once to Alan.

It was easy to see how things would be between the two of them—Alan lost in a situation he could neither soothe nor negotiate, approaching things reasonably, with logic, warm in his new love, so confident in its power. It must have been hard for him to believe that barriers would not fall to pieces, like sand mountains, before its force. Alan's love was everything to Alan, but it wouldn't seem like much to her father, just easy, selfish desires, enflamed by challenge and unlawful proximity in a bored, immoral man who was too used to getting what he wanted.

Staring into the red, dirty heat of the forge, her father had said, "If you love her, then don't become her damnation."

Though Alan didn't come to see her after he left the haymow, she felt his presence without respite.

So lonely, wanting him, wanting him . . . he doesn't come . . . Thank God he doesn't come, or I might weaken . . .

Daniel came with her to talk first with her parents; after, with leaders from the church, the Bishop and others, men she trusted as she would her father. Those hours she wanted to strip forever from her memory. Her father kept shaking his head. He'd shake his head, stare at his hands, murmur, "Susan, Susan . . ."

Her mother got so wan, then wild with anxiety. She'd had one daughter taken; she wasn't going to lose another. It just wasn't going to happen. This wasn't Susan.

Anyone could see this wasn't like Susan. There were reasons—her grief over John's death, and losing that tiny baby so soon after. She'd had no time to get over that before Rachel left them. It had been too much for Susan—she was troubled; she didn't understand what she was doing.

The charges against her were serious: sins against the rules of dress, of separation, sins of pride and fornication. It was a sickening nightmare to hear them on the Bishop's lips. She confessed immediately. She couldn't stand to have it go on. But to her horror, she was just saying the words.

As usual, Alan's emotions weren't for public consumption. He wrapped up the final days of his location work at Greyling, his efficiency mechanical, cruise control switched on. But everyone close to him had a glimpse of the turmoil inside in his rare moments of unguarded abstraction, when he let the facade slip, and the blank twilight of his unclothed anguish showed on his face.

Joan had heard about the pigs from Alan, in language so stark, it made the hair rise on the back of her neck. She was furious for him, furious for Susan; angry, helpless, and more than a little taken aback. What were these people going to do next, burn crosses on Susan's lawn?

Saturday night Daniel picked her up in his buggy, and she was so upset that she did one of the two things she had promised herself she wouldn't do: She got into a fight with him about it. Or rather, she tried to.

They stopped in a deserted park near the dam. Starlight sparkled on the indigo water, but somehow the peace wouldn't penetrate, and she kept harping on the subject until he took her hand and brushed it over the tree bark and said, "Rough"; held her hand in the water and said, "Smooth and wet"; brushed it over the grass and said, "Soft."

His touch, as always, was gentle, and as always it made her pulse beat in counterpoint. "What's that supposed to mean? Are you imitating someone?"

He held onto her hand. "Anne Sullivan."

"Anne—teaching the blind? I'm not that bad."

Smiling, he leaned back against a tree trunk, his hat tilted over his face, shading his dark, expressive eyes.

"You're leaving in a couple of days. This is the last time we can spend together. Let's have one night clean."

Beautiful and not knowing it, clever, natural, he was more than she could resist, and she did the second thing she'd promised herself she wouldn't do. She bent forward and kissed the warm satin of his mouth. She felt a slight motion that might have been surprise, a breath indrawn, and then his mouth remained still, a gracious captive.

By no one's definition was she an insecure woman, but the failure washed deep down into her most primal fears, and she drew away, frost growing under her skin. She tried to take back her hand; he kept possession of it.

She asked, "Are you a virgin?"

He had to think it over. He actually had to think it over, and she felt the frost in her cheeks turn to flame, wondering what kind of angles he had to consider. With a half-smile, he said, "Technically."

If he had the decency to be embarrassed, she couldn't tell it from his face. *She* had the decency to be extremely embarrassed. She turned to stare at the moon cups in the water, and in a moment she felt his hand moving slowly in her hair and realized with an exquisite leap in the pit of her belly that the touch was no longer sexless.

His breath swept against her ear. "I'm trying not to take advantage of you."

She paused incredulously. "*You* don't want to take advantage of *me*? If your friends put pigs in poor little Susan's bed for sleeping with a man she loves, I can't imagine what they'd decide to put in mine. Maybe a brontosaurus."

His soft laugh wavered on her cheek. Barely breathing in surprise, she felt his callused hands shift tenderly on her, lowering her to the warm, tickling grass, and he followed her down, covering her mouth in a long, erotic kiss, sublime, unselfconscious, questing.

"You're so very beautiful," he murmured. His fingers wandered with delicacy over her face, her brows, her eyelids, over her nose and lips.

Even more softly, she said, "I can't imagine what you believe you're protecting me from."

"I'm not trying to protect you. I only want it to be different for you once." He sat with his back against the

tree, taking her head gently onto his lap, placed his hat
playfully over her face, set it on her stomach. Then he
asked, "How's Alan?"

"Dying by inches. How's Susan?"

"The same."

"Maybe she should just—I don't know. Go with him."

"To Los Angeles?"

"He'd treat her like a jewel. He'd ease every step of
the way. She might be very happy."

"It isn't only a religion, being Amish, it's a way of life.
It's her way. She grew up in a church where women don't
speak in service, with no divorce, no contraception. We don't
bear arms. If she left and had sons, they would be subject to a
military draft. . . . Susan's never been more than thirty miles
from home. Almost everyone she knows is a relative."

She stirred and sat up, wearing his hat. He tipped it
forward over her nose. "How did the movie end?" he
asked.

"What do you mean? The filming?"

"No. The story."

"As a matter of fact, he's changed it. And changed it.
First time he's done anything like this."

"What changes?"

"Well, there were technical changes in the way the
film looks. Color film is very . . . rich. It makes things look
bright and pleasing, and Alan originally wanted it more
subdued and moody, so they prefogged the film. It's a
subtle effect; the audience probably feels it more than
notices it, but it makes a big difference in terms of impact.
Anyway, Alan saw Susan on film and right away he
wanted full color. That meant they had to waste some of
the stuff they'd done already. That was just the beginning.
It's not the same film he started out to make."

"In the end?"

"There's this—I guess you'd call her a sorceress, some
kind of demon being that controls the man Susan loves.
The man *Polly* loves. The demon wears his soul in a ring
on her finger. Whoever wears the ring will control him
absolutely. Now, when Adam Burke, Polly's husband, is a
monster, he has to eat living flesh. He can't stop himself.
Polly learns about all this and has to go through agony to

get hold of the ring—if she gets it, she can wear it and free him from becoming the monster. In the original, it's just too much for her, the burden of this other soul, and it kills her, and her true love is frozen forever in the form of a monster. He goes crazy with grief and carries her off to this cave far underground and stays with her, hovering over her until he dies of starvation."

"Alan wrote that?"

"The darkest imagination since Poe, the critics say. *He* says, 'For God's sake, it's just commerce.' I think he sees himself as the missing link between H.P. Lovecraft and the *Rocky Horror Picture Show*."

"Lovecraft? *Rocky Horror Picture Show?*"

"Sorry. English weirdness." She kissed him. "In the rewrite, the monster trusts her so completely, she's able to endure his possession of her in that form and they both live." She put the hat on her knees and stared into it. Moments passed before she spoke again.

"Daniel, tomorrow morning when she has to do that truly barbaric and repugnant thing that we won't discuss again—has she told you what she's going to say?"

"No. I don't think she knows."

Chapter 21

*O*n Sunday morning, Susan's father came to take her to service alone, as he had on her baptism, her wedding, and on the day of John's funeral. She met him in the kitchen, and found him eating one of the doughnuts she'd made yesterday. She brushed the powdered sugar out of his beard and he gave her a guilty grin.

"Too much baking around here. You'll wear yourself out and get Daniel fat." He smoothed her hair back from her face. The motion was clumsy for all its gentleness, and he accidentally dislodged a strand, which came dangling over her nose. They smiled a little at each other. "*Ach*," he said, "big, *dopplich* hands . . ." He brought his other hand from behind his back. "Look what's out. Wild roses."

"You picked me roses, Dad?"

"On the way over." His smile became shaky. "Do you remember the last day your sister was to church?"

He would not say her name. But that he spoke of Rachel at all amazed her. She nodded.

"There was blue flag out," he said, "and I thought, I ought to pick some of that for her, she was so fond of them. She had my dander up, but I thought of it anyway. I didn't do it, though. I don't know why. A man gets too late smart. . . ." Then he began tucking the roses into a jar on her counter, and she stood there with hair over her nose and a pain in her middle.

"Dad, aren't you mad at me?"

He was concentrating hard on the flowers, as if it were the most important job he'd ever had to do. She saw him swallow. His voice was rough. "When I had more hope I was mad. Now I can only worry."

Hoofbeats drummed on blacktop, bringing the line of buggies to service at the farm of Ezra Peachey, John's father. Susan tried to close her mind, to endure it all as she must endure it, with humility and submission. Here there were not a thousand paths, choices like a field of pretty stones to hunt among. Here there was one course—repentance followed by forgiveness.

Ezra's deep white barn rose from its skirt of green foliage toward a shimmering blue sky. When she arrived in the rig, her eyes strayed to the steep-pitched gable roof, toward the shed dormer. John had sat there, his long legs dangling over the eaves as he waved cheerfully to her. Five minutes later he was dead.

Her father followed her gaze, and his broad hand left the reins, and, smelling of leather, came to lay over hers.

"Still you look," he said.

Half past eight in the morning and it was already hot. Bright, moist sunlight made the shadows cool oases. In the pools of shade that dotted the farmyard, folks had been greeting one another, men shaking hands, children with scrubbed, shiny faces finding friends and cousins, leading toddlers. Here was every living being she loved in creation—except two.

Talk had died. Group by group everyone had become aware she was here and had gone quiet. Only the smallest went on as they had been, and the pretty babble of the very young became clear and seemed loud, like the clatter of cutlery at the table when there was an uneasy silence. Faces were especially clear today. She had never seen them so well. At no time had they been more dear.

I should have lived every day of my life in thanksgiving for all that you'd given me, Lord. . . .

For she was no longer dear to them.

Some had turned their backs on her—Seth's sister Ada, two of John's brothers, Shem Whetstone. It was better to see their backs than their faces. Worst of all were the small mercies, the resolute acts of kindness. Fanny, with her chin up, came forward to greet her in that terrible pall of silence just as if nothing had happened. Her own family slipped toward her, to touch her arm protectively, to smile at her. Ezra brought forward his sons Dan and Isaac, and watched grim-faced while they made lifeless apologies for their act against her home. With hard-held balance, she learned that it was not Seth who had thought to soil her bed with shoats—it had been her brother-in-law Isaac.

Preaching service was in the barn. For air, two wide doorways on either side stood opened, dazzling squares of light. Between the rows of benches rolled the scents of the pasture, warm oats and alfalfa and sun-soaked wood, and the hymns held a faint echoing murmur, as though the earth herself gave praise. The final tone of each song stayed with Susan, richly vibrant to her ears. She could hardly hear the spoken words of the service. What she heard she could not interpret, for even the holy passages of scripture were formless anagrams. She clung only to rhythms, the slow meter of the hymns, the fluid chant of the sermons. She saw the heat, clear, wandering ripples of distortion that arose from the sandy drive beyond the door, but her senses rejected warmth also. She felt sticky and cold.

Katie grew restless near her mother, and Susan drew her little sister onto her own lap, cuddling the pleasing roundness of childhood, playing silent finger games to amuse her, rocking her, her own cheek pressed to the smooth plump one.

Katie fell deeply asleep after the final hymn. Children were released now, and with them, those, like Daniel, who had not accepted vows of baptism. She did not look up to see them leave. It took all of her concentration to realize she must open her arms to allow Anna to carry Katie off.

Sound remained as eerie whispers on the edge of her consciousness, and in time it was her mother who held her close and told her softly that she must go to the Bishop now; they were ready for her.

She walked forward blindly, and as she knelt, she could hear with startling clarity the solemn quiet within the barn. So many were here, and yet she heard the feathery flurry of pigeons in the open mow above her. She felt the heat in a thick wave, threatening sickness. Light perspiration pooled on her breastbone and between her shoulders, turning cold on her skin and she began to shiver under her clothing. She recalled briefly the day of her baptism, at eighteen, kneeling like this, the air warm and spicy with mystery, the concrete rough against her legs, the utter silence as the deacons gently removed her *kapp*, and the Bishop's hands on her head, then above it, cupped to receive the baptismal water, which flooded through, trickling in cool joy and grace into her hair, into her lashes, to sparkle with her tears on her cheeks and throat. . . . That was the memory, but now . . .

"I am no longer . . ." Her voice weakened and broke. In a moment the Bishop softly murmured encouragement. "I am no longer easy with myself."

Where were the words? Did they exist?

"I have allowed myself . . . to be employed in worldly ways so that I could give the money to my sister Rachel. I couldn't stop myself thinking, 'What if she gets sick? What if she loses her job?' I have offended God in ways I cannot count. I confess to the sin of fornication with—"

The pattern of flecked straw on the floor blurred, grew white spines of light.

"I saw in Alan Wilde . . . his compassion, but he had none for himself. I saw that there was love in him, but he couldn't recognize what it was. He had so much vision, and at the same time he was blind to his real gifts. He thought he was like a machine that could only say, 'Put a camera here, put a camera there—'" *I am wandering*.

Her clasped fingers were damp, cold as icicles, her face stinging hot, the contrast sickening.

"If I saw a child in a wilderness lost beyond hope, would I say, 'No, there's nothing I can do, he isn't Amish'? Would I pass by a man in chains and say, 'I can't help, I'm separate'? God loves the unbelievers. Their welfare is precious to Him. Doesn't the scripture say that God is like the shepherd who finds one lamb has gone astray and goes to hunt for that lamb, leaving all the others? As much as He loves me, more than He loves me, He loves this man."

She drew a breath, her heart lurching. "I knew Alan might try to lead me into sin. He has no idea about salvation; he wouldn't be able to help himself." Her breath sped almost as fast as her heartbeat, and the words came faster too. "And I thought, 'I'm strong, nothing can happen to me,' but that was pride; I didn't understand how temptation would be. It wasn't like I thought. It doesn't feel like evil with him, and I can't find a way to deliver myself of thinking that if I had it to do over I would do the same." She broke off, forcing an end to the babble, trying to swallow, and clenched her hands together, shaking hard. So wrong, so hopelessly unacceptable, the defenses, the admission that she could repent of only the consequences of her actions and not the actions themselves.

Down to the side she could hear someone weeping, a woman, her aunt, she thought. She looked up and found it was John's mother. Again the world dissolved behind a tattered veil of brightness, and when that cleared she was looking up past the ivory-colored cloud of the Bishop's beard, finding his eyes. Briefly she was confused—she was back at her baptism, kneeling, awaiting the moment the Bishop would extend his hand to her to help her rise, welcoming her into the body of Christ. So would he extend his hand now if he were to pardon her. But this time, the moment did not come.

She was past listening after that. Others had begun to weep, the sounds too terrible to hear. The Bishop was speaking to her, the words too terrible to hear. She saw the shock the words caused in the faces around her. It was an awful thing to shock people. There was something indecent about it. She felt stripped naked before them, felt that she didn't own enough clothes to cover the shame.

It went on for a long time, like childbirth, longer than she could really bear, and when it was over, she was left with nothing but a sickened feeling.

Outside the sun hit her like a hard wind, and she walked chin up into it, and kept walking, squeezing her middle. Her brothers and sisters had been waiting near the door. She heard Carolyn say, "What's the matter, Susan? Levi, why is Susan crying?"

Close beside her, running to keep up, Anna whispered, "Susan, what's happened?"

"I've been excommunicated." She didn't want to stop to breathe or think. She walked across the farmyard until her legs lost their strength, and then Daniel was there to catch her.

Running hard, Fanny caught up to them before they passed the first bend, and she said, "I won't shun you, Susan." Those were the words Susan took with her toward home.

Luke and Levi came with her, and Daniel and Anna too. They should have been sent back—it would cause trouble. But she hadn't the heart for it. Partway home, they stopped under a bridge, took off their shoes and stockings, and put their legs in the cold creek. Susan wet her apron and pressed it to her face and hot throat, taking long breaths through the saturated cloth. Beside her, Luke was shredding marsh grass into thin strips.

"Daniel?" Luke's voice was hesitant, on the verge of discovery. "Is one reason you haven't been baptized that you don't want to support the ban on Rachel?"

"It's one reason."

"Then it's one of the things that has Dad beside himself about Rachel going off."

It was, of course. Susan came to a terrifying awareness: This morning had ended nothing. Nothing had ended, only begun.

She was desperate to be alone, half-crazy with it. Daniel knew, and finally he was the one to urge her to go off for a walk if she wanted, and although it was difficult for him to do it openly, he gave her a bear hug, the funny, bone-compressing one, and said, "Be back soon. Please?"

So she walked, looking up mostly toward the northwestern sky, where storm clouds piled lazily in an immense floe shot through with pencil lines of escaping light. Her thoughts and emotions kept up a quick, nauseating fluctuation, and she felt over and over the numbing surprise that *this* was her life, this oddity, this was happening to her.

In time she realized she was near town, near the public telephone, and she ran there, her breathing agitated, closing herself in the glass walls, carrying out the strange sequences of operations. He might be gone already. He was leaving sometime today. She heard one ring, a second ring, and then Alan's soft, inviting voice, inattentive, indifferent.

"Hello."

Unbearable longing. Too much, too much. She fell back against the glass, cradling the phone close to her face, her mouth on the receiver, her blood frantic. She heard him repeat the word, now making it a question, his attention beginning to focus, and she waited another moment, savoring the dreamlike connection, before she returned the receiver to the hook.

Susan left the telephone box, blinking at the sunlight, startled that it was still there. The mighty pyre of a thunderhead filled up the western sky, and its moisture reached out to touch tiny chills down her spine.

She wished she could go back and call him just once more to hear him say one word, just one more word. . . .

She had to be careful now. This was the time coward-ice might try to creep in. Nothing could defeat her like her own fear. She must make her will like steel.

The Fellowship after service had ended. Rigs passed her, leaving her in silence, with the taste of dust in her mouth. She walked along the shoulder of the road, taking the burden of avoidance upon herself.

Most of the children didn't know yet. They'd hear gradually. The truth was a slow sieve. Their parents wouldn't want them to hear everything, and she remem-bered how it had been when she was young, how the ones who strayed became sunk in myth and speculation. So the children still waved at her, her scholars, the cheery ones, the mild, passive ones, the ones who couldn't get out of mischief. They called her name, and she returned their smiles, her chest aching.

The wooded hillside was fat like a sleeping cat where it curled around the Amish cemetery. Only spirits were here today, and a peaceful wind, the grass nodding. Wan-dering through the aisles of white arched stones, she heard buggy wheels strike gravel and her name being called. In the outer yard behind the wire gate, Levi drew up in his rig with her grandmother. Susan was there to help her descend. Levi stayed in the rig.

Arm in arm they walked up the hill together, retracing the path Susan had begun, the sun a many-speared star on the top of the trees.

They stopped once by a pair of sunburst locust trees that draped on each side of two stones.

"My, these trees have grown since they were planted." Grandma patted the bark, and Susan thought about how beautiful people became when they got older, how her grandmother's hair was light as a cloud, how her eyes had a child's brightness that people lost in midlife, how her skin tissue was so fine, rayed with life, fascinating in its transparency, wonderful to touch. Grandma found the familiar headstone without help. "Forty years since Grand-pa's been gone. And my folks longer yet. Here I am ninety-four. Think how long they've been gone." She put her hand on the stone beside it, then stepped backward looking toward what she couldn't see, smiling a bit. "Used to be I'd come down here and stare real hard at my stone, at that number that isn't there yet, and there'd be times I had the feeling, if only I looked close enough, I'd be able to read it."

She tucked her arm around Susan's waist. "Sure wish you could've known your grandpa. I tried to pass on a little of him. Daniel reminds me so of him. Whenever he could, he'd be out there at night with that telescope, looking up at the sky. He saw all kinds of things up there, comets, meteors, knew all about them. Only one thing he ever had wrong. He said, 'Man will never make it to the moon.'"

Susan had her eyes shaded, scanning the sky. "It's something, what they've done, sending things up there...."

An old straight wire fence wound with grape leaves ran along a lily-covered slope at the edge of the woods. Branches overhung the fence, letting the sun through in spots, and moss grew thick under the grass, creeping up lichen-freckled stones. Only two headstones up here were new, without the worn inscriptions of the others—a white arch, and beside it, a tiny one.

"Look here, a little oak tree is coming up." Susan showed Grandma with her hand.

"A nice little tree..." Then, "Listen to those birds."

"Grandma, do you remember how funny John's dad got when I told him John had asked to be buried up here?"

"Some don't care for it up here. They say it gets so messy under the trees—the leaves come off, and the branches are so dry."

"John pointed up here when we were walking once, and said, 'That's where I want to be, right up by the woods,' like his mind had already been made up for a long time. He had this funny thing he used to say about how a cemetery was the place to learn about democracy."

"He had a way about him, he sure did. Those were the days, him riding over on that high-life horse of his. How he liked to kid you about how small you are. Said he could carry you around in a thimble. He'd put his arm straight out and it could go over your head."

Inside she felt soft as the moss beneath her toes. "Sometimes he bent his knees down when we walked, to be the same size. It looked so comical."

She sat by the little grave, fragrant with scatterings from the forest, and wrapped the stone in her arms, resting her cheek on the cool granite. The coolness went through her; the wind tugged wisps of hair from under her *kapp* and set them to motion on the sides of her face. She whispered, "I wanted to pick flowers with her."

"I know you did." Her grandmother's hand lay against her hair, her open cheek. "You just remember, she has John with her."

"Do you think children grow up in heaven? I want her to be able to run and learn about things, and to play. . . ." Breezes flowed over her lips, into her mouth and throat, catching there. "I'll never forget the day she was buried. Remember how it was just starting to snow lightly and a young deer came to the edge of the woods and stood there looking at us? It was so pretty." She came suddenly to her feet, enclosing her grandmother in a hug. *She's so frail under her clothes. Ninety-four, and last winter was so hard on her. She's lost weight. I could lift her myself.* "I don't want to leave you." The words came from her heart like a prayer. "Grandma—"

"I know you so good, Susan. You don't have to tell me."

The wind blew their skirts together, making them bob as one. Inside she was nothing, only hollow, hurting like an animal. "Thank you for always loving me."

Her grandmother's smile was tight against her face, and Susan drew back to see it, the narrow mouth, the lips that unusual color, like the flower of a milk thistle, but bluer these days than they'd been once. The clear pearl of a teardrop pooled in one corner.

She put a hand on Susan's *kapp*. "You never did get no bigger than a hollyhock."

She managed to answer, "Runt of the litter."

"Pick of the litter." The gentlest, gentlest hands took hold of her face. "We'll all be together again one day and then the separation won't have seemed long, and I'll be able to see this sweet little face again. You and I, we've got our star all picked out."

On Sunday morning, during his last hours at Greyling, Alan found himself at the window often, gazing across the open field toward the gap in the woods showing the path Susan had often used to come to the set. Day and night had become the same to him, equally without meaning. He didn't know what to do with the pain of worrying about what she must be suffering. The pain was there all the time, chattering at him.

The air had turned cool, that strange Wisconsin warmth with a bite in it. The sky was darker than a blueprint. A black thunderhead spread over the countryside, puffing to an impossible height.

He wondered if she was watching it, too, alone in her battles. The only thing left that he could give her was the gift of his absence, his discipline.

He sat in front of a reel of film outtakes of her, watching her face, the forthright smiles, the moody ones, the intuitive and knowing ones. His mind gave him the taste of her mouth and the feel of the texture of her hair against her skin. He lived for minutes in the fairy tale of the flickers of colored light.

When the Lop wandered over to snuggle up to his ankle, he lifted it without thinking, and the second his hand brushed over the warm fur, a terrifying sense of loss gripped him. The film ended and he was not able to recognize that he was looking into a square of empty light.

Another image entered his mind, of the ragged desperation on her face when he'd asked her to come with him to California. Dear God, her eyes . . . Help me, they'd said, you can't help me.

He had the feeling he would never readjust to life without her. He felt as though most of him had been torn away, all the good parts. There were no words to describe it. He missed her . . . he missed her. . . . There were no words anywhere to describe his longing.

The bottom of the thunderhead fell out in a deluge that thrashed the trees and peppered the carpet through the screen. Weeds and grass were packed flat. Lightning chained the clouds, and he went to the window, closed it, and put his hands to the glass, feeling the sepulchral shock of answering thunder. Rain struck the glass in blasts. Staff after staff of broken light stripped back the darkness.

Something moved near the trees. A small figure hunched

against the rain hurled from the gap in the forest, running into the bleak field.

He felt himself backstep, whisper something, hope tearing at him. He knew he was speaking, couldn't control it, couldn't stop it.

By the door he realized he was saying her name. Fear made him slow, fear that what he wanted to see wouldn't be there. Heartbeats ripped up into his throat.

Then he was outside, running in the downpour, heavy raindrops like marbles soaking his clothes, and he saw her, pallid in a blast of light, waving her limp bonnet at him, her skirts saturated, taking the shape of her legs, her hair down and soaking, water vapor flying like smoke around her. And then he had her in his arms, really holding her, the narrow, graceful body pressed to his through the wet clothing, finding warmth. With the sky blowing up above them, they kissed, water running in their eyes and mouths, desperate, thirsty kisses, her skin sweet as honey glaze. His mouth moved in disbelief over her face, drinking rainwater. His hand curved under her breast to experience the pace of her heartbeat.

Lightning snaked out of the sky and struck in the woods, filling the air with a geyser of sparks. Sound split and perished in the crackling thunderclap. They watched it together, shaken and elated, shivering.

Catching her hand, he tried to pull her toward shelter, but she lingered, head back, eyes closed, letting the rain wash over her smiling face.

Laughing, he dragged her close again, kissing her until he made himself drunk on her.

"Isn't the rain wonderful?" she said, holding tight.

"Why is it wonderful?"

"Because . . . Because when it comes down as snow you have to shovel it. Because it makes plump berries. Alan, I love you. I need you."

She was everything he wanted in this life and the next, sodden, piteous, and fervent in his arms, and he held her tight, as if he were holding onto a dream, and said, "I need you, I need you too."

Chapter 22

Coming in from the rain, Alan felt cleansed, purer than he'd ever been. He cherished every second, undressing her in the warmth and brightness of his bedroom, sending her clothes to be dried, rubbing the moisture from the brilliant drift of her hair. She smiled often at his love talk and gentle teasing, but it took a long time for her to stop shivering. In the car to the airport, on the plane, he could feel the tremors chatter under her skin.

She came to him with nothing beyond the clothes she was wearing, and it hardly surprised him. When he'd asked her if there was anything she'd like to bring, she'd looked surprised, and laughed.

"I've never been anywhere before. I suppose I don't know about bringing things."

He suggested that if she'd like to, they could stop by her house. She shook her head, the smile frozen, and he hadn't urged her. Parting with her family was not something she seemed able to tell him about. It was easy to believe she wouldn't want to go through any of it a second time.

That one aspect was the only blot on his happiness. It felt so good to be with her, he couldn't come down, and she was so fierce to protect him from her sorrows, maybe to disguise them from herself, that he saw her stress only in glimpses.

Her image of the outside world was made up of myth, a collage of inexperience, science fiction, hearsay, innuendo. Plucky and positive, she was composed, almost prosaic, about boarding the plane. He had almost forgotten this was new to her, when she asked, "Aren't we going to wear parachutes?"

When they were high in the air, she balanced a pen on her palm, waiting for it to float.

It was right to laugh. She encouraged it. She laughed, too, at her misunderstanding. They shared it, discovery and self-discovery, and they shared the unreal quality of being here together, the feeling of surprise that repeated itself minute by minute.

For someone who had never been more than thirty miles from home, Los Angeles might as well have been Baghdad. He was an Angeleno, born there, and in his rootless way fond of the city. Less than a melting pot, Los Angeles was a sprawling confederation of interests—pilgrims who had come west, like wide-eyed Goldilocks, looking for a place that wasn't too hot or too cold, a place that was just right all the time.

Other extremes flourished here—the full flower of bourgeois opulence in the hills; the entertainment community, with its laid-back zeal and parlor Bolshevism; the seekers after truth; the hand-to-mouth beautiful people waiting to make it big; the weird; and the masses, trying in their extraordinary ways to be ordinary. It all managed to look a little sleazy to the rest of the country; to him it was uncomplicated, comfortable in its neurosis, people trying to make room for one another.

No one knew better than he what an adjustment it would be for her. He knew better than she did. That she would like it here meant everything in the world to him.

Gazing out the window of his silver Mercedes, she was very much herself. He watched her for signs of revulsion. Surprise was all he saw, an amazement so profound, he could only catch echoes of it. She spoke little, but she smiled at him, and nodded at his explanations. What she did say was cheerful; strained, of course, but he had expected that—the trip, the change... He had hope, real hope.

That lasted until they were at his home, late in the evening after dinner, when he came quietly into a room where she sat unwary and alone. She had removed her *kapp*, and held it to cover her face, the cords on her wrists standing out tautly. Her body bowed like that of a punished child. The shudders she had controlled for many hours ran through her unchecked.

He felt a hissing blankness.

"My grandmother used to rock me in her arms." Her head lifted. She stared at the crushed *kapp* with an expression of simple curiosity. "Do you think you could?"

He took her in a light grip. Her hair caressed his cheek, carrying in its mass the fragrance of a Wisconsin rain. "How? Show me. Like this?"

"You do it just right," she said, and fell asleep within minutes, so quickly that it scared him. He stayed as he was for many hours, holding her, wishing he could protect her from her dreams.

Being Susan, she didn't tell him for days about the circumstances under which she had left her family.

Susan woke with a sense of struggle, of fighting her way out of a dream. But then she felt warmth against her back and breathed in the scent of clean skin that was not hers. Alan. She sat up and tenderly watched him sleep, with the feeling of mild shyness that had come gradually to life since she'd left Wisconsin with him the day before.

Now she'd spent a full night in his arms. It meant something; a watershed . . . like baptism.

Her stomach compressed into a knot. She had a task she'd set for herself, and she wanted to do it quickly and have done with it, with no drawn-out agony or faltering. She was going to change to the English way of dressing.

There was no question that it had to be done. She'd seen the half-hidden smiles at the airport yesterday, and felt the curiosity. Then, at the restaurant where he'd taken her, when she'd left him to comb her hair, one of the men who waited on tables had grabbed her by the arm.

"Who let you in? You can't come in here hassling our guests!" he'd said, and put her out the back door. When they found out whom she was with, they just about wrapped themselves around her knees apologizing, or around Alan's knees, anyway. They had thought she was soliciting for a cult. As protective as Alan was toward her, it took her a little while to get him to see in it anything to laugh about.

It had been somehow important to put a good face on things, more important than it might have been on the safety of her home ground. She'd pretty well hidden the panic that came at her like tides in a windstorm, one behind the other, always one more. She no sooner weathered one but another would rear to replace it.

By late evening she had been unable to brace herself anymore. She'd gone to lie down because she didn't know what else to do. To rest, she'd told him. She had been pretending to sleep when Katelyn Fisher came by. She dimly remembered the lawyer Alan had sent to draw up a contract with the movie company. Odd, she'd thought at the time, to bring someone all the way from California to have a part in an agreement she and Alan could have come to on their own. Alan had gotten a peculiar smile when she'd said that, and she had seen that it offended his sense of how the world was, with her assumption that people would keep their word to each other without having it written down and made into law.

She could barely hear Katelyn speaking to Alan. They were quiet, probably so as not to disturb her. Their voices had a soothing quality for her, making her feel the way she had as a child lying in bed, hearing adults talking late in the kitchen when times were hard, after a death or a fire. Mostly Katelyn spoke. Once, Alan laughed. Presently she heard Katelyn say something like, "I wasn't sure if anyone's had time to be practical," and then something about "getting Susan's measurements from wardrobe."

Then Alan's voice came more clearly. "Maybe it's because I've come to associate it so completely with her, I don't know. They don't look medieval to me anymore. She says the skirts are warm in winter and cool in summer. Amish girls ice-skate in them, play softball in them, run races. . . . Anyway, it's part of her religious practices. Her life's so screwed up right now that the last thing I want to do is push her into anything."

Then she'd understood. Katelyn had brought her clothes. English clothes. Quietly relieved, quietly depressed to have the decision over and done with, she'd gone to sit alone in Alan's bedroom, waiting for him to come up.

Before releasing herself to sleep, and then on waking, she thought about the clothes. Maybe it would be like having a whole new skin. Maybe she'd feel itchy and new and brave, like coming wet from a chrysalis. So she let Alan sleep and went to the small, sumptuous room that belonged to his clothes. She found what was meant for her and dressed quickly, avoiding looking in the mirror that stretched right from the floor to the ceiling. She didn't like the sensation of that much mirror. It couldn't watch her, any more than a piece of furniture could, but it gave her that feeling. Furniture that watched people—it might have been one of Alan's thoughts, a piece of one of his movies. She almost smiled.

She turned her attention to the new clothes, looking down at herself, at the pale peach-colored linen skirt fine as handkerchief linen, and the soft clinging top. If there was going to be a feeling of metamorphosis, she didn't want to miss it.

Nothing came.

The new clothes felt like a costume, something to wear in a play. Real clothes weren't made by strangers. It was a part of impersonal English ways.

Yet when she took a step, the linen was light against her, and comfortable. Her hands went to her shoulders, rubbing the weightless fabric against her skin.

She wandered toward the living room, touching the expensive mysteries there, the rich fabrics and brass-trimmed table, the lights hidden as decoration, the paintings and sculpture she didn't understand though they stole her breath away with their unexpected beauty.

So far from home. She couldn't conceive of it, being in Wisconsin and California all in one day. The plane had hardly seemed to move. It hung up there while land flooded away, the fields and farms broken bits in a dusky kaleidoscope. Toy miles, but try and walk them . . .

She was gone. Well and truly gone.

This morning Daniel would deliver the letter she'd

written to her father. She could see in her mind how her father would look when he saw it, the raw flush that would burn his skin, the way his hands would tremble when he opened the paper, making it tremble too. She hated the thought. How could she live with it? There were moments when she wondered how she could live with any of it. Removed completely from its familiar surroundings, the self she'd always known might be such a stranger, she wouldn't recognize it.

Familiar things. Daniel. He looked south, mornings, when he went out to chore, toward Rachel. Maybe today he'd look west too.

In the downstairs bedroom Anna shared with Grandma, they'd be getting up. First thing, Anna would put up Grandma's hair. Susan had done it for years, and there wasn't much that felt nicer than Grandma's hair when it hung loose. It was like puffy fleece, and smelled sweet and milky like new lambs in a field. She tried to recapture how it was to touch Grandma's hair, softer than soft mostly was. Threading her fingers into the weight of her own hair, she lifted on her toes, slowly arching her stiff back, breathing in deeply, stretching muscles that felt cold and unwell, closing her eyes and remembering.

When she opened her eyes, she saw Alan. He had leaned his shoulder up against the edge of a white wall, and he was watching her as if it were the most important thing he'd ever done. Bare except for a pair of jeans, his hair mussed from the pillow, he had about him the heart-lifting sensuality that had frightened and excited her from the beginning. His eyes carried a sleepy delicacy, their color very bright, like light through colored glass above the faint pink slumber bands on his high cheekbones. On waking, his skin was marked like that; and sometimes also when he made love to her, when he made both of them feel fiery and desperate and joyous with need. She'd looked up at him at those times and seen his eyes brilliant, his cheekbones tinged with fever colors. She'd paid with burning coins to see that.

"Do I look English?"

"No." He walked to her. "Like Rapunzel or Snow

White. A myth fighting its way to life." He kissed the tips of his fingers and slid them over the side of her face.

Her heartbeat became hard and uneven.

His thumb smoothed along her jaw, moving back and forth, testing the skin, his gaze searching. His hand came to rest under her chin and lifted her face. He spoke softly. "What's happening in you?"

She tried unsuccessfully to put her thoughts into words and tried to turn her face away, but his hand brought her inexorably back.

"Susan?"

She hadn't meant to back away from him. It was the strange dizziness that made her pull back. The sliding glass door to the garden stopped her. It was cold against her shoulders, and she lay against it as if it were a chilly sheet. "Are you going to take me to bed?"

So much was in his face: desire, pity, a kind of gentle amusement. "Oh, yes."

But instead of moving, she slid down the glass and sat on the marble floor, her hands sinking into the skirts fluffing between her raised knees. The knot in her stomach pushed up into her chest and turned hot. She'd never been more fascinated by his eyes, by the delicacy of their color, the cool blue-green, lighter than his sun-warmed skin. "I guess after all this, it would be pretty . . . pretty crazy not to."

His expression changed, and he came down before her, saying something she didn't hear, maybe wasn't meant to hear, that soft, worried exclamation that she'd decided was his substitute for prayer.

"The world's a pretty crazy place," he said, "full of tricks. You can tell me things, Susan. You can tell me anything at all. Everything."

"I was thinking . . ." The words didn't want to come.

"You can tell me."

Her eyes were stinging hot, her vision blurred. She realized with overriding self-disgust that she was going to cry. She'd had enough of emotion, and wanted to push it away. Anger almost stopped the tears, anger at the continuing surprise of her own turbulent nature, at how she couldn't get it organized, but his voice broke her again. He said her name, the sound so gentle, it came inside her like a shadow and sent soft quivers down her spine. He used that same voice sometimes when they made love, and the timbre brought up a new heat patch spreading over her chest.

"About things. About how things are. People just get so hurt, do you know? My mother—" Her voice broke. "When Rachel left, Mother couldn't keep her food down for three days. She was nursing then, and her milk wasn't right, and the baby cried all the time. When I think back to then, that's what I remember, I remember the baby crying and crying..." Choked sobs tore at her words, pulling the syllables apart, making their rhythms frightened, uncontrolled. Tears ran into her hair and left hot, sparkling tracks on her skin. His palm slid over them, clearing them away. "I can't pray. I just can't. It's like drinking from a spring I've poisoned. I talk to Him, but it's like there's no one there."

She just cried then. It was too hard to think, too hard to talk. Her throat became peppery. Her head ached. Around her ears, her wet hair had turned cool and ticklish on her skin. In a moment she became aware that he had taken hold of her hands, had penetrated the tightly curled fingers. His flesh felt good. The sobs decreased, hoarse whispers of breath.

"You've never poisoned anything," he said.

"I don't know." Her throat was dry. She opened her mouth to cough and two tears ran in from the corner of her lips, tasty, salty on her tongue. "How can this work? What happens to a sheep that goes to live with dogs? He'll stay a sheep—he can't change like that—but he'll take on the ways of a dog. What's left then? He has no place."

His gaze found their joined hands and fixed there before returning to her face. His fingers didn't tighten their hold, but she felt the gathering pressure in her imagination as if it had happened.

"I'll make a place for you, Susan. We'll make a place together."

Thoughts she didn't speak came and went in her mind.

"Don't ask me to take you home," he said. "I can't."

She sighed, and shuddered. "Who says I want to go home?"

"Oh." He got something close to a smile, of pure relief. She touched one of the smile lines that edged his mouth, when he said, "Are you afraid you'll be unhappy?"

"I think I'm afraid I'll be happy." Her voice was raw, hoarse.

"Afraid because you have all this guilt?"

"I've got this guilt and that guilt over there, and the guilt in the next room, and the guilt all the way to the moon."

"That's impossible. I've got the guilt all the way to the moon. Wait. I'll be right back." He returned shortly with a cool cloth to touch her cheeks, her chest, wherever emotion had left heat stains. When it was done he drew her up and close. "I'll make it right for you. Whatever it takes, I'll make it right."

He would if he could. She knew that now. If he could, he'd take the earth apart and rebuild it for her piece by piece. He would have tried. He had faith in the power of their love; faith that was so real she could almost see it, like something she could hold in her hand, except that it would be too big. too wide, too lovely to touch. It wasn't like the old kind of certainty he had. She remembered a time not long ago when he wasn't much but cynical. Now he believed in something outside himself.

She had given him this. In some mysterious way she knew it came from her, as though from a mother who'd given birth to an awesome and wonderful supernatural child. And that was something that had to be good.

It's good, Lord. Isn't it good?

She felt the beginning of an answer like a smile that started way inside in her chest, more a sensation than an emotion. And then the good feelings were outside too—his hand stroking her face.

"Do you remember once you told me you wanted to feel what I feel?" he said. "I want that now. I want to take it all. Every place that hurts. To have it and hold it and keep it away from you . . ."

"You can't."

Under her cheek she could hear his heartbeat, steady and a little fast. "Maybe I can," he said.

She stood back, shook her head, wondering at her odd smile, which still hovered way down.

"Let me try," he urged. "I want your guilt. Give it to me."

"I can't. How can I?"

"Pretend it exists. Pretend that it's a physical thing. What would it look like?"

"Oh, bad. Terrible. Dark. Black. If you held it up to the sunlight, you couldn't see through it. There's nothing living in it. It's a black, greasy, quivering blob, like a jelly."

"Give it to me."

"I couldn't. It's a terrible thing. I couldn't give it to anyone. It's too awful."

"Give it to me." He put out his hands.

She laughed suddenly, softly. "Then it's yours. Here. Take it." She put her hands within his, then drew them back. "What will you do with it?"

"Leave that to me. You don't have to worry about it anymore. It's gone. But I can't leave you empty. I'm going to give you something in return. Close your eyes."

"What is it you're giving me?"

"Good things. Love. Sunshine. Happiness."

"What do they look like?"

"Close your eyes. You tell me what they look like."

He was pretending to put things into her hands, one by one. She began to see them. "They look like peppermint sticks. They *are* peppermint sticks, and each one has stripes on it of a different color."

She opened her eyes and looked into his, and found they were tender, whimsical.

"Maybe we can find new ways," he said.

"Not dogs or sheep?"

His smile grew. "Maybe sheep dogs."

Something in the way he said it stuck with her and made her smile the rest of the day whenever it came into her mind.

She learned something about Los Angeles that day. You could find peppermint sticks there in many colors. He took her to a store and found them for her, these things she'd pulled out of her imagination. There was a sudden moment's uneasiness when she stepped outside and the flash of awareness struck her, like a hard, clear light, that all around her, even to the horizon on all sides, were strangers and strangeness, and surprises, and ideas that were wrong and worldly. But then there was Alan beside her, and sun on her arms, and new flowers and endless variety, more than she could have thought up in a lifetime.

I have to do this right, he thought. No slipups. Like music that couldn't be turned off, the history of the things he'd brought into her life kept playing in his mind. It couldn't go on the way it had. The cycle of hurt had to stop. It had to get better. He had to make it better.

He was a family now, with her. A family—that unit he'd never understood, the legend invented to sell cereal and station wagons. What a crazy world. Finally he saw what it was like to be alive in it.

He was careful where he took her that first morning. There were things to avoid: crowd, paparazzi, places where his appearance would draw attention. Beyond that, he chose at random.

He showed her the small Japanese house he'd built in the back part of his garden. She'd smiled, surprised at the Zen austerity, the paper walls, and tatami floor mats, and said, "It's plain!"

He drove her to buy candy, and then to a public garden with rambling fragrant pathways. He drove her to a ranch outside the city where friends raised and trained animals for movies and television. An anteater ran its tongue over her toes. She rode a camel. An ostrich took food from her palm. She helped bathe a baby elephant, and it teased up her skirt with its trunk.

In a seaside town, he took her to lunch at a Chinese restaurant. Teaching her to eat with chopsticks—feeding her, mostly—he thought she had the prettiest mouth he'd ever seen. Outside, she became entranced by a Christmas shop, one that carried ornaments year-round. The Amish didn't have Christmas trees—she'd seen very few—and although she could hardly bring herself to leave, she only allowed him to buy her one ornament, a little skunk in a

Santa hat. Maybe it startled her more than it might have someone non-Amish, coming, as she did, from a culture that didn't sentimentalize animals, or maybe it was simply the incongruity, but it made her laugh. She laughed in that way she had when she was utterly charmed by something but couldn't figure it out, and in the car on the way to his oceanside house, she took it out of the bag to look at again and was sent off into fresh streams of laughter.

"Why is it so funny?" he asked.

"Well, it's a skunk. As a decoration! A *skunk*!"

She was tired by the time they neared the beach house, and she slept part of the afternoon in his white-walled bedroom, with the sea making its clean sounds outside an open window. He walked on the sand while she napped, and was back by her side when she awoke.

She didn't know how she looked to him, opening her eyes, smiling lazily, her limbs relaxed, her hair loose and curling over her upper arms and breasts. One dark curl crossed like a satin ribbon over her neck. Her lips were parted, just enough, and he wanted that mouth, wanted that taste on his tongue, those soft lips open and hectic under his. He hadn't made love to her last night; she was too sad, suffering, her senses numb and blind. But it hadn't shut off the need in him. All night, her breasts rubbing his flesh with the softest invitation when she breathed, it had been almost more than he could bear, and he'd put his hand on her breast once as she'd slept and held her, just lightly, and made himself crazy inside. And when he couldn't stand it anymore, when he'd been desperate to have her, to turn her on her back and press open her lips with his mouth and take the form of that soft breast again and again in his palm, when he was at the far edges of control, he had only gently brushed back the hair over her ear and whispered to her in her sleep, "I love you."

It was right to wait—right for her. For him it was like giving up oxygen for a few days.

She sat up slowly. "I had such dreams. Have I slept long?"

"A little more than an hour."

"So many things have happened. So many events. I can't get it all straight."

He picked up a curl and let its own weight pull it down, letting it slip over his fingertips. "Could you handle one more event, do you think?"

Her gaze fought free of his, and she stared at his hand, her mouth anxious; she seemed half-wary, as she'd been this morning.

"Hey," he said, "not a seduction."

She focused on his hand. "Why not?"

"Because you became ashamed," he said gently. "I don't think you wanted to, but it happened."

"No, I wasn't ashamed. Not that."

"Uncertain, then."

Her gaze returned to his face. She put her hand on his hair and began to stroke it. "If I am, then I must be all turned around in the head." Then she whispered desperately, "Fix me. Please."

His heart seemed to jump in his body. He was light-headed from wanting her. His smile was slow. "Oh, I will. I'm going to fix you so good."

Her flush could have come from pleasure or alarm, or a powerful and disturbing combination of the two. His need flamed, but he subdued it once more. He offered her his hand. "Come out with me. I have something to show you."

"On the beach?"

"Farther down the beach."

Outside there was a redwood deck, with steps leading down a cliff above the ocean. All around was the delicious splashing sound of the waves, water slapping on water over sand.

She stopped on the deck by a straw basket of shells and lifted one out. He had the impression that to her, shells were something rare.

"Can you really hear the ocean in them?" she asked. "Try."

"I can hear it, yes."

He held up a tiny shell. "In this one you can hear the sink." Then he picked up two large conches. "Walkman headphones for whales."

She laughed and pushed at his chest, and he grabbed her wrists and held her hands there against him, moving them slowly, but his breathing was rapid. He had to force himself to release her.

She halted again at the base of the steps, staring over the ocean, her gaze sweeping over the horizon. What a grand thing, she thought. What a beautiful thing. The water was all different colors, not merely values of the same color, but color bands in blue-green, gray, green like new leaves, and deep blue. An opening broke through the piles of immense clouds and let down a shaft of sunlight that altered an area of blue-green into yellow. Far out, waves were bobbing white buds that appeared on the water like the delicate paw prints of a giant unseen cat. Waves chased one another to shore—a peak, a curve, white flowers blooming, then a shining smear on the sand. The wind was different from other winds she'd felt. It seemed to get inside her more, penetrating her hair and skin.

She dug her feet in the sand where it was warm and dry, filling up the spaces between her toes with warmth and luxury.

He linked her fingers with his. They walked on the beach with their shoes off. He rolled up the bottoms of his jeans so the water froth could flick at his ankles. Little sandpipers ran back and forth before them in front of the waves.

"I couldn't have left you in Wisconsin, Amish."

"Would you have hired kidnappers?"

"In L.A. they probably have a listing in the yellow pages."

"They probably have one that specializes in Amish."

He slid his arm around her back, pulling her closer to him, his hand just under her arm, his fingertips stroking ever so lightly upon the upcurve of her breast, his touch subtle and skillful.

"Shall I stop?"

There was a new tightness in her chest. "No."

"Hungry?"

She looked up. Smiling, he produced a gold-and-pink peppermint stick from the pocket of his jeans and handed it to her, then watched her as she licked it. The wind took her hair, and he wound it around his neck like a garment.

It spilled down his chest, blew against his cheek, rubbed against his mouth.

"I didn't think I'd like it so close to the sea," she said. "Years ago I saw this drawing in a book. It was a map of North America as it is; then right next to it was another map of how it would become if the icecaps melted and the sea came higher and covered up part of the land. It fixed the shore in my mind as a disastrous, temporary sort of place. Now that I see it, it looks like it could go on and on. . . ."

They continued to walk on, keeping close, listening to the heavy percussion of the waves, her hair softly beating him in the wind. She had the sudden sense of being on the verge of learning a powerful secret.

"It whispers to you," she said.

"It's the same sound I hear in my head whenever I'm near you," he answered. He took her hand, wind-bound with his by her hair, and carried it to his lips. He kissed her fingers and then lifted it, indicating a crack in the cliff wall where a pillar of rock had split from the craggy face and tumbled in a hundred megalithic fragments onto the beach and into the sea, blocking the beach. It was made passable by a wooden bridge, ten sandy steps up, a small platform, and then a second set of steps that led down the far side to the interrupted beach.

He said, "Stand at the top, please."

She smiled curiously. "Is this what you brought me to see? What shall I do when I reach the—"

But she had reached the platform, and what she saw below on the sand made her draw a breath and stand as she was.

"MARRY ME, SUSAN," said great letters in sand, framed by a heart.

He watched her from below, capturing the image in his mind, wanting to keep it forever. Behind and around her, the sky and clouds had colors from Chagall. She was quite still, her feet apart. Sunlight glowed between her legs, making them gleam in outline, cupping in light the prettiness of her buttocks. Sunlight sparkled in sand on her bare feet, on her long bare calves. Wind scattered her dark, gleaming curls.

Oh, so beautiful, dear God, she was so beautiful, so fine.

He said, "I love you."

She turned back.

He leaned over and in the honey-colored sand drew a sweeping question mark.

The smile in her eyes said yes. Yes yes yes . . .

He put out his hands and she ran down the stairs and stood on the bottom step, so that her face was level with his.

He took her hands. "I want to marry you the way your people marry. With all my life. For all my life."

She rested her brow on his and they stood so, her hair rubbing up and down his arms in slow, voluptuous caresses. Then she released his hands and in giant letters wrote "YES" in the sand.

He would have taken her in his arms, but she began to run backward, blithely, her heart jumping. She weighed nothing; she was nothing but joy, every bit of her buoyant with it.

She saw that he was looking at her that way again, part heat, part humor, the generous mouth tugged up at the corners as if he could taste her with his eyes, and the scary-shaky feelings she'd had that morning were gone, changed to shaky feelings that felt friendly.

His smile carried a wealth of sensual meaning. He beckoned with a crooked finger.

Desire came at her as a thud in her stomach, making her feel tight and flighty there. He must have sensed it; his smile widened.

"Come here," he said. "I want to kiss you."

A new wildness seized her, and she turned and fled, anticipation delicious in her, her feet pushing down on the cool custard sand, her breath like a chant in her ears, her filmy skirts flying up to tease her thighs and belly.

He caught her from behind, and she gasped at the contact of his hips, remembering the hardness and lean-ness of them, their strength in love.

She turned in his arms, lifting herself onto his body, and felt him helping her, one hand between her shoulders, the other much lower in a sensuous caress that made her press into him of her own need. Her pulse came hard in her throat. His hand moved up and down her back, flooding her spine with shudders.

"Before I met you, I didn't know I could be like this," she said.

"How?"

"Passionate."

He smiled, a tender crook at the corners of his long mouth, and ran a finger in a slow line sinking from the very tip of her ear down her throat in a gentle stroke between her breasts. "How passionate?"

Heat followed his finger and went on its own into the low part of her stomach. "Very passionate."

The deep rhythmic rush of the sea filled her ears. She took in the scent of him, sunny, sandy, and laid her head back into his supporting palm to prepare herself for the descent of his mouth. His lips touched her throat, the tip of her ear, and then found her mouth in long, beguiling kisses that went on and on, massaging her parted lips, then going deep, and the low ache in her stomach became fiery for him.

He sensed it, she thought; or perhaps it was a response to some powerful need of his own that made him raise her higher on his body, and with gentle hands he drew open her legs and helped her to wrap them around his hips, clasping him. He held her that way, her arms around his shoulders, his arm under her skirts pressing her up and into him. The pressure of each of his hands drove her to an intoxicating surrender. She wanted to feel his hands on her flesh, to tear off the brief band of fabric that was his only barrier to her. She pressed herself more tightly to him, taking a sharp breath, another, another as the uncovered sensitivity of her thighs recorded the faint abrasion of his aged-cotton jeans, and then, beneath, the lovely pattern of him.

They clung together, the wind tossing her hair around them like many garlands. With scant breath, hardly knowing what she said, she whispered, "Am I heavy?"

"You don't weigh enough to donate blood." He kissed a tendril of hair on her cheek, nuzzled the corner of her mouth. "And you've got enough hair for three people."

Again a kiss, hungry, deep, hardly patient, shudderingly sweet.

She began suddenly to laugh. Against the curve of his throat she said, "Maybe you'll fix me up sooner than you thought."

Chapter 23

*H*e married her in a week. He couldn't have waited longer than a week. A week had driven him half out of his mind because he'd decided—out of guilt, belated, misfiring chivalry, or some impulse of demented tenderness—not to make love to her until after the wedding. Denying himself that first afternoon on the beach had seemed a fate worse than death. But it had to be better not to be with her again in a state that was less than right to her. Nothing should hurt her. Not the faintest shade should touch her life again.

The problem was, he couldn't stop touching her. Kissing her, running his hands over her, engaging in endless hours of love play, he took himself right to the limit. Her too.

"You're so noble," she told him once, "it's terrible."

And then she lay back in the tumble of her disarrayed clothing and laughed hard at his expression, ruffling his hair with her hand. He could tell she was relieved.

She hadn't been to a wedding that wasn't Amish. She knew vaguely that it would be different. She'd seen the fluffy wedding dress in the window of Betty's Bridal Shop in Greyling. Years back Betty had passed away, and her husband had taken over the shop, grown peculiar in his ways, and let the window go. Sun and heat had turned the gown yellow and had faded the the mannequins' red lips to a grimy pink. So over the years of half-noticing those dusty yellow gowns and bleached plastic flowers, Susan had come to see English weddings as rather forlorn and shabbily extravagant affairs. And so she told Alan pretty firmly that she didn't care to have a bridal dress. Except then she'd thought, well, maybe. Just maybe.

A voice in her that she didn't understand, that she'd never attempted to understand, made her want to try things. She couldn't even decide if the voice came from herself or was a spirit voice—and if it was a spirit voice, whether it was good or bad, God or demon. It was like voices she heard on the radio and didn't know where they were coming from, how far away they were, or even if the speaker was talking now or it was an earlier recording. She'd brought it up to Alan. Did he think Satan was holding the world toward her like an apple, whispering, "Come bite"?

And then she remembered that Alan didn't believe in the devil; in fact, that he didn't quite seem to approve of the devil, which seemed to her so naive and droll and rather haplessly rational that there didn't seem to be much to do but kiss him wildly and be glad all over again that she was here with him. Heaven knew what could become of someone who didn't believe in the devil. "What am I going to do with you?" she said.

It turned out he had a couple of good ideas. But he had willpower. Oh, boy, did he.

By the day of their wedding he had a permanent tightness in his chest and a body temperature that felt as if it were about a hundred and three. His head felt light, floating in a sea of happiness.

They married with his closest friends there, Joan, Dash and his family, and others Susan had gotten to know on the set. The ceremony took place in the garden, the acres of exuberant California flora and foliage that Alan had rarely spent time in and that had already become a boundless delight to Susan. They made their vows to each other under the canopy of an oak. Azaleas in luminous rose pink and ruffled lavender grew with pale green fern clusters, bordering the sweeping white lace of her gown as she stood next to him. She wore nothing in her hair. Her shoulders may as well have been bare under the fine, transparent gauze that fell into the lacy foam of her bodice. He could see the barest tease of the lush vanilla surface that began her breasts.

Ivory-colored light wove through the leaves to dapple her skin, her shoulders and breasts. Near them was the tile fountain he'd bought in Seville, and as they spoke to each other, the splashing water made peaceful music. Light caught in the water, and beads of reflected sunshine danced on her like a spray of silver at unexpected moments and played at times upon her mouth. Desire rippled through him like the hard backwash of a wave.

Her way to marry and his were so different, so they each agreed to say what they felt, and that would be their vows.

She sang to him first, an Amish wedding hymn in German. She did not have a strong voice, or a trained one, but it had a bell-like clarity from the years of singing a capella in Amish services, and an affecting sweetness. It was the kind of voice he imagined murmuring a lullaby by the cradle.

Then she said, "Whether this is an Amish service or not, it makes no difference to me. I promise to you the same thing I would promise a man of my own faith." She took his hands, the words coming slowly, with care, and he understood she was translating them as she spoke, and hearing them for the first time in English. "I believe it was ordained by God for you to become my husband, and I promise before God that I will not depart from you in my life, and that I will hold you dear and care for you until God will again separate us from each other."

The love he felt for her was so intense, it bordered on being painful. "I love you, Susan," he said. "This is the strongest, most complete emotion I've ever experienced. Nothing else has ever come close. I didn't know I had this capacity. I'm going to make you happy. This is so new; we've barely begun. I don't know everything that it will mean. But whatever it takes, I'm going to discover it and do it for you.

"And I promise that I will not depart from you in my life."

Serene during the vows themselves, she became shaky the moment he kissed her, a long, hard kiss that made her lose her breath entirely.

There was to be a party, which Alan had tried with great tact to prevent, at Ben Rose's house, nearby. They had only a minute together, and she took him aside to give him the handkerchief she'd stitched for him, white on white, two doves carrying a furling banner with her name and his entwined. And he scooped her up and carried her to the atrium, where red and yellow rose trees grew in clay containers, and showed her another tree, a new one—a small evergreen. On the cheerful, feathery branches he'd hung every Christmas ornament from the shop they'd seen that she'd laughed over or admired—porcelain angels, wreaths of satin ribbon, crystal animals, camels wearing holly. Her first Christmas tree.

"Merry Christmas in the summer," he said, gathering her in his arms.

"Merry Christmas," she whispered, and kissed him.

They were both smiling so hard, it was difficult to kiss properly. He lifted his head, his mouth so tempting only inches from hers. "Chloe said to ask you about the present she gave you."

"Chloe?" So many new and difficult names.

"Dash's daughter, the oldest one. She helped you dress."

"Oh, yes, that! Is it safe here? Do you think anyone will come in?"

Vivid images materialized in his overheated imagination. Heaven have mercy, there are too many hours before I can be with her alone, he thought, and began to laugh.

"No one will come in without warning us, no."

She sat down on the broad edge of a low brick wall around a raised bed of deep purple fuchsias, her eyes bright with an excitement that caused a powerful sensual arousal inside him. Her hands went to the base of her cloud of skirts, the tip of her hair brushing her lap as she

bent those beautiful shoulders forward. With her gaze
warm on him, she uncovered white satin slippers, tossed
them off with her legs comfortably outstretched and toes
slightly pointed, and then bared her legs clear to her
thighs.

"Fancy stockings!" she said. And they were: sheer
frosty silk embroidered in semitransparent pale, dewy
roses, her legs lovely beneath. She seemed to read something in his expression; a bit of a smile stretched her
mouth. She leaned back on her elbows into the mound of
blooms that billowed up to caress her arms and bare neck.
One blossom nodded, barely skimming the upcurve of her
breast only a finger's width above where its delicate peak
must be.

His heart slammed into his ribs. One of her feet
arched. Her toe drew slow, wide circles on the sunny
stones. Her smile got bigger.

High on his own adrenaline, he came down beside
her, up to his elbows in a profusion of fuchsias, his hand
on her thigh, tracing up and down on the smooth silk and
the long, firm muscle beneath. He bent and kissed the far
upper edge of her stocking.

"You like them then," she said in a tight whisper.

"I envy them. I want to be where they are." His
fingers kept up their play, higher.

She took a breath, and whispered, "I want you to be
where they are too." His fingertips traced just higher. "*Oh,
Alan.*" Her eyes squeezed tightly shut. "Would you like to
know something else? Something about this dress?"

His fingers followed the edge of the stocking, slipped
up and under, caressing the skin beneath. "I'd like to know
every one of your secrets."

"Look, then." She made a slight movement with her
shoulders, half a shudder and half a shrug, and drew the
lace down her upper arms. As he watched, the exquisite
frothy bodice fell, and she was bare to the waist but for the
transparent silk that lay over her arms and chest like a mist
falling from the pearl-and-lace necklet at her throat. Her
skin was the softest, prettiest pink; her breasts, snowy
slopes with a dainty, deeper pink at the tip.

"Oh, you are so . . ." His hand curved around her

waist, moved upward, stroking all over her, between her
breasts, over her stomach, and she pulled his head blindly
downward until he enclosed one of her nipples in his
mouth, his tongue pressing her through the ethereal fabric,
making it wet against her, and he was lost as he pulled her
under him, like lying on a cloud. "Sweetheart, sweetheart..."

He kissed her, tasting the lace at her throat first, then
that soft, responsive mouth. He kissed every part of her
face; he rubbed his lips gently over her eyelashes, stroked
her brows with his mouth, planted soft, open kisses on her
temples. He chanced to look down at her face, and it was
like seeing a vision—the dark, love-hazed eyes, the dusky
wet-cherry lips that were slowly reshaping themselves into
a crooked, sleepy grin.

"You feel married, Alan?"

"I've felt married from the first moment I saw you,"
he whispered against her mouth. He would have kissed her
then—he wanted to kiss her again—but her grin persisted,
and he found he was wearing a drowsy smile of his own,
and the floating, blurred images in his mind settled in a
moment on the thought that he was about to begin his
married life making love to his bride in a fuchsia bed. And
maybe she had the same thought, because she began to
laugh, a breathless sound as contagious as her smile. He
couldn't help it; he began to laugh with her, in sheer
shared joy. They lay in each other's arms, drowning in
hilarity, wild desire, and euphoria.

Presently she murmured, "Party."

With desire, with amusement, he agreed. "Party."

At the party David Thorne took her aside. Glamorous,
unfamiliar in a gray suit and red tie, he kissed her cheek.
"What in heaven's name do you think of Los Angeles?" he
asked.

"Well...It has a thousand different kinds of water
taps that I can't make out how to work. It's a beautiful
place, but it's hard to get over how big it is. But I guess I'd
be happy knee-deep in a bog if I could have Alan with
me."

"I'm not sure I buy that. There's a lot you haven't

seen yet. It's hard to believe Alan's done anything so irresponsible as to drag you into the twentieth century."

"I suppose you've told him that?"

"You have the most magnificent eyes. I can't count the times I've purposely aggravated you to make you flash them at me. No, I didn't tell him. He knows. But I have things I'd like to tell you. First, about that day in my room. I've let you know I regretted what happened there, what you saw, the things I said. But I didn't let you know how deep my regrets go. I felt idiotic; I took it out on you. I'm sorry in italics."

"I wasn't so happy with what I said to you either— about other ways to make you feel good. It maybe sounded like preaching. No wonder you felt like giving me the dickens. You get preached at about something, it just makes you want to go and do the opposite."

"Yes, there were my delicate agnostic sensibilities to be considered. What's funny?"

"Joan. One time she told me that agnostics think that when you die, you go to limbo and do the limbo. That's a dance, Alan says."

"My closest brush with a religious experience was having my I Ching cast once. Did you know that Alan and I met when we were both working in Japan?"

"He's told me. He lived in Paris, then spent three years in Japan."

"I have a wedding gift for you from Japan. I left it back at your home. You might not know what it is. Alan will be able to tell you about it."

"I'm sure he will." She smiled mischievously. "You'd be surprised at the good ideas about some things I get on my own."

His expression became suddenly kind full of the goodness in him that she'd only glimpsed when he showed it as her lover before a camera. Then he said, "I think the closest Alan's come to having a religious experience has been loving you."

After David, she was folded up again into the gaiety of Ben's party. All around her were white columns and flowers and statues, colorful tile-work, sunlit spaces, and the scents of champagne and perfume and food she'd never seen before. The food—she couldn't even tell what some of it was; it was strange and wonderful, like things your lost loved ones must be eating up in heaven. Everyone was beautiful here. She'd never seen anything like it. Everyone wore fabrics like rainbows and had tanned skin and soft hands with polished nails and perfect, perfect teeth.

Alan's animal-trainer friends came with their cockatoos. They had one bird dressed in sunglasses, like a movie director, and the other in a tiny Amish bonnet—the movie director courted the one in the bonnet and gave kisses, and then they both did tricks and made her laugh.

She met another friend of Alan's, who was a "comedian." She'd never heard of that before. He was a man who made his living by making people laugh. It was a wonderful thing. The English would get together in a theater or in front of the television and watch something called comedy and laugh and laugh. Alan's friend sat with her for a long time and told her stories, and she had a very good time, about the best time she could have had.

There was music at the party, too, on instruments she didn't know, which made the most amazing, thrilling sounds. Alan taught her to dance, and it was wonderful being clasped in his embrace, catching the sounds with the rhythm of her body, glancing down to mind her feet and watching instead her knee moving in and out of her skirts as they danced.

He took her home as soon as it was decently possible and he saw that her eyes said, "I'm tired." She was ebullient by nature, but he'd learned that his culture—or the newness of it—wore her out much more quickly than her own. He tried to place himself in her mind, to understand the maze of stimuli, the kisses from urbane strangers, the abundant strangeness of sounds and manners and faces. She'd met all that with great charm, and now she was tired.

"I want to go to the plain house, please," she said.

Then they were together, alone with each other in the small Japanese house in his garden, and he thought, I want you now, Susan, right now, with your big, tired eyes and meters of pristine imported lace and fancy stockings. He'd often imagined life as having a sound track, and he was hearing the Pachelbel "Canon" played by a vast, spectacular string orchestra.

She sank down on the clean tatami floor mats in the exciting mound of her skirts and closed her eyes. He knew that look, that backing-up-from-a-too-fast-world look.

He kissed her fingertips, and the smoothness of her skin against his mouth set his senses on fire. Only once, he stroked his hand over her hair, and then made a bath for her in a pool of azure tile in the small courtyard. On the clear, shining water he floated gardenia blossoms from her bouquet.

He waited for her just outside, on the wooden veranda that overlooked the arched sod-covered bridge separating the bamboo-fenced Zen garden from the rest of the grounds. His gaze touched on the fine white gravel placed here and there, and the islands of uncut stone encircled in starlike moss. The house itself was low, the corners uptilted, the walls made of translucent shoji.

The sun fell, blazing, in the west, and light struck the latticed paper, turning it into leaping sheets of scarlet, and he thought, the way the paper seems to burn, I burn.

In the gathering shadows, the gaslight inside the courtyard where she bathed grew stronger, and he began to see her, a magically darkening silhouette upon the rich ocher paper, her beautiful nudity exposed in profile. Half-seated on the edge of the pad, her legs extended, she was patting dry her thighs. Putting back her head, her hair fell behind her, giving her the look of a Beardsley sprite, and she touched the towel to her throat, to the soft curve of her breasts. His pulse became like running water.

He watched her until she came into the open doorway in a shaft of rosy-blond light to lean her head against the frame. She had wrapped herself in a silk robe of brilliant embroidered crimson, and her hair was cast over one shoulder in a rippling cascade. His expression made her tip up one side of her mouth in a smile. She plucked at a fold of the robe.

"From David," she said.

"It's a kimono. A special one for brides."

"Brides wear red?" she asked.

"It's traditional."

Ah, tradition. That she understood.

A breeze lifted over the bamboo fence, and she saw how it tumbled his hair like teasing fingers. Behind him the moonlit garden had become soft and dusky and mysteriously fragrant. He was half-reclining in an easy way against one of the porch supports, but she sensed he was not so relaxed inside as he looked, and the knowledge excited her. The nearby glow of a stone lantern made an orange line on the severely handsome curve of his cheekbones and spread like a flame along his clean white shirt sleeves, down his legs to his long, tanned bare feet. His trousers were rolled up at the cuffs, so she could see his legs. He'd opened his shirt collar and discarded his jacket.

After all the times she'd thought of him as her husband, she could hardly grasp now that he really was. He didn't look like a husband. He looked like someone she'd hardly dare to let herself dream up. "Domestic" was not the word that came into her head, not when she looked at him, not with his ease and elegance, his sensual, strong-boned body and erotic smile and clever mouth and pleasure-giving hands and his soft, hypnotic manner of speaking. No, "domestic" wasn't the word that came to mind.

The thought hit her that she'd like to make him drop his veneer of poise and handle her in that wild way he had that could make her drift in a sea of sparks.

She was breathless, her voice languid with the quality of a woman speaking to her lover, as she smiled and indicated the Japanese garden. "It's like a child's sandbox."

"It's more. Look closely. It becomes a small world outside of time. Do you see the patterns in the gravel? The rocks might be islands rising from a tranquil sea. They might be mountain peaks above a field of clouds. If you let your thoughts wander through it, it gives you a rest." His eyes never left her face, though he'd set a gardenia on his thigh and his forefinger absently, repeatedly stroked one curling petal. "When I work, I look at things all day. Sometimes I have visual fatigue, and I come down here to see symmetry. There's nothing to stop my thoughts. It's meant to purify the soul."

"I see. It's the plain way. Like Amish."

His finger continued to gently prod the petal. "Just the same."

"Maybe you have a little Amish in you."

"One little Amish in particular. I have one little Amish way down inside me." Ever so slowly, his thumb was moving over many petals, barely touching, rubbing them, and a new feeling of weakness came over her, a dizziness that took her in the throat, the legs, the stomach. Her gaze dropped from his face. She seemed able to watch only his finger in its unhurried exploration of the flower.

His voice came again, softly touching her skin. "In China, the poets write that one should enter a garden in a receptive mood."

Her heartbeat was strong in her throat, making her ache. The wanting became suddenly like an illness, leaving hot patterns on the surface of her skin, radiating deep within the vital parts of her.

"You're cautious when we love, aren't you?" she said. "I mean, sometimes in your practices, because I'm not worldly?"

His finger went still. "Yes."

"I know you'll only give me good things. Teach me," she whispered. "While I was bathing, I could see you in the garden light. I knew you could see me. I wanted you to." She relaxed her arms and let the silk robe fall, caressing her breasts and back, settling in whispers around her legs, and the night air breathed over her skin, making a light, sensual sting where it wasn't quite dry.

She heard his involuntary exclamation, a soft and passionate word, and then she had the fleeting impression of him as a shadow, big and dark with the full moon over his shoulder before she was pulled hard into his arms, her mouth crushed under his, the flower pressing forgotten against her cheek. Fervent sensations filled her head along with the lush gardenia scent. She felt the rough pressure of his body, and the fire of his mouth moving against hers, opening her, his tongue tracing her lips, penetrating her mouth, making her gasp and gasp.

He swept her up, the robe tangled in her legs, and carried her inside to a wide, airy room with lattice-and-paper walls, his breath harsh and seductive against her ear. Under his feet the thick hay-colored mats of woven rush gave off their half-heard creak and sweet grass smell. He laid her down on a flat floor cushion, the red silk of the kimono spread out under her. His hand was firm on her jaw as he lay beside her, and his thumb began to rub against the swollen surface of her lips and a little inside. His skin had the scent and taste of gardenia, luscious, distinctive.

She felt like something that reminded her of bubbling water. "It's written in the Bible about two together," she said, "that they shall have good reward for their labor. The words go on—again, if two lie together, then they have heat; but how can one be warm alone?"

Between the slow, open kisses he was pressing in a descending strand upon the side of her face, he whispered, "Where is it written?"

"In—" she drew a sharp breath as his tongue followed the inward swirl of her ear, "in . . . in Ecc—Ecclesiastes."

"Very wise. Shall I tell you something too? What would you like to hear?"

"I—I . . ."

"About the kimono?" His hands had moved under her, under the silk, stroking it against her back, massaging the slippery lining against her spine. His mouth arrived above hers and hovered there. "This golden crane and her mate mean happiness, long life, and faithfulness." He spoke the words with his mouth on hers, each one becoming a hungry caress. "The star shapes are maple leaves." They were low on her back, under her buttocks, and he lifted her silently, sliding his open hand beneath the fabric, shaping it to her. "And these are plum blossoms. . . ." Under her thighs, his hand moved there, and she shivered. There were pine boughs, also, long curves that he followed across the fabric, pulling it over her ribs, the silk a sensual tickle on the underside of her breast.

Her fingers sought his shirt and began with the clumsiness of desperation to open it. She needed to feel his skin, she needed its nourishment; it made her blood a new, richer mixture.

"Cover me with yourself," she breathed.

Clear blue-green eyes alight, he laughed softly, the laugh husky and charming, as if he'd been running hard, breaking in an involuntary murmur when her hands brushed over his chest as she pulled off his shirt. "I can't," he said. "I'm sorry. Not yet. It would be . . ."

"No fun?"

He half-laughed, half-groaned. "Too much fun, too quickly. Oh, dear God, your sweet little mouth. I can't get enough of it. . . ." Touching no other part of her, he took her face in his hands and brought his mouth down on hers and kissed her until the breath was painful in her throat and her ribs hurt and she moaned each time his mouth came down on her and each time he entered her mouth with his tongue.

He lifted her hand, spread her fingers wide apart, and stroked with his forefinger on the center of her palm. "This," he said hoarsely, "put this on my skin."

"Yes, yes . . ." Under her hands, with their heightened sensitivity, she discovered the erotic tension in the muscles of his shoulders, the drive of his pulse, the uneasy contractions of his rib cage as he breathed. She relearned his skin, supple firmness underlaid with iron, and every flexure of muscle when he moved drew a sensual response from her, the feeling that her body was rising and sinking at the same time.

The gardenia had fallen against the curve of her neck, the new-cream whiteness tangled in the dark snare of her curls, its scent surrounding her like the aroma of pleasure. He freed the blossom with gentle, unsteady fingers, withdrew a petal, and used it to caress her cheek while he kissed her, then drew it slowly over the dampness of her barely opened mouth. The petal had a tantalizing softness, subtle in texture, like sensitive flesh.

Ever so slowly he began to pluck the petals and drop them on her skin. They made the lightest erotic blows, cool, napless velvet against hot, love-ready flesh; little love pats on the delicate plane of her shoulders, the palm side of her wrists, the vale between her breasts. Petals struck the outer swell of her breasts, skittering on the surface of her skin, and she couldn't keep still; she felt the stammer of her heartbeat all over her body. She closed her eyes. Weightless as pollen, one petal, then another, hit her erect and aching nipples and brought the shock of a sharper ache low in her, and it took her to anguished delight.

His voice also was a caress. She heard him murmur, "Everywhere the petals touch you, I'm going to kiss." And his mouth just touched a spot on her shoulder, so delicious and light that she shivered. Passion made a rich rushing sound in her head, like the whistle of a hard wind through many leaves. And his light, rapid breathing, his own whispered passion words, were heart-catching accents.

It was more than she could bear. She hardly knew what she was doing when his mouth reached her breasts and traced a halo of kisses edging them, then the island of rose that surrounded her nipple; and she was arching herself up, wanting his mouth, hearing herself whisper his name, and his tongue made a slow, stroking circle where his lips had been, creating a warmth that cooled instantly from his breath. His mouth closed around her nipple with the most exquisite pressure, giving her chills.

Her thoughts were a restless blur. She hardly understood when he let the petals fall in a line down her stomach, a petal and a kiss upon her toes, her ankles, strewn over her legs; but when the gardenia petals fell with their brushing, damp-skin texture on her inner thighs and between, she came up on her elbows, her eyes wide with shaky-hot uncertainty.

"Alan? What will you do?"

His lips returned to hers, his kiss soft as the powder on a moth's wing. "I want to love you with my mouth," he said gently. "There's nothing to fear. It's the same as when I kiss you . . . only one more way to give you pleasure, and I love you, Susan, I love you so dearly. . . . You're too delicious, too delicious. . . ." His voice was nothing more than a ragged whisper, his kiss setting fire to her senses as he slid lower on her body. His hair stroked over the tips of her breasts, caressed her navel, and his arms were warm and strong on her thighs, his hands gentle, as they'd been on the flower, making her wild.

His mouth discovered her, tender and urgent on her just-washed skin, and her heart was pounding, her body feeling loose and hot as her head fell back onto the cushion.

"You're so soft, Susan, soft as down. . . ." His tongue made a slight eddying circle on her, and she dug her head back, gasping, her breath chaotic. "Being close to you . . . touching you is . . . the sweetest thing, the very sweetest . . ." His hands were gliding over her thighs, under her bottom, moving her hips so she was caressed by the silk beneath her. His ragged words were like honey poured on her skin, soothing her, exciting her. "Each touch has life ... like the strokes of a brush painting. When the brush meets paper ... the stroke awakens. It's called *kititsu*...." His cheek caressed the tender inner skin of her thigh. He slid upward to draw lightly on the tip of each breast. "Then ... *sohitsu* ... the brush is sent on its journey...." His lips touched low on her stomach. "And *shuhitsu* ... the brush leaves the paper; the line melts back into the eternity that brought it...."

He lowered his mouth to her and her veins became channels of flame, feeding fire to the inside ache, and a pulse began to beat there, spreading back the fever, filling her head with the white heat of rapture. She couldn't stop herself; she was frenzied as the north wind, working her hands in and out of his hair, pressing herself upward, opening herself more to him. She whimpered and he slid his fingers inside her, deep inside, and she couldn't tell his dampness from her own. His breath came in continual shivers.

Trusting and helpless, she felt him lift and turn her, exposing the milky softness of her nape, to put his mouth there and kiss her again and again, his lips caressing her flesh, his arms around her, his hands filling themselves with her breasts, pulling her back full length against him, stroking her breasts to the feverish rhythm of his kiss. And with him tight and hot against her back, the hard lines of bone and muscle and burning skin there, his hands moved downward to caress her until her breath came as sobs and she cried out, "Please, please, please ..." and he turned her on her back and filled her slowly with the goodness of him.

She saw him like a vision above her. Lamplight had given his skin the tint of pale amber, desire had left a mark like a child's sunburn over his nose and cheeks, and his enraptured eyes had a smile that made them a densely saturated blue-green, the color of an Easter egg patiently left to sit in dye. He looked so young, she would have smiled, but could not, because he said, "I adore you ... adore you ..." and put the palm of his hand on her far down and pressed, and she felt nothing but burning enchantment....

Later she lay enclosed in his arms in a wondrous state of peace, tasting his breath in her mouth, feeling his hands cherishing her body. He kissed her just over her heart, and said, "Back in Wisconsin, before we became lovers, I didn't want to sleep at night. I didn't want to dream you were with me and wake to the pain of an empty bed."

She answered, "I wanted to dream you. It was the only way I could be with you without blame. Once I dreamed I was the moon and shone on your bed."

His arms brought her so close. "Everything I feel for you, I would never have dared to dream."

In the morning, sitting on the veranda, having breakfast amid flowers and sparkling crystal and linen napkins, she leaned her chin on the heel of her hand, looked him directly in the eyes, and said, "I've never heard of this before, this loving of people with the mouth. Is it a common English way?" She watched him choke on his orange juice. "Maybe it accounts for why the English seem to have such a small number of children."

And then, at his expression, she burst into laughter and punched his arm.

Chapter 24

She hadn't been able to tell him about her last hours with her people. He'd asked; she'd evaded. He waited.

On the second morning following their marriage, she

was a long time joining him for breakfast. He found her in the room where she dressed. She was facing herself in the wall of mirrors, fully clothed. But she held another dress against her—the Amish one in which she had come to him. Her face was rapt, tense, and pensive, and he realized she was looking, not at herself, but at the dress.

Then understanding came, like a weight landing on him. She wanted to see one of her own kind, someone Amish, even a chimera. She had no photographs, no drawings. . . . And the quality that had seemed pensive to him was a loneliness so vast, so bewildered that it formed a frost layer under his skin.

Their lines of sight made sudden troubled contact in the bright mirror.

"Homesick, Susan?"

"*This* is my home now."

"You had another one before. It's all right. You don't have to pretend." He smiled. "Would you like to fly back for a visit? You can, you know. As often as you'd like."

"No!" Her eyes filled with horror, shocking him. Then in a strained tone, she said, "I've been banned, you see." She paused; a long, terrible pause. "Well, they had to. There was nothing else they could do. I had been with you and I was not contrite."

"Susan, isn't there some way our marriage would rectify—"

"No. In our marriage, in coming to live in the world, I've cut myself away. I no longer live in *ordnung*. There is no rectifying. For church members to associate with me would bring on them a ban also. It would be impossible to visit. How could I cause my parents the pain of avoiding me? It makes your soul feel like it's being cut in two parts. And my friend Fanny, she's stubborn—she won't turn her back on me. What would happen to her if she were banned, too, with her own husband shunning her, not even being able to have marital relations with her? And Daniel is angry already; he could become bitter. Even now he won't join the church. He might become estranged from it completely, and some of the younger ones with him."

The hurried, impassioned words seemed torn from her throat. She looked at the dress in her hands. "I can never go back."

He came to hold her from behind, holding tight, his face nestled in her hair, and spoke softly. "Did you come with me to spare them?"

Her answer was spoken even more softly. "I came with you because a life without you would be like a life spent shut in darkness."

Wilde wondered why ancient philosophers had seated love in the heart. He felt it in the marrow of his bones.

He remembered back to the day after Susan told him she had been banned from her community. He had bought Rachel's book, and read it as if it were a doctrine, trying to understand. She had written: "We are an optimistic family. When bad things happen, we are less prepared than most. We anticipate sunny days."

He saw it in Susan. Even now she lived with grace. If her ease of manner was only on the surface, he tried not to mine beneath it often. He couldn't bring himself to claw at her defenses. When he did urge her to tell him how she felt, she said she was content. If she'd told him anything else, he might not have been able to bear it.

The days were to savor... Susan wearing a Halston, sitting in the living room and talking to Dash on the phone, shouting, because she thought that was the only way he could hear her... Susan sitting on the marble counter of the kitchen, opening a package as if it were the most complicated thing on earth, saying, "I've never had a boughten cookie before"... Susan kneeling in prayer beside the bed, something he'd never known an adult to do. He had to control a flame of panic that he'd brought her into a place where she would always be different.

But then, the difference was so delicious. He took her to sign papers at Katelyn's office, and when they stopped in the lobby to meet one of his friends, he saw Susan staring mesmerized at the elevators. Alone with him, she said, "Where do the people disappear?"

"Which people?"

"The people who go into that little room in the wall and vanish before the doors open again." A second elevator opened and disgorged a couple. She looked startled. "How long have they been inside the wall?"

He couldn't stand it. He pulled her into the elevator, and when the door closed them in together, he kissed her buccaneer-style—he couldn't help himself.

Emerging breathless from the kiss, she said, "If *that's* what these rooms are for, it's no wonder people can't wait to get inside them."

That was one of the things she'd learned about Alan. Whatever she did, he thought it was great. On her second day, she sat by the pool while he was on the phone, dangling her legs in the water, and a violently buzzing machine attacked her. It looked like a robot. There wasn't time to think, so she grabbed up the long-handled net used to pick leaves from the pool water and tried to fend off the machine. It rushed past the net, cackling angrily, and she followed it along the poolside, beating it to pieces. Alan arrived in time to watch it wheeze and expire, and explained that it was a pool cleaner set on a timer.

"I thought it was a robot," she said.

"You make me so happy," was his reply.

What could she do but be happy too? The pain of exile would heal. The sense of being cut in parts, the longing for other smiles and faces, would fade. She'd get used to it. She was determined. But, oh, boy, what a place it was, a sunny, hazy, jangly town. The air had a taste to it like licking a metal pole on a park swing on a cold day. Everywhere there were cities, blending one into the other without country in between. She never knew where she was—it looked so much the same everywhere. The highways didn't take you anywhere, just back inside more city, like being trapped in an endless maze. Watching the cars made her dizzy; they went on and on by the thousand, no two alike. They seemed to be taking over the place. The noise they made awed her. Though Alan lived in what was considered a quiet area, she could hear the vibrations at all hours, even in the dead of night—an undertonal hum, as though the city were a great engine that couldn't sleep. But she'd get used to it. David had a word for what she was. Crazy in love, he said—and she liked that. She was crazy in love with Alan.

Alan began to work on postproduction of the film, pulling it from the ungainly alloy of rough assembly through editing and mixing—tedious, obsessive work. He dispatched permanently the love scene that had been filmed with a double to make Susan appear nude, watching it with satisfaction as it wound off the reel and coiled on the floor. He couldn't recall now the squalid ethics that he'd used to justify doing that to her. The person he'd been then was a fading nightmare.

Other projects occupied his days, the ghosts of past and future. The effects people for his next picture were trying to unload a werewolf on him that looked like a schnauzer. The "improved" version reminded him of Benji. In a couple of months, one of his previous films would be opening; there were discussions about advertising and distribution and talk about sending him to do promotion in Europe.

He had to force himself to remember that he'd once been challenged by these repetitive minutiae, for now he wanted only to get back to Susan, estranged in a technological and cultural puzzle, so unwary and vulnerable that it terrified him.

He'd read about people who claimed to have spent years in the entertainment industry without seeing drugs used. He didn't doubt it. In a world of infinite possibilities, anything was possible. It had been otherwise for him. The circles he traveled in were fast, wealthy, corrupt with privilege, thrilled with beauty and status, aggressively street-smart, and not wise. He knew where the recreation got heavy and what to avoid with Susan, and in the beginning he thought that would be enough. A month went by, two months, and he knew it would not.

What had been only amusing in the past—the level of illusion here, the trivial snobbery, the bitchiness—became increasingly ludicrous to him. Susan had an indifferent way of looking at someone's thirty-thousand-dollar Cartier bracelet that made it seem like a sideshow trinket. Poised, not shy with his friends, she was still uneasy in the eager, unstable relationships that made up the procession of his social contacts.

The sadness and badness began to filter through to her, the elegant coldness and unfettered interest in self, the men and women who bought land they never visited and bore children they never saw, and who anesthetized themselves, with drugs and drink and serial affairs, against the lives they discarded.

One of his ex-lovers encountered Susan at a party and tried to let her know about the long-dead relationship with innuendo and smiles. Susan came home quiet and sat on the garden steps. He went and sat just behind her, closing her in his arms, drawing her back between his legs.

"I've never felt for another woman what I feel for you," he said.

A long pause followed. She tucked her head back against the hollow of his shoulder. He thought she was considering his words, but when she spoke, it was to say, "Did you know that Ann Cutler had a car accident on the way to the party? Someone ran into her bumper from behind. She wasn't hurt, only shaken. You didn't see it, but when she came in, she said, 'I'm a wreck. Does anyone have a Valium?' Three, no, I think four people did. People seem to take a lot of pills here." Then, "My grandmother used to have a pill she took for her eyes, so they wouldn't get dry. There doesn't seem to be any harm in it."

Thinking back months later, he couldn't remember what he'd answered, something minor, the way he'd respond to a commonplace. He only remembered his relief that she seemed to have missed the other, uglier hurt.

For months he didn't see that it was failing. Her curiosity and resilience, her droll mood swings, the way she'd been raised not to make complaints: These things disguised the truth.

She never could quite adjust to his long work hours. Farm hours were long, too, but the family remained close, a field or two apart, meeting for three meals, the stretch of work broken by frequent intervals of visiting. There was a kind of solidarity in the way they shared caring for the farm together, not vanishing into the separate cells of mysterious lives and goals removed from one another.

She was disconcerted by his household, too. Everything was done by others, a cleaning crew that swept through in two hours, a staff to cook and shop, caterers to bring van loads of food if they entertained. She was at a loss to know how to contribute.

She could have done a film. He began looking for a vehicle for her, one they could work on together. Friends were sending scripts. He was committed to two projects first, so it would be awhile. But she didn't seem in any hurry at all to pursue a career. *Career* was hazy to her. She hadn't grown up thinking about men and women having careers. Any way one looked at it, it would be a major undertaking for her to rethink the entire course of her life.

She thought sometimes about writing to Rachel, but in the end she didn't. "I should wait for her to write to me," she would say. "With Rachel, it's better to wait until she comes to you."

Afternoons of tennis or shopping were more leisure time than she was comfortably able to digest. Instead she read fiction, nonfiction, anything; taught Amish games to the children of neighbors he hardly knew he had, letting them play with the lop-eared rabbit Luke had given him in the spring. She volunteered her time in one of L.A.'s vast public gardens, making her own circle of friendships there. She worked in their own garden also, pursuing her own exotic drifts of imagination. Three college-age men worked part time under his head gardener, and all three fell completely and obviously in love with Susan.

"I'm going to fire those drooling kids," he would say, to make her laugh. He taught her to drive and worried about her in the sea of erratic traffic, worried more about her becoming lonely.

She explored his culture, connecting in unexpected ways. She delighted in sequoias and flamenco guitar and wok cooking and reruns of "The Beverly Hillbillies." The representations of human figures in classical art were graven images to her—that prejudice hung on—but she admired abstract artists like Rothko and Pollock. The expression of mood and theme with color she understood at its most obscure and esoteric. It was reminiscent of what she had been doing for years with quilts at home.

Many things she "didn't care for." Billboards. Perfume. Horoscopes. He'd given up trying to predict. Mimes, he would have guessed. But when they walked in a downtown park on Sunday and ran into a small troupe, Susan watched them, smiling. When it was over, one of the mimes, a young man with his hair in a ponytail, handed her an imaginary flower. She took it home, planted it in their yard, and every morning he saw her going outside to pretend to water it. Once he asked her what kind of flower it was, and she said a lily. He never could bring himself to ask her if it grew. There was a passage in Rachel's book:

> To the casual observer, an Amish home will seem colorless in its lack of ornament. But take a spring walk with me around my sister Susan's garden. That rose of Damascus by the corner there is nothing more than a thicket of sticks recovering from a hard pruning. Nothing will tell you that it was a wedding gift from Fanny, planted for a surprise out of the blue while Mother kept Susan distracted on the old farm. From the petals of the very first rose, Susan made Fanny a sachet that she keeps in her linen drawer. The apple tree bears a graft John tended with care to give Susan the same sweet Macintosh apples she'd eaten as a child. It's too early now for apples, too late to see buckets on the sugar maples catching sparkling ribbons of sap, but I can hear the trickling sound as the bucket fills with bright, transparent sugar water. At the boiling, the scent of maple steam reaches far out in the fields and down the road, and neighbors come with their kids in hay wagons for fresh maple candy.

The cellar doors are closed over the new staircase my Dad built when he'd become anxious that the steps were too steep to be safe. The Persian lilacs by the paddock—those are softwood cuttings grown especially for Susan by John's mother from her own bush. Under the birch are blue irises that grew on Grandma's farm. There are other flowers, too—day lilies along the walk, coral bells, cornflowers, daisies. I could pair each with the name of the neighbor or relative who'd shared a garden with her, as she was starting to share now with the younger ones who followed.

In this way, we bond.

Harvest time arrived back in Wisconsin. Susan stopped talking about her family. She became quieter, pining, hiding it.

The way an American student of the Orient remains an American, Susan remained Amish. Learning more about his world had not made her a part of it. In her own society, she had been a complete person. In spite of her struggle to assimilate in his, he could feel she was always navigating. She was separate.

He tried, with every last atom of his love and intellect, to find ways to dim the faraway voices that called to her. So often he would succeed, and they would spend long halcyon hours together, and the world was nothing to either of them.

Yet when he awoke at night, he found her still and wakeful, her eyes a subtle sheen in the darkness. Sometimes he made love to her until they were both drained and silly and exhausted, and then she slept. Other times he took her in his arms and rocked her, his cheek on her hair, and when she fell asleep he stayed as he was, holding her.

He hoped it might help her to get away, so they flew to Arizona, to Dash's ranch, for the old cowboy's thirtieth wedding anniversary. Susan blossomed there in the cluster of kids and grand-kids and messy, happy celebration. When they came back she was quiet, sad again. At the airport, photographers caught them and she walked close to him, her legs unsteady, her hands cold and bloodless. Afterward she rubbed her eyes until the lids were sore and told him she kept seeing the print of the strobe flashes. That night, neither of them slept, and he went to the piano to smother the strain in brilliant sound.

The morning was cool and misty, wet enough to need the windshield wipers. He had to work, and he drove away with the agonized sense that he was leaving behind the immeasurably more important work of his life. At Armageddon, the last man and woman would find themselves balancing their checkbooks.

He had day meetings, then a night meeting. She drove to his office to meet him for dinner, charming him, caressing his hand with her fingers. Her smiles were wistful. She was cheerful when she kissed him good-bye, and wandered off to visit David, where he was filming a thriller on a sound stage. That old monster, she called him.

Alan was preparing to leave his own office, when David appeared at the door, the famous slough-black hair windblown, his clothes smelling of makeup, hot lights, and movie smoke.

"Alan, have you talked to Susan in the last couple of hours?"

"Wasn't she with you?"

"She was, but—" David went to the telephone. "How do I dial your house? Never mind, I see—" After a minute he cradled the receiver. "She isn't answering. Look, Alan, she might be in trouble. Tonight she ran into one of the kids who was with us in Wisconsin, Brian something. He was a grip, and I'm not sure if you were aware of it, but he's been dealing drugs in a minor way. Apparently he overheard her talking to me about having trouble sleeping, so he gave her some pills."

Alan was on his feet. "What kind of pills?"

"Maybe Seconal. Maybe Quaaludes. He's changed his story a couple of times. She asked him how to get to Griffith Park Observatory and left, but he saw her stop by the coffee machine on the way out and swallow the pills. She must have had no idea how they work. He tried to catch her, but she'd left very quickly, and for two hours he was too scared to tell anyone."

Ice spears pricked along Alan's spine. He heard himself say, "Griffith Park."

It would mean headlines, but he called the police. There was no alternative. Griffith Park could be a bad place after dark—a very bad place.

They came across her car almost immediately, but there were four thousand acres of park to comb through, looking for her, and Alan spent more than an hour listening to his heartbeat before she was found unconscious under a tree. They let him come and wake her.

They had wrapped her in blankets, and dense red from the revolving emergency light on the ambulance pulsed on her still face. There was no trace of movement under the blanket. He couldn't see her breathe. Far away, at the dim end of a long tunnel, someone was speaking to him, telling him that the officer had found her wearing no shoes or stockings and that her feet were bleeding.

He was kneeling, and felt cold, cold as though he were dying. He wanted to hold her and weep. He wanted to take her place, to be the one lying in the open with chilled skin, and have her be somewhere else, anywhere, to have her safe and warm, not here in a world where she had no defenses.

He touched her icy cheek.

When she opened her eyes, his heart contracted. He said her name softly. She didn't seem to know where she was at first. She was bewildered, like a bird blown from a nest.

"Susan . . . How are you, my love?"

"It's nice here . . . like home. I got lost, I think. . . ."

He stroked the fragile wing of her cheekbone. "Did anyone hurt you?"

"Hurt me? No. I—Do you have my shoes? I took them off. . . . Barefoot is—"

"—the best feeling." He kissed the damp bluish chill of her mouth and gently uncovered her feet. They were torn and bleeding, cut by litter and glass she'd stepped on, not able to feel the cuts in her anesthetized state.

She slept again, drifting in the heavy chemical trance.

At home, clean and warmed in bed, she stirred. He took her hand. For a long time they stayed so.

She spoke quietly. "I've been dreaming they're dead. My family."

The cold, crushing sensation sharpened in his chest. He slid his arms under her and held her against his pain.

"I see their graves so clear," she said. "Dad and Mother, my brothers and sisters, the babies too . . . Carolyn, Katie. They're all gone." Her fingers moved with drugged languor on his shirt buttons. Her head rested heavily against his bare skin. "I've buried them."

He murmured something, a comfort, a protest.

"I have, though. I'll never again tug Dad's beard, or taste Mother's bread, or touch Grandma's hair. And when Anna and Luke and Levi and all the others have children, I'll never know them and they won't know who I am; I'll be like someone in the far past who died before they were born and you can't even miss. . . ."

The pain in his chest was so deep, he could hardly breathe. His hands moved blindly in her hair.

Presently she said, "Do you remember the night we chose a star together?"

"I remember."

"Last night I tried to see our star from the garden. I hadn't seen it in so long. It wasn't there, Alan. It was just like it had vanished right out of the sky. I thought, maybe those flashing lights from the cameras at the airport did something to my eyes. Or maybe it was all drowned out by the city lights. Light pollution, you called it once. I thought I would find the observatory and try to see the star from there."

"Could you see it, Susan?"

He waited.

Finally, with wonder, she said, "No."

When she slept again, he brought over a chair and sat watching her, feeling a love for her so strong, it burned with every breath. A truth occurred to him, a simple, certain truth, and he said aloud, "I've got to get you out of here."

In the morning she went outside to water the imaginary lily and found that he had planted a real one in its place.

Chapter 25

*R*achel knew that Alan Wilde was coming. He had sent her a telegram.

He couldn't have called. She had no telephone. She'd had one for a while after she left home, taking uncanny pleasure in the act of mild defiance, proving she *could* have a telephone if she wanted. There, see, I have a phone. Haha. Except that she began to meet people and the phone began to ring. When she was in the shower, it rang. When she was writing, it rang. She discovered she didn't like the sound of it, so she got rid of it.

Alan Wilde wanted to come talk to her. Alan Wilde had to send a telegram. No, a cable. Maybe she should call it a cable. Maybe "telegram" was an outdated word, one of those that still spotlighted her Amishness.

Her first cable. There'd been an old-fashioned B-movie drama about its arrival. She imagined herself in grainy black and white, tearing it open and fainting. She hadn't fainted, of course, though it had been rather exciting. She decided to send one to Daniel sometime, for fun. DEAR DANIEL STOP HOW GOES IT STOP YOUR SISTER RACHEL.

Being excited about Alan Wilde's cable didn't mean she was excited about Alan Wilde's visit. When the initial confusion cleared about why he wanted to talk to her, worry set in. There were no subjects he'd want to talk to her about that wouldn't be painful. Talking to him carried by extension the same emotional hazards as contact with her family. It had taken weeks for her to recover from that one visit to see her parents, from the unhealthy triumph of confronting her father, from the crashing depression that came after. She was tired of hurting, impatient with it. She'd left them behind to become fully herself and here she was, perpetually entangled. One ought to be able to divorce one's family. You ought to be able to say, "I divorce thee" three times like a Moslem and have done with it. Why did she keep loving them so?

She'd had just the one letter from Susan since Susan's excommunication, that sweet, punctilious, economical account of her expulsion from the church and her subsequent marriage.

She'd put some time into thinking about how to respond to her distant exiled twin, and finally decided to send a plant. Heck, it was perfect; after the uneasy years together and the spectacular soap opera of their various departures from faith and family, the gift seemed an appropriate and funny anticlimax. Maybe Susan would take it as a gesture of reconciliation. Maybe Rachel wanted her to.

Except the plant never made it to Susan. The Los Angeles florist couldn't deliver it—there was some code; it had to be marked personal, or something. Faceless minions whose job it was to accept or not to accept offerings to the famous director hadn't recognized her name and had rejected it, politely.

She said, "Screw it, then."

Anyway, she didn't have to gear herself up to dislike Wilde. She merely assumed she wouldn't like him. His callous seduction of the chaste sister she had loved and rebuffed since birth would have been enough to make her hate him. Even without that, she didn't think she approved of people who allowed themselves to make a fortune in the arts. Artists should be outlaws, stragglers, chronic misfits, filled with pity, accepting none. They shouldn't grow rich and complaisant and lose their passion. Perhaps no one should own a disparate share of the world's resources. Perhaps she was a communist. DEAR DAD STOP JOINED THE COMMUNIST PARTY STOP LOVE RACHEL.

She laughed out loud. That was how it had been before she'd begun writing seriously, the lonely search for that moment of self-discovery, the way to justify in a word all the rebellion and tiresome sensitivity that had made growing up such a pain in the neck. Oh, those wonderful, absurd revenge fantasies where she said, "Dad, I'm gay," "Dad, I'm psychic," "Dad, I'm from another planet." She could imagine trying to explain "gay" to her father. Anyway, none of it had turned out to be true, and when her book was published the seeking vanished. She was a writer, and that explained everything, and she had a vocation and a place in the universe.

When Alan Wilde arrived, she was cleaning her typewriter keys.

She opened the door, unexamined tension curdling in her stomach, a cup of lukewarm coffee in her hand.

The face was familiar, but newspaper photos showed only one more polished celebrity. They masked the fascinating smile and warm skin tones, the hinted strength of mind and humor. He was incurably sexy. She spilled coffee on her fingers.

She made a welcoming gesture, shut the door behind him, sucked the coffee from the back of her hand, and found herself under his light, discerning scrutiny.

Okay, you, she thought, let's see how easy you are to embarrass. "Yes," she said, "Susan is the undisputed beauty of the twin set."

She'd misread him. Rather than apology, his eyes held a self-deprecatory amusement that would have warmed cold ash.

"Did I stare? I apologize. I was thinking how well you'd film. It's something I do. A bad habit."

It was nicely done. The delivery was so easy and charming that, barring polygraphic analysis, you'd have no idea if the words were sincere. She wished suddenly that she hadn't read the harrowing unauthorized biography of his childhood. We're all Christs, she thought. We've all been crucified. She could sense it in him.

In the brief silence, she heard Ginny, in the apartment downstairs, beginning to practice her harp. The song was "In the Mood." Rachel took a breath.

"I find meeting you under these circumstances to be extremely uncomfortable. Left with the initiative, I'll probably make it harder on both of us. Since you're clearly the more socially able, I'd be grateful if you'd put me at my ease, if you can."

She gave the man credit. If he was disconcerted to have the whole thing dumped like wet pudding in his lap, he didn't show it. He glanced around the room and focused on Blister, sunning himself in the front window, and said, "Ugly cat."

Talk about disconcerted. Surprised into a smile, she looked at the cat, sprawled like a balding feather boa on the narrow ledge. "Yeah," she said, "he's ugly, all right." Then there was the second surprise, his hand in a persuasive, yet matter-of-fact grip on the sides of her face, his lips in a brief, sexless visitation of her brow, his breath cool and pleasant on her skin. He stepped back smiling and she understood why Susan had lost her head.

"If that's how you put chance acquaintances at their ease, what do you do when you want to really relax someone?" She watched the voltage of his smile soar.

"Excuse me," she managed to say, mumbled something about preparing some refreshment, and went to the kitchen to recover. She spent several minutes gloomily examining the color spots on her cheeks in the refrigerator chrome before it occurred to her that she'd better produce something to eat or drink, or she'd have to go back out and say, "There's to be no refreshment after all."

She returned with hot tea and found him gazing out the window, one long, beautifully shaped hand stirring the cat's marmalade fur. In the powdery sunlight, the room began to seem to her like the interior of a dream.

Downstairs, the harp had begun to produce the "Blue Danube Waltz"—la da da da *da*, plink, plink, plink, plink. She remembered reading that he was an accomplished musician. She'd better face the music.

"I tried to arrange weeping violins for your arrival, and look what happened. I hope you like the harp."

"It's . . . heavenly." He was grinning, damn him. "So you live above a harpist?"

"A harper. She plays folk harp. If you play a pedal harp, you are a harp*ist*. If you play a small folk harp, you are a harp*er*."

He gave that a moment's cheerful thought before he added, "If you're part bird and legendary, you're a harpy."

"And if you leap at whales and try to stick them, you're a harp*oon*." *Chalk one up for me*, she thought. "When she plays in the evening while the birds sing, I feel like a mouse in a cartoon that gets hit on the head with a mallet. If you'd like, you could come back tomorrow. Fridays, she practices her accordion."

"Well . . . How are Saturdays?"

"She has friends over to sing madrigals."

"You'd better move." They were smiling at each other again, which was crazy and not what she'd anticipated at all.

"But on Sundays and Wednesdays she bakes bread and gives everyone in the building a loaf. Sit down, if you'd like."

He did. He picked up his cup and she saw suddenly that she'd forgotten to add the tea bag. It didn't seem to perturb him. He looked like one of those Californians who wasn't surprised by anything that happened in Middle America. Probably he thought it was a regional custom, serving hot water. They were frugal out here.

She went into the kitchen, found a tea bag, dunked it in his cup, and, with "Never On Sunday" seeping through the floorboards, said, "I expected to hate you."

"I don't blame you." Then, "I love her, you know."

"If you're talking about the kind of love that hits you like something that comes out of a ray gun, I don't believe in it."

"Neither did I."

Their gazes held, and then he looked down and began rather thoughtfully to drown his tea bag. Here was a man used to brewed tea, she could see. She steadied herself to ask the difficult question, and was pleased with the even tenor of her voice when it came.

"How is Susan?"

"She's . . ." His face revealed that the question was difficult for him also. A smile interrupted his thoughts. "Last night we ate in a dim restaurant. She ordered filet of sole and a flashlight. Mostly she's the same. Changeable, funny. She takes piano lessons. She studies poetry." He lifted the cup, cradling it in his hands as if he welcomed the warmth, seeming to concentrate on the simple action. He slowly gave up the smile, and said, after an extended pause, "But the black moments for her are very black. Daniel told me not to take her, and he was right."

The hurt was too great, too many-tiered to allow her to speak quickly. "Dammit, why did you come here, then?"

"Susan is an observer, not a critic. I need to know more than she tells me."

He'd spoken her name as if it were some sweet melody forever in his heart. Yes, she could understand someone loving Susan that way. She felt too full inside, like a cat with a hair ball in its stomach.

"Maybe," she said, "you should have tried harder to learn about my family before you made my sister into Hester Prynne."

He was too honest a man to defend the indefensible. Instead he looked at her steadily. "I've read your book, you know. It touched me very much." Then, gently, he said, "You didn't explain why you left."

"I wasn't ready."

"And now?"

"I try. It isn't easy to capture."

"If you would try for me, I would be very grateful. There's a possibility Susan will return. I have to know what there was about life with your family that made it intolerable for you."

Her mind froze around the words "a possibility that Susan will return." Her palms were sweaty. She grasped her knees. "I've spent most of my life torn between two worlds. The thought of Susan's having to endure that makes me physically ill."

He set down the tea he wasn't drinking. "There's another thing we have in common."

She spent a moment feeling unspeakably vulnerable, before she levered herself up, drying her palms on her jeans. She searched through a file on her desk and handed him two typed pages.

If human beings experience emotion in different degrees, the way they do bodily pain, I would be said to have a low threshold. I know this about myself. When I am very angry or afraid, I become silent and appear withdrawn to those around me. I cannot permit myself to speak or I know I will become inarticulate and perhaps tearful.

I worry about the world. It seems to me too cruel on a grand scale. In the intimate relationships in my life, I find I am no more elastic. Petty injustices and minor tyrannies disturb me. I don't like to be teased or startled or jostled. This is difficult to avoid in a large family.

Susan likes all those things. The suddenness and commotion of life with many adults and children is not offensive to Susan. She doesn't carry resentments or need long periods of quiet. She forgives easily. It is nothing to her to forgive someone; it's just done, instant, complete.

My mother is like this too. It used to make me angry. It seemed to show a lack of personal dignity, too little concern for what was just and owed to one.

I know differently now. They have a gift. The ones who accept life as it is—they're the free ones. The rest of us carry our emotions like weights.

When I left, I wrote this to my father: I will never return to live by the ways of the church. I love children; that much is bred into me. But I cannot have child after child, like Mother. I can't clean and sew and feed animals and people in an endless cycle. I can't have my reading material censored, my appearance made to conform, or my behavior patterned after the standards of the seventeenth century.

When he had finished reading, she said, "I love my family. Now I walk around with a permanent lump in my throat, but even if I have to grieve for the rest of my life, that's a price I'm willing to pay. I want to write and study and be responsible to no one but myself."

She sat opposite him. She looked at the pages, at the dull haze of light coming in the window, at his face, his clear, bright eyes, so tolerant, so filled with comprehension. You could tell anything to a man like that. She said, "Did Susan tell you that a long time ago I was attacked, out of spite, by boys from town?"

"She only told me a little. Why didn't it make you turn from the outside world?"

"I read. I knew it wasn't all like that." She swung her feet up on the couch, tucked them under her. Her legs were stiff puppet parts. "Do you know, they didn't take me to a doctor until a week after it happened? It didn't occur to them that there could have been anything sexual in the assault. They couldn't imagine that in relation to a child, and I didn't have the language. . . . City people think farm kids know everything, because we see the cycle of life in animals, but often we don't, especially girls. It isn't something we talk to one another about much, and even when you see animal behavior, you don't necessarily equate that with humans."

She didn't touch her face. It would be hot, she knew. He said only, "Of course you don't." She found the words oddly comforting.

"Anyway, what had happened had happened, and nothing could change that. They did everything they knew how to for me, but you see, it wasn't enough. This was an unheard-of thing. They were completely unprepared. I can't describe to you how I felt. When the bruises healed I could still see them on my skin. I wanted to get out of my body, to escape somewhere. . . ." Her gaze had strayed to the window. She closed her eyes. When she opened them again, she saw him looking at her, and saw the intelligent, unshockable compassion there, and remembered what he'd endured as a child. Here was one to whom explanations were needless.

"There was an anger in me so powerful . . . just a rage over what had been done to me, and there wasn't a thing I could do about it. Terrible things had happened to me, and I had no way to fight back. My parents wouldn't have allowed me to take an oath and give testimony against my attackers in court. It would have violated their beliefs.

"I stopped eating, stopped talking, and my parents became more and more frightened. They sent for the Bishop to speak with me, and he said that I must not hate, I must forgive those who had trespassed against me. He read from the Bible about forgiveness, and he took me down on the floor at his side and told me to pray with him for their salvation. Well, I prayed, all right. I've never prayed so hard in my life. I prayed that God would strike down the English boys. I got some relief then. To my parents, I seemed to improve. They didn't know I was waiting. Time passed, the town went on without pause or pestilence, and I was beginning to wonder about God. He began to seem ineffectual. But I thought, well, all right, maybe He's just biding His time.

"I had begun to spend time with a retired schoolteacher, an English lady who bought her eggs from us. She gave me books secretly, talked to me about places she'd been. One day we were talking about religion, comparing what we'd been taught, and I learned that in the town's church there was no public confession of sins. In other words, the boys who attacked me would never have to face public shame in order to be absolved. One private moment between them and God, and it would all be in the past. That easy. Even in everlasting life, I'd never be avenged.

"That's when I knew that life was irrational, and if there was any justice, it came about by accident. I was elated when I found books by English philosophers that had the same idea. It was so obvious, so clear to me that the world was God-less. It explained everything. It was the only believable story."

Rachel was quiet by nature. It had been, for her, a lengthy explanation. Silence was a relief.

Downstairs the harp had launched into "Rock Of Ages." It was positively macabre, she thought. He'd noticed it, too, because he grinned at her, but when he spoke, she thought that rarely had she heard a kinder, more soothing voice. "Did you keep your new insight to yourself?"

"No. I went to tell my father. He locked me in my room for a week. You can imagine what that did to Susan.

I'm not sure why I fought my dad so hard. It might have been because I was so attached to him, I had to fight that hard to get free. But I've learned one thing since I was banned. I've learned what it's like to go without forgiveness. I don't despise forgiveness any more, even when it's not linked to justice. In fact, I can see there's all too little of it in the world."

Chapter 26

*S*usan didn't mind waiting for him in her hotel suite.

They'd come in late last night, and she'd been fast asleep by the time Daniel had called, responding to Alan's cable. Alan hadn't said much about the call, just that Daniel was coming into the city to see them this afternoon. She was so glad about it, she could have played like a kitten. She wanted to sit in the lobby with a newspaper and see if he knew her in English clothes, her hair cut to her shoulders.

She hadn't gotten over being amused by the way Alan did things when he wanted to: *zip, zip*. She'd needed this trip—funny, she hadn't thought even how much.

She was halfway amused also by the way Alan had volunteered to see Rachel first on his own. "When she tells me I'm a degenerate and that she hates me for what I've done to you, you won't have to listen," he'd said. She told him to go without her, not because she was afraid of Rachel's tongue—she'd never been that—but because she wanted them to become friends on their own, not just out of duty. It could make all the difference with Rachel, how you approached her. Alan would know the way.

While she waited, she dressed herself in a bedgown of burgundy-colored silk and lace, one new to him. She just wanted to see what he'd do. Then she studied the jagged city skyline and the sparkling surface of Lake Michigan, picking out what the city guide said she ought to be impressed by. She contemplated the world's tallest building and tried to assemble an appropriate response, finally setting on, "Well, that's one big building." The world was getting bigger and bigger to her.

When Alan let himself into the room she said, "How'd it go?"

She couldn't tell if he'd heard the question or not, the way he was looking at her. He only said, "Wow!" and started toward her.

She fended him off with the guidebook. "Was she cruel to you?"

"There were no streamers of confetti, but I think she tried to be gentle. We're picking her up tonight for dinner. She sent this for you."

She recognized Rachel's hand on the note, the letters carefully formed—you could always tell she enjoyed the act of writing for its own sake.

Dear Susan,

I was weighted down by guilt, thinking it was my fault you were seduced by a movie director, that you went through the whole thing to earn that money for me. Now that I've met Alan, I can see maybe I did you a good turn.

I can hardly call it rivalry, what was between us while we were growing up. You were better at all things. I know you did your best to equal things up and count me in. I guess it didn't work because I didn't want in badly enough. We were stuck in that cycle of generosity, rejection, and regret.

You were the one I wanted most to understand how stifled I felt, but it couldn't be. You lived fully; you were too complete and satisfied to know the kind of hunger I felt. I know you always had the feeling you were disappointing me, and in a sense you were. I wished you were angry too. You know me. I always felt as if I talk to people through one of those screens in prison. I'm not warm like you; I don't have the knack.

I wish I were your friend.

Love,
Rachel.

Susan felt a quiver inside, a part of her beginning to relax that had been tensed for a long, long time. She swallowed.

Alan said, "Come here."

"First you have to tell me more."

"If you're going to look like that, you probably won't get much sense out of me."

The sensual heat in his eyes began its work on her pulse. She got that funny smile only he knew how to produce in her. "What's going on in these private talks with Daniel and Rachel that you haven't told me about?"

"Nothing might come of it. I don't want you to worry."

"That won't work. I sense things. What are you going to do?" She grinned. "Let's communicate."

"Tomorrow Daniel and I are going to talk to your parents."

What a way to lose a smile. "Oh, no. Please. I've told you nothing can come of it. It's no good talking—it only causes hurt. They won't accept me while I live in the world. What good to go there and have them—"

"But they could accept you if you came back to live."

The air around her tingled like winter. "What are you saying?"

"I want to tell them I'm willing to live with you in a new community where you can practice your faith if your parents will agree to accept you back as their daughter."

She heard the guidebook hit the floor before she knew her fingers had released it. His image softened to a glassy blur. "What—" The word didn't come out well. She had to try again. "What can you be thinking of?"

"That you look magnificent. The rest is censored."

She tried to decide whether she was holding in laughter or tears. "Alan, you can't adopt a view of God because you care for a woman."

"I know that. It might strain credibility to pretend to a conversion. Daniel thinks we might be able to find another Plain community that would accept your marriage to an outsider."

Her legs were poor support. "There's nothing like that near Greyling. Maybe not even in Wisconsin."

"Maybe not. It could mean your family would have to move if they wanted to live near us."

"*Daniel* had this idea?"

"He's wanted to leave for some time, Susan. In fact, he flew out with Fanny's husband to look at land near liberalized groups in Indiana and Pennsylvania. He's ready to go with me to your parents."

"It couldn't be . . . it's just too . . . Mother and Dad would have to leave everything they know—land Dad's worked since he was a boy. For Daniel it's not so much. He's always wished he could have the farm more modern, but for my parents . . . The differences between Plain groups may seem small to you, but to us they're vast. There are no small acts of faith. Each one has meaning." A wet track tickled its way across and down her cheek. "Oh, my dear, even if they were persuaded, how could you think you'd be happy in the country, after the way you've lived?"

His smile burned her to the soul. "It doesn't matter to me where I live any longer. It only matters that it be with you."

Love filled her like the swell of wind in a tree crown. She stood so until her smile grew like his, and then she said, "Come here."

She understood why he had to try. But she had also understood from the beginning that leaving home would be forever. Hope was too dangerous. She permitted herself no more than the most frail flicker—and that way it was merely searing when he came home late the following day and held her in silence and she knew he had failed.

Two days after the visit by her banned daughter's English husband, Rebecca Hostetler had a troubling recollection.

It had nagged at her all day and stayed with her that night as she lay in the darkened bedroom beside her husband.

The sun had come up on the finest morning in her memory, and after breakfast Levi had gone off behind the tool shed to burn leaves, and she'd taken Katie out to the yellowing grass to play catch. When the ball rolled under the blue spruce by the porch, she didn't want Katie scratched by the needles, so she herself had crawled under the evergreen's heavy skirt. As she'd knelt breathing pine resins mixed with the sharp scent of burning leaves and the sunless dust under the porch, the strangest feeling came over her that this had happened to her once before. Once before she'd been like this, the branches sweeping down around her, her knees up by her nose, smelling pine and leaf smoke. It wasn't a recent memory, she knew. It came from way back, perhaps even from her early childhood, a memory that had vanished totally over all the years of her adult life. Why would she have been crouched so, as if she were hiding? Why had that moment been so important that it would come back to her after so much time?

She couldn't place the memory, and it bothered her, and then it came back to her while she'd been dusting the German Bible—it came clear, complete, as if it had happened yesterday.

She couldn't place her age at the time, but she'd been little, real little. It'd been Church Sunday, and the preaching had been on the faith of Abraham.

She heard for the first time about the terrible day God had asked Abraham to kill his own child. She remembered the horror of each detail, the distraught father lying to the curious child, telling him that they were walking up the mountain to sacrifice a goat, how he had covered the child's eyes so that he might not see the knife, how he had bound him and laid him on the cold stone altar.

Sickened, not a bit consoled that God had sent an

angel at the last to stay Abraham's hand, she'd been good
and scared after service. She hardly knew where to turn
for comfort. Not in her worst nightmares had she guessed
that the cruel streak God showed the heathen could come
out against His own people. Her father was a godly man.
Suppose God got the idea to test her dad's faith, maybe to
ask him to take her out to the field and take her life, just to
see if he'd do it. And her dad would do anything for the
Lord.

She'd hidden herself under the porch lattice by the
yews and stayed there until evening, when her folks found
her and brought her inside for supper. They'd fussed over
her, asked her why she'd done such an odd thing, and,
when she wasn't able to tell them, they'd loved her up and
put it down to childish nonsense. Set to her chores, the
familiar tasks of her family life had begun to seem normal
once more, and in a few days she forgot her terrifying
thoughts, the way children will. Something had erased
them as surely as if they'd never been there, and then
returned them to her now, just as if they'd never been
gone. Why?

Might be because she wasn't sleeping good. All kinds
of strange things came into your head when you didn't
sleep, things you'd never think of otherwise.

Amos wasn't sleeping either. That was unusual. Most
nights he slept hard even if something was disturbing him.
The long hours working outdoors took care of that. But he
was awake now. When he slept she could hear his breathing, and the peaceful rhythm carried her into sleep more
than half the nights of her life. Tonight he was quiet.

She had to get herself to sleep. Last night had been
like this, and in the morning it had been real hard to get
herself out of bed. She'd felt old, and she wasn't used to
that.

She wasn't used to thinking of Amos as old either.
Funny how many years went by and you didn't notice the
extra weight and the lines, and then one day you did, as if
they'd come overnight.

She rolled up on her side and began to stroke his hair,
up and away from his brow, following the wave in it with
her fingertips.

What she knew about giving, she had learned from
him. She'd come to the marriage a little spoiled from her
family. He'd never said much, but still she'd watched him,
to be like him. She always especially admired how he
didn't ignore his daughters in favor of his sons, the way
some did. No matter how hard he worked, he could find
the time for a little fun. And in their most private moments, like this one, he'd never put a hand on her that
wasn't tender; he was never in a rush, although she
wouldn't have complained if he had been sometimes. What
might have been duty between them was a joy, and it was
his doing.

So close they were, and yet she kept her secrets, and
she imagined he had his too. There was the dark-brewed
tea she used to rinse through her hair to shade down the
white tones. She got and lost a smile, thinking back to the
awful thing she'd kept from him, that horrible night when
she'd found Rachel gone from her bed and waked up
Daniel to help look for her, and they'd found her by the
creek on a blanket with Seth. Seth had been the scared
one. Her fey, moody daughter, twenty years old, had said
calmly, "I wanted to know how it would be with him.
Maybe it's not a sin. Maybe God is the devil and he wants
to keep it from us."

For herself, she'd been too numb to speak. It was
Daniel who asked her, "So how did you find it?"

Rachel answered him with cold contempt. "God is
right. It is a sin."

Rebecca wondered if it was different for Rachel now.
She'd asked Daniel once in private if there was someone in
Rachel's life. Yes, he said.

She knew why Rachel had been drawn to Seth. He was
like her, severe and unsentimental, and he'd left long ago,
been outside, come back. There was that streak of rebel in
him.

There used to be a question in her mind whether or
not Rachel would have stayed if she'd been with a better
man. What had gone wrong to make her so different? Was
it something in the seed, some flaw in herself she'd passed
on, a hidden moral weakness that had deformed the spirit

of her daughter? One thing didn't change: No matter what, she didn't find she could love her daughter any less.

She stirred restlessly, and Amos turned in the dark, drawing her head onto his shoulder. She put her arms around his strong neck and buried her face in his whiskers. His big, rough hand touched her on the cheek.

"What are you thinking of?" she asked into the quiet.

"It got to me today when Beachy said how we shouldn't grieve over the girls because we had so many others." His voice was very low. "Like they was puppies for replacing."

"They don't understand," she whispered back. "Sometimes I have to bite my tongue, not to say anything back."

Wind came through the window, stirring the strings of her *kapp* on the side table. In the same low voice he said, "I've been thinking back to when Rachel started to school." His whiskers tickled her nose with each word. "She used to say how she was going to run off and live in a hollow tree, you remember? Like there was hollow trees all over just waiting for her to move in."

He rarely spoke of Rachel, only like now, in the dark. Only to her. She said, "Remember when they were born— all the attention we got? Everybody was so excited to see twins. They were the funniest-looking babies, so little, and all that black hair and round brown eyes. When I think about them, I see their child faces mostly, not their grown-up ones."

"We never dressed them alike," he said.

"Maybe we should have."

His face nestled to the side of hers. His beard curled like a small scratchy animal into the curve of her neck. "We just couldn't get them straightened out. Rachel got led around by the head; Susan got led around by the heart. You know, of the two, it was Susan I worried about more. She had that streak of wildness in her, how she liked to be out walking by night." His sigh cracked as though the very air he breathed were too sharp. "I never thought we'd lose them, Rebecca."

Longing caught in her chest. "Just when they got old enough to really talk to, they're gone."

Outside the wind switched direction. Pine scent puffed across the bedclothes, carrying a faint reminder of the leaf pile. The troubling images of Abraham and Isaac crept into her mind, teasing at her. She tried to push them out, but they clung and clung, and then suddenly they were bleached in sudden, blind understanding. She knew. Just like that, she knew. The memory hadn't come without purpose. She knew why God had sent Abraham to the mountain, why the story was so important that it had been put in the Bible, what lesson God had meant to teach for all time on the day He had stopped Abraham's hand.

For the first time, she saw her way clear.

Aloud she said, "He wouldn't ask it of us. God wouldn't ask us to deny our own children."

On their fifth and last morning in Chicago, Alan was tied up on the phone, so Susan kissed his nose and went out to get her last view of the tallest building on earth.

The streets were torn up, and at the corner there were men in work clothes pouring a concrete sidewalk. They stopped to watch her walk by, and when she smiled at them, a young man wearing a red kerchief headband slapped his hands over his heart and pretended to collapse. That kept her smiling for a bit.

She looked up at the massive structures where people lived like cliff dwellers. When her neck got sore, she watched the different kinds of people. The human museum, Alan always called it. Homo Sapiens Metropolitana. There were infinite paths to follow. She knew she would always be like an explorer out here, excited by what she saw, wearied by it.

The scrawny stick trees struggling out of the concrete were shedding leaves that cartwheeled off down the streets like withered golden butterflies. She wondered what happened to leaves in the city, with no earth to sink back into. Maybe they rolled through the streets as vagabonds until they turned to dust.

At least she and Rachel could be orphans together. That was something. That was a lot. For the rest of it, she would have to be careful. She would have to be tough. You made decisions, you must stand with them. It was important to live with all the dignity one could muster. The raw sorrow inside was an inconvenience, nothing more, and she would shove it off again and again until it too was dust.

A long black automobile with dark window glass waited outside the hotel, the kind Alan rode in often. He thought nothing of it; he'd earned a million dollars before his eighth birthday. It was a way to find some privacy. But it suddenly put her in mind of Rachel, talking to the world from behind a prison screen.

She looked pale to herself in the glass doors, but her shoulders were firm, right up there, and her chin was good and high.

Inside, the hotel lobby was quiet. She saw the suitcases, and then Alan, who smiled at her. With him was a man in a freshly brushed Amish Sunday coat, his back to her.

She knew him even before he turned around. Her stomach flipped over, and she wanted to cry.

The man took off his hat and stood with his hands at his sides, gazing at her as though he weren't going to stop looking for a long, long time. She took two steps toward him, hesitated, and he began to walk toward her, fast, and then she was walking fast, too, and he put out his arms. As they came around her, drawing her in, against his broad, comforting chest she whispered, "Dad."

When we are small, my father takes each alone into the woods and teaches us to follow a path. Don't wander into the trees, he tells us. Keep on, even when the way narrows. Beyond the curve, you find a fallen tree. Sit there and wait for me.

He can see us through the trees, of course, but we don't know that. The first time we get scared, and stop and call out, *Dad!* But there comes a day when we do it, we take off and wait alone until he comes smiling, and we know we've learned something very special.

Chapter 27

Amos Hostetler watched the rain dwindle.

Best kind of rain, this, coming down like snowflakes. It sunk straight into the soil. In an hour, you'd be hard put to find a puddle. July rain was nothing like spring rain, with the cow yard turned to swamp. Tonight he wouldn't have to hear Luke and Levi grumbling about the time it took to wash caked mud off of dirty teats, or cussin' when they got slopped in the face with a wet tail. It would be quiet, cows chewing, milk hittin' the pail, one of those nights when he might get talking to the boys and forget the hour. They'd had some of their best talks that way. Separated by the cows, the boys couldn't see his face, just hear his voice, and they seemed to open up easier that way. They'd let him know if something was troubling them, or if they had a question for him they would have been embarrassed to ask another time.

Maybe he should have had his daughters milk. Could be those hours in the barn were why Daniel had stayed, when his two oldest girls had left.

It was in the cow barn that he'd begun to care for Alan. When they'd first moved to be close together, he wouldn't have thought that was possible. He'd had no use for the man back then. The articulate tongue, the charm, grated on him. Those engaging manners had worked too well to pull Susan into the mire. When he saw Alan, he got a picture of Susan on her knees before her community trying to explain why she'd fallen in sin with a man she'd barely known a month. Alan's efforts to reunite them with Susan were small enough compensation for the anguish he'd caused.

Even just after the move, when he got to see a lot of them and noticed how good Alan was to Susan, how he thought the world of her, he could bring himself to feel nothing but cold toward the man.

It had been far into the spring before they got the farm sold and made a move to the new one, eight hundred miles away, and they had to settle in and get a late corn crop into the ground. On top of it, Levi got his arm crushed—broken in two places—when they were moving the bull, and a week later, Luke came down with glandular fever. Daniel had fields of his own to see to. So, reluctantly, with his boys laid up, he'd accepted Alan's help. They plowed thirty-five hours straight through, stopping only to eat and for him to bark orders at Alan. They got to milking late, by lantern light. Things had gotten quiet, the way they do. Then quieter yet. "Alan?" he'd called out, and got no answer. He'd walked around a Holstein and found Alan fast asleep on the milking stool, his head resting against the big cow's broad belly.

He'd had to chuckle, but then something took hold of him inside. God had planned it that way, he saw later. The Lord had let him see Alan that way. In the innocence of sleep, his hair in his face, the startlingly handsome face relaxed, his son-in-law hadn't looked more than fourteen years old. A fresh view of what had happened between Alan and his daughter came into his mind: the possibility that, instead of being a bad man, Alan had only been a lost one, who'd found hope in the goodness he saw in Susan.

As if Alan were one of his own, he'd woken him up and led him to sleep on a pile of clean straw, with a blanket over him.

The seed of affection planted that night took hold, and had grown in the two years since, and by now he'd come to love this unlikely son-in-law as though he were one of his own boys. The other bitterness began to dwindle that night also, just as if it were a thorn drawn out.

He'd come here so as not to lose his daughters, and at first he hadn't seen much good in the new community. There was a lot to get used to, too much change, and from what he'd seen of change, it brought plenty of bad with the good. Even the look of the Amish here was different— the men's hair a little shorter, the hats a little wider. They even sang their hymns a little faster.

He couldn't see so much to like in the way they farmed, either. Most had tractors. He didn't approve of that. It was too hard on the soil; those heavy machines packed it down, and the roots couldn't get air, the way they should. And the cost! How many more acres to plant, how many more head to milk to pay off the bank note and buy gasoline. So what did Daniel do the first week they arrived, before he'd even gotten the furniture in his house? He'd gone off to pay money down on a tractor, just as if he'd been waiting to do it all along! Amos had had words with his son over it, that's for sure. Not that it did any good to have words with Daniel over anything. He'd just tell you, "I can see your point," and go off and do what he wanted anyway.

At the time, he'd had some suspicion Alan was egging Daniel on to the new ways, but it hadn't turned out that way at all. Daniel and Alan had bought land together— good land, too. There was a partnership between them, with Alan putting up a greater share of the money, taking part of the day from his writing to help with some of the labor. What got to everyone, though, was the way Alan liked the old ways best himself. When he plowed, he liked to work the horses. It was quieter, he said.

That had been another worry when they'd first moved. Alan's money. Rebecca in particular had feared that Susan might not be accepted because Alan was so well off. He might build himself a great big house and drive some fancy automobile, and that would cause hard feelings. You saw a lot of people with that fault in them. It was human nature to be covetous. But here again Alan had surprised them. He bought a one-hundred-year-old farmhouse, and everybody in the new church said, "Oh, poor Susan, she's going to have to live in that old house." Then he and Susan got it all fixed up inside, so it was about the most beautiful house you ever saw, all refinished oak and some fine furniture brought from California and overseas, and everybody just said, "Isn't it nice what those two have done with that old house? That took a lot of work."

His own new house he'd liked right away. There was another bedroom, for one thing, and that meant Rebecca's sister didn't have to share a room anymore, and that put her in a good frame of mind. And there was indoor plumbing and electric. He didn't use the electric much, but he had to admit he didn't miss the trip to a frosty outhouse on a January night. It was easier on his mother, too. He liked best the screened-in porch facing west, where they could sit out after supper and not get bit up by mosquitos in late summer, and watch the sky change to gold and red and pink while the sun sank down behind the woods. Or on days like today, he could sit out and watch the rain and let his dinner settle before he went off to the field in the afternoon.

Sitting right here on the porch, as he was today, he had the one view of which he'd never tire and that each day he wanted to explore again. He could watch over his family.

The clouds had thinned out enough to let sunshine sift through with the last drops of rain, and the kids were out already. Norman and Chester were halfway to the creek with a watermelon, to leave to cool for supper. Freeman and Carolyn were tearing around on the wet grass, slipping, sailing pie plates for each other to catch. That clump of white birch was at its best with rain and sun bright on its leaves, and Carolyn stood beneath it with her legs crossed, itching her nose, watching her turtle cropping grass. If he leaned almost to the screen he could see Katie's little head where she was playing in the flowers, squeezing the snapdragons to make them talk to her.

"And how are *you* feeling today?" she asked a snapdragon.

"Oh, not so good," answered the snapdragon in a squeaky voice. "I got the measles last night."

"Oh, that's too bad. Well, I'll get you all better soon," she said soothingly. She pinched the petals open and peered inside. "Let me look into your throat. And now I'm going to take your temperature. . . ." She closed the snapdragon's jaws around a tiny stick.

He chuckled softly to himself, and thought about

what Susan had told him last week. She had read a quote from an English painter who said all the gestures of children are graceful.

He had to look over his shoulder to see the barn. There was Jacob with a big, old black king snake in his two hands. What a big one. Four feet if it was an inch. For the life of him, he couldn't figure out what Jacob was doing, sneaking around with that snake. Then he remembered how Luke and Levi had taken off for the mow after dinner with a checkerboard to lay up there and listen to the rain on the barn roof and play checkers. Jacob slipped in through the side door to the barn. Amos listened for a minute or two, and then yelling erupted, screaming like you'd never heard, and Jacob came racing around the side door laughing his head off, and a second later Luke and Levi came tearing out after him with red faces, and they weren't laughing a bit. They all disappeared around the back of the barn.

Yah, he thought, *you better run good, Jacob. Boys who throw snakes on their brothers really got to know how to run good.*

Rebecca came by the kitchen window that let out on the porch and asked what the racket by the barn was about.

"Just the boys in the mow," he said.

She cut off a peach slice and leaned out to give it to him on the end of a paring knife. She was putting up peaches today, bushels of them, he didn't know how many, and besides Mary, she had Susan and Fanny over, and Rachel, who was staying.

The move had been good to Rebecca. He was glad about that. She'd missed some of the folks and things they'd left, but she'd found plenty to like here, and the electric in the kitchen was a big help to her. She got through work a lot faster with some of the new gadgets, the mixer and what Katie called the chopper-upper. It made him warm up to electricity, seeing how it made things easier for Rebecca. He wanted things nice for her, as nice as could be. He watched her going back to working with the girls and marveled, the way he did sometimes, that so many children could come from that one little body. It was a miracle. He'd just like to know how anyone could keep from admitting that it was a miracle. When he looked at his children and thought about how they'd come from her, he felt his chest swell up with gratitude to her and pride in her.

But I've never told her that, he thought. I've never said that to her. Tonight I will. Tonight I'm going to say to her, "Thank you for all you went through to have my children."

Laughing came from the kitchen—howling, more like. Susan had said something to make Fanny and her aunt Mary and grandmother laugh hard, and then Rachel put in her bit of a joke and bent them double. And then Anna murmured something thoughtful.

Like a mending wound, it was getting better between Rachel and the rest of the family, although when she came to stay it was for no more than a day or two, almost as though she didn't dare stay any longer or she might not be able to leave again. And with him she kept up a barrier that neither of them seemed able to breach. When they tried to talk to each other, they fought. He couldn't get over how tough his twins had been, those oldest daughters of his, how they'd stuck to their guns no matter what, one to choose the life she'd wanted, the other to choose the love.

He had Susan back now, and was thankful for that. With Rachel, he didn't know. He just didn't know. He prayed every day that she'd be saved. It was awful hard looking at her, belligerent, desperate, and plucky, to think God could harden His heart against her, that He had to know how she was and maybe make allowances.

It had been a mistake to blame her writing. That wasn't what had made her leave. The writing was a talent, God-given. It was her spirit that had made her go, to see what was outside, and if it was better.

Two writers in the family. Think of that. Once he'd said to Alan, to make him smile, "Two writers is too much for one family." It was strange how Rachel had gone in one way looking for freedom and Alan went in the other, and they'd both found it. It meant something; he couldn't think what. He'd have to get it sorted out in his mind.

Rachel had turned around in the kitchen, and she was staring at him, just as if she had the idea he was thinking about her. She hesitated. She wiped her hands on her apron, taking longer than it should have.

Again he felt that helplessness and that yearning. He smiled at her. She stayed solemn, like she was thinking about something else. Then she swung around and marched from the kitchen. His heart sank.

Something made him look over to the screen door, and he saw her there behind it. She pushed open the door, let it slam at her back, and sat down at his side.

"Hi, Pop," she said.

It was the first time she'd sought him out since her banning. He felt thrilled and at a loss. "Hi yourself."

"It was a nice rain."

"It was just what we needed," he said.

And because they couldn't talk, not without a fight, they sat there side by side and were quiet together, watching the sun come out, and in a while his hand came over and held hers.

From the window above his desk, Daniel watched the breeze comb wetness from the alfalfa, wrinkling the hay in wings of white shadow. It'd be dry enough to mow later, and in the meantime, he could put his accounts up to date . . . unless Joan came back from riding in the rain with Luke and distracted him, which would be fine too.

For him, life was nearly perfect.

He was able to worship in the gentle, severe faith of his ancestors, one that had brought him serenity since childhood, in spite of his reservations, and if he could do that, and farm, and read, and have love, that was perfect. And he had love.

Susan and Alan had plenty of company, old friends with luggage tags stamped LAX, LGA, CDG. They came out of curiosity at first, now for the fun of it, as though to a chicly rustic resort, to mock and admire and find rest and talk late into the night.

Joan was the most frequent visitor. She came when she could between films and Susan's refrigerator filled with Pepsi and Perrier and the hall outside the guest room

332 SHARON AND TOM CURTIS

smelled of face powder and perfume. She adored the children, brought them whimsical expensive presents, fairy tale games from Germany, Scandinavian puzzles, chocolates in gold foil.

Most of all she came for him. She played at farming like a French queen at a Versailles dairy. She followed his footsteps while he plowed, went sledding with him by moonlight, cried when she left.

He'd tried to keep it in perspective in the beginning, and for him perspective had meant that he would not bring his passion for her to physical completion. Except then one night he'd come into his bedroom to find her wearing nothing but his hat, and she'd asked him if he thought black felt flattered her. He'd discovered then there were limits to his virtue.

"Oh sweet girl," he'd said, sometime during the night, "will you marry me?" He'd stopped her answer with his kiss so she wouldn't have to refuse him aloud. He knew her answer already. *Wife is a four-letter word* he'd heard her say sometimes, and *I could never give up the glitter*.

They didn't make it harder for each other by planning tomorrow. They loved in the fullness of the present.

He didn't anticipate a miracle. He'd never thought it was easy for God to intervene in nature. There was a balance to things. Maybe to answer a prayer for rain in Ohio stuck Kansas with a drought.

So he must learn to accept the idea that he wouldn't grow old being able to wrap himself in red hair.

Daniel looked up from a seed bill when he heard his screen door creak open and crack shut. He came into the kitchen to find Joan sitting on the kitchen table beside a cherry pie. Her legs were flecked with damp grass and her halter top was shining wet. Luke grinned and gallantly put up his hat to cover her chest.

Then Luke left and she took off the halter and squeezed it out in his hair. When he took her in his arms, this time he didn't shake away the hope that if there were any miracles floating around up there, he and Joan just might snag one.

The rain had ended.

Early-afternoon quiet crept into the old upstairs bedroom. Sunlight broke through a side window, channeling in a wand over the plain bedstead, the cotton quilt, and Alan Wilde's denim jeans.

He was, in every sense, at peace.

He lay at an angle, hands under his head, his son a pleasant chunky bundle on his chest. Everyone should have moments like this, when time had no importance.

He heard the breeze in the corn, the muffled chirr of the refrigerator. A dove crooned near the woods. His little boy hiccuped in his sleep.

The baby wore only a diaper. His warm, rounded limbs were outflung in sleep, and they felt to Alan like an embrace. He loved every detail of this small body, the puffy bottom lip, bluish-pink eyelids shut over Hershey-bar eyes, the curls as soft and as bright as rook feathers nuzzling his skin.

The baby had been born in this bed. Alan had thought that Susan would be safer in a hospital. It had been his only serious conflict with her family since he'd bought the farm. How could he be so hard, they'd wanted to know, surrounding Susan with strangers at a time like that? What was so safe or comfortable about making a woman take a trip to the hospital in the midst of her labor? The baby had ended the argument by coming quickly, and two weeks early, right in the middle of Christmas dinner. As Susan's mother said, there was scarcely time to get off her apron. "I just did it to get out of doing the dishes," Susan said after. Carolyn's crayoned card, with every letter a different color, was still tucked in the frame of the mirror. It read: "WELCOME, I LOVE YOU, DEAR BABY."

There'd been a time—he could barely remember it now—when he couldn't understand how people could bring children into the world, when it had seemed like a cruel and selfish act, when families had seemed to be a combination of fable and Freudian nightmare. That was a different him.

Contrary to popular wisdom, native caution, and hard experience, he'd given up everything to be with her in the Midwest near her family. He had let go the career, the houses and cars, the jazzy perks of fame. "Dear Katelyn," went his note, "I'm checking out of Hotel California." No one he knew was quite able to assimilate it. Studio stock had begun to fall minutes after his agent had made the announcement.

It was just as well for the movie that he'd allowed it to open first. By everyone's definition, it was a good one to ride out on. It made money and netted Academy Award nominations for screenplay, score, set design; it took an Oscar for special effects. *Nothing for direction—that was appreciation for you,* Alan thought. It meant little to him now. It only amused him.

He'd even scored with the critics. They'd dubbed it Alan Wilde's eerie fairy tale. "Each shot so lovingly framed, so visually arresting, so intimate, one almost feels embarrassed viewing it. No director has ever approached technique with more originality. But newcomer Susan Peachey runs away with the film with her sheer playful charm and abounding joie de vivre." Those less enamored of the film said it was a closet Gothic, "Alan Wilde in a public identity crisis." "Alan Wilde has discovered sentiment, God help us all." And his favorite: "Never have we seen a director more carefully restrain his impulses toward greatness than Alan Wilde. In this film, it almost catches up with him. We still wait for the man to find himself."

For the man himself, the wait was over. For his old friends, the change had been difficult to accept.

Susan had just learned she was pregnant when Katelyn arrived by surprise one morning, in response to an open invitation. By chance, and maybe it was a little much, she had her first view of Alan behind a horse-drawn plow. Making a corner, he saw the rented white Chrysler New Yorker, with Katelyn, in a black Persian-lamb hip-length jacket, staring at him over barbed wire.

When he'd gotten close enough to hear she said, "Oh, dear God, Alan, how can you?" Taking in the Levi jacket and boots: "You've only done this because you know it's such superb theater. If you have suspenders under that, I've done with you." He had flashed open his jacket to show that he didn't wear them. She'd pointed at the plow. "Is that difficult?"

"The horse does it all. I'm strictly luggage. Come and try."

Lamb jacket and snakeskin heels went into the Chrysler, and in her stocking feet she let him put her ahead of him between the shafts and position her hands on the plow handles. He clucked to the bay mare, flapping the lines. With her meticulously cared-for chestnut hair blowing in his face, he was showing her the way the furrow of rich earth grew from the pasture, saying, "You don't have to bear down on the handles. The plowshare is designed to cut into the ground by itself," when he realized something was wrong. He turned her around, and found she was crying, her face white and furious.

"It's such a waste," she said. "It's such a bloody waste. This is not a sane way for you to spend your time."

He pulled the horse to a stop and stood with her like that, resting his elbows on her shoulders; then, with affection, his chin on her head.

"I can't make horror movies, Kate. I don't feel any more horror."

"For God's sake, who asked you to? Characterization is your strength. You can make any kind of picture you want."

"I've left a lot of money back there, invested in good movies."

"Throw a stick at the San Fernando Valley and you'll hit a thousand fools who want to lose money making movies. But try to hunt up someone with honest creative energy and you'll go begging. They need you, not your money, and all you want to do is grow vegetables and turn into one. You came here for her, but what are you doing for yourself?"

He smiled. "I'm writing a play."

There was a long pause. She rubbed her wet nose against his jacket sleeve, and said thickly, "Is it any good?"

"You read it and tell me."

She read it later at the farmhouse, her coffee turning cold. Set before the Civil War, the play was about a feisty and intrepid family escaping slavery, making its way north to freedom in Canada on the underground railroad, staying with Quaker farmers, under taverns, in the back room of a bordello. It was a story about liberation, and, surprisingly, a comedy.

When Katelyn was finished, she kissed Susan and said, "For this he was born."

One year later, the play had opened on Broadway, and it was still playing to almost full houses.

The baby made a tense movement and woke up, depositing a shiny thread of drool on his chest. Realization must have hit that he'd been tricked by Machiavellian stratagems into napping, and his pixie face puckered to cry. Then he seemed to change his mind and poked his fist in his mouth, teething drowsily on it with sore gums.

"Hi, mouse."

The baby chewed ruminatively, staring thoughtfully at him before glancing suspiciously around the room.

"Ma-ma?"

"At Grandma's. She'll be home soon."

The baby pulled the soggy hand from his mouth, examined it, and used it to explore his father's face.

Slowly stroking the satiny hair, Alan said, "Let's get up and get you a new diaper."

"No." The long-lashed eyes were stern. He was entering a negative stage—normal, Susan said. Alan gazed back at the baby, marveling that anything so small could have a distinct personality.

"Want to get dressed?"

"No."

Really fascinated now, Alan asked, "Want to play?"

"No," was the quietly satisfied answer.

"Want a million bucks?"

"No."

"Want to grow up and have hot sex with starlets?"

"No."

"Want a cookie?"

"N—" The gears of a year-and-a-half-old brain clicked silently into action. Eyes narrowed briefly in cunning, and then the face ignited into the fabulous smile that never failed to make Alan's heart feel as if it were turning over in his chest. Susan's smile.

"*Yes!*"

*   *   *

When they were done with the peaches, Susan walked with her grandmother west of the barn to the slough pasture to look for black raspberries—black caps, Grandma called them. She had a special way she liked them, made into sauce for dipping bread in.

Grandma told her about the old days, when Susan's great-uncle had been a bee finder. He'd chase those bees through the woods to get to a bee tree, and when he did, he had such a way with bees, he could reach right down into the hive without getting stung.

Images from the story took hold in Susan's imagination while she rode home on horseback. She liked that about living, that just when you thought you'd heard all the stories, new ones came along. Rachel would write the story down, Alan might too, and it would be saved, while it might not have been otherwise. When you saved stories, you held onto time.

It was important to hang onto time. She felt a little blue, because when she'd taken Grandma home, it had been hard for the frail legs to climb the steps, harder even than last month. After each step, they'd had to take a rest, and Susan had wanted to hold her grandma and hang on tight.

Lord, thank you for giving me these days with her.

Warmth and a murmur of comfort surrounded her.

When she got home, she wanted to be with Alan and her son.

Her house had kept a good smell from the rain, fresh and cedary. Wooden houses had a way of reminding her that they'd come from a living thing.

She came in quietly, on the off chance that Alan was writing, though that wasn't likely, not with the baby. He usually wrote early in the morning, tapping the fertility of his mind, where there'd been dreams only moments before. That was a change. Back in California, he used to get out of bed to business and coffee and write tired. Now the writing came first, catching his best.

No. He wasn't in his office. The word processor was off.

She sat at the Steinway and began to play her half of the Pachelbel "Canon." It was something Alan liked to do, make up one-piano duets they could play, and they often played for her family. *Ordnung* wasn't so strict here on instruments in the home, so it was all right. Alan said the people here were the most appreciative audience he had ever seen, instrumental music being so rare and special to them. Alan had even coaxed her dad into accepting a record player and some albums of band music, and she'd caught him sometimes listening and tapping his toe to the melody.

On winter evenings she and Alan played in front of a bright, fragrant fire and the music seemed to stay close and wrap them in warmth. When they played in spring at sunset, the music seemed to stretch far out and become part of the pink and gold and violet of the air. Both parts of the duet were complete in themselves, but brought together they expanded with new life and richness. Because the farm covered a lot of space, whenever one of them needed to call the other, a loud piano solo would do the trick.

Before long Alan came into the house, with the baby under one arm and the Lop under the other. He held the baby up to her face for a kiss, and then put him in the playpen with his toys. Alan joined her at the piano, sitting close.

He came right in with his part, knowing where she was in the piece. Each time he played differently, altering the mood and flavor. Three years she'd been playing and still she felt all thumbs. She never could get over his ease and excellence.

He liked to play so their hands would touch, cross each other, caress, but today that didn't last, because he began to play with his hands covering hers. Lightly, thrillingly, he played his fingertips up her bare arms and then lay her down slowly backward on the piano bench to bring his mouth down over hers in a long, sensual kiss.

Her sisters came by for the baby. Her mother wanted to spend some time with him. So Susan walked with Alan, soaking up the summer.

The sky was hazy on the horizon, blue as chicory flowers higher up. Below, the earth had turned the raw, powerful colors of summer. Cardinals made scarlet flickers in the cottonwoods, and turk's-cap lilies nodded over the

creek bed. Sometimes one of them stepped on a fallen
plum or a crab apple, and the scent would stay on their
shoes. Farmers had gotten back to the fields, and the
pungency of new-mown hay ascended from the raked
windrows to make floating bands of fragrance in the breeze.

Her hands were around his waist, her head tucked
into his shoulder.

"Are you crazy yet?"

She still asked sometimes. When they'd left California, in his elation and self-doubt they'd made an agreement
that if he became bored or restless they'd return, or return
part of the time, or work something out.

"Not crazy. Happy."

When he experienced the infrequent itchy pangs of
loss, when he missed briefly what he'd been, he took short
trips back, pursuing business for two or three days or a
week. Each time the old interests seemed more trite, and
he was grateful to escape the synthetic excitement, the
alienation of pleasing strangers, and the burned-out reality
of the only form of success he'd understood all those years.

Nothing he'd learned in his life had been a clue to
what he'd needed to know in the country. It hadn't taught
him how much grain to feed a fresh heifer, how to catch
alfalfa in the bud to hold its protein, how to tell when the
soil was in need of nitrogen, potassium, or lime.

He'd had to become like a child, to see and touch and
taste in a new way, and it had changed him. The pinched
soul had become whole. He knew things he never might
have known about the unexpected luxuries and complexi-
ties of country life. He'd seen how snow stays white on an
open field and packs hard and trackless, how the coat of a
newborn calf will steam in a cold barn, how the woods
glimmer at night when you walk through them with the
only light a jar of fireflies. He'd felt the wonderful softness
of a Clydesdale muzzle. He'd learned the smell and heat of
an applewood fire, and how woolen underclothes froze stiff
on a winter wash line and entered the kitchen like giant
gingerbread men. When he found himself in a barn of
hungry calves and delivered feed to those bawling mouths,
he knew what it was to feel important. He learned the
romanticism of helping a woman alight from a buggy, and

of eating dawn lamplit breakfasts of home-skimmed cream and homegrown grain. And Thoreau was right about the woodpile. It did warm you twice, the first time when you chopped it.

There'd been life to learn in California, too, but never the time. There were the plays now, and the new creative satisfactions, strong, direct ones, discovering the slow dramatic cycles of growth and fertility by which the world was fed, discovering the texture of a warm and clever extended family. And, most deeply, he had the satisfaction of bringing their child into the world, and the anticipation of the sons and daughters who would follow.

"We *could* have a small family," Susan had said. "Maybe seven."

He looked at her. Her cheeks were soft, her eyes bright as sequins.

"You missed the excitement this morning," she said. "They had a photographer out at Fanny's clicking pictures over the fence, and he got chased by the bull. Poor man, he got mixed up and thought he had our place and all he got was a half hour up a tree with a cameraful of Christ's overalls on the line." She winnowed her fingers through his hair. "I thought you said they'd forget about you if you were out of circulation for a while."

"May it be soon. May my name be stricken from all obelisks and pylons."

"From the entertainment section of *The New York Times* . . ."

"From the underside of the freeway overpass . . ."

They admired a field planted in corn, and he was able to imagine it as it would become in another month, the light catching red-gold across the tassels, winking lower on the sleek hanks of corn silk—one strand for every kernel. Some of the rows—his rows—were crooked.

"I'm not much of a farmer."

She said, "For a writer, you're a pretty good farmer."

Across the young stately rows were the scarecrows she'd made in the spring to surprise him, replicas of themselves embracing, hers dressed Amish. Then he kissed her, pulling her close, his hands gentle on her back, stroking up and down.

Above them, a dense-crowned maple still held raindrops on its leaves. Tilting sunlight penetrated the glassy pearls that became prisms to create bright rainbow strands on the wooden fence, on the white gravel, on her face. Magically created from white lights, here was color at its purest, red, orange, yellow, green, blue, indigo, violet—colors richer and fuller than he usually saw them.

He turned her face slightly to catch a many-colored ribbon over her soft mouth, and lowered his mouth to hers to sip the sun colors from her lips.

She was redolent of sunshine and peaches. The scents nested in her hair, spiced her skin, made her kiss nectar, and he was lost in the enchantment of loving her. Tenderness ran through him, hot, honeyed, familiar, irrevocably strong, still startling in its wonder.

He nuzzled the side of her face. "I didn't know happiness came in this color."

She smiled up at him, hypnotized by the joy she had in him. In time she put a finger on his lower lip, and said softly, "I wish to feel you as close to me as my skirt would be wet."

He gave her the kind of smile that made it hard for her to swallow and whispered a word or two into her hair that made it even harder.

"In a waist-high cornfield," she answered. "As if I would."

"One of my strange English practices."

She dragged him back into the kiss, standing on her toes, arching into him, making him breathless. "A good many of which I like very much," she whispered.

Smiling against her ear, he said, "Then how about the haymow?"

She spun around laughing, tossing her *kapp* back at him, running toward the barn. He caught up to her and held her again, because it felt too good to stop. He rubbed his face in her hair, touched her parted lips with his, and then framed her face in his hands and just looked at her.

Then they began to walk again, together. He lifted their clasped hands to kiss her fingers.

High in the west the sun sparkled off the silver dart of a jetliner, and he looked at it and thought, Down here is one who got away.

ENTER THE BANTAM
"SUNSHINE AND SHADOW"
AMISH QUILT SWEEPSTAKES

Official Sunshine and Shadow Sweepstakes Rules

1.) NO PURCHASE IS NECESSARY. Enter by completing the Official Entry Form below (or print your name and address on a plain 3″ × 5″ card) and send to:

> Bantam Books, Inc.
> SUNSHINE AND SHADOW SWEEPSTAKES
> Department Mktg—SR
> 666 Fifth Avenue
> New York, New York 10103

2.) One Grand Prize and 50 Runner-Up Prizes will be awarded. There will be no prize substitutions or cash equivalents permitted.

* GRAND PRIZE is one authentic, handmade "Sunshine and Shadow" Amish Quilt. (Estimated retail value $1,000.00)

* RUNNER-UP PRIZES will be one free copy of Bantam's fabulous new novel *Privilege* by Leona Blair. (Retail value $17.95)

3.) All entries must be received by Bantam Books no later than December 15, 1986. The winners, chosen by random drawing, will be announced and notified by January 31, 1987. Odds of winning depend on the number of entries received. Enter as often as you wish, but each entry must be mailed separately. Limit one prize per household, address or organization. Bantam Books is not responsible for lost or misdirected entries.

4.) Each winner will be required to submit an Affidavit of Eligibility and Promotional Release supplied by Bantam Books, Inc. Winners' names, addresses, and likenesses may be used for publicity and promotional purposes without compensation.

5.) Employees of Bantam Books, Inc., its subsidiaries and affiliates, and their immediate families are ineligible to enter. This sweepstakes is open to residents of the United States and Canada, except Quebec, and is void where prohibited by law. All federal, state, and local regulations apply. Taxes on prizes, if any, are the sole responsibility of each winner. Canadian winners will be required to correctly answer a skill question in order to receive their prize.

6.) To receive a list of winners, please send a self-addressed, stamped envelope, entirely separate from your entry, to:

> Bantam Books, Inc.
> SUNSHINE AND SHADOW WINNERS
> Department Mktg—SR
> 666 Fifth Avenue
> New York, New York 10103

- -

OFFICIAL ENTRY FORM

Name_____

Address_____

City_____ State_____ Zip_____

Heirs to a great dynasty, the Delaney brothers were united by blood, united by devotion to their rugged land . . . and known far and wide as

THE SHAMROCK TRINITY

Bantam's bestselling LOVESWEPT romance line built its reputation on quality and innovation. Now, a remarkable and unique event in romance publishing comes from the same source: THE SHAMROCK TRINITY, three daringly original novels written by three of the most successful women's romance writers today. Kay Hooper, Iris Johansen, and Fayrene Preston have created a trio of books that are dynamite love stories bursting with strong, fascinating male and female characters, deeply sensual love scenes, the humor for which LOVESWEPT is famous, and a deliciously fresh approach to romance writing.

THE SHAMROCK TRINITY—Burke, York, and Rafe: Powerful men . . . rakes and charmers . . . they needed only love to make their lives complete.

RAFE, THE MAVERICK by Kay Hooper

Rafe Delaney was a heartbreaker whose ebony eyes held laughing devils and whose lilting voice could charm any lady—or any horse—until a stallion named Diablo left him in the dust. It took Maggie O'Riley to work her magic on the impossible horse . . . and on his bold owner. Maggie's grace and strength made Rafe yearn to share the raw beauty of his land with her, to teach her the exquisite pleasure of yielding to the heat inside her. Maggie was stirred by Rafe's passion, but would his reputation and her ambition keep their kindred spirits apart?

 LOVESWEPT

YORK, THE RENEGADE by Iris Johansen

Some men were made to fight dragons, Sierra Smith thought when she first met York Delaney. The rebel brother had roamed the world for years before calling the rough mining town of Hell's Bluff home. Now, the spirited young woman who'd penetrated this renegade's paradise had awakened a savage and tender possessiveness in York: something he never expected to find in himself. Sierra had known loneliness and isolation too—enough to realize that York's restlessness had only to do with finding a place to belong. Could she convince him that love was such a place, that the refuge he'd always sought was in her arms?

BURKE, THE KINGPIN by Fayrene Preston

Cara Winston appeared as a fantasy, racing on horseback to catch the day's last light—her silver hair glistening, her dress the color of the Arizona sunset . . . and Burke Delaney wanted her. She was on his horse, on his land: she would have to belong to him too. But Cara was quicksilver, impossible to hold, a wild creature whose scent was midnight flowers and sweet grass. Burke had always taken what he wanted, by willing it or fighting for it; Cara cherished her freedom and refused to believe his love would last. Could he make her see he'd captured her to have and hold forever?

THE SHAMROCK TRINITY

*On sale October 15, 1986
wherever Bantam LOVESWEPT Romances are sold*